THE MIDNIGHTS

The Midnights

SARAH NICOLE SMETANA

HARPER TEEN

An Imprint of HarperCollinsPublishers

HarperTeen is an imprint of HarperCollins Publishers.

The Midnights
Copyright © 2018 by Sarah Nicole Smetana
All rights reserved. Printed in the United States of America. No part of this book may be used or
reproduced in any manner whatsoever without written permission except in the case of brief quota-
tions embodied in critical articles and reviews. For information address HarperCollins Children's
Books, a division of HarperCollins Publishers, 195 Broadway, New York, NY 10007.
www.epicreads.com

Library of Congress Control Number: 2017949555
ISBN 978-0-06-264462-6

Typography by Sarah Nichole Kaufman
18 19 20 21 22 PC/LSCH 10 9 8 7 6 5 4 3 2 1
❖

First Edition

For my parents,
and for Justin

ONE

THE FIRST TIME I woke at midnight and stumbled out of bed, drawn into the yard as if by a magnetic force, I was eight years old. A warm breeze had blown down from the mountains that day and pushed all the clouds out of Los Angeles, revealing a fat full moon that drenched our lawn in a puddle of light. My feet itched against the dry grass as I moved forward, lured by the secret whisper of wind through our avocado tree. I knew my father spent his nights in the studio if he wasn't down at Joe Thompson's bar, but I'd never gone out there for any other reason than to call him back in. My mother always made me the messenger.

"Oh good, you're here," my father said when I entered the

garage, still drunk with sleep. "I need you to help me out with something."

As though he'd been expecting me, he sat me on a folding chair and placed an electric guitar across my lap. Its body was so much bigger than mine, the wood dense on my legs, the metallic scent of the strings both exotic and intoxicating. He maneuvered my clumsy fingers into a C and I held them there, or tried my hardest. I strummed. It sounded terrible.

"Keep at it, Susie Q. Try to make it so your fingers only touch the string they're holding. And strum along with this beat, okay?"

He slapped his palm against his thigh, tapped his foot against the oil-stained cement. I struck the pick down the strings and cringed at how harsh it sounded—but I knew this was a test, a way into my father's mysterious world, and I wanted to pass, so I kept going.

I nodded my head each time I strummed and soon my whole body moved with the beat. After what seemed like an eternity, I managed to play the chord without muting any notes. I pushed the strings down harder, afraid of losing the sound, but it felt like I was holding down the freshly sharpened blade of a butcher knife and my wrist ached from the odd angle. Still, I continued, propelled by my father as he picked up another guitar from its stand and cried, "That's my girl! Keep going! Keep going!" He ran around turning knobs, flipping switches, changing the sound of my strumming into something euphoric and haunting. Then he began picking a solo so hypnotic that I seemed to move out of my body, into the sound, disconnected from the pain in my fingers and the unexplored depth of night outside in the real world—a place that suddenly seemed so insignificant.

And even as time passed, as my fingertips hardened into cal-luses, as I slipped into those awkward early teenage years and began to sense the scrim of my childhood lifting, my father's stu-dio remained the sole place where I felt most extraordinary, and most alive.

Inevitably, I grew up, but I never grew out of that feeling. It was the reason I continued stealing away to the studio throughout high school. It was why I found myself there on that sweltering August midnight, less than a week before my senior year started.

That summer, I had one goal: I wanted to write a great song. I'd filled an entire notebook in the pursuit, the pages brimming with perfect rhymes, chord progressions, and notes carefully plot-ted across the six lines of hand-drawn tablature charts. I'd made lists of harmonious chords, and scribbled potential lyrics in the margins. And yet, despite all the nights I spent in the studio with my father, despite the songs I had finished and the fragments that consumed my daytime mind, I hadn't shown him any of my attempts. I'd written some good songs, surely. But not great ones. Not yet.

So we spent that night working on one of his new pieces—a rock ballad built around heart-wrenching shifts in delay. And after what must have been a few hours, I began to feel the pull of the sun in the east, even though I couldn't actually see the sky outside and had no exact idea of what time it was. Long before, after my father lost the practice space his band had rented in Silver Lake and decided to convert our small detached garage into a music studio, he'd soundproofed the walls with scraps of shipping foam and covered the windows with cardboard and old, heavy quilts. The only light came from a single bulb hanging directly above us; the other side of the room, where my mother insisted on storing opaque plastic bins full of unnecessary things like my baby clothes and her old college textbooks—that had always been cloaked in darkness.

Without warning, my father switched off his delay pedal and leaned back in his chair. His fingers glided over the neck of his favorite guitar: a maple Fender Telecaster. It was one of the only things he brought with him when he first came to LA from some place he never talked about.

"All right, Susie Q," he said, examining me. "Your turn. Show me what you've got."

"Right now?" I asked.

He nodded. "When else is there?"

I pulled my flimsy composition notebook into my lap and flipped the pages, rejecting song after song. I wasn't sure what to play for him, what would be good enough.

My father muted his strings, plunging the room into static silence. "Whatever's there, on that page. Play it for me."

"This one's not ready," I told him, a nervous crest of sweat gathering between my shoulder blades.

"Fear's not going to help you, Suz. Maybe the song's shit, but maybe it's not. You'll never know unless you let it live."

My heart drummed against my rib cage. "But I haven't even finished—"

"Play it," he said.

I bit my lip, and brought my hands to the strings.

The song, so far, was simple: just a few barre chords and a verse. I strummed slowly through the intro and took a deep breath, preparing to sing. Though my voice lacked the flexibility of drifting between octaves or into a smooth falsetto, often snapping like a power line during the Santa Anas when I tried to reach a high note, I'd written vocals just slightly out of my comfortable range because I knew they would suit the song better. I closed my eyes and leaned my head back, hoping to propel the words from my chest:

The longer I stand here waiting,
the less I understand why.
You're only an illusion,
a mirage on the horizon line,
and I can never get any closer to you.

When I finished, my father nodded to himself, thinking. My stomach tightened as I waited for his verdict.

"About a boy?" he asked after a moment, reaching for the glass of whiskey sweating by his feet.

My skin flushed. I'd always been inspired by that place of longing, of love, but had never actually been in it. Not reciprocally, anyway. "It just sort of came out."

"You're holding back."

"Well, I might not rush to bring him home for dinner, but if I had a boyfriend I wouldn't lie about it."

My father cleared his throat. "I was talking about the song."

Between us, the amps buzzed.

"So you wouldn't bring him home for dinner?" My father narrowed his focus on me.

I shrugged. "We're not exactly the family-dinner type."

"See? This is what I'm talking about. Fear. You have to let go of that. You've got a lot of potential here, Susannah—I mean that. But when you're afraid, you try too hard. And that stops the song from evolving organically, from being what it wants to be."

The tension in my stomach climbed toward my throat. My father continued: "Don't get that look on your face. I'm talking about the universal 'you,' okay? No one can force a song to be great."

"I know," I said, though having this knowledge didn't actually help.

"You have to shake your notions of good and bad, and create outside of judgment. Follow the instinct, not the convention. Listen only to here." My father pounded his fist against his chest. "Because who's to say that a song you think isn't very good, or isn't the right style, isn't in fact the best fucking thing you'll ever create? That's what happened with 'Love Honey.' We had hits before, but nothing even close to that. And all because of your mom. Because I decided to say fuck it, and take a chance on something different."

I knew this story well. My father met my mother at a show his band, the Vital Spades, played at the Troubadour. He'd seen her from the stage, and only because one of the spotlights had been knocked loose during a punk concert the night before. Instead of swiveling forward, the light shone directly down into the crowd, illuminating the freckles on my mother's cheeks, haloing her honey-colored hair. They'd been dating just a few weeks when she decided to call off the relationship. He wrote the song to win her back.

Then, it became the Vital Spades' biggest hit.

A smile flashed across my father's face as he summoned the memory, one hand glancing off the guitar's strings, the other clanking ice around in his glass.

"After 'Love Honey,'" he said, gazing into the dark half of the room, "everything changed. There was always some suit-and-tie coming by to chat with me after shows. They never knew the first thing about music, only cared about what kind of money we could make them, like that was all I had done it for. And you know what I told them?"

Sometimes, he told them to go fuck themselves. And sometimes, he spent hours discussing philosophical approaches to music, until he had the label guys practically converting to his pseudo-religion. There were a number of variations, any one of which he could have run with that night, but as I waited for the insurgent punch line, his expression shifted and became distant.

"I said that all I wanted was to be able to do this for the rest of my life." My father motioned to the guitars and the cords, the clutter, the storage bins. But I knew he saw something else. "To keep writing songs and playing shows," he said slowly. "That's all I wanted."

As the room filled up with the amps' idle hum, I couldn't stop the guilt from burning through me. I knew I was the reason why my father left the Vital Spades. No one had ever said so, but I'd long ago filled in the rest of the story on my own: when my parents married at the chapel in the Beverly Hills courthouse, she was already pregnant. The Spades' final performance was six months later.

These were the facts. I couldn't change them, but I could do my best to sever my father's regret before it festered.

"Maybe we should pick this back up tomorrow," I said, stretching my arms over my head. "I probably have to leave for work pretty soon."

My father glanced up at me, blinking, like he had just been shaken from a pleasant dream. His eyes looked bluer than they had in weeks, but his face was tired and slightly crinkled. I wondered if he'd been sleeping at all, and whether this particular wistfulness had anything to with Lance and Travis—two boys a few years older than me who had appeared at our house earlier that summer, obsessed with the old Vital Spades tapes they likely bought on a whim from the sale rack outside some used record store. They claimed to have tracked him down on the internet, and for a while, they'd shown up frequently, invigorating my father's ego, shadowing him like a low-angled sun. Two weeks had passed since I'd last seen them. Truthfully, I hoped we'd never see them again.

"We should both try to get some sleep," I said as gently as possible.

My father nodded. I rested the Stratocaster I'd been playing back in its stand.

"You're getting better," he said then. "Every piece you write is better than the last."

I smiled and said, "Thanks, Dad."

As I eased the door shut behind me, I caught one final glimpse of him: swirling the last inch of whiskey around in his glass, staring into it the same way that fortune-tellers on the Venice boardwalk look into their murky crystal orbs. Then I waded back through the sultry night.

A current of static electricity tingled through the air as I tiptoed across the living room, sliding my fingers over the spines of my father's record collection before rounding the corner to my bedroom. Beneath the stillness, I sensed something stirring. In my chest, I felt a throb of hope.

TWO

I'D BEEN WORKING at the Last Bean for a year and one month, since the day after my sixteenth birthday. My mother basically forced the application upon me, but for a part-time job it was pleasant enough. Unlike our house, the building had air-conditioning, and when shifts were slow my boss, Lou, even let me change the café's standard jazz CD to something far more agreeable, like the Band, or Smokey Robinson and the Miracles. Otherwise, I worked to a score of steaming milk, the soft hiss and drip of espresso. And while I sometimes hated the slick smell of coffee that coated my hair and the way the grinds clung beneath my fingernails, worse fates were certainly imaginable.

"Hey, girly," Lou called that morning as I flew through the

door, a plume of dust kicking in behind me. Sometime after leaving my father in the studio and waking twenty minutes earlier, the Santa Ana winds had started blowing.

A grunt was my only response.

Lou shook his head. "Is that any way to start a Wednesday? Let's see some enthusiasm. Up top!"

He reached for a high five, his smile too wide for the time of morning. Though Lou was in his late forties, he acted much younger; he still spent all of his off days surfing, and wore his beach-glazed hair long. Most of the time I admired him for this. I smacked his hand with what little strength my body could muster.

"You're especially chipper today," I noted through a yawn.

"What can I say? It's a beautiful morning."

I turned back to the window. "I think this still counts as nighttime."

In the dark glass I saw the Bean's interior reflection: the chalkboard menus where I had painstakingly written prices, the silver espresso machine gleaming against the dusky sky. And yet, I knew what he meant; everything seemed so calm and quiet from inside the empty café. In here, I could almost forget that California was crushed beneath another unrelenting heat wave, all the hillsides brown and brittle. I could almost forget that the winds had started blowing, so much earlier than usual—and what might happen if they didn't stop.

"It's all about perspective, Susannah, about seeing the glass as half full." Lou poured coffee beans into the grinder. "You've only got one life. And today, I see good things on the horizon."

I said, "You can't see anything in the wind."

Over the next few hours, our morning rush came and went. Lou retreated to the storage room to check inventory, and between customers, I wrote down new ideas for my song on a strip of blank receipt tape that I kept tucked in the pocket of my apron. I tried to follow my father's advice, listening only to instinct and my heart. I tried not to judge too quickly. None of it worked.

I was scratching out a line so hard that the paper began ripping, when someone else's voice penetrated my concentration: "Can't a guy get some service around here?"

I glanced up to find Nick Fletcher smiling at me. In the new-morning sun, his eyes looked the same bright aquamarine as a swimming pool.

"We don't serve the likes of you in here," I said, waving him off with a flick of my wrist.

He clasped his hands at his chest and bent over the counter toward me. Because of the way his blond hair swooped across his forehead and the faint scent of chlorine wafting from his skin, I knew he had just finished water polo practice. "Come on, Hayes, please. I'm dying for one of those blended mochaccino-whipped-cream concoctions. A tall is a large, right? And can you double the mocha but hold the whipped cream?"

"You want what?" I asked, scrunching my nose. Nick usually kept his order simple: an iced coffee with a dash of cream.

His cell phone buzzed then. He glanced at the screen before sliding it back in his pocket. "I'm only messing with you," he said. "I just want an iced coffee. But I'm a little disappointed at how easily you cracked."

I laughed, allowing my gloom to peel away. "Thank God. I was beginning to question what all that sun is doing to your sanity."

"You just looked so painfully serious. What are you working on?"

"A new song."

"Let me see."

"It's not ready," I said automatically.

Nick snatched the receipt from my hand. "Who cares? It might never be by your standards, anyway."

As his eyes swung across the paper, I scrutinized his face for an honest reaction. His brow furrowed in concentration, and I noticed his lips moving, as though testing the weight of the words on his tongue. Nick was not a musician—he was a filmmaker, or hoped to be one day—but he knew how to navigate a piano, and had created surprisingly beautiful soundtracks for each one of his short films. When it came to music, I trusted him. Besides my father, he was the only one.

He handed the paper back. "This is really good, Hayes."

"That's what you always say," I told him, but a warm rush of gratitude surged through me.

"I wouldn't say it if I didn't mean it. The end—" He reached out to reclaim the paper, but I shoved it back into my apron. "What was it again? 'Expiration dates tease me, and other possibilities tempt only pain, but I can't let go. I can't let go.' And then how it keeps repeating? I can feel the momentum building just from the words. That's gold-record material right there. Have you written the music yet?"

I turned around, grinning in front of the fridge for a few seconds before extracting the iced coffee. "It's still a work in progress."

Then, anxious to change the subject, I said, "How's the first day planning, Mr. VP?"

At the end of the previous school year, Nick had been elected vice president of our student body. No one had opposed him, but he still put hand-painted posters all over the hallways with silly slogans like "Vote for Nick to do the Trick!" Cara Allen had helped him while also managing her own successful campaign for treasurer. She tried to get me to run, too, arguing that the year would be more fun if we were all on ASB together, but the whole process seemed way too exhausting. And anyway, I'd never seen myself as the student council type.

"We've been meeting every afternoon this past week to get ready for the assembly," Nick said. "You would never believe how much effort goes into it."

I handed him the coffee. "You're right. Our school's assemblies suck too much for any effort to have been exerted."

"But that's why we're working so hard, you know? We want it to not suck, for once. I'm even making a video for it. Only a few more days, though, and I'll get my life back. You're coming on Saturday, right?"

"Saturday?" It was my last free night in the studio before resuming eight hours of daily classes, mounds of homework, and my mother's constant lectures about the importance of a college education.

"Cara's party," Nick said. "Didn't she invite you?"

"Yeah," I said, the lie emerging before I even considered the truth. "I'd just forgotten about it."

Nick's phone rang and he looked down at the screen again,

frowning. "Hang on a second," he told me. As he answered, he walked over to the window, angling his body toward the parking lot.

"You'd better not be giving your boyfriend free drinks," Lou said, suddenly behind me. He plopped a box of sugar on the counter.

"He's just a friend," I said.

"Nobody buys the cow if they can get the coffee for free."

I shook my head. "That doesn't even make sense."

But Lou was already headed back to the storage room. "And don't forget to mop," he called over his shoulder.

I looked around the lobby, from the milk spills on the counter to the dirty mugs adorning our haphazard arrangement of tables and chairs. In the sudden quiet, I heard Nick tell someone he was at home. "Yeah, practice was pretty intense today," he added. "I'll just see you at the meeting." Then he hung up the phone and called out to me: "Hayes, I've got to run, but I better see you Saturday!"

He rushed through the door before I had a chance to reply.

Less than ten minutes after Nick's departure, Cara Allen arrived at the café. I was sweeping the floor when I saw her black Jetta curve into the parking lot, her curly hair exploding from the restraint of a ponytail.

"I thought I might find you here," she said.

"You know me." I shrugged. "Forever a slave to the Bean."

She leaned across the counter to give me a hug. It was only nine in the morning, but already, she wore a pink bikini beneath a white crocheted sundress. Coconut tanning oil glistened on her arms.

"I can't believe you *still* don't have a cell phone. I think my mom would have a heart attack if she couldn't call me every five seconds."

I didn't want to waste my own money on a cell phone, or ask my parents for something I didn't need—not to mention that my father adamantly opposed them (and computers, and email, and MP3 files, for that matter. "Technology will destroy us," he'd tell me, "the same way it destroyed rock and roll"). But this was not something I liked to talk about with Cara. Besides, I kind of enjoyed being disconnected. Analog, almost. Vintage. So I began scooping ice into a blender, and deflected her question with another: "I'm sorry I haven't called back yet. How was Hawaii?"

"The islands are incredible, Susie. I wish you could have come. Our place was literally two blocks from the water, and super close to this volcano, which, obviously, terrified me at first, but then this whole group of us decided to hike up there so I could face my fears, and . . ."

As she described her trip, I tried to listen—I honestly did. Cara and I had been friends since fifth grade, and until that June, no more than a week or two had passed without us talking. But then she went with her parents to Maui for two months, followed by ASB camp, and I became entangled in my songwriting, and suddenly the whole summer was gone and I'd been too distracted to remember to miss her. The thing was, she just didn't care about music the way I did; she didn't understand how a great song could shake you all the way down in your bones when the chorus swells in for the first time, or how the right album could turn an ordinary experience into something transcendent. She didn't understand the way a certain sound could be so striking that it gives your arms goose bumps, even as the rest of your skin sweats.

So I let her talk, my mind whirring back to the lyrics tucked inside my apron. Nick's reaction had galvanized me, and I yearned to set the new words to song. Instinctively, my hands added the rest of the ingredients to the blender: milk, coffee extract, chocolate powder.

". . . but if I told you, Nick would probably kill me," she said then. "He's been working so hard, and the whole thing is supposed to stay classified until Monday."

At the mention of his name, my eyes shot up. I caught Cara's expression changing in a way I didn't recognize—just a slight slant of the chin, a strange pucker to her lips.

"Sounds like fun," I said, wishing now that I'd been paying attention.

"Way more than I expected." She fidgeted with her phone. "But what about you? Tell me everything you've done this summer."

"Mostly just working," I answered after a pause. "Busy, but boring."

"Well it's time for that to change. My parents are going away for the weekend, so Josh and I are throwing a party on Saturday before he goes back to Santa Barbara and school starts. You have to be there."

"I might have to work," I said, turning on the blender.

"I know this place isn't open all night," Cara yelled over the crushing of ice. "And the party probably won't start until like nine, anyway."

"The next morning, I mean. I think I have to open."

"So come for an hour. Come on, Susie, we haven't hung out in months."

The blender stopped. I said I'd try, and topped off Cara's drink with a generous swirl of whipped cream. Like Nick, she always ordered the same thing.

"Is this for me?" she asked.

"Extra whip, as usual."

"Oh, Susie, that's so nice of you." She gazed uncertainly at the drink.

"Isn't this what you always order?"

"I'm trying to cut out unnatural sugars. But I can bring this to Josh. He'll love it." Grinning, as though everything had worked out perfectly, she added, "Can you just make me an iced coffee?"

As Cara diluted her drink with milk and raw sugar, a silhouetted figure stepped into the café. Light painted his body, illuminating his tight jeans first, then his T-shirt, his narrow face. My heart leapt. Even though he had a different haircut and his eyes were hidden behind boxy black sunglasses, I recognized him instantly: Cody Winters.

He'd been a senior at my high school when I was a freshman. Back then, he walked around with an acoustic guitar strapped to his chest, singing songs like "Crimson and Clover" in the hallways. I'd craved him in a way that felt savage and frightening, dragging Cara with me as I trailed him around campus, and now here he was, removing his sunglasses, ordering coffee.

He looked directly at me. "Make that a medium," he said.

This was the first time he had ever spoken to me. I glanced at Cara, who was mouthing *Holy crap!* and gesturing at Cody Winters's back.

"Room?" I mumbled, trying to ignore her.

"What?"

Heat spread through my cheeks. "Would—would you like room? In your coffee. For cream."

"Nah," he said. "Black's cool."

My hands trembled as I took a paper cup from the stack and filled it with coffee. When I turned back to hand it to him, sunglasses once again covered his eyes.

"How much?" he asked. He pulled a Marlboro from his pack and placed it between his lips.

"A dollar seventy-five," I said.

He handed me two. "Keep it, uh . . ." He trailed off, squinted at the name tag on my chest. "Susannah." I put the money in the register and took out a quarter for the tip jar, but then Cody walked over to the condiment bar for a sleeve and Cara focused on stirring the raw sugar in her drink, and I decided to shove the quarter in my pocket.

"You're Cody, right?" I heard Cara say.

I looked up, horrified.

"I'm Cara Allen. You probably knew my brother, Josh Allen? From high school?"

"Sure," he said, cigarette bobbing between his lips as he reached across her. "I knew Josh."

"Well, Josh is throwing a party on Saturday before he goes back to school, and you should totally come."

Cody nodded. I couldn't tell if he was looking at her. "Cool," he said, and then left the café.

"Oh my God, Cara," I said, unable to suppress a burst of laughter. Though I could hardly utter a sentence in his presence, Cara had made Cody Winters just another guy who used to go to our high school, who knew her brother, who might come to her party. Her speech hadn't ever faltered. I covered my face with my hands.

"I can't believe you invited him," I said.

Across the counter, Cara shrugged, as though the idea of being embarrassed hadn't even occurred to her. "Well, I guess now you have to come."

Later that morning, I walked home through wind-scrambled streets. Fallen palm fronds littered the sidewalk and garbage cans had toppled, the loose trash fluttering between fences, hedges, and cars. In front of a Spanish bungalow, a cracked ceramic pot spewed bone-dry soil across the previously immaculate porch. In the gutters, white plastic shopping bags banked like snow.

As I walked, sweat dripped into my eyes. For a moment, I closed them. And that's when I felt it: a rhythm, hidden amid the disarray, itching across my skin. I paused, listening carefully to the peculiar din of my windblown streets—the clattering of trees and crash of overthrown lawn furniture, a choir of defiant birds trilling from an unstable telephone wire. The sounds converged, playing harmoniously off each other, and all at once I found myself deep in the previously inaccessible marrow of my new song. The opening began with the same simple chords I'd played the night before, but this time a drumbeat swooped in underneath and the verse burst into the chorus, fast and unexpected. I sang out loud, fitting my lyrics into the patterns around me. "Don't Look Back," I decided to call it. Joy strummed in my chest.

As I came upon my block I began walking faster, anxious to get inside and grab a guitar. I was halfway down Catalina Street before I noticed my father's truck was still in the driveway.

Inside the house, my mother sat at the kitchen table alone, gazing out the window. Bright sunlight illuminated the strands of her yellow hair, the modest diamond adorning her wedding ring. She had one hand clasped around a mug of coffee. The other was fingering our telephone.

I crossed my arms, trying to offset the growing stir of uneasiness in my stomach.

"Where's Dad?" I asked.

"Where do you think," she said.

"Doesn't he have work?"

My mother smiled, but her eyes remained dim. "Sonja should be here any second," she said.

Sonja was one of my mother's coworkers at the catering company. She lived nearby and offered to pick my mother up whenever they served the same shifts. Briefly, I wondered why my mother didn't just take the truck, but of course, the answer to that was obvious. The truck wasn't supposed to be here. My father wasn't supposed to be here.

Outside, Sonja double-tapped her horn. My mother sighed and rubbed her temples. "I should be home around eight," she told me.

"I'll bring leftovers if I can, but there's some spaghetti sauce in the fridge if you get hungry." She kissed my forehead before she left.

After, I sat in her chair. The seat was warm. Through the window, I could see the front of the garage. To confirm my suspicions, I clicked on the phone and hit redial.

"Finch Electronics," a woman said. "How may I direct your call?"

My mother only called my father's office for one reason: to tell them he was sick when he wasn't. I'd witnessed these deceptions numerous times throughout my childhood, after my father fell into a spell of depression and locked himself inside the studio. Each time, I expected my mother to bang down the door, drag him out, and force him back to the office, but she didn't. Instead, she'd invent an illness, something banal like the flu. It's been going around, she'd explain. It was bound to catch up with him.

But no. That didn't make sense this time. He hadn't been depressed last night; he hadn't been vehemently complaining about the stifling monotony of his job, or had an explosive fight with my mother. We'd worked on my song. We'd talked about the Spades. Nothing was wrong.

And yet, even in that moment, I suppose part of me already knew this wasn't true.

"Hello?" the woman said. "Are you there? Can I help you?"

I wish, I thought, and hung up.

After a while, when my legs grew tingly and I finally stood from my mother's chair, I decided to make my father lunch. I put a baloney sandwich, some potato chips, and an apple in a grocery bag, then headed out to the garage.

"Dad?" I said. I knocked on the door but there was no answer. I tried the handle. Locked.

Placing my ear against the wood, I knocked again, this time listening for movement inside the studio. "I have food for you," I said. Somewhere out of view, a siren wailed. When nothing else happened, I left the bag on the doorknob.

Back inside, I picked up the guitar my father kept in the living room: a 1974 Martin dreadnought acoustic with a big glossy body and steel strings. It was a beautiful instrument, and something about playing it—the surprising lightness, maybe, or the fact that it could very well be the most expensive thing we owned—had always made me feel powerful.

Now, when I sat down on the sofa with the guitar, I felt nothing. I heard nothing but the hot, dry winds whipping down from the desert, rattling our avocado tree, tipping the city on edge. Whatever harmony I'd imagined before was gone.

For three days, my father stayed in the garage. My mother called his boss every morning to update him on the progress of the "stomach bug," and every evening I left a new bag of food outside the garage's side door—whatever I could scour from our house without her noticing. She didn't want me to encourage him. In fact, she hardly seemed worried at all. Like she knew something I didn't.

During those days, hours slunk by. Cara called on Friday to see if I wanted to go to a movie, but I didn't feel comfortable leaving my house unless I had to. My father had never remained isolated for so long, and I wanted to be there when he surfaced.

So I told her I might have the flu.

"It's been going around," I said apologetically.

"Well, it better be out of your system by tomorrow," she warned. "Worse comes to worst, we'll just set you up with your own personal barf bucket, because let's face it: my mom would kill me if you puked on one of her rugs."

Truthfully, though, the excuse didn't seem like much of a stretch; I'd felt in some fundamental way off-kilter ever since my father locked himself in the studio and I lost the rhythm to my song. I hadn't given up on "Don't Look Back," but the harder I tried to wedge the pieces together, the less they seemed to fit. Only one partial line had stayed with me, its euphony jangling, useless, in my head: *I can't let go, I can't let go, I can't let go . . .*

By Saturday, I'd grown restless.

Our house sealed in heat like Tupperware and it was too stuffy that day to do anything useful, so I decided just to lie on the couch, in the direct line of fan-churned air, and listen to my father's records. His collection was massive; he had everything from the Allman Brothers to the Zombies, stacked six shelves high and over two hundred wide. I put on *Rubber Soul* first, followed by *Rumours* and *Surrealistic Pillow*, hoping that immersing myself in the enduring brilliance of my favorite albums would help dislodge the fragments of "Don't Look Back" from deep within my memory. But by early afternoon, all I had to show for my efforts was a pervasive sheen of sweat on my skin and the twang of a sitar stuck in my head. I put the records back in their alphabetical places on the shelf and switched to the radio, nudged the dial to K-Earth 101. "It's Too Late" crackled through the speaker.

"Oh, I used to love this song," my mother said from the kitchen, where she'd been scrutinizing the *Los Angeles Times*. She started singing along, her voice ambling over the music with a polished, stunning softness. For a moment, I almost forgot about my father, my lost song.

Then she stopped. "I think I've found one for you, Susannah. Sales associate at the new Nordstrom they're opening in the mall."

"My job's fine," I said.

"The possibility of commission, too," she continued. "That could be much better than the tips you get over at Lou's."

"You're the one who wanted me to apply there in the first place," I reminded her.

"And I think the job has been really good for you. But that doesn't mean you can't keep an eye out for something better. It's important to have options." With a false note of casualness in her tone, she added, "By the way, have you looked into any of those colleges yet?"

I crossed my arms. Perspiration puddled in the creases of my elbows. "I haven't really gotten to it."

"If I remember correctly, UCLA has an early admission deadline. Long Beach might have one too."

"Do we really have to talk about this right now?" I moaned. School had never been more than a job to me—I went, completed the requirements, and came home. But my mother had gone to UCLA for two years, and she'd always harbored the fantasy that I would complete what she didn't. Once, after she forced me to take the SATs, I made the mistake of asking her why she didn't go back and finish her own degree instead of pressuring me about mine, and for a week after she refused to do anything for me. "This is what it would be like if I went back to school," she had said. Because I couldn't cook, I ate nothing but peanut butter and jelly sandwiches until my mouth felt permanently coated and parched.

Now, I had a desk drawer brimming with the application forms she'd collected for me. A few times I'd even seen her add money to an envelope titled "Application Fees" kept beneath the silverware holder.

"Your senior year of high school is starting in a few days," my mother said. "Summer's almost over."

"But it's not over yet."

My mother frowned. "Just tell me you'll look into it."

I said, "I'll look into it." Then I picked up the Martin and began strumming over the radio.

I didn't blame my mother for continuing to seek something better, something steadier and with higher wages, but I was sick of her wanting "better" for me. She just couldn't see that her definition of the word did not align with my own. To me, "better" meant a shadowy room alive with the sway of close-pressed bodies, the din of a hundred synchronous voices chanting the lyrics to "Don't Look Back." Only one more year of high school, I reminded myself, and then freedom. But at that moment, I felt like my life was on hold.

My mind flashed to Cara, how outgoing she'd become, and the rasp of my name as it rolled from Cody Winters's tongue. Maybe it wouldn't be so bad to become a little more like her, I thought. To just let go of my fears. I could start by going to her party. I *wanted* to go to her party.

I knew I probably wouldn't.

I turned to the window, watching as children splashed in the futile spray of wind-flung sprinklers. That's when I saw my father burst out of the garage.

He marched across the lawn so quickly that he looked supernatural, his skin strikingly pale against the sun-swathed landscape. The sight of him, after all that waiting, was startling.

"This is it," he said when he flew through the front door. "This is it, sure as hell. They can't ignore this one."

My father held up a cassette tape and shook it between his fingers. He still recorded analog, everything on eight-track or tape deck, because he thought the sound quality felt more authentic.

"Can I hear it?" I asked, the guitar mute in my hands.

"No can do, Susie Q." He crossed the entryway and plopped down next to me on the couch. "I don't want to jinx it. I'm putting this bad boy in the mail first thing Monday morning."

"On your lunch break, you mean," my mother said from the kitchen.

"Yeah," he said, leveling her gaze. "On my lunch break."

My mother did not seem convinced by his response, but she didn't argue. Instead, she walked to the sink. She filled a glass with water and drank while standing there, staring out into the yard. She said, "Michael needs an answer soon, James."

My father leaned into me. "I mean it, Suz," he said. I could smell the tinge of whiskey on his breath. "This one's for real. I've never written anything like it."

Smiling, he plucked a small orange canister out of his pocket and dropped two white tablets into his palm. He swallowed the small pills dry.

I squinted at the label, but the wording had been scratched off. "What are those for?"

"Headaches," he said. "Been getting these awful headaches lately."

"For how long?" I looked to my mother, expecting her to share my concern, but her expression was unaffected.

"You're not supposed to drink with that," she said.

"Do you see a drink in my hand?" he said.

I repeated: "For how long?"

"Oh, I don't know," my father said to me. "Now and then. It's probably all the loud music. Your mom always said it would be the death of me."

He laughed, and I wanted to believe it was over—that my father just needed a break from work, from responsibility, a few days to immerse himself fully in the thing he actually loved. And yet, unease continued creeping through me; I couldn't help but think that he looked dangerous in his elation, no different from a panhandler at a freeway off-ramp. His face seemed gaunt as he spoke of the studio like a sanctuary, the tape like a time machine—but the fear only lasted for another moment, because then he stood up, put Stevie Wonder on the stereo, yanked my mother out of the kitchen, and began twirling her in his arms.

"What are you doing? James, stop." My mother tried to wiggle out of his grip, but it was no use. He only held her closer.

"C'mon, Diane," he said. "Just dance with me here for a second. One song."

I expected her to start yelling, to fight until free of him. A few seconds later she rested her head on his shoulder.

Though I still believe she really did love him then, as much as ever, I also think that she was tired of fighting, tired of trying to change someone who didn't want her help. It was easier just to dance, barefoot on the linoleum floor, and forget he had ever been anything other than what he was in that instant—a father who was trying to do right by his family in the only way he knew how, and a husband who could still make his wife smile when he had one hand on her slender waist, his mouth barely moving as he whispered into her ear: *I'll give you all my love, honey, pull the moon down from above, but I know that it will never be enough.*

THREE

THAT AFTERNOON, WHEN the sun began to droop in the sky, my father decided to hike out to the hills. He said he needed to stretch his legs. Though physical exertion in one-hundred-degree heat sounded torturous, I offered to go with him. I didn't want to wait until midnight to get him alone.

The smell of slightly charred hot dogs permeated the air as we crossed through the neighborhood. Then we turned left, followed a private road under the freeway overpass, and made our way up forged paths. At the top of the hill, my father sat on a large boulder that hung over the side of the cliff. He let his legs dangle.

"Doesn't everything look so calm from up here?" he said. "It's much smaller than it seems."

To me, the city looked infinite. The winds had thinned out the smog that usually blanketed the horizon and I could see the outline of downtown jutting into a volcanic sunset. To the east, the dark gray plume of a fire spiraled skyward. I sat down next to my father, slightly back, not comfortable so close to the edge. He sang something under his breath and I couldn't help but think that even when we were alone, he was never fully with me.

"When you were little, your mom and I used to bring you up here a lot. Whenever we couldn't get you to stop crying we'd just pack some sandwiches and hike up here and I don't know what it was, the quiet or the view or something else, but it would soothe you. You'd fall asleep instantly."

"I don't remember that," I said. "Why'd you stop?"

He shrugged. "Guess you stopped whining. Haven't said it much, but you've been a good kid, Suz."

Sometime before we left, he must have stuffed a bottle of beer in the waist of his jeans because he pulled one out and struck the top down on a sharp rock. The cap flew off, bounced across the boulder's surface, and fell over the edge. I watched until I could not see it anymore.

"When I was a kid," he said, and took a long pull from the beer, "I whined about everything, especially guitars. I was five the first time I asked for one. Could barely speak a coherent sentence yet, but man—you should have heard me trying to express how much I wanted that Tele."

I could hardly breathe, the air stunned in my lungs. My father never spoke of his life before Los Angeles. For all I knew, he was born of this city, driven into existence on a Greyhound bus headed for the depot in Chinatown. Of course, I wanted to learn about his past, had asked many times. I'd even tried to trick him once by asking about his oldest records. I pulled one of the most tattered spines from the shelf and held it out, imagining its history, a shaggy-haired little boy saving pennies for a year just to purchase that one album: *Pet Sounds*.

But when I asked my father where it came from, he just pointed back at the shelves.

"You see this, Susie Q?" he said. "This is my family, my history. These people may not be related by blood, but we've got something stronger. You want to know where I came from? Listen to this." And then he put on the record and started singing.

On the cliff, my father stared at the skyline, a muscle twitching in his jaw.

"They didn't make little-kid guitars like they do nowadays," he continued, "at least not where I was from, and my ma said no for a thousand different reasons. I wasn't big enough. It was too expensive. I'd get sick of it the way I got sick of those plastic toy soldiers she'd bought me. But I kept on whining." He paused, took another sip of the beer. "Don't tell your mother about this."

I said nothing, my silence complicit. I wanted to believe that this was my father's way of apologizing—of making amends for his secrecy, for cutting me out of his process and not playing me his tape. Now, though, I sense it was those pills, that they made his tongue far looser than liquor.

"A year went by, and I didn't ask for anything I didn't need to live. That was the only way I could think of trying to show them I was serious. About a month before Christmas, Ma started acting weird every time I mentioned the guitar. Changed the subject. Man, I knew right then. I knew they'd bought it, and I knew where they were keeping it, too.

"I raced home every day after school, before my parents got there, and snuck into the closet where they hid the guitar so I could mess around with this instructional booklet I stole from the library. I was learning kiddy shit, like 'London Bridge Is Falling Down,' because the only beginner books they had were full of nursery rhymes. By the time I unwrapped that Tele Christmas morning, though"—he whistled—"you better believe I knew how to play the damned thing. I just picked it up and started plucking the notes to 'Joy to the World.' Everyone thought I was some sort of prodigy." He laughed out loud. "They were amazed for a whole half second before deciding the guitar was a waste of time."

Without turning around, he handed the bottle to me. Though alcohol was not hard to find in my house, my father had never offered to share. I'd never had much interest, either, aside from some sugary wine coolers Cara's brother had given us sophomore year. But for the first time in my life, my father had willingly told me something that happened before the Vital Spades, and though it wasn't much, it felt like the key to his entire existence. So I took the bottle and drank.

Emboldened by the new knowledge, or maybe just the taste of alcohol, I decided to ask for more. I could feel the air straining around me as I sorted through the possibilities.

When I opened my mouth, an entirely different question emerged. "Are you sick?"

"Nothing I can't handle," he said after a moment. "Your mother just likes to make everything seem worse than it actually is."

When I didn't respond he turned around, his expression momentarily inscrutable. "I'm not dying, if that's what you mean."

I nodded. Silence settled between us as the wind kicked up, blowing my long hair around my face like a blindfold. I handed the bottle back to my father. The day continued to darken, and slowly, one pinpoint of light at a time, the city became electric.

"We should head back down," he said, casting a shadow over me as he stood. The sun was directly behind him, outlining his body with a tangerine glow. "Don't want to be up here when the coyotes come looking for dinner."

I was not ready to go yet. There was still so much I wanted to ask him, about his childhood, about his tape. But my father started walking and I followed. Later, I thought, in the studio. We'd have all the time in the world.

We walked home through the lengthening dusk. Beneath the sunset, heat continued shimmering, bending the air in squiggly lines that made our neighborhood look like it was filled with puddles. And when we turned onto Catalina Street and I saw two figures sitting on the curb in front of our house, I hoped, with a growing ache in my gut, that this was another mirage.

The figures only crystallized as we drew near.

Lance and Travis.

"Well, well." My father grinned, his dour mood evaporating like water. "Look what the coyotes dragged in."

It astonished me how casual he acted around them, as if he hadn't spent the past eighteen years waiting for other people to appreciate him—as if these two fans hadn't appeared out of nowhere and vanished just as quickly. But then my father sauntered toward them, and I began to wonder if maybe they hadn't vanished at all.

He said, "What are you doing down here in the street?"

"Your wife wasn't too thrilled with the idea of us hanging around," Travis said, standing. Though they both had unkempt hair that fell in tangles down to their shoulders and wore the same grungy uniform as so many of the boys at my high school, I knew this one was Travis because he was shorter, with cheeks still vaguely corrugated by acne scars. "She threatened to call the cops if we stepped on the property again."

My father chuckled under his breath. "I wouldn't put it past her. She's always been a woman of her word."

"We stopped by Joe Thompson's last night, hoping to catch you," said Lance, who was tall and lanky. "People there are still talking about us, you know. Had a couple of guys even ask when our next show is."

"Is that right?" my father asked, obviously pleased.

"What show is he talking about?" I asked.

"It wasn't really a show," my father said. "I just brought the Martin over to Joe's, had these two back me for a bit. We played some old Spades stuff, a couple covers. Nothing major."

"Come on, man," Lance said. "It was more than that. The place was packed."

"There were even people out in the parking lot," Travis added.

My father laughed. "It really wasn't that big of a deal."

"Why didn't you tell me?" I asked. "I would've come."

"You know you couldn't have, Suz. You're not old enough."

This, of course, was true, but that didn't make it any less painful.

"We were just playing for a bunch of drunks," my father said through a smile.

"Even so," Lance said, "it was epic. But that's not why we're here. We wanted to get your thoughts on something."

"Shoot," my father said.

"Our band has been talking about this for a while, but we wouldn't do it without first getting your permission. So . . ." Lance and Travis exchanged a nervous glance. "What would you think about us covering 'Love Honey'?"

A wave of panic roiled through me. "Love Honey" was my mother's song. It was *my* song, my history, practically part of my genetic makeup. My father sang it to me when I woke up from nightmares as a child. It was the first song he ever taught me to play on guitar.

My father scratched his chin, considering the possibility. I tightened my arms into a knot and felt my mouth tensing. He couldn't give our song away like this. He wouldn't.

"What do I think?" he said uncertainly. A moment passed before he broke into a grin. "I think it's a great fucking idea. Of course you should play it. You should play it every goddamn show." My father clapped his hand on Lance's shoulder. "Why don't we go down to Joe's now and talk some more about this?"

"Hell yeah," Lance said.

"Drinks on us," Travis said.

My father turned to me. "Tell her I'm going out for a bit, will you?" He motioned toward the house.

"But you just got back," I muttered, startled by how ragged my voice sounded.

"Come on, Susie. We'll only be gone a bit. Don't be like your mother."

Though he stood still in front of me, it felt like he was already walking away.

"Please," he said, quieter, the hot breeze dragging his words down the street. "Just do this one thing for me."

A bitter taste bloomed in my mouth but I must have nodded, because the next thing I knew, he folded his body into the front seat of Travis's car. The engine sputtered to life and they rumbled down the street. In my balled-up fists, I felt my pulse throbbing.

All summer, I'd wanted to eradicate Lance and Travis from our lives—to prove to my father that I was a valuable band member and not just his daughter. And all summer, I had failed. But now, finally, I knew what I had to do.

I was going to cover "Love Honey." And I was going to cover it a hell of a lot better than Lance and Travis.

The whole process took little more than an hour; I began with the skeleton of my father's song and translated it to the twangy drawl of open chords on acoustic guitar. I had no interest in performing some bland, basic copy of the original, as Lance and Travis probably would, with the same tempo, the same harmonies, and even the same solo after the bridge. I wanted to reinvent it, break it down, explore the song's hidden intricacies in a way that only I—as an artist, as James Hayes's daughter—possibly could.

So I clamped a capo on the third fret, tweaking the key to match my range. I slowed the song down to better embroider the raw simplicity of acoustic guitar and vocals. While my father's version was infectiously upbeat, I sought to emphasize the lyrics' introspection, building my progression into a final crescendo that brimmed, instead, with frustration and longing. And it was easy. God, I was surprised by how easy. Not once did I stop to wonder whether I was making the right decision or whether I was any good, because I knew. This was the sound of my childhood, as coherent as my heartbeat. And without even trying, I'd relinquished my fear.

But the elation didn't last long; seven thirty turned into nine, and still my father did not come home. All the triumph I felt funneled into a fresh surge of rage. I was sick of it—always waiting for him, always being the second choice. So I made a decision: I wouldn't wait anymore.

I marched down the hallway.

"Mom?" I said, pushing the door to my parents' bedroom open.

"Yes?" she replied without looking up. She was sitting cross-legged on the bed. An array of papers covered her like a blanket, rustling each time she took a breath.

"I'm going to Cara's," I said.

"How nice. I was hoping you two would connect before the summer ended." She picked up a page, her eyebrows creasing as she examined the tiny lines.

"She's having a party," I said.

I expected those words to shake something in my mother. She knew I never attended parties, or at least that I never told her so, and I thought she'd inquire about a chaperone, instill a curfew. Give me a lecture about the dangers of underage drinking. Perhaps there was even some part of me that wanted her to make me stay home. But my mother had always adored Cara and her proper manners, the way she offered to help with the dishes on the rare occasion when she came to my house. Cara was a good student. A good influence.

When my mother finally lifted her eyes, she said, "Is your father still out?"

I nodded. Outside, a car wove through our street, up toward our house. My mother and I both turned to the window, and even as the engine rumbled past us, fading back into the night, we didn't move. We kept staring, though we could not see anything other than our half-rendered reflections—two pale oval faces, differentiated only by the color of our hair.

In that moment, I felt something inside me crack.

"Well, have fun," my mother said, breaking away. She turned back to the bills.

"Mom?" I said again.

"What is it, Susannah?"

Her body hunched on the bed and she began rubbing her temples, a shadow of impatience clouding her eyes.

A few seconds passed before I found my answer. I said, "Can I borrow a dress?"

I knew exactly what I was looking for: a 1970s pale blue peasant dress with a cinched waist, low shoulders, and faint pastel flowers that swished against my knees when I walked. I'd tried it on in secret many times over the years, but I'd never seen the dress on my mother. Not in person, anyway. The dress had only ever appeared in a photograph.

The image was actually of the Vital Spades onstage—something I'd commandeered from a shoebox under my mother's side of the bed during one of my snooping crusades as a child. In it my father stood front and center, illuminated beneath a crisp fan of spotlight. His eyes were closed tight and his mouth was open, grinning slightly as he sang. Around him, the other Spades were rendered mostly in shadows. And perhaps it was because of this, the biased effect of the lighting, that I didn't even notice her at first: the figure dancing in the background, blurred and partially hidden by a Marshall half stack. She looked so different then, with short hair and a veil of straight bangs covering her eyes, her slender arms suspended in the air, her hips cocked playfully to one side—but I knew it was my mother. She was wearing that blue dress. The fabric dripped off her left shoulder, caught, with her body, in motion.

When I was younger, I had marveled at the photo. Sure, there were some differences between the man in the spotlight and the man I knew as my father, but for the most part, he looked the same. My mother, on the other hand—she was almost unrecognizable. The animated girl in the background was a stranger, like my mother from another planet. Another life.

But I suppose that was the difference between them. While my father proudly built his mysteries into an aura, put them on display and let them define him, my mother buried hers like evidence of a crime.

So I dug out the dress from the depths of her closet. I invaded her bathroom, painting my lips and sketching black liner around my eyes. Then I stepped back and studied myself in the mirror. I'd always thought I looked like my father; we had the same blue eyes, flecked with green, the same dark hair and smooth cheekbones. The same squinty smile. Now, with the makeup, the way my eyes softened against the pale fabric of the peasant dress, I looked like somebody different. Somebody stronger.

I walked back into the bedroom and stood in full view of my mother.

"What do you think?" I asked, holding the hem of the dress in my hands. When my mother peered up I did a slow spin, snapping my head around at the last second like a ballerina.

As she examined me, I searched her face for any traces of the stranger in the photograph. I thought that maybe if I looked hard enough, I would glimpse the place where the two people intersected, like the center of a Venn diagram.

All that crossed her face was a tired smile when she said, "You look lovely. Don't stay out too late, okay?"

Cara lived on a quiet street at the top of a hill, where the houses were wide and remodeled and had backyards with pools. The fifteen-minute walk there was familiar, but the night seemed brighter than usual. Overhead, without the thick filter of smog, the stars winked and blazed. I found Orion, the only constellation I remembered, and sang him my version of "Love Honey," because I didn't want my work to go to waste. I sang it over and over, all the way to Cara's house, knowing that against the wind and the din of traffic, no one would be able to hear me.

Inside Cara's living room, people clumped together. Their voices overlapped in melodic discord, rising above the thump of a stereo, the thundering bass. I pushed through the crowd, standing on tiptoe until I spotted Cara near the kitchen. She said something to the people around her, gesturing with her hands. Her face glowed with their laughter. And maybe it was because of the giant, lovely house I knew as well as my own, or the way Cara spotted me and cried out, "Susannah, you made it!" as though I was the sole person she'd been waiting for, but I was suddenly very glad I had come.

Cara glided toward me, throwing her arms around my neck in a tight, sloppy hug. "I *love* that dress. Boho is so in right now. Do you want a drink? Josh bought a keg, but it's totally cool if you just want Coke or something."

The night air had left my skin dry, my mouth parched. I asked for the first thing that came to mind. "Have you got any whiskey?"

Cara laughed. "That's such an old man drink. Here, try this."

She gave me her cup, began filling a new one with the contents of various bottles from the makeshift ice chest in the left half of the kitchen sink. I looked around the room.

"Cody's not here yet," Cara said. "But I have a good feeling. I really think he's going to come."

"I think that's the alcohol talking," I said, trying to temper the flurry of my heartbeat.

"Liquid courage." She splashed her cup against mine.

"For me or you?" I asked.

In another part of the house, something crashed. A collective cry surged from the living room—the same noise that arose when a fight broke out in our high school's quad.

"Oh crap," Cara said, looking behind me. "Josh!" she yelled. "I'll be right back, Susie. Josh!"

She rushed off, shoving her way into the crowded hall. I glanced at the clear fluid in my cup and sniffed, detecting a hint of something fruity. Then I drank. I drank it all. It was surprisingly sweet, and yet throat-scalding. I coughed.

I tried to refill my cup with whatever Cara had used, but there were too many bottles and I didn't know the difference between them. I hoped that Cara hadn't known, either, and began pouring. When I took a sip, I had to hold my hand over my mouth to keep from spewing it back out, but after the initial shock I felt light and tingly. Taking a deep breath, I plugged my nose and drank again. At some point, while my eyes were closed or tearing, Nick Fletcher appeared at my side.

"Someone's on a mission," he said through a smile. "What's the rush, Hayes?"

"I'm playing catch-up," I said. I traced my tongue over my teeth, my body feeling warm and loose.

"Maybe you should drink something a little less toxic. I can smell that from across the room."

Though I halfheartedly resisted, Nick took the drink from my hand and we both watched as its contents slipped down the drain. The sink gurgled in response. Examining the bottles, he chose one with gold letters and began refilling my cup while I picked at a fingernail that had grown slightly too long.

"I wasn't sure if you were going to show," Nick said. "How'd Cara do it?"

"Do what?"

"Get you here. I want to know so that next time, I'll be able to lure you out."

I shrugged, scanning the crowd one last time for Cody Winters, but of course, he hadn't come. I felt a pang of disappointment. "Guess I just felt like doing something different tonight," I said. "Cavorting with my classmates. Acting uncivilized."

He gasped. "Uncivilized? Is that what you think of us?"

I pointed to the scene of the fight, which Cara's brother had finally contained, and said, "Exhibit A." Then I pointed to a group of guys near Cara's chrome refrigerator who were arguing about whether or not olive oil would work as a lubricant, and, if so, the likelihood that it would make them ejaculate faster, dubbing this "Exhibit B."

"I'd argue that Exhibit B might actually fall in the civilized category because of creativity," he said. "After all, evolution can work in mysterious ways."

I said, "God help us if those are 'the fittest.'"

Nick laughed, his eyes squinting into slivers, and I caught a glimpse of the little boy he had been when we met in elementary school. He'd had big plastic glasses then, and short spiky hair. As kids, we'd passed many hot, smog-saturated afternoons playing kickball on the cul-de-sac in front of his house. Though Cara just sat on the sidewalk and watched, Nick always invited me to play because I was one of the few girls who wouldn't cry if she got pushed down. It had been a long time since I'd last thought of that. For some reason, though, the memory suddenly seemed important, and I grabbed on to it, let it rise with the flush in my cheeks.

Nick handed me the cup. "Vodka Sprite," he said. "Simple, tasty, effective."

I sipped. My head floated, light and airy on my shoulders, and something about Nick—about that moment—made me want to tell him everything I'd spent the summer withholding. I wanted to tell him about the days my father spent locked in the studio. I wanted to tell him about Lance and Travis, and how they were ruining everything. And above all, I wanted to tell him how those lyrics he'd read at the café had almost turned into a song that I thought was good—*really* good, maybe even great—but I had lost it to the winds and the emptiness of my house without my father and I feared I'd never get it back no matter how hard I worked or how many nights I lay awake, sleepless, watching the sky lighten into another wasted dawn, because it felt like my father was disappearing, chasing some distant force the way the tides chased the moon, and without him I had nothing—just a notebook filled with half-rendered phrases and predictable patterns of chords. Not even my interpretation of "Love Honey" could change that. My father was my teacher, my mentor. But he needed nothing from me.

My mind flattened, unable to support the weight of all the words I left unspoken. I gazed out at the party. In the shadowed corners, couples pressed up against each other with an intimacy so public it alarmed me. I felt the bite of tears in my eyes.

"What's your dad like?" I said suddenly.

"What do you mean?" Nick asked.

"I don't know. Do you get along?"

"I guess, yeah." Nick gulped his beer. "We've had our moments, but he's not around much."

"He still works a lot?"

"He's never too busy for his students, but for me?"

Nick's bottom lip curled down as his head shook. His father, I knew, was a highly regarded professor of environmental studies at Occidental University. I'd only seen him a few times, always at mandatory school functions. He had a mustache and stood plank straight, with his hands clasped behind his back. I'd never spoken to him but he seemed like a nice man, wise and understanding. I imagined him to be all the things my own father was not.

I stretched my palms across the strange, soft fabric of my mother's dress and wondered if my father had shown Lance and Travis his tape. I said, "Mine too. I mean, it's not exactly the same. But kind of."

"I always thought your dad seemed so cool."

"Turns out he's just the same as everyone else."

"Parents can be such assholes sometimes," Nick said, glancing at his phone. It was getting late. Though he probably had practice in the morning, I didn't want him to leave.

"Speaking of assholes," Nick continued, "Chris Crowley has developed some weird obsession with his own nudity, and every time he drinks, he announces that we're all going streaking, then passes out naked by himself in the front yard. I've seen his junk so many times this summer that it haunts me in my sleep, and if we aren't careful, you might get the full frontal, too."

I laughed. "You're bluffing."

Nick checked his phone again. "Give it about . . . one more minute."

I looked back out at the party. The faces had begun to blur.

Nick and I were standing so close that I could feel the heat of his body. A strand of hair had fallen into his eyes and I felt the urge to reach up, to push it aside for him, but my hands were too heavy. The minute slipped by.

Then someone yelled, "Who wants to go streaking?" and Nick pushed me playfully on the shoulder.

"Told you," he said, his hand lingering.

A chorus of cries amplified across the room, and the crowd began swaying, jumping, trying to see what was happening and snap pictures with their phones. I anchored my gaze on Nick's sunburned nose, at the spray of freckles there, but I couldn't focus. The room began to spin.

"You all right?" he asked.

"Fine," I said, but as I leaned back against the counter for support, my grip slipped. Nick caught me right as my knees buckled.

He wrapped my arm through his elbow and leaned into me. "Let's go sit down."

My legs were moving but I could barely feel them as Nick led me toward the staircase and we climbed higher, past the school portraits of Cara and Josh, one from every grade in chronological order up the stairs. It looked like a flipbook—I could see them aging right before my eyes and even after we reached the top and the end of the hallway and the guest bedroom, the one door still standing ajar, I saw their faces getting older and older until they were gray and wrinkled and their skin started melting like wax. Finally, we tumbled down onto the bed.

"Thanks," I said, rolling onto my back. I tried to focus on the ceiling fan but the blades were tilting, even as the air felt sultry and still. Nick lay down next to me.

"You look really pretty tonight," he said quietly.

My pulse quickened. I wanted to thank him, to say something true and real in kind. But so little felt real right then. My world had become crooked—a place where anything could happen, where everything could fall apart.

"I'm afraid of the winds," I told him. At least that's what I said in my head, the words I thought I had formed, if I formed any at all.

A moment passed, then Nick said something else I couldn't hear. Our proximity had turned his voice to a whisper. I tilted my head toward him. Closing my eyes, I breathed in his scent (beer and peppermint ChapStick, the faint chlorinated tang of his skin) and thought about how badly I wanted to be close to him. How natural it felt when he lowered himself down and pressed his mouth to mine.

The kiss was gentle at first—both clumsy and fluid, familiar and new. Then the full length of my body pressed against him, and when my lips parted, his tongue reached for more. My skin felt liquid as his hands roamed over me, beneath my dress. I grasped for him, fumbling. For an instant the world was motionless.

Then a fresh cry of voices seeped under the closed door and a flush of clarity zoomed through me. I heard the thumping bass of a stereo downstairs, the smash of someone dropping a bottle on the tile floor, the low groan of movement in the next room. I opened my eyes. On a side table, Cara's face popped out from the lush green landscape of a photograph. Nick continued kissing my neck, soft lips fluttering across my collarbone. I shut my eyes again but even then I saw her smiling, joyous in her pink bikini, her face rotating with the blackness behind my lids.

"Wait," I said.

"What's wrong?" Nick asked.

"We can't do this." Dizzy, my skin damp with our sweat, I sat up.

Nick sighed, rubbing his hands over his face. "Because of Cara?"

"Yes," I said, and only then did the answer feel true. We were in Cara's house, at Cara's party, with a hundred people roaming around us. My stomach smoldered. I did not want my first time to happen like this.

Nick pulled his body up next to mine and said, "There's nothing between me and Cara."

"What?" I looked back at him, my head moving too quickly, my body unable to settle.

"We both agreed. It was a mistake, and what happens at ASB camp stays at ASB camp."

"Oh God." I stood up. A wave of nausea spun through me. "You and Cara?" I shook my head again. "Oh God."

Nick reached for my arm, trying to stop me, saying something about how he and Cara only ever made out, but I had seen her face shift and soften when she spoke of him, had heard the lazy way his name lingered, sweet on her tongue. I said, "I have to go."

Spilling down the stairs, I refused to stop—not when someone called my name, and not when Cara's smile flashed before me, transposed on all the faces I passed. Acid rose in my throat as I pushed out of the house. When I was far enough away that the sounds of the party had faded, I stumbled to my knees and vomited.

The next morning: head pounding, mouth parched like a desert wind. I stumbled out of my room with little black dots clouding my sight. I couldn't remember getting home but I was still wearing the blue peasant dress, my eyes red and puffy and crusted together. The previous night swirled around me. The pit of my stomach was heavy and empty at once.

At first, I panicked, unsure of what had happened, if I'd thrown up on my mother's dress. But with the exception of the hem, where I must have kneeled on it, the fabric was unsoiled. After struggling into a T-shirt and pajama shorts, I made my way toward the kitchen.

A wedge of sunlight plunged through the open windows, drenching the place where my father sat at the table, reading the paper. I squinted in the glare.

"Good morning, sleeping beauty," my father said. "Looks like you had a rough night. Is that makeup?"

I noticed immediately that his eyes were red too, but they had a misty sheen to them, a contented edge that had been absent from the gaze staring back at me in the mirror minutes before. "Is Mom working?" I asked, ignoring his question.

"Beats me," he said.

I dropped a piece of bread in the toaster and stared as the orange light grew brighter inside the machine. With each tick of the timer, fragments from the previous night bombarded me: the affection in Cara's smile, the roar of the crowd and the flash of cell phones. Nick's lips like a butterfly against my skin. Blood rushed to my head while the snippets materialized and grew coherent. I hadn't done anything wrong, I told myself. You couldn't betray what you didn't know.

The toaster continued clicking. When the bread finally popped up, it was burnt.

"Where'd you get to last night?" my father asked, and for a moment, my mind twisted away from the party. Maybe, I thought, my father had come home for me after all. Maybe he'd been waiting for me. There was still time to show him my cover of "Love Honey." To work on the lost rhythm of "Don't Look Back."

But then he continued: "Lance and Travis came in to jam for a bit. I was going to invite you out there with us, but . . ." He shrugged. "You weren't around."

The words filled my head like a poisonous gas and the dizziness rushed back, expanding in my stomach. It was one thing to take Lance and Travis out to Joe Thompson's bar, but it was entirely different to bring them here, into our studio—the one place that was ours.

Anger coursed through my body. I locked my jaw to keep the lump in my throat from rising as my father's eyes fell back to the paper. His thoughts were already traveling from our conversation, and this time, I didn't bother trying to reclaim them. Tossing the toast in the trash, I turned from the kitchen.

As I passed behind him, he reached out and grabbed my hand. "If you could start something over," he murmured, his gaze tearing into me, "start fresh with what you know now, would you do it?"

A cold fear crept up my spine. "Why are you asking me this?"

"Something's changing, Susie. I can feel it." His lips twisted into a smile, and his grip tightened. My skin pinched beneath his fingers. "I'm so close to understanding, to figuring out what I need to do to get it back. It's all going to be different this time."

I wanted so badly to believe that his words came from a place of hope, but I knew better. He was untying his tether, loosening his weight, floating away. Soon he would be up above the palm trees, the hills, getting smaller and smaller until he became one with the sky and the smog. Until I couldn't see him anymore.

"Why does everything have to be different?" I snapped. I felt furious and sick, could taste the acid burning again in my mouth. "Why can't you just be content with what you have?"

For another moment, his eyes burrowed into mine, begging me to listen. Then he let go of my hand and looked away. Like that last night we had spent in the studio, I knew he saw something else, something beyond me. He wanted me to see it, too, but I was caught in my own disappointment and didn't care when his expression shadowed, or when he began shaking those little white pills into his palm. I left him there, back rounded beneath the harsh rays of sun, consumed by a burden I didn't try to understand.

FOUR

ON MONDAY I returned to the hallways of my high school feeling dazed and out of place. Cara already knew everything. "Don't," she said, turning her back when I approached in the morning. "I saw you." She ignored me as I tried to explain, to remind her that I didn't know she'd had any feelings for Nick because she hadn't told me—but of course, this was also my fault. I'd been too preoccupied to call her, to see her. To be a good friend.

When the first bell rang, I was almost thankful that a crowd of students parted us, and I had no choice but to walk away.

The rest of the week, I felt like I'd been submerged in water; I was holding my breath, drifting between classes. Leaving the cafeteria at lunch on Thursday, I spotted Nick across the quad. He must have felt the tug of my gaze because he looked up, and our eyes locked, and for a moment neither of us moved. Then Nick raised his hand in a wave, an uncertain smile rising on his lips. My body turned hot. All I had to do was walk over and say hello the same way I had hundreds, maybe thousands, of times before—but that exchange seemed suddenly huge and terrifying. I hurried in the opposite direction.

After that, I spent my breaks in the library.

Home wasn't much of a reprieve, either. During the torrid afternoons, I retreated to the studio, trying to reappropriate my anger and loneliness in a song, but any potential I felt immediately eroded beneath the rough gleam of the studio's single working lightbulb. Without my father, the room seemed foreign and hostile. And even if I had forgiven him, if I wanted to pretend that nothing had changed, I couldn't. He spent his nights down at the bar.

I didn't see him again until Friday.

That evening, while the Channel 4 news murmured about a fire and my mother sautéed ground beef in the kitchen, I lay on the sofa, annotating *The Remains of the Day* for advanced English. Secretly, I actually liked English class; I enjoyed unraveling the stories, identifying metaphors—and anyway, as long as my songwriter's block persisted, I had nothing better to do. I might have even blown through the whole novel that night if my father hadn't decided to finally come home.

He cruised through the front door and into the kitchen, all the while whistling some soft, easy tune I didn't recognize. Something new. I lowered my book, peering over the top of the pages.

I wanted to hear the fresh wave of sound forming inside him, to tell him about "Love Honey." But I refused to be the one to speak first.

My mother finally broke the silence.

"Dr. Brown called this afternoon," she began. The beef hissed, sizzling in the frying pan. She jabbed at it with a spatula. "He said you missed another appointment."

"That was today?" my father asked, opening the pantry.

"Yes," my mother said. "That was today."

This seemed like a strange way to begin a conversation between two people who had barely seen each other in days, but as my mother stabbed the beef and my father poured a drink, I had the feeling that I'd once again missed something essential.

My father stooped to slurp from the nearly overflowing glass. "Huh. Guess I forgot."

"I rescheduled it for Tuesday at eight," she said. "You can stop there on your way to work."

My father sipped.

"Did you hear me, James?" my mother asked. She turned to look at him as she flipped the meat and a spray of grease jumped out of the pan, stinging her forearm. "Shit," she said, rushing over to the sink. She held her arm beneath cold water. Unattended, the hiss of cooking beef grew louder. My father took a jar of peanuts out of the pantry and began eating them by the handful.

"Please," my mother said, barely loud enough to be heard over the cacophony of sounds. "All you have to do is see Dr. Brown and get this whole thing straightened out. Michael will take care of the rest."

My father didn't respond. He just kept eating peanuts.

She said, "He's offering you this job because he believes you can succeed there."

I looked back and forth between them. "What job?"

"Your father's work has offered him a new position."

"Offered to ship me off," my father grumbled.

"What?" I asked. "Where? When?"

"It doesn't matter," he said. "It's not happening."

My mother watched the water stream from the faucet. "You know, the pay increase alone is worth—"

My father smacked the jar against the table. "It always comes back to money with you, doesn't it?" he snapped. But it wasn't really a question; before my mother could say anything else, he jerked up from the table, forcing his chair back with a screech, and said, "I'm going out." When he left, the front door slammed with such fury that the molding around the frame began to crack.

For a moment, neither my mother nor I moved. Only after the sound of his truck faded down the street did she turn off the faucet, the stove. Water dripped from her fingers. She closed her eyes for several long seconds and I focused on her hands, hung limp over the sink, the slight shudder of her shoulders. Frustration clogged my throat. It wasn't fair that my parents could choose when to listen, and when to let my voice slip unnoticed through the half-opened window like the smoke twirling up from the frying pan. It wasn't fair that they could decide my future without ever giving me a choice.

"I'm not really hungry anymore," my mother said. Then she grabbed an open bottle of red wine and shuffled down the hallway to her bedroom, grazing a palm against the wall to steady herself. Outside, coyotes yapped in the black-clouded dusk. I couldn't see it, but I heard them talking about it on the news: not far from us, fire swallowed a hillside.

For what seemed like a long time, I just stood there, watching through the window as the moon moved in and out of view, the faint outline of Orion fighting to break through the smoke-wrapped sky. Here and then gone. Here and then gone.

Later that night, I watched the fire coverage on TV. A fast-moving brushfire in the Sepulveda Pass had been contained after burning through more than ninety acres, but that morning's wind had knocked loose two new electrical wires in Calabasas Hills and Scholl Canyon—the latter of which was just a few miles north of our house, not far from where my father and I had hiked. According to the reporter, local firefighters struggled for control, the flames gaining fuel with each gulp of straw-like vegetation. She said something about evacuations: still voluntary in most places, but please stay tuned. Then the screen switched to an aerial view.

Never before had a fire that large come so close to where we lived, and I went outside to gauge its proximity. I couldn't see any actual flames but the night was lit up in oranges, canopied in smoke, looking more like a volcanic eruption than a wildfire. Wind groaned through the canyon and gusts crashed through the palms. When a police cruiser rolled up the street, I ran toward it.

"Officer," I yelled, flagging down the car.

Inside sat two men, both with crisp navy shirts buttoned up

to the neck. They regarded me suspiciously, looked past me at the dark house.

"Officer, do we need to leave?" I asked.

"Evacuation is still voluntary at this time," the man in the passenger seat recited. "But we're advising all residents to gather any important belongings and clear the area as a precaution. If you have somewhere you can go, any friends or family you can stay with, we suggest you do so as soon as possible."

But what if we don't have any family, I wanted to say. What if we're alone? My heart heaved as a caravan of cars and trucks coasted down the opposite side of the street. One of them honked as they passed and the officer behind the wheel waved. Elsewhere in the valley, a chorus of sirens whined.

The officer must have seen something cross my face then because he sighed and added, "Just pay attention to the news reports, okay?" They started to drive away.

"Wait!" I yelled. The car stopped. "How likely is it that the fire will jump the freeway?"

At the north end of Eagle Rock, just beyond where Cara lived, the 134 Freeway cut through the hillside, ten paved lanes separating our neighborhood from the small expanse of wilderness beyond. If the fire made it over, Cara's house would be one of the first to go. Then Nick's. Ours would surely follow.

The officer shrugged. "It's unlikely. I've never seen it happen. But if the winds keep up . . ." He shook his head. "Let's hope it doesn't come to that."

A number of my curious neighbors had also emerged from their homes and were now approaching the cop car, hoping to learn more about the degree of danger. I took a few steps backward and noticed the Murphys, the family that lived across the street, piling suitcases into the back of their SUV. Both parents and the children moved briskly in and out of their algae-green house, stuffing every available crevice of the car until there was barely enough space left for them all to sit. The only one not moving was Beth, the smallest child. She was wearing pink pajamas and clutched a stuffed rabbit to her chest, staring, mesmerized, at the smoke oozing into the sky until her father scooped her up and strapped her into a car seat.

Once the family was situated in the SUV, Mr. Murphy ran back inside. A few seconds later, a piece of white paper with *EVACUATED* written in bold red letters appeared in the front window.

Where was my own father? Why wasn't he here, packing us into his truck? The fires must have been on every news and radio station in the county. If he were driving, he would have been able to see the orange outline of the hills, the surging black smoke. He would have heard the sirens. He had to know that without him, we were stranded.

Across the street, Mr. Murphy locked the front door and drove his family away.

Inside, my mother clutched the phone to her chest and looked out the window.

"Susie," she said, her words slow and deliberate. "Honey, what's happening?"

The TV was on, as it had been all evening. I looked from my mother to the screen as the reporter discussed the violent, erratic winds, the flying embers.

"There's a fire," I said. "What's wrong with you?"

"Are we being evacuated?"

"Not yet."

She nodded. Her whole body swayed with her head as her eyes drifted to the window, dull and heavy. She looked half asleep, or like she'd forgotten why we stood stiff in the living room, the phone in her hand, the white light of the TV bathing her skin.

"Some people are already leaving," I told her.

"I'll go pack some things, then, in case. You'll keep an eye on it?" she asked, as if we were talking about a cake in the oven and not a brushfire burning just beyond the 134. Yes, fires were normal in Southern California, and my mother had lived with the risk of a singed world her whole life. Still, I was surprised that she hardly even considered the matter. Maybe she knew something I didn't, or maybe she was losing her mind. I wanted to ask her about my father's job. I wondered if she drank the whole bottle of wine.

She put the phone on the table and walked back down the dark hallway.

After her door clicked shut, I grabbed the phone and called Joe Thompson's. The line was busy. I called Cara's house too, then Nick's, and felt a glittering relief when both answering machines picked up.

Then, not entirely sure of the precautions for a fire, I did the few things that felt natural: I closed all the windows to keep the smoke out and set the fans on high so we wouldn't suffocate; I found the flashlights and spare batteries in the junk drawer and set them on the table, next to a box of crackers, a jar of peanut butter, and half a loaf of bread; I filled cups and bottles with water; and, finally, I pulled out a few of my father's records that I would want to take if we had to go, stacking them by his Martin near the front door. When all that was done, I turned back to the news.

The anchor droned on about the acreage already burned and I was lulled into a state of calm, eyelids fluttering in and out of sleep until the sound of tires rolling up the driveway jostled me. A door slammed shut.

It was nearly three in the morning when my father crashed into the house, bringing with him the smell of smoke. He did not look like himself; his skin was soiled, and flyaway pieces of his graying hair stood erect with static. Behind his eyes, something reckless flared.

"Where have you been?" I asked. "I tried to call Joe Thompson's, but the phone was busy."

He breathed heavily and put his hands on his hips. "Goddamn devil's wind tonight."

"I think we should leave. Some of the neighbors have evacuated already."

"No," he said, his face darkening.

"But the officers said—"

"It won't cross."

I waited for an explanation. "How do you know?" I finally asked.

I'd spent the week wishing for everything to be back as it was before our fight and Cara's party, before Lance and Travis, the tape, the winds. I wanted my father to look at me the way he used to, eyes brimming with potential and mystery. I wanted him to need me again.

But that night, when he finally raised his eyes in my direction, I felt only the urge to look away.

"I know," he said, voice thick through gritted teeth, "because I listen." He turned and went into the kitchen.

Even from where I sat, I could smell him as he passed—like oak, like the Redwoods, the burning flavors of spices and rye. I felt the inebriating effects of his scent as if I, too, had been drinking, and though that already made me dizzy, it was not enough for my father. He took a new glass from the cabinet and dropped in three ice cubes that cracked beneath the warm rush of whiskey.

"Now, it's people," he called over his shoulder, fishing the orange pill bottle from his pocket. "People that I can't figure out. Just when you get everything back on track, people want to derail you. They're more dangerous than anything Mother Nature can create. If the world burns, it will be our own damn fault."

I wasn't sure what he was talking about anymore, wasn't even sure he was talking to me. Afraid of trying to understand, I stayed quiet.

As he walked down the hall, the liquid sloshed over the rim of his glass and dripped into a constellation on the floor. He entered the bedroom where I thought my mother was sleeping. A thin haze of light fanned out beneath the door.

"Are you happy?" I heard my mother say. "We've been worried sick."

It surprised me to hear her voice; she had not stirred in hours. I stood up and crept closer, bracing myself for whatever fight was destined to come.

She said, "Oh, James. Can't you see how this place has ruined you?"

"Do you remember what you said," he asked, voice low and dangerous, "all those years ago, when Vivian threatened to cut you off? She said if you stayed with me, you would have nothing. Do you remember?"

Vivian—the name sparked in my mind before fizzling out. I recognized it, but could not remember who it belonged to.

"You said that you didn't care. That money didn't matter. That this"—he paused—"was bigger than any amount of zeros on a check. Your exact words."

"This is our last chance. Don't you realize that? And if you turn it down . . ."

My father was silent.

"Michael said he knows a great Realtor who will help us find a house. We could have a yard big enough for a pool. Can you imagine?"

"We live a half hour from the goddamn Pacific Ocean. Right there is a giant body of water we can access, free of charge. And we don't need to buy supplies or pay to maintain it."

"Well, if you consider our taxes—"

"You think Phoenix is going to be better, Diane? Phoenix has nothing. You may as well move us to fucking Antarctica."

I pulled back from the door, a knot of dread expanding in my throat. Phoenix? *Arizona?* It was impossible. My father would never leave Los Angeles.

"I guess I'm the only one trying to do what's best for our family, then," my mother said. "For Susannah."

"This is not about her! This is about your life not being good enough. About me not being good enough."

There was a long pause—nothing but the sound of the Santa Anas as they kicked up dust and threw the smoldering cinders around the city. I was about to turn away, when my mother spoke again: "You're right. It's not. And you can't keep doing this, James. You're ruining any possibility of a future for this family."

"And you've given up on me. Do you have any idea how that feels?"

"I've done nothing but sacrifice for you."

He let out a sharp laugh. "Oh, now you want to talk about sacrifice?"

My mother started yelling something else but my father interrupted her. "You know what, Diane? I changed my mind. You win. I'm going to give you exactly what you want."

As I stood there outside my parents' bedroom door, I thought that was it.

I thought we were moving to Phoenix.

I closed my eyes and tried to picture it—a wide stretch of dehydrated brown land punctuated here and there by a cactus. It would be hot there all year. No occasional ocean breeze. No ocean. But maybe it wouldn't be so bad. Maybe our house would be brand-new, two stories, like the homes in the Inland Empire but with an orange-shingled roof and a rock garden instead of grass, a blue tiled pool in the backyard. We could have a basement—a new studio. Maybe all we needed was a change of scenery, a place where there were no Santa Anas, where no one had ever heard of the Vital Spades.

Then a crash resounded inside the bedroom and my eyes flapped open.

"Where are you going?" my mother shouted. "Don't be ridiculous. Sit down, James. *James.*"

The door flung open and my father stormed past me, through the living room. I ran after him, outside to the driveway, but he refused to stop. Ash fluttered down from the sky, flakes so white you could mistake them for snow. Somewhere in the distance, flames paraded through the hillside, and though many miles still separated us, I could have sworn I felt the heat against my cheeks.

"Dad," I yelled. "Wait."

"I'm going for a drive," he said.

"I'll come with you."

He put his hand out to stop me. "Go back inside, Susannah."

It scared me to see him like that, his eyes wild, his voice rubbed threadbare. And yet I couldn't turn away.

"But the fire," I said. The words came out as a croak, unfinished.

"Everything's going to be fine. Go back inside. You're in charge."

I stood paralyzed, uncomprehending. My father opened the door of his truck.

"You can't go," I said.

Not entirely sure of what to do but certain I had to do something, my body jolted forward. Whether I was going to wrap myself around his leg like an ankle monitor or buckle myself in the passenger seat and refuse to leave, I'm still not sure. Before I had even crossed in front of him, my father pushed me away. I staggered backward, lost my balance, and fell to the concrete.

His eyes widened while the rest of his face sank, pallid as the ash pooling around us. "Susie," he said in a whisper. Inside my chest, something began to close. Neither of us moved. My hands stung from where they had scraped against the ground and my heart thrashed against my throat, rising like bile, blocking my speech. He reached toward me, just barely. "I'm sorry," he said. Then he ducked into the cab of his truck.

The headlights dazed me as he backed out of the driveway. I dropped my head and shut my eyes. Behind my lids I saw two yellow circles floating in an endless stretch of black nothing. When I opened them again, my father was gone.

I don't know how long I stayed there in the driveway. Even as the minutes passed and the ash fell around me, I could not get up. I watched the white specks sifting over the street like a fine powder. I listened as the coyotes wailed, flushed down from the fiery ridge.

When I finally returned inside, anger spilled over. I wanted to scream, to break something. Instead, I took my father's whiskey down from the top shelf and, hands throbbing with each movement, unscrewed the cap. Less than an inch of brown liquid flashed up at me from the bottom, and I drank all of it. I did not like the taste of whiskey yet, but once the liquid scraped its way down my throat, I started to feel better. When it was gone, I walked over to the records.

My skin felt hot as I slid my finger across the soft, tattered spines. The Doobie Brothers, Emitt Rhodes, Little Feat—these were the people my father called family, but none of them knew a thing about him. Maybe I didn't, either.

I put the Kinks' *Lola Versus Powerman and the Moneygoround: Part One* on the record player—side two. "This Time Tomorrow" began playing. I sat back on the sofa. My eyes grew heavy.

The next thing I remember is waking. The sun radiated through the glass window above the couch where I had fallen asleep, illuminating the specks of dust in the air. A moment passed before I recognized a woman's doughy voice floating through the still room. I searched for the source of the sound, but was alone.

"After a full night of battle, firefighters can finally sigh with relief as the Santa Ana winds show a drastic decrease in speed. Were it not for Mother Nature's mercy in the early hours of the morning, many residents of Eagle Rock would have faced a mandatory evacuation as their homes became directly threatened by the fire."

The TV was off, the record player open but not spinning. I felt a pounding in my temples as I turned toward the kitchen where a bulky black boombox sat on the counter.

"The fire department has confirmed that the flames are now under control," the woman continued, her voice trained and unaffected. I stopped listening. My father was right—the fire did not jump the freeway. Of course it didn't. He would not have left us if that were even a possibility. Somehow, I felt certain of this, and as I headed into the kitchen for a bowl of cereal, I decided I would forgive him. After all, I'd been selfish and stubborn too. If I had to be the one to bow down, make a compromise—fine. I just wanted our lives to go back to normal. I wanted to return to the studio, finish "Don't Look Back." And I didn't even care whether any of that happened here, or in Arizona.

As I scoured the shelves of the mostly empty refrigerator, the cuts on my hands burned. The woman on the radio said something about power outages, and I realized that the fridge was dark. Oh well, I thought. I sat at the table, picking individual *O*s out of the Cheerios box, wondering where everyone had gone.

". . . winds will likely keep up through the winter, so we urge all of our listeners to be prepared for the worst. In other news, a black Ford pickup was found overturned on the eastbound side of the 134 Freeway this morning, just before the Fair Oaks Avenue exit."

I stopped eating and looked toward the radio.

"The police have yet to release any information regarding the cause of accident or the identity of the deceased, but it appears at this time that no others cars were—"

"Morning, honey," my mother interrupted, nudging the front door closed with her hip. She had a big red cooler in her hands. We used to take it to the beach when I was a child. Now, it was covered in a fine fur of dust, one of the handles broken. It must have been buried somewhere in the garage.

My heart began thudding in my chest. "Where's Dad?" I asked.

"Not sure," she said. "Probably down at Joe's."

Dread coursed outward, numbing my hands. My mother walked toward the refrigerator. The radio continued: "The traffic on the eastbound 134 will likely remain backed up throughout the morning as rescue crews try to clear the scene of the smashed vehicle. Alternate routes to the eastbound 210 are suggested."

"Mom," I said, voice wavering.

My mother switched off the radio. "I'm sure everything is

fine." She put the cooler down and began transferring perishables from the fridge.

Outside, a car pulled into the driveway.

"See?" she said.

I nodded as she moved apples, cheese, a head of lettuce, and half a package of baloney into the cooler, methodically placing each item so everything would fit. By the time she reached the orange juice, my father still had not come inside. I saw her hands quaking as she considered the best spot for the large carton. Someone knocked at the door.

"Probably just the Murphys looking to borrow some matches," she said, but I already knew the Murphys were gone, and I remember, even then, detecting the truth wash over her with each slow step. Regardless of whether or not she actually knew, I have come to believe that my mother was trying to elongate that last moment before our world imploded. Until she opened the door and saw the two police officers standing there, she continued clinging to our last shard of hope. Then one of the officers said her name and looked over her shoulder at me before bowing his head, and I wondered if they were the same men who patrolled our neighborhood the previous night, but I couldn't recall their faces. My breath caught in my throat, and all I remember thinking in that instant was that my mother's skin had turned such a miraculous color—the color of moonlight.

FIVE

THERE WOULD BE no funeral.

"We don't have the money," my mother told Detective Melendez when he asked us whether or not we needed a recommendation for help with the arrangements. Her voice was strange and flat, with an inflection that made each statement sound unfinished. Or maybe I just thought this because of the way all noise and movement seemed to occur apart from me, on the other side of a thick fog.

"There are special loans you can take out," he said, and told us about our options. Periodically, he cast me split-second glances, as though my presence in his office made him anxious, but I refused to leave the room.

That afternoon, one of the officers—a young man who wore blue-tinted sunglasses even though the sky was a dense layer of black and soot clouds—drove us to the station. I can't recall what happened before we left, or even how much time had passed. All I remember is that the squad car smelled like sweat and stale coffee, and that all the way to the Pasadena Police Department, I couldn't help but feel that we had done something wrong. That we were the convicts of a crime, being delivered into the custody of the state. And now, as Detective Melendez eyed me like some rogue weapon he worried would start firing spontaneously, I knew it was true. In the blackness behind my eyelids, I saw a burst of headlights and flaky white ash, yellow orbs floating in the dark, the gasp of an apology in the distorted O of my father's mouth. The cuts on my palms had burned too much to push my body up, to stop him. I didn't even try.

Suddenly, all the what-ifs flooded me, shoving the air from my lungs. I forced my hands into fists. My palms pounded like heartbeats.

"And a lot of the local funeral homes have payment plans," Detective Melendez was saying, but what I heard was: *This is all your fault.*

"Susannah?" he said suddenly. "Can I get you something? How about some water?" His eyes darted to my mother, then landed again, uneasily, on me. "It's important to stay hydrated when the air is smoky like this."

I could feel my head getting light from the pain. I released my fists and motioned toward the crumpled copy of that morning's *Los Angeles Times* lying on his desk. "Is he in that?" I whispered.

"Not today's issue." The detective cleared his throat and turned his body back to my mother. "What I'm trying to say, Mrs. Hayes, is that they are very accommodating for folks in your situation."

"That's kind of you to suggest, Detective," my mother said, "but a simple cremation will be fine."

At the time my mother's decision seemed like the right one. No burial, no grave, no giant hole in the ground to remind us of the giant hole we were left with. I turned to the window. Out on the busy street, wind roamed through the traffic. A grocery bag got caught on someone's windshield. The driver turned on his wipers, but the bag just swayed back and forth with the motion.

"I don't understand," I said, interrupting the detective. "I don't understand how . . ." I looked down at the cuts on my hands, unable to say the words out loud. "How it happened."

"Based on what we know so far," he said slowly, "it appears that Mr. Hayes—your father—lost control of his vehicle going what we'd guess to be about eighty-five miles per hour. The truck hit the guardrail and flipped onto its side before finally crashing into the telephone pole."

"The power outage," I said.

"I thought the wind knocked a wire loose," my mother said, her eyebrows pinching together.

"That's what the electric company thought at first," Detective Melendez said, "but once they were able to identify the source of the outage, they discovered the crash was, in fact, the cause. However, if it weren't for that pole, his car would have plunged through the barrier, down onto the westbound on-ramp beneath."

He offered this last part as a consolation, as if what mattered were the circumstances of death rather than the death itself.

"So that makes it all better?" I said.

"Susannah, please," my mother said, but her voice was too tired to sustain any authority.

Detective Melendez sighed, studying a framed photograph on his desk. "Sometimes," he said, and stopped. The thick bristles of his moustache curled over his top lip as he frowned. "Sometimes, families have to bury empty boxes."

For a moment we sat in silence, as though in vigil for the families whose situations were worse than our own. But I couldn't imagine them.

My mother pushed herself out of her chair. "Are we done, Detective?"

He stood, the worn leather of his own chair groaning. "There's one more thing," he said, lowering his voice, "but I'd really prefer to speak to you privately."

My mother sighed and said, "She's old enough."

Detective Melendez glanced at me once more, and I made my face hard and blank to show that I could handle whatever he had to say. "We uncovered some evidence of alcohol in the car. We're not sure yet whether the crash is alcohol-related, but it is being investigated."

"Do what you must," my mother said. "Anything else?"

"Yes." He breathed heavily. The sour scent of coffee wafted on his breath, and I realized how humid it was in the office, how flushed I felt. He said, "There were no skid marks on the pavement leading up to where he hit the railing."

I shook my head. "What does that mean?"

"It means," he said, "that the driver didn't slam on the brakes when he lost control. Right now, the information could still point to a number of different explanations. We haven't yet ruled out the possibility of a coyote running in front of the vehicle, causing him to swerve off the road. We know a whole pack of them were forced out of the hillside last night and have been showing up all over the area. He also could have fallen asleep at the wheel. Or, well . . ."

"Or what?" I asked. My heart contracted. I thought about all the nights my father and I spent in the studio, building songs out of silence until morning snuck up over California. I knew what those midnights meant to him. He would not have fallen asleep in the hours when he felt most alive.

Detective Melendez said, "There is a chance he had intended . . ."

"Thank you, Detective," my mother said, cutting him off. She put one hand on my arm. "I think we've heard enough for today. You have my number, should you need anything else."

The coolness of her skin startled me as she steered us into the hall, and all at once I remembered the fight. Phoenix. The unwavering resignation in my father's voice as he said, *I'm going to give you exactly what you want.*

But no. No one wanted that. He wouldn't have left us. There had to be another explanation.

"What about the headaches?"

"Headaches?" Melendez echoed.

"What if he got a headache while he was driving, and he leaned over to try to get his pills out of the glove compartment or something. Maybe he didn't even realize he was swerving." For the first time, I wondered if he had been wearing a seat belt or if he had shot through the windshield like a cannonball, the way dummies do in those videos shown during driver's ed.

Detective Melendez gazed at my mother. She said nothing, her eyes locked on his, her expression unreadable.

"You have to consider that as a factor too, right?" I asked.

He gave a swift nod and said, "We'll be considering every possibility." Then he led us to the front desk, where he shook my mother's hand and promised to be in touch. We followed the same young officer back to his squad car.

We were halfway across the Colorado Street Bridge when my mother finally broke into long, shuddering sobs. I wanted to lie and tell her that everything would be okay. I tried to touch her but my limbs, like my mouth, wouldn't move. She pressed her face into her hands, and the officer flicked on the beacon lights. We accelerated, cars parting around us, the streets blurring in dusty smears of color and wind.

It wasn't fair, the sameness of everything, the way the world hadn't changed. To everyone else it was just another Santa Ana, but when I looked out the living room window, I saw pieces of my father in the skeletal branches clumped in the gutters, in the guts of clawed-open garbage bags gushing out into the street. He was the shredded paper scraps, the chalk imprint of gray ash, the sharp, jagged trunk of a tree torn in half. Everyone else would clean up the mess, replant their front yards, and forget that a fire had ever come so close. But what about us? How could we possibly sweep up the debris and move forward?

In the kitchen, my mother filled the teakettle and used a match to light the stove. "We should take out some candles," she said as steam rose from the spout. "We don't know how long this power outage will last."

I nodded, but after a while, when the light started fading, neither of us moved.

Inside our house, my father's presence clung to everything. Even his whiskey still coated my teeth, though the taste had eroded into something only vaguely acidic. In the dark, at least, I wouldn't be confronted by the records and the loose picks and the indent on his side of the couch. And thank God my mother had done the dishes that morning; the sight of his used coffee mug in the sink might have undone me. I drank my peppermint tea quickly, sloshing it around with my tongue before swallowing. The liquid burned the roof of my mouth, but I kept drinking, wanting to feel the heat, to focus on something small and understandable.

I couldn't tell how late it was because all of our clocks were electronic, connected to the telephone, the microwave. I worried that we might remain in limbo forever, just sitting at the kitchen table as the daylight disappeared, waiting for someone to tell us what we were supposed to do next.

"Why can't we have a funeral?" I asked. My voice seemed too loud in the still room.

"Your father never wanted to be buried," my mother said.

"How do you know?"

"He told me." She looked into her tea as if searching for a way to explain. "A long time ago."

"What did he say?"

"Just that he didn't want to be buried."

I tried to picture them, the faces from the photograph: twenty years old and lying on the hood of a car at twilight, discussing death as if it were something romantic. She was right—he would have hated being confined in the ground, reduced to a plaque and a prescribed speech in some dank, pink-walled funeral parlor. But *I* needed it. I needed the veneered cherrywood of a coffin and flower-lined aisles so sappy and pungent that the scent nearly suffocated me. I needed a ceremony at some sun-filled cemetery, like the Hollywood Forever, near the duck pond and the statue of Johnny Ramone. I needed a place where I could keep him, because he already felt so faint that I feared losing him completely.

I said, "A burial is different than a funeral."

My mother traced her fingers over the table. "We'll make sure to do something. Just the two of us."

"What if someone else wanted to come?"

"Like who?"

The Vital Spades, I wanted to say. But then I remembered: I'd never actually met them. I did not know where they were, or how to get in touch with them, or if they even wanted to be found.

"Joe Thompson," I offered after a while. "And the guys from the bar."

My mother frowned at the table. "Those people fueled your father's habits. That's all."

"Then what about us?" I asked.

My mother stood up and walked to the window.

"We didn't stop him," I said. "We're just as much to blame."

"I need you to know," my mother began, concentrating hard

on some point beyond the glass, "that I never wanted this. Not for a second. Your father and I had problems, but never—even during the worst of it."

"I know," I said.

She stayed there for a long time, staring out into the yard, but from where I sat the night was already too dark to see anything.

"Where was he going?" I asked.

My mother reached a hand up to her face. After a moment, she turned back to look at me. She had just opened her mouth to speak when something clicked and screeched, a skidding sound like worn-out tires. Then music began to play.

Startled, I jumped up, searching for the source of the noise. The record player had started spinning in the living room. Only after I shut it off did I consider that the song might have been a sign from my father. Miniature bumps rose on my arms. I turned around to ask my mother if she felt him, too, his ghost passing through her—but then I noticed the glint of her hair beneath the overhead lights, the green zeros blinking from the microwave.

The power had come back on. That was all. And it occurred to me then that the record must have started playing from where it stopped the night before, during the last track of the album, at the exact moment my father's car crashed into the telephone pole and disconnected the electricity.

I lifted the record from the player by its edges and put it back in its sleeve, in its rightful place on the shelf. Even though most of the spines were indecipherable, worn and frayed in a familiar mosaic, *Lola Versus Powerman and the Moneygoround: Part One* stood apart from the rest. I yanked it back out of the lineup and hurled it at the floor, willing it to break into a thousand little pieces—which of course it didn't. The floor in the living room was carpeted.

I began moving then, tearing the records from the wall. First one and then a dozen, I pushed them off the sides, threw them back, clawing at the covers until my mother grabbed my arms from behind and, surrounding me, pulled me down to the floor. "All we can do is keep living," she whispered, and put one cold hand on my cheek. My tears pooled in the spaces between her fingers as I thought about the impossibility of more life after this, and how wrong it felt that in another minute, when my body stopped shaking, we would pull apart and pick up the records and without saying anything, stack them back on the shelves.

That night, from the center of a thick, black dream, I woke to the sound of my mother whispering. My eyes opened in slits, too tired to pull apart any farther. I vaguely remembered that at some point earlier, she had coerced me to the sofa, rested my head in her lap. She weaved her fingertips through my hair until my throat hollowed and dried and my mind emptied into sleep. Now, the living room was dark except for a thin slice of yellow light cutting through the hallway. Her words spilled out, soft, intangible.

"I never would have thought," she began, and stopped. "No, of course I did, but not the extent of it. How can anyone ever really know what is going through someone else's mind?"

For a while, she was quiet. A heavy silence pushed into the living room, sinking me back toward unconsciousness before her voice grasped me again. "But this—nothing prepares you for this."

I guessed she was on the phone, but could not think of a single person whom she would speak to with such frank, unguarded sincerity. She had no close friends, no remaining family. My grandmother (who existed in my memory as vague, bony fingers and silk) died when I was a baby, following her husband, who passed a few years prior. My mother rarely spoke of them. At some point I must have decided the memories were too painful, because I didn't push her for any further information. She only had the two of us, my father and me.

"What do I do now?" my mother said after a moment, her voice coarse and raw. "I need you. We both do."

I heard the squeak of the bed as my mother's voice faded to a murmur. In the darkness, I imagined she was talking to my father. They were lying on top of the bed, facing each other, their noses an inch apart. His eyes still held blue. His smile crooked. She said, "I need you." When he reached out to touch her face, a feeling like wind in her veins.

SIX

I WOKE EARLY to an empty house dense with heat. My arms were sore and my mouth tasted like dust, but during those first few blissful seconds, I didn't remember anything. It was just another morning.

Then I noticed the records.

Though they had all been restacked neatly on the shelves, even a split-second glance revealed their scattered spines and arbitrary order. The memories roared back. My father's absence felt crushing, dizzying—like I had lost him all over again.

I waited for something else to happen: a knock at the door, a record to start playing, a fault line to split beneath my feet and suck me straight down into the earth's core. I closed my eyes, bracing myself. Nothing.

After a minute, I noticed a soft grunting noise coming from the yard, so I went outside. Sun glared through the smoke-stained sky and I raised one hand to shield my eyes, squinting at the shape of my mother squatting in the flower bed. She wore loose cotton pajamas, muddy sneakers, and a ratty SeaWorld cap with her hair pulled through in a ponytail. Dabs of moisture clung to her chin.

"What are you doing?" I asked.

"Pruning," she said. She gripped the base of a thick stock of weeds and jerked the roots out with all the force of her upper body. "You want to join? It helps—" Her voice faltered, caught in her throat. "It helps to keep busy."

I shook my head and went back inside, watching from the window as my mother clawed through the soil for her next victim, grabbed it with both hands, and yanked.

For the next few days, she worked in the flower bed while messages from the outside world accumulated on the answering machine: the cremation was complete, the high school wanted to extend their deepest sympathies, the rental car was ready, and would we like that delivered to our doorstep for a small extra fee? The catering company wanted my mother to know that a third missed shift would result in termination from the company. Detective Melendez also left one brief message, requesting that my mother contact him as soon as possible. I suppose she must have; after that, we never heard from him again.

All the while, my mother labored with a maniacal fixation that likely should have worried me, but in some small way, I think I understood: this was how she kept living.

Truthfully, I envied her. If I could have thrown myself into some mundane activity, separating my mind from the pain for just a minute, I would have. Nothing worked—not even the guitar. I attempted to play "Love Honey," but couldn't make it through the first verse without something going wrong. In less than five minutes, I lost three of my father's tortoiseshell picks into the sound hole, split one of the cuts bridging my left lifeline, nearly smashed the guitar through the living room window when I couldn't shake the picks loose, and finally shoved the Martin between unused winter coats in the hallway closet because I couldn't even bear looking at it.

I couldn't go in the studio, either. I tried once, on the second or third night, unable to shake the possibility that somewhere inside was a clue to what really happened the night he died. But when the door clicked open, a strange, musty smell slammed into me—a hodgepodge of metals and rye. My father, I realized quickly. Preserved inside the sealed-up room his scent had swelled, and I closed the door immediately, afraid of losing it, the essence that had already vanished from our house the way the smell of cheap laundry detergent fades from your clothes as soon as you put them back in the drawer. The realness of it—him, in there, the lack of him everywhere else—knocked the wind from me.

In fact, the only distraction I seemed to tolerate was my mother, so I spent most of my time that week sitting under the dappled shade of our avocado tree, in a lawn chair half-broken by the winds, watching her jab at the dirt. I didn't think about school. I didn't think about work. I didn't wonder why my own boss hadn't called.

One day, I woke from a nap to a silhouetted body blocking the sun above me. An extended hand clasped a piece of crumbled paper.

"What's this?" I asked, taking the note from my mother. In crisp blue pen she had scribbled the names of half a dozen flowers.

"I'd like you to pick these up from Home Depot," she said.

As a child, I hated Home Depot. I looked down at the list and felt lost already among the foreign names. *Alyssum. Lily of the Nile.* "Wouldn't it be smarter if you went? Maybe you'll see something you like better and change your mind."

The phone rang inside the house. My mother paused, mouth half-open in the formulation of some thought, and craned her ear in the direction of the living room window. Neither of us moved. I felt my heart accelerating as the answering machine clicked on, wondering if this would finally be the call from one of my father's friends, someone from the Spades or Joe Thompson's bar who had heard about our loss and wanted us to know how sorely my father would be missed. Then, I wondered if the caller was Nick. A moment of suspended silence clogged the line before the person hung up.

"I trust your judgment," my mother finally said, eyes still trained on the window. "And getting away from the house will do you some good."

"Maybe you should take your own advice," I mumbled.

"What?" She turned to me.

"I said, 'A car ride actually sounds kind of nice.'"

As I cruised down busy side streets in our sterile rental car, purposely avoiding the 134 Freeway, I flipped through the local radio stations until I found the familiar, slippery bass line of "Ob-La-Di, Ob-La-Da." I turned up the volume.

Paul McCartney crooned about Desmond and Molly and their simple little family, and I was suddenly transported back to this time my father came to Career Day at my elementary school. Ms. Hopkins, my fourth grade teacher, had expected him to talk about working in corporate computer distribution. I could still see her eyes widening as he sauntered up to the front of the room in his blue jeans and biker boots, the Martin strapped to his back. He started playing without any introduction, nodding to the other parents in the back, a signal for them to join in. By the end of the song everyone had started singing, even Ms. Hopkins and the kids who wouldn't know the Beatles from bees swarming the playground. But not me. I was consumed with pride, watching the other fathers—stern-faced lawyers, accountants in stiff suits—transform under his spell.

Then someone behind me honked. The light had turned green, and my reverie was shattered, and for those first few seconds I could not accelerate—could not even remember where I was going. The car continued honking as it swerved around me and whizzed by.

Turns out my mother was right: It did help to keep busy. So when I returned home I decided to help in the garden.

We worked side by side for most of the afternoon, hardly speaking, lost in the monotony of digging and filling holes. At one point, as I sat back on my heels to take a break, I looked across the street and noticed that the *EVACUATED* sign remained in the Murphys' window. I was wondering why the family hadn't returned, when a sleek black Jetta pulled up in front of their house. For an instant, I marveled at the coincidence. Then Cara stepped out of the car.

She crossed the street, waving hesitantly, and waited on our curb as though unsure of whether or not she should come closer. A blurry, heat-twisted image of Lance and Travis clouded my mind but I stood, shaking off the memory with the dirt on my hands. I shuffled down the driveway to meet her.

"Hi," Cara said, perching her sunglasses up on her head. Her curly hair had turned wild in the static breeze.

"Hi," I said.

Cara glanced at my face, at the ground, down the street, where a mailman puttered from door to door, whistling. I crossed and uncrossed my arms. An uncertainty had bloomed between us and we stood in silence for what felt like a long time before Cara finally shook her head and looked back to me. Her eyes had welled with tears.

"I only just heard," she said, bottom lip trembling. "I'm so sorry." She stepped forward and wrapped her arms around my shoulders.

My face caught in the net of her hair and I inhaled hairspray. I said, "It's okay," though it wasn't, and all at once I was glad we hadn't had any sort of funeral. I didn't think I'd have been able to handle the flood of grim, pitying expressions and tilted heads that assured me *he's in a better place now*. All I wanted was the tiny luxury of questioning everything—to be allowed to feel weak and tired and lost.

Cara said, "He's in a better place now."

The phrase made me wince. I knew she believed in heaven, but other than the sweeping, unending emptiness that slogged through me, I found it hard to believe in much of anything. Silence expanded between us, and I felt a weight pressing against my chest. I was exhausted. Nothing seemed more important right then than going inside and falling asleep.

"The school," Cara said suddenly, brightening as she offered me a binder neatly divided with colorful tabs. "They wanted someone to bring your assignments so you don't fall behind. We tried to organize everything so it'd be easier, but I'm warning you in advance: some of this stuff is such a snore, especially for Mr. Burnell's class. I swear he speaks in monotone on purpose."

Opening the binder, I flipped through the pages.

"Nick helped," she said.

My heart lurched. I remembered how his eyes glistened, splashed with hope, when he waved at me across the quad. The words on the paper blurred together.

"We're just friends," Cara continued. "Honestly, it's better this way. People always say not to mix business with pleasure, you know? And sometimes ASB feels like a full-time job."

She laughed awkwardly and drew something on the ground with the tip of her shoe. I nodded, or tried to. I continued flipping through the handouts.

"Is there anything else I can do to help?" she asked after a minute.

"No," I said. "Thanks, though."

"Well then I guess I should . . ." She gestured over her shoulder.

"You'll call if you need anything?"

"Yeah." I closed the binder.

"Okay," she said. She waved to my mother and started back across the street.

"Cara?"

She turned around. Behind her, clouds rose up from the mountains like smoke from a fresh fire. I said, "Thanks again."

A faint smile crossed her face before she got into her car and drove away.

"How nice of Cara to drop by," my mother said when I walked past her on my way into the house. "You two should go do something this weekend. See a movie. I think there's some money in my wallet."

"I'm going to take a nap," I said, and continued inside.

In the kitchen, I shoved the binder into the recycling.

SEVEN

WHEN MY TWO-WEEK approved leave of absence from school ended, I didn't return. My principal must have called, or the guidance counselor, someone—but by then, our answering machine was long past full. All my mother said on the subject was "If you're not ready to go back yet, I get it. But if you choose to stay home for the time being, you have to help out around here. Deal?"

The compromise seemed fair enough. Besides my willingness to do anything if it meant staying out of school, I'd taken a liking to the slew of simple errands my mother sent me on for her newest obsession: deep-cleaning the house. I followed her whims without hesitation, content to retrieve Drano, sponge rollers, and even a big carpet-washing machine she had reserved from a hardware store way out in Pomona. And when she mentioned one Tuesday that she was not looking forward to the congested drive down to the crematorium where my father's urn was waiting, I grabbed the keys and told her I'd be back in a few hours.

Returning home, I set the urn down on the kitchen table next to my mother's visual to-do list—a towering mound of receipts, mail, and miscellaneous clutter. She'd been inspecting a letter when she heard the thud, and she jerked up at the sound.

"Jesus, Susannah," she said, one hand over her chest. Then her eyes floated down to the urn. "What is that?"

The white ceramic vase looked fake, like a prop in a movie, with little peach flowers frolicking around the rim. If it weren't so heavy, I might have thought the whole thing was a hoax—that he wasn't in there, wasn't even dead.

But there was no mistake; the mortician had his wallet, along with a few of his other belongings. I put them on the table. Most of them, anyway.

"I guess we should've answered the phone," I said.

"You didn't . . ." She pointed in the urn's general direction and swirled her finger through the air, unwilling, I suppose, to say anything more specific about the ugly thing. "I mean, this wasn't your choice, was it?"

"Please," I said, and sat down next to her. "The guy told me they chose their most popular style when they couldn't reach us. I guess their entire customer base is made up of old ladies survived only by their cats and doily collections."

The left corner of my mother's mouth curled up before drifting back down again. "There's something so eerie about it. Just knowing he's in there, beneath those hideous flowers." She sighed. "Where do you even put something like this?"

"On mantels, I guess."

"If he saw this . . ." My mother slipped into laughter. She covered her mouth, trying to hold in the sound, and I remember thinking she looked a little bit unhinged right then, yet at the same time, a little bit free.

The next thing I knew, I was cracking up too.

"He would hate it," I said. Hot tears spilled down my cheeks. "It would seem more personal if we kept him in a coffee canister."

My mother smacked her hand on the table and a few unopened envelopes slipped to the floor. "Maybe we should transfer him. Can you imagine what he would do if he saw those flowers?"

I shook my head, jaw aching. But the truth was that I *could* imagine.

"You think this is funny?" he would say, feet planted wide, trying to look menacing. "Yeah, go ahead. Laugh it up. It's goddamn hilarious, as long as it's not happening to you. How would you like spending eternity inside this hunk of shit, huh?" And for a second I thought I could actually see him, right over my mother's left shoulder, fighting the smile that tried to break free of his taut lips.

A shrine did not suit my father any better than a burial, so in the end, we took his ashes up to the ridge. It was my mother's idea.

"Is this legal?" I asked, cradling the urn like an infant.

"Probably not," she said. "But it's all ash up here now, anyway."

Blackened grass crunched beneath our feet as we climbed, past the signs warning of coyotes, of fire hazards, of the newly restricted area. At the top, I took the urn to my father's boulder. The summer heat had finally broken and a brisk evening breeze swooped down at us from the marbled sky. Sometime that week, all the remaining smoke clouds had been blown out to sea, and the city was back to normal. I closed my eyes and imagined my father sitting there at the edge, chucking pebbles out into the canyon. When I opened them, there was only the city, the sunset, a two-dimensional image reproduced on a million postcards lining the shop fronts of Hollywood Boulevard. A sprawling city that my father had fought for, that I hardly even knew at all. Right then, Los Angeles just seemed like another piece of him I could not claim.

I walked out to the ledge, lined up the tips of my shoes with the lip of the rock. My body wavered, unbalanced.

"Be careful," my mother said. "Maybe you should move back a little."

"I'm fine," I said, and opened the urn.

I let my fingers glide through my father's remains before extracting a handful and flinging him into the air. For a second he hung suspended, a beautiful haze of gray dust. Then the wind rose up from beneath and the cloud dispersed. Some particles took flight, out toward the freeway, while others dove down into the valley or gathered around my feet, immediately blending into the charred landscape. I threw a second handful. A third. A fourth. And I thought about how easy it was to vanish.

"He's part of the city now," my mother said. "He always wanted this."

I nodded, but now that it was over, I couldn't help thinking she was wrong. We both were. I felt a frantic urge to scoop some part of my father back into the jar, to take him elsewhere, do everything over. Maybe he would have wanted to become the ocean instead, one portion lapping at the California shore while other specks floated out to Hawaii, to China, slipping through tributaries into the Amazon or the Black Sea. Looking down at my feet, I couldn't distinguish between my father's ashes and the ashes of burned trees. As the silence around us deepened, I realized we hadn't even given him a soundtrack.

How had I not thought of that before? He'd envisioned a soundtrack for everything else, even joking about the songs I should play when he retired. "At my party, Suz," he'd said, "I need you to play some Sly and the Family Stone for me. 'Dance to the Music.' When I'm finally done with this shit once and for all, I'm going to dance. I'm going to dance all damn night."

And if his retirement—something I can't imagine he thought that seriously about—had a soundtrack, why didn't his funeral?

That's when I knew. Without a doubt, I knew, as soon as the question formed in my mind: my father had not intended to die.

I turned back to my mother, tears lumping in my throat. "He didn't do it on purpose," I said. "I know he didn't."

"Oh, honey." She hugged me—not arguing, but also not agreeing.

When we pulled away, I shoved my hands in my jeans to keep from clawing at the earth for fragments of my father. And there, in the front right pocket, was the matchbook.

"We found a few things on him," the guy at the crematorium had said before handing me what little was left of my father—the inadequate urn and his brown cowhide wallet, so worn it felt like velvet. "We tried to reach your mother to verify whether or not these items were supposed to be cremated with him, but when we didn't hear back, we decided to save them for you."

Then he placed the matchbook on the counter, a small packet of twenty sticks with red-dipped heads. The card stock may or may not have been white at one time but now appeared a sort of brownish cream, water-stained, with folds on the verge of tearing yet still, surprisingly, intact. On the front, the facade of a building had been drawn in thin black lines. Music notes floated from the second-story windows, out into the soft blue night.

I picked up the matchbook and turned it over in my palm. On the back, in the bold, loopy font of an old magazine ad, were these words: *Live music till 2 a.m. The Sea Witch. Ellory Plains, IA.*

Walking back to our house, my mother and I were quiet. The daylight had nearly vanished and I couldn't stop thinking about the Sea Witch. My first idea was that this place, Ellory Plains, in my mind little more than a cornfield with a general store and saloon popping out of the farmland, must be my father's hometown. Or, I thought, perhaps Ellory Plains was a place he passed through on his way to California, the Sea Witch a bar he felt some sort of lingering connection to. The Joe Thompson's before Joe Thompson's.

"Dad ever say anything to you about the Sea Witch?" I asked my mother as we rounded the last corner onto our street.

"The what?"

I didn't look at her for fear of seeming suspicious. "The Sea Witch."

"It rings a bell, I guess, but I can't think of the reason. It sounds like some scary children's book. Why do you ask?"

"He just mentioned it once. I didn't know what it meant and thought you might."

My mother stopped. "What the hell?"

I kicked a pebble with the toe of my sneaker. "I was just asking," I mumbled. But when she didn't respond, I glanced up to find that she wasn't looking at me.

Following her gaze down the street, I saw the candles before anything else—how they hovered in the dark air, only the white flames visible. It wasn't until after she took off speed-walking toward our house that I noticed the people, each body dressed in black, cradling the candles in their palms. There were a dozen of them sitting in a circle, holding what appeared to be a vigil on our front lawn.

"What the hell do you think you're doing?" my mother yelled as she approached our driveway, but the group didn't seem to hear her, or else they didn't care. One of them was playing a guitar as another sang the words to "Contradictions," one of the Spades' earliest tracks.

My pulse filled my head as I recognized them.

"You." My mother pointed and wove her way through the small crowd. "I remember you. I let you off with a warning last time, but you better believe that I'm going to call the cops now."

"We just want to pay our respects, ma'am," Travis said, an

alarmingly sincere edge to his voice. "Mourn the passing of a legend. But since his resting place hasn't been released, we came here."

I expected my mother to start screaming then, to tell them about the ashes and the hills, the exact place where we had scattered him and left his urn like a tombstone. Or, I figured she would at least reveal that the powdery residue of his bones had likely fluttered across much of Los Angeles by now, and they could—quite honestly—honor him anywhere. I waited. The wind whimpered through the trees.

"Why tonight?" she finally said.

"We just found out," Lance said. "It was only posted yesterday."

"Posted where?" I asked.

"Online."

My mother turned to me. "Did you do this?"

"No!" I cried. Strangely enough, the thought hadn't even occurred to me. Of course I wanted the world to remember and appreciate my father's music, even if only posthumously, but I hadn't the foresight to do anything about it.

"Then who?" my mother demanded. "How?"

Lance and Travis glanced at each other, confusion budding between them while the rest of their group remained sprawled out in the dead grass. I wondered who they were, if they'd ever met my father, if they even knew his music, or if they'd just come along for the show.

"I don't know," Lance said. "It's the internet."

His dark eyes caught mine, as though asking for help, and I thought I saw genuine sadness in him.

"We just want to pay our respects," Travis said again.

At the end of the street, the moon wrestled with the last dregs of sunlight. I wrapped my arms around my chest. "Maybe we should just let them stay," I said to my mother.

Her expression was hard. "That's what you want?"

I shrugged. I didn't know what I wanted anymore. The last time I'd been certain was when I decided to cover "Love Honey," but where did that get me? My father never heard it, and these two boys continued appearing in our front yard like drought-resistant weeds. I didn't know how else to get rid of them.

"They'll be done in an hour," I whispered, "and we'll never hear from them again."

My mother's lips tightened, but she nodded. "One hour," she said to Lance and Travis. "If you're not gone by then, I'm calling the police." Then she stormed toward the house.

I hesitated. I thought I saw Lance smile at me. And I thought that maybe, just for now, for this one hour, I could set aside everything I had previously felt toward him and Travis. I wanted to ask them what they knew about my father's final days. Had they heard his last tape? Had he ever mentioned the Sea Witch? Maybe we could help each other, comfort each other.

Maybe we could be friends.

The air shivered with a sharp gasp of wind, and Lance turned back around. Travis started strumming another Spades song. Their group reanimated, raising their candles as though in salute, and my sentiment slipped away into shadow. A murky, hot aversion began to burn in its place. I followed my mother inside.

That night, after the sounds from the front yard finally receded and the gatherers blew out their candles and went home, loneliness descended. I lay on the sofa with the TV on mute and tried to imagine a time when I wouldn't feel so sick and isolated. It wasn't fair that Lance and Travis knew what to do, how to mourn and move forward while my entire life felt upended. Even my mother had her daily activities, and whoever she'd been secretly talking to on the phone. But I had nothing.

With each day that passed, the lack of my father became a little more normal, and any hope I had of unearthing the truth about his past, his death, felt a little further away. If only I could travel back in time, read his mind, discover what that matchbook truly meant to him. If only I could speak to the rest of the Vital Spades.

I sat up, stunned by a solution so obvious that I had never considered it before. While my father was alive, finding the other Spades—the mere suggestion of it—would have felt like a betrayal. Now, it was the only path forward. If Lance and Travis could find my father online, then surely I could find the other Spades.

Too anxious to sit still, I turned off the TV and headed down the hallway to my bedroom. I hadn't spent much time in there lately, falling asleep instead on the living room sofa, and I was struck by the impression that the room belonged to someone else. The shelves were decorated with childish knickknacks and a handful of dingy stuffed animals my father had won for me years earlier at the county fair. On the walls, old photos had been haphazardly taped. My eyes paused on a photo-booth strip of Cara and me at the Santa Monica pier, thirteen years old, smiling, our tongues out, making eyeglasses with our fingers. We had done it twice: one strip for each of us.

Tomorrow, I thought, when my mother sent me out on the next errand, I would detour through the public library and begin my search for the Vital Spades. But right then I was still alone, and all I wanted was to find a way to exist—even momentarily—outside of the sadness. So I closed the door and clicked on the house phone.

I listened to the blare of the dial tone for a long time before I finally punched in a number.

For the ten minutes before Nick arrived, I sat on the driveway with my back against the garage, gazing at the wild universe of diffused stars. There was so much I wanted to tell him—about the crash, and Lance and Travis, and my decision to find the other Spades. I wanted to tell him I'd meant to call sooner. I wanted to tell him I was sorry. And I was so consumed by this menagerie of thoughts, my eyes fixed on the shine of a slow-moving satellite, that I didn't even notice him until he was halfway up the driveway.

"There's a satellite" was all I managed to say. I pointed into the dark sky.

Nick sat down next to me. For a while, we both watched as the tiny white dot moved, almost imperceptibly, across the night.

"How are you?" he asked.

"I'm not sure I know how to answer that," I said.

"Fair enough."

A kink of hair swung across his eyes as he looked down at the cement. I continued staring at the sky. If not for the bulk of our sweaters, our arms would have been touching, and I felt a glow spread up my neck at the thought of his tan skin, his sunburned cheeks, the way he smelled when he held me close. He drew in the dirt with his finger. The satellite snuck forward.

"Tell me something," I said.

"Like what?"

"Like—" I paused. "A joke."

"A joke?" Grinning, he took a deep breath. I felt his wide shoulders rising and falling. "Okay, okay. I got one." He shifted, sitting up straighter. "Why did Beethoven kill his chicken?"

I thought for a moment. "Why?"

"Because it kept saying, 'Bach, Bach, Bach.'"

Scrunching my eyes closed, I laughed—silently at first, and then with a burst of sound. I clasped my hands over my mouth, afraid that my mother might hear me. "That was terrible," I whispered through my fingers.

He shrugged. "You didn't ask for a *good* joke."

Finally, I turned to look at him. Even in the murky gleam of a streetlight, his eyes were luminous, gentle and wide. This was not the first night we had sat with our backs against my garage, laughing at silly jokes. Years ago, when Cara and most of the other boys our age were called home early for dinner or unfinished homework, Nick and I would ride our bikes back to my house and eat sour candy we bought at the liquor store as we waited for our own curfews to expire. Both of our fathers worked late (at least that's what I told him, because it felt close enough to the truth). We never really talked about them, though. Somehow, we just knew.

"We spread his ashes today," I said.

Nick opened and closed his mouth. I waited for him to apologize, to offer some artificial sentiment. Crickets sang from one of the neighbor's bougainvillea bushes.

"Up on the ridge past your house. And when we got back there was a group of people holding a vigil on our lawn, led by these guys who've been following my father around all summer, acting like they're his spiritual children or something. My mother was livid."

"And you?" Nick asked.

A breeze twirled down the street. I pulled my sweater tighter around my chest. "Lately I keep thinking about this time he came to Career Day at our elementary school and played 'Ob-La-Di, Ob-La-Da' for the class, and all the parents, even the lawyers, were singing along, completely transformed from whatever they had been moments earlier. It was like he allowed them to remember something about themselves that they'd forgotten. It sounds ridiculous, I know."

"Not at all," Nick said. "I remember that, actually. Fourth grade with Ms. Hopkins."

"You were there?" My eyebrows knotted as I tried to remember the room that day. I saw Ms. Hopkins in her Thanksgiving-themed attire, and the sticky desks lined up in rows five deep. But despite the lucidity of these other memories and the fact that Nick had always been vibrant and gregarious, appearing to me a shade brighter than everyone else, I could not find him anywhere in that classroom.

"That's how I first heard of the Beatles," he said. "I was so mad at my own dad for not being there and I just kept talking about yours, and how he totally changed the dynamic in the room. Anyone can pick up a guitar and play a song, but it was like he was speaking to both the kids and their parents, and not separating them the way most adults did." Nick paused, glancing up. The satellite was gone. "Anyway, my dad eventually figured out I was talking about the Beatles. We reconnected over *The White Album*, and he introduced me to all these old bands he liked." He smiled then, looking out at the empty street.

"That's a good album," I said.

We fell silent for a moment. I leaned my head back and watched Nick from the corner of my eye. His expression softened, drifting somewhere between me and a memory that I could imagine easily enough: the jolt of that connection he had once felt, that he built up and relied on and savored all those other nights when his father wasn't around.

"It sucks," Nick said, rubbing the heels of his hands hard against his eyes. It was a school night; he must have been tired. "It really fucking sucks."

Though I wasn't entirely sure what he was referring to, I nodded. It did suck. All of it. I said, "I wish I could just have a new life and start over."

"In less than a year, we'll be at college," he said. "I just keep thinking that. Less than a year, and everything will be different."

"College," I repeated, somewhat bewildered by the word. I had forgotten about it, all my possible futures scattered across the Golden State, currently shoved and wrinkled in the bottom drawer of my desk. My mother hadn't mentioned the applications since that summer afternoon when I heard the soft lilt of her singing along to Carole King, and my father finally emerged from the garage. How long ago that day felt.

"People always say that you don't really know who you are or what you want before college," Nick said. "That it's one of the most important times in your life."

"You believe that?" I asked.

"I don't know." He swam his fingers through his hair, guiding the thick blond strands back from his forehead. "Maybe it's less that you find your true self, and more that you feel okay allowing others to see it. But I do think there's some truth to the idea that you can't fully be you until you leave home and have to deal with the world. I've heard from many reliable sources that the process of doing your own laundry can be very enlightening. I've already started saving quarters."

I laughed and scooted in closer, rested my head on his shoulder. A strange confidence inhabited me in the dark, knowing that Nick wouldn't be able to see me blush. Down by our hips, the backs of his fingertips brushed against mine. I felt his hand twitch, unsure, before settling. His pinkie finger slipped just slightly under my palm.

"Will you still visit me when you're in college?" I asked.

"Are you kidding?" he said. "We're obviously going to the same school."

"Is that right?" I smiled.

"Yup. We'll live in adjacent buildings. And your roommate will be in some sorority, so she'll never be around, and I'll come to your room with Sour Patch Kids and we'll watch the entire Hitchock filmography, in chronological order, on your tiny dorm bed."

"Why Hitchcock?" I asked.

"Dunno, really," Nick said, the warmth of his breath tickling my forehead. "I'll be studying film, so it seems sort of appropriate."

I wanted to kiss him. I knew that all I had to do was lift my head and I would find him there, waiting. And yet I couldn't help feeling that the timing was wrong. It wasn't right that night in Cara's guest bedroom and it wasn't right now, while so much of my world still seemed irreparably broken. So instead I kissed him in my head, on the tiny dorm bed in my tiny dorm room, our mouths sour and sugar-laced. In college, I thought. That would be the right time for us.

For a while longer, we sat in the driveway, the far-off stars flickering overhead. Nick never asked why I suddenly called, or why I hadn't for so long, or why I'd asked him over in the middle of the night to sit in near silence, but I felt some understanding pass between us. And after he was gone I went back into my bedroom, pulled all the applications from my desk, and began to fill them out, one at a time, starting with the easiest questions: my name, my birthday. The only things I knew for sure.

EIGHT

UPON FIRST ENTERING my local branch of the Los Angeles Public Library—an uninspiring room bathed in browns and steeped in the scents of stubborn dust and old paper—this was what I thought: I could have been, quite literally, almost anywhere else. Depending on the direction, an hour's drive from the center of LA could put you at the majestic, white-capped mountains, the ocean, the barren expanse of desert. Any of these places would have been preferable. But if I wanted answers, I didn't have a choice.

So I parked myself at the computer farthest from the noisy kids' section and made my peace with the incessant buzz of the low-hung lights. I logged on, and began to search.

I assumed the process would be simple; I didn't expect to find much information about the band online, but I hadn't thought it would be that hard to track the other members down, find their phone numbers and addresses. And yet, after four separate afternoons of clicking, I was no closer to any answers. There were hundreds of Jason Millers and Dan Lees—dozens of each in LA County alone. Fewer men were named Kurt Vaughan, but even then the handful of candidates seemed impossible to sort through.

The problem was, I'd always felt like I grew up with the Spades, the swell of their instruments so often trilling me to sleep. Plus, I knew all the stories. My father had told me in great detail about the time Jason, the bass player, fell off the stage at a festival in San Francisco and broke his wrist in two places. And I knew that when Dan's drum set was stolen from a dive bar in Murrieta, he dragged in metal trash cans from the street as a replacement. I could practically hear the awful clamor made when Dan struck them, because my father's stories had been painted with such vibrancy into my childhood that his memories began to feel like my own.

But as I scrolled through the search results, I understood: They weren't mine. I didn't actually know these people at all. Though the internet could reveal many things, it could not tell me which men were the costars in my father's life, or which men would give me the truth.

"I only need to find one of them," I said to myself. "And at least there's air-conditioning in here, right?" I shook out my arms and legs and cracked my fingers, trying to rejuvenate my resolve. Then I smacked my forehead against my palms and let out a long, frustrated groan.

The woman who'd been sitting at the next desk over shot me an annoyed look before scooting two chairs down.

My luck was no better with the Sea Witch. A search for this phrase resulted in a thousand images of fantastical undersea creatures, including Ursula from *The Little Mermaid*. Apparently, there was a Sea Witch Tavern in New York, but no other results came close. I tried searching for *the Sea Witch Ellory Plains*, though this yielded nothing. I even tried just *Ellory Plains, Iowa*, and then finally *James Hayes Ellory Plains*. All that came up then was the city's outdated welcome website, and links to articles from their local paper. They were having a rainstorm. An elderly man also named James was lost, presumed dead.

And then, finally, on a hot cloudless afternoon, I found him: Kurt Vaughan, resident of Pasadena, California, and part owner of Vaughan Construction. I had clicked on his company's website, unsure of what exactly I thought I would find among the before-and-after photos and testimonials from satisfied clients until I saw, on the "About" page, a photograph of two men smiling. *Richard and Kurt*, the caption read, *the father/son duo behind Vaughan Construction*.

The photo must have been at least a few years old, but maybe that's why I knew. This was the Kurt who, according to my father, refused to wash his hands before a gig so that his pick wouldn't slip out of his fingers, and who always wore the same pair of argyle socks onstage, cleaning them afterward by hand so as not to wear them out. In the picture, he had on a heavy canvas coat and blue jeans, his arm slung across the shoulder of his father. The same loose smile that I recognized from the band's promo photos stretched across his face.

It took another hour of searching before I found what appeared to be a home address. I scribbled the directions onto the back of a research request form, and rushed out into the bright parking lot.

The drive east to Kurt's house took less than twenty minutes. He lived in a nice neighborhood, upscale but unassuming, on a quiet street shaded by the lush stretch of deep-rooted trees. Warm air sifted in through my open window as I counted down the addresses. Just a few more to go—two, one.

My stomach whirled when I spotted it, a simple two-story home with an American flag swishing over the porch, a mud-splattered truck parked at the curb. I wondered if my father had known that Kurt was here all this time, only a few freeway exits past us. Had they been in contact since the breakup? Did Kurt know about my father's death? Would he welcome me like distant family, admit he wished we'd already met?

My car inched closer, and the rest of the house lurched into focus: a young boy shooting basketball hoops in the driveway. A dark-haired woman unloading groceries in the garage.

The next thing I knew, the house was behind me. I had kept going.

Bad timing. That's what I told myself after. I'm not sure what I expected to find when I arrived at Kurt Vaughan's house, but I did not anticipate seeing his wife, his son, his well-adjusted, normal life. In fact, I hadn't even realized he would have these things, or that he wasn't still, in the most fundamental ways, the same person who'd shared a stage with my father. I hadn't considered that he might actually be happy with the course his life had turned.

Besides, they'd just gotten home from the store. His wife probably planned on starting dinner. I'd try again later.

But later took more time to come than I expected.

It was an overcast Tuesday morning when I finally felt like I'd rallied the courage to return. My mother had not yet bestowed a task upon me, so I sat on the sofa watching a rerun of *The Price Is Right*, thinking about what I would say when I introduced myself to Kurt. *You don't know me, but I think you knew my father. . . . Why yes, I* am *Susannah. And how interesting that you mention "Love Honey," because I actually just wrote an acoustic version. . . .*

Yes, today felt promising. Today, I was going to meet another member of the Vital Spades.

At the corner of the kitchen table, my mother sipped her coffee and stared out into the street. Every few minutes she scribbled something on the yellow legal pad in her lap, but between notes she didn't shift, shoulders rigid, eyes alert. The crowd on TV yelled out answers. I wondered where she'd send me today. I wondered what Nick was doing.

"Susannah," my mother said. The sound of my name in the still room startled me. "There's something I want to—"

Someone knocked at our door before she could finish.

"I'll get it," I sighed.

At the door, I put my eye to the peephole. I had expected a man—the UPS guy in his brown uniform, or a debt collector in a wrinkled suit. I even considered that Doug, my high school's guidance counselor, might be making a house call and would appear at our door in his familiar thrift store tweed and belted blue jeans, a few bagel crumbs still stuck in his beard from breakfast. I did not expect to see an older woman.

She had platinum hair—not the wispy, shriveled gray of TV grandmothers but a styled white-blond that glistened, crisp and light, beneath the bright shimmer of sky. Pearls adorned her ears and a bright floral scarf had been tied loosely around her neck. She looked familiar, but I wasn't sure why; she certainly didn't work at the school. She put one honey-colored eye right up to the glass, as if she knew I was standing there on the opposite side, watching her. I stepped back and opened the door.

"I was beginning to think no one was home," she said.

"Can I help you?" I asked.

She laughed. "No, dear. I'm here to help you."

Of course, I thought. She must be selling something. "I'm sorry," I said, trying to sound polite. "We don't have any money."

I began closing the door, but the woman had already slipped into our living room. She eyed our old furniture, the empty walls, the heap of mail on the kitchen table. "Cozy, isn't it?"

"Mom," I said, unsure of what to do.

"You look good," the woman said to my mother. "Considering." She waved her hand through the air. Now, standing in front of me, I could see that her black slacks were pressed. Shiny red leather flats peeked out from beneath the hems. She looked so foreign in our home, surrounded by our things.

"You know each other?" I asked.

"Well . . ." my mother said.

"Oh, *Diane*, for God's sake. You didn't tell her?"

My heart began stomping in my chest. "Tell me what?"

The woman rubbed her temples. "What a nightmare this day has turned out to be." Her head fell to one side, thin lips turned down in a look of expected disappointment that reminded me of my mother.

"What's going on?" I asked.

"Ever since your father . . ." my mother began, and then stopped. She looked around as though for help—for something to tell her the right combination of words that would make whatever was happening okay.

The woman sighed and said, "I'm your grandmother, dear."

I looked between them, trying to understand. "You've known where his family was all along?"

"No," my mother said. She pressed her palms together, held her fingers in front of her mouth. "*My* mother."

Cheering erupted from the television, but the sound seemed far away, as if the air in the room had thickened. I shook my head in what felt like slow motion. "But," I said, my thoughts spinning together. "You told me your parents were dead."

"Why does that not surprise me?" The woman opened her purse and began digging around inside. "Thought you could wipe your hands of us, is that it?"

"Jesus, Mother. Must we start with this already? And for the record, I never actually said that. Susannah just assumed."

So this is my fault? I wanted to say, but words had deserted me.

"I couldn't have predicted how this all would end up," my mother said, though I wasn't sure to whom.

The woman pulled a tube of lipstick and a gold compact mirror from her purse. "Well, there's no point beating around the bush now." She began reapplying the color to her lips. "Or were you hoping to spin some new tall tale about me before I showed up? Claim that I've risen from the grave?"

"I was only trying to make it easier for Susannah—"

"Been reincarnated?" She rubbed her lips together. "Hare Krishna, or whatever else they're singing about these days?"

Their voices overlapped, colliding discordantly in the air as the room warped around me. I felt dizzy. I'm not sure how much time passed while I stood, speechless, but when I finally found my voice again, I shouted, "Will someone please tell me what the hell is going on?"

They both grew silent, and turned to me.

"Susannah." My mother said my name slowly, delicately, as if improper pronunciation might break me. Then she put her hands over her face and inhaled through the cracks in her fingers. "Your grandmother and I weren't in contact for a long time. Until recently, I honestly didn't know if we'd ever talk again."

"Well, I'm here now, so let's not dwell. Dwelling gives me a headache." The woman—my grandmother—lowered her petite frame down onto the couch. She frowned as her body sank into the cushions. After a moment of trying to adjust her position, she stood up again. "I suppose you can call me Grandma if that makes you feel better about the whole thing, but I'm perfectly content with Vivian."

The name hit a nerve. I remembered my father mentioning her but the context of the conversation was blurred. To my mother, I said, "Why is she here?"

My mother took a deep breath. Vivian spoke again.

"Your mother's obviously having a hard time articulating this to you, so here's the long and the short of it. She can't pay the mortgage, and there haven't yet been any bids on the sale. Therefore, I have agreed to let you both live with me."

My mind stuck on that one word: "Sale?"

My mother walked over to me. I stepped back. I wondered how I hadn't felt it, how a secret that big had slipped by me undetected. But of course, I'd been immersed in a secret of my own. Though the rational part of me knew I was to blame for my own ignorance, right then, I blamed my mother.

She said, "We can't afford to stay."

"But we can't just leave. This is our home."

"As far as I can tell, I'm your best option," Vivian said. She looked at her watch. "It's almost noon, Diane, and we still have to return your rental car. We should hit the road now if we want to avoid traffic."

"Why do you get a say in this?" I said, my pulse quickening. "You don't know anything about our lives."

Vivian smiled. Her eyes were soft with pity. "Oh, honey, trust me. I know more than you."

She must have skipped a word, I thought, the last one: *I know more than you* think. There was no possible way that she would know more about my father than I did, about the woman my mother had become. About me.

"Go pack some things," my mother said, her voice heavy in a way I didn't recognize. She stood rigid in the middle of our living room—uncomfortable, I remember thinking, as though she had already shucked this life off like old skin and was now left standing in the filth. "Just the essentials, enough to get by. We'll get the rest later."

For a moment I was frozen, my mouth open and unbelieving. My bottom lip trembled with anger as I said, "I'll never forgive you."

I stormed into my bedroom. Tears clawed their way to the surface and I tried to force them down, but my throat burned and my head was swirling, astounded by my mother's cruelty. *How could she?* I kept thinking, until finally the tears broke from my lashes. Until I remembered what I was supposed to be doing.

Briefly, I considered barricading myself in the room or running away, but I knew that wouldn't solve anything. In the end I'd still have to leave. I took a deep breath, blinked the final tears free, and began to pack.

I placed the items in a duffel bag carefully, folding each piece of clothing into a neat square, piling the toiletries in the front pocket one at a time. My eyes were so bleary that I could hardly see what I was doing, but I managed to grab two of my father's old shirts that I'd been sleeping in and the notebook where the lyrics of "Don't Look Back" lay dormant. I slid the photograph of the Spades onstage inside the pages. The book of matches from the Sea Witch I slipped in my pocket.

Done packing, I surveyed my bedroom one last time. I wanted to remember everything: the way the silvery sunlight streaked in through the window, the discernible patterns in the spackled ceiling and the strange arrangement of photos on the walls. My heart felt like it was collapsing. I thought about Kurt, how he'd been right there, how I'd waited too long. Now, I might never get the chance to meet him.

Back in the living room, I saw that my mother's suitcase had been placed by the front door. I wasn't sure if it had been there all day and I was just too preoccupied to see it, or if she had been hiding it beneath her bed, in the back of her closet, and only now allowed it out into the light. I wanted to know, but refused to ask. I couldn't even look at her.

"Let's go, then," I said to Vivian, not even caring where we were heading, or how long it would take to get there. At the time, the overwhelming act of leaving eclipsed everything else. So the three of us filed out of the only home I'd ever known, past the studio where I would never again hear the soaring sustain of my father's guitar. And then we drove away.

I soon found out that Vivian lived just south of LA—in Orange County, in the city of Orange, only three freeways from our home in Eagle Rock—but on that first day, I felt like I'd entered another world. Her property sprawled at the end of a long driveway that snaked back to the base of the foothills, behind the sparse yards that lined the main road. And though her ranch-style home stood just one story tall, by no means the type of stereotypical mansion that I'd always assumed to populate Orange County (in fact, so far, I'd hardly seen any of those), it was still big enough to make the house I grew up in seem like a shipping container.

"It looks the same," my mother said. "Mostly."

"When have you been here?" I said through gritted teeth, but as soon as the words emerged the answer was obvious. I'd always sensed a sort of settling in the way my mother presented herself, in what she wanted for my father, and for me. Before, I'd thought it was because she longed for more than our meager life. Now I knew the truth. This was where she came from.

The irony stung in a way that felt physical, like touching hot metal that had been baking in the sun. After trying so hard to locate the roots that led to my father's past, I ended up here: in a world that existed before him. Without him.

"Well come on, then. I'm not going to leave the AC running while you two brood," Vivian said. She slipped the key out of the ignition and opened her door, ushering in a wave of warm air that left me light-headed. My mother turned back to say something but I jumped out of the car and followed Vivian to the front door.

"I know this is hard for you," Vivian said when we were alone. I waited for her to continue, watching my mother's slow movements as she hoisted our suitcases out of the trunk, but she didn't. The front door swung open, revealing a bright-lit foyer. Vivian motioned for me to enter. "After you, dear."

Inside, everything smelled like citrus. Soft waves of sun twinkled up from the polished tile floor, and the walls, sparsely decorated with art and antique mirrors, were painted a lush desert cream. Vivian headed toward the hallway that led to the left half of the house as I trailed behind. Because of the tall ceilings, each room seemed monstrous.

"Cozy, isn't it," I said, louder than intended. My voice echoed through the corridor.

Vivian laughed. "Yes, well, it's certainly a change. But you'll get used to it, I'm sure." She led me to the kitchen, another wide room with broad bay windows that looked out over a placid pool and the unfenced hillside. On the left, a structure the color of rust peeked through a tangle of wild green growth, nearly invisible.

"Those were horse stables," Vivian said. "But all you'll find in there now are weeds. Termites, undoubtedly. I really need to tear that old thing down."

"You rode horses?" I asked.

"Once upon a time. But the horses we had here were your mother's. Her father always spoiled her."

"She's never mentioned horses," I said.

"Are you hungry? I can make you a protein smoothie, or rinse off some grapes."

"Just water," I said.

"Please," Vivian said.

"What?"

"You should always say 'please,' especially when you're a guest in someone's home."

I said, "I thought I lived here now."

Vivian's lips rose in a half-moon smile, and an unexpected softness overcame her. It lasted only a moment. The front door slammed shut, and Vivian's smile faded. She pushed her fingers against her forehead. "She still does that?"

I shrugged. My father was the one who slammed the doors in our house, but I didn't want to tell her that. I put that fact in a section of my brain labeled *Things I Know That Vivian Does Not*.

When my mother found us in the kitchen, me drinking a glass of water while Vivian sorted through the afternoon's mail, she spent a minute orbiting the room, touching everything lightly with the tips of her fingers. She appeared to be checking for dust, but of course the place was spotless. Her hands glided over the granite countertops, the smooth wood of the cabinet doors, the pink pencil erasers that poked up from a faded white coffee mug advertising the Orange Park Acres Equestrian Alliance.

"I decided to put Susannah in your old room," Vivian said as she opened an envelope. "I couldn't imagine you'd be comfortable there, though the place hardly resembles what you'd remember. You'll be in the guest room, the one that connects to the front bath."

"Fine," my mother said. Then, after a pause, "Thank you."

"Susannah, you're staying down at the other end of the house, last door on the left. I've set out fresh linens for you both."

"I can't believe you kept these," my mother said, spotting the poorly crafted macaroni and marker magnets adorning the side of the refrigerator. Her fingers gravitated toward one of the more elaborate pieces—red-and-blue-painted pasta glued onto a Popsicle-stick picture frame. "I never was much of an artist, was I?"

"Yes, well, I need magnets," Vivian said. "Never saw a need to replace them, since they work perfectly fine."

Back home, my mother had decorated with a similar flourish. The knickknacks I had handcrafted in grade school, holiday decorations made with pipe cleaners and colored felt balls—she displayed these items proudly. Now, as she brushed her fingers against the pasta frame, gazing at the photo in the center, she smiled. She brought one hand to her cheek. Her other hand lifted the magnet, unintentionally spilling a slew of loose papers onto the floor.

"Damn it, Diane!" The severity of Vivian's tone made me jump. "Those are important documents."

My mother's voice sounded crooked as she apologized. "I'll put them right back," she said meekly, scrambling to replace the pages. But Vivian bumped her aside.

"You must have lost one under the fridge. It's important," she said again, and then, under her breath as she bent down to look, something else I didn't quite catch. My mother's face turned pale. Vivian said, "We can't keep bothering him with these tiny tasks, Diane."

"Mom, he's not . . ." my mother started. Then her eyes darted, momentarily, to me. She shook her head. "I'll fix it," she insisted.

"There's a broom in the garage. The handle might be slim enough to slide under there."

My mother nodded and headed back through the hallway.

"Who can't we bother?" I asked Vivian after a moment.

She turned to me, blinking, with an empty expression as though she'd forgotten I was there. She said, "Would you like to see your room?"

My mother was everywhere. She had long hair and short hair, broken arms and ballet recitals, softball games, scrunchies, and, later, jean miniskirts beneath bright-colored crop tops. She rode horses in wide arenas that sprung from the middle of densely foliated fields. She crouched down at the rocky tide pools of Crystal Cove wearing torn jean shorts and soiled Keds. One time, when she swam with a stingray, the photographer even captured her mid-laugh. I could see her molars; she had a silver filling, back left.

At first, I found it odd that she was ubiquitous in Vivian's house, the journey of her life chronicled along the wide hallway that led to my new bedroom, and yet Vivian was entirely absent from ours. But my mother had no siblings, no one else to share the space on Vivian's walls with except the occasional appearance of a tall, slender man who I assumed to be my grandfather. I guessed that displaying a lost family was better than having no family to display at all.

Still, one thing continued to bother me: Vivian did not act as though she had just discovered my existence. I wondered if my mother had sent her my annual school portraits in crisp white envelopes with no return address, nothing more than a caption. *Susannah, age seven, second grade.* None were found. And I was not the only one absent; I scrutinized every image, every blurry background, for some trace of my father, but he wasn't here either. There was not even one photograph from their wedding day. The few shots I found from my mother's time at UCLA must have been taken before they met because her hair was long and straight, tucked behind her ears to display her whole face. In the photograph of the Vital Spades onstage, her hair had been cropped short, draped like a curtain across her eyes.

After wandering through all the neatly made bedrooms and the bright-lit office where a bulky old computer skulked, I went to find my mother and Vivian. They were still in the kitchen. A piece of paper—presumably the one my mother had fished from under the refrigerator—rested between them on the table.

"She deserves to know," my mother insisted in a hushed voice.

"I've made up my mind about this, Diane," Vivian replied.

"I deserve to know what?" Crossing my arms, I leaned against the door frame. A look that I could not translate shot between them.

"You're going back to school tomorrow," my mother said.

"Tomorrow?" I almost laughed. "That's a joke, right?"

My mother's mouth plunged into a frown.

"I haven't even moved in yet, and you already want to send me back to school? Don't I get a transition period? Some time to adjust?"

"This *is* the best way for you to adjust, dear," Vivian said.

"And of course, I get no say in the matter."

"The longer we wait, the harder it will be for you to catch up," my mother added, though her words had grown hesitant. "You were doing so well before—"

She paused. I waited, wanting her to say it, to bring my father into the room and make him real again.

"It'll be good for you to make some friends your own age," Vivian said. "I'm not going to flatter myself by pretending you want to spend all your time with me."

"This is completely unfair," I said. When no one responded I turned away and strode out the back door, letting it slam behind me.

Outside, I sat in a dusty lounge chair and watched the pale stars flicker into view overhead. I thought about my father, trying to imagine what he would think of this place, of Vivian, of me, and how easily I went along with it all—not fighting or resisting. It seemed like I'd been doing a lot of that lately. I'd given up on my father, given up on "Don't Look Back," locked the Martin away in the hall closet and not thought of it since, not until right then, in fact, when it was too late. Now, I was stuck in Orange without a guitar. I was stuck in the wrong part of my parents' past. I was stuck without ever having spoken to Kurt Vaughan.

Right then, the what-ifs came rushing back, pummeling me like an avalanche. All the anger that I felt toward my mother and Vivian was usurped by the hot, visceral fury I had for myself. I picked up a jagged rock that rested near my feet and hurled it at the pool. The turquoise water only broke for an instant before reconfiguring, flawless again.

I stayed outside that night until the sky turned black and the coyotes began cackling, not bothering to respond when my mother called me in for dinner. Then, once it seemed that everyone had gone to sleep, I crept back inside, snatched the phone from Vivian's office, and called Nick.

"Something's happened," I said when he answered, my voice low and wispy in the quiet night.

"What is it?" he said. "What's going on?"

I tried to remind myself that only three freeways separated me from my old home. I'd memorized the route that afternoon. At night, if there wasn't construction, I could probably make the trip in an hour. Nick wasn't that far, nor the Martin, the studio. Kurt. I just had to figure out where Vivian kept her keys. . . .

"Susannah?" Nick said through a yawn. "Are you there? What's happening?"

It must have been late, and while I didn't know what Nick's plans were tomorrow—if he had an important water polo match or some ASB assembly, a major test during first period—I knew that if I asked him to drop everything for me, he would. Which is why, in the end, I decided not to do it.

Instead, I let out a long sigh and fell backward against my pillow. "I've been exiled to Orange County," I told him. "Three freeways and a universe away."

NINE

MS. GROBLER, THE guidance counselor at Santiago Hills High School, was a big, old woman with thick convex glasses that made her copper-colored eyes look like fossils preserved in amber. Her office smelled like garlic, and she wore a beige sweater that spilled over her chair's armrest in a way that made me think, uncomfortably, of pizza dough. In addition to last night's dinner, I had also refused breakfast. My stomach grumbled.

"I want you to know that we are very sorry for your loss," she said once I had closed the door and settled myself in the worn-out vinyl chair across from her. "Losing a parent, especially at your age, is a terrible thing. And I'm here for you, if you ever want to talk about what you're going through."

I had expected Ms. Grobler to have a soft, nurturing tone, and her booming voice surprised me. Though I didn't want to talk about it, I nodded anyway.

"Good. Now, let's discuss the future—particularly your future here at Santiago Hills. My job is to help you make it the best future that it can possibly be, to navigate those rough, weedy paths that life bestows upon you. . . ."

Ms. Grobler's hands circled the air as her metaphors spiraled away. I knew she would not be able to mend the blistering hole that ripped through my chest every time I heard the mysterious, ametrical opening chord of "Hard Day's Night" on the radio, or even thought about how careless I'd been to leave the Martin behind—but for her, success meant only that I listen. So I let her talk, bobbed my head periodically, and allowed my mind to wander out of the room and down the open hallway. I didn't miss my old school, but I wished Nick were here and that our conversations weren't relegated to the opposing ends of phone lines. And it occurred to me then, sitting there in her office, that I had never been the new kid before. I tried to think of some from my old school, tried to remember how they were treated, but not one face materialized. In a way, I felt the anonymity would be comforting—and yet part of me wasn't so sure that I wanted to be invisible.

"You know," Ms. Grobler said abruptly, "I was your age, a senior in high school, in 1969. Do you know what kind of things happened in 1969?"

A swarm of facts dashed into my consciousness, like a newsreel my father had spun into my mind: In 1969, Led Zeppelin released their first album. The Beatles filmed their rooftop show. Creedence Clearwater Revival put out both *Bayou Country* and *Green River*. Neil Young and Crazy Horse released *Everybody Knows This Is Nowhere*. The Who, *Tommy*. Muddy Waters, *After the Rain*. And, of course, there was Woodstock. Ms. Grobler must have noticed a spark of interest cross my face because she smiled and sat back, waiting. I thought about which answer to give.

Then I remembered that even though the summer ended magically, the year did not.

My father had told me stories. He knew every detail of Altamont, the Rolling Stones' poorly planned attempt to re-create Woodstock on the West Coast. He knew of the terror in Mick Jagger's voice as he threatened to stop playing, and the gun Meredith Hunter wielded before being fatally stabbed. He knew of the other deaths, too, the ones that had been overshadowed: two in a hit-and-run; one drowned in a drainage ditch. My father even held the same bitter grudge against the Stones as the dismayed fans who had been there. But he wasn't there. He wasn't even born yet.

My stomach began to tumble with something other than hunger. I looked down at the grungy gray carpet, crossed and uncrossed my legs. I didn't want to remember the violence, the ending, the memories that my father had always claimed as his own. I only wanted the good.

"Woodstock," I said finally.

"Exactly!" Ms. Grobler roared. She slammed her palm on the desk. The pencils in her pencil holder jumped. "Just picture it, Susannah: Woodstock Nation! The first man on the moon! The largest antiwar protest in our country's history! I've seen some pretty amazing things in my day"—here, she put a hand beside her mouth and feigned a whisper—"but it wasn't all pot-smoking hippies and daisy-chain crowns then, and it sure isn't now. Over the years, I've had kids dealing with situations that no one should ever have to deal with. But you know what else? I've helped them through it. Those kids got out of here, went on to better things. Some of them went to Ivy Leagues, to Stanford. UCLA."

My heart skipped and I glanced up, struck by the possibility that my mother had known Ms. Grobler. Attempting small talk on the drive to school that morning, she'd told me that she, too, attended Santiago Hills, and though I was still too angry to grace her with a response at the time, I now wondered if she'd sat here in this same office, in the same sticky vinyl chair, and confessed her dreams, her fears.

"Now, I'm not trying to say that you're this type or that type," Ms. Grobler said defensively. "I don't judge books by their covers. But I've seen your academic record, and I'm concerned. You had a steady B-plus average into your junior year, consistent As in English, and then your grades plunged. Three Cs last semester."

I picked at my too-long fingernails.

"I know you've been through a lot, but from here on out, you're on my turf, and I'm going to keep track of you whether you like it or not. We'll meet weekly for the first month, and see how it goes from there."

I shrugged in a way that suggested I would comply, even if I didn't like it.

"Now, I know from experience that students perform better when they're learning something they're interested in. There's no way to get out of math class, so don't bother asking, but I do see some potential wiggle-room in your schedule. So tell me, Susannah. What do you like? Do you play any sports, or have any hobbies? Were you involved in any clubs at your last school? What makes you *happy*?"

Happy. The word hadn't even stumbled into the periphery of my thoughts in weeks. I didn't know how to be myself without my father, let alone be *happy*, and the fear that I wanted so badly to banish came rushing back to me. Every day, I lost a little bit more of him, and I was afraid that he would slip away until nothing remained but an old photo and a faint longing, a half smile as I struggled to remember some thing he once taught me on a midnight long ago. I had to find a way to hold on to him. I had to find a way to hold on to myself.

"Music," I said. "Music makes me happy."

"Perfect!" Ms. Grobler leaned back in her chair. "I have just the class for you."

I pictured the jazz band at my old school, an ensemble of twelve talented musicians who played at all the assemblies. I'd always marveled at their skill, and how easily they performed in public. Ms. Grobler was right: it *was* perfect. And I wouldn't let anything hold me back this time—not shyness, not fear of inadequacy. I would be different now. Stronger. Focus only on the music. Surely the school would let me borrow a guitar until we retrieved the rest of our things from LA.

"We'll put you into sixth period choir," Ms. Grobler said next, and just like that my shiny new future disintegrated into a mass of itchy gowns and too-tight buns.

"I don't really think that I'm the choir type," I said, scratching at the invisible crushed velvet dress around my neck. "I was thinking of something more like jazz band. With real instruments and amps and stuff. I'd even do xylophone band. Do you have one of those here?"

"I think you should give it a chance."

"I just don't feel like that's the place for—"

"If," she interrupted, "in a couple of weeks you really hate it, then we'll reevaluate. Deal?"

Sensing I had no choice in the matter, I shrugged. "Fine."

"Mr. Tipton is in charge of the program this year, and the students adore him. I really think you'll be surprised. And—" Once again, she raised a hand aside her mouth. "Just between us gals, I've overheard many a student say he's quite a looker. Nothing wrong with a little eye candy to pluck some life out of a boring class, right?"

And then Ms. Grobler attempted to wink at me.

The day passed quickly until lunchtime when, on my way to the cafeteria, I noticed that the quad was segregated into something reminiscent of the nine circles of hell. My fourth period advanced English class had just finished a discussion of Dante's *Inferno*, and the gruesome illustrations of hell were still tattooed in my mind. Instead of classifying my new school's social cliques by popularity or the often obvious after-school activity, I couldn't help but identify groups by potential sin: the lustful, the gluttonous, the heretics. This made it much easier to spend my first lunch break at Santiago Hill High School alone.

At least, I thought I was alone. I'd taken my greasy slice of pizza out to a secluded corner of campus and flipped back through *Inferno*, engrossed in the idea of the treacherous, the only sin that could not be identified in the quad. The treacherous were hidden, unknown to the innocent bystander, asking you to pick up paint samples and toilet bowl cleaner while they conspired to tear your whole world apart. And I was so consumed by this concept, and all the ways we can never know the people we think are closest to us, that I started to write a new song about it—or tried to, anyway, scribbling fiercely in my notebook before changing my mind and scratching everything out.

I was so consumed that at first, I didn't even notice the sound: two jangled guitars filtering out through a veil of nearby trees.

Closing my notebook, I strained to hear. I could make out the dueling rhythm, built around a purposely disjointed upstroke, and a singer's battered voice just detectable above the chords. I could not make out his words, but that didn't matter. The music soared through me. I crept closer.

In the center of the trees, I saw a group of boys sitting in a circle. The two closest to me faced the opposite direction, strumming acoustic guitars, while another lay back on the dry grass, one arm draped across his face to block out the bright columns of sunlight. For the most part, they were identifiable only at their legs: jeans with a set of worn leather boots, jeans with frayed canvas sneakers, and one pair of dirty, wiggling toes. I continued listening, but did not recognize the song they were playing. They might not have even been playing any real song at all, and surely, something was out of tune, just barely sharp—though somehow that made the music more seductive.

I was already imagining what the song would become with a full band behind it, the harmonies augmenting the singer's rough voice, when something unexpected happened: a girl's laugh punctured the music. I understood immediately that it was a private sound, its silky tone intended only for those in her company, but I didn't care. I inched forward, trying to see around the trees without making any noise and upsetting the harmony of the music, or the privacy of the girl I could sort of, almost, barely see.

Then the bell rang. It was alarming how fast they cleared out— the clumsy clanking of nylon strings, a flash of red and suede, and the group dispersed, scrambling through the trees like a pack of wild animals. Only the grass, flattened in whiskery brown patches, and a small plastic wrapper no bigger than a cigarette pack indicated that anyone had been there at all.

All throughout fifth period and on my way to sixth, I couldn't stop thinking about the musicians in the trees, the soft melody of the girl's laugh. Who were they? How could I meet them? And, most important, what if they never came back?

What if. Those two torturous words still haunted me, burrowing deep into the marrow of every chance I didn't take, and I was sick of always wondering what would've happened had I just done something different, been different. I already felt a boulder of regret beneath my rib cage, its weight suffocating. Any more, I thought, would crush me.

So as I entered the choir room that first day, I made a resolution: I would banish *what if* from my vocabulary. Not even an army of my past mistakes could stop me from approaching the musicians tomorrow at lunch.

But tomorrow, as I imagined it, never came, because then one of them entered the choir room.

The girl.

"Class started fifteen minutes ago, Ms. Chandler," Mr. Tipton announced lightly, trying to sound unfazed by the interruption. "I don't suppose you heard the bell?"

The whole class turned to look at her. Even now, I remember that instant so clearly: the first time I saw Lynn Chandler, I thought I was seeing a ghost.

This was not because of her complexion, pale as it was, nor the fact that a brisk, relieving breeze seemed to float into the stuffy room with her. The whole effect might have been a coincidence, after all—the air-conditioning kicking in at precisely the right moment, or a gust of mountain-chilled wind whirling down from the hills where Vivian and my mother likely sat with coffees, plotting their next coup. Regardless of science or magic or whatever I felt that day, the reason for my first impression was simple; she looked remarkably like the young Michelle Phillips—a member of the Mamas and the Papas—immortalized on the cover of a seven-inch single my father owned for "California Dreamin'."

I stared as she strolled up the row beside me. She had that same slender face, the same icicle eyes. Her hair, despite its deep red color, was also long and straight-parted, pooling in the collar of her lovely (but unnecessary) suede coat. A furry cuff grazed my desk and I noticed her nails were blunt—purposely short. I wondered if she played an instrument.

"Sorry, Mr. T," she said, taking a seat near the back. "Female problems."

In the front of the room, the muscles in Mr. Tipton's face tightened. "Better late than never, I suppose," he said before retreating to the whiteboard.

Though my classmates did not settle back into routine as easily as Mr. Tipton, covertly pulling cell phones into their laps and doodling in the margins of their textbooks, I tried to focus. The day's lecture centered on pitch and its place on the treble clef, something my father's less technical teachings had never even referenced. But my effort was pointless. Like an itch somewhere unreachable, my mind kept returning to her.

I can't quite explain the effect that she had over me, except to say that Lynn Chandler, the exact apparition of a figure on the cover of an album I once loved, lured my mind in a strange, forgotten direction. My father disapproved of singles as a concept, so it was a wonder that the "California Dreamin'" seven-inch ever made its way into our home. The problem, he claimed, was that you couldn't fully understand a song without also experiencing its composite parts. You needed to know the album's arrangement, its movement, the spaces of silence in between. What came before, and what followed after.

But despite my father's intentions, this only made the song more alluring. At ten years old, I was fascinated by the mysterious idea of ghostly cogs existing between what can be seen or heard or felt. And when I listened to the song, I detected a dark layer beneath the sugary harmonies, a sinister allure in the gospel-like croons. I became consumed by the obvious contradiction: I had lived my whole life in Los Angeles, and yet the song evoked a shadowed paradise I could not recognize, a place that didn't even exist in my world. It was an invisible in-between that I could sense but could not see—just like my father's California.

A similar feeling emerged from Lynn Chandler. I felt a latent connection to her, like she'd been in that place, or in some abstract way understood. And I knew right then, only twenty minutes in, that Ms. Grobler had been right. There was no way I'd be asking to transfer out of choir class now.

When the period finally ended, everyone hurried from the classroom. Mr. Tipton called Lynn up to the front while I lingered, shamelessly eavesdropping.

"That's seven tardies so far this semester," Mr. Tipton was saying, "and two absences."

"But I've had good excuses for all of them," she pleaded.

"Excuses don't make up for missed classes, Lynn. The last thing I want is for you to fail, but you've got to meet me halfway here, and actually start participating in this class."

"Is there some sort of extra credit I can do? Make-up assignments?"

"The point is not to bog you down with busy work. I already know you understand the concepts. Your first exam proved that."

"So how can I make it up, then?"

"You tell me," Mr. Tipton said, sitting casually on the corner of his desk.

He waited. The room grew silent. I saw my opening, and this time I didn't let go.

"Excuse me, Mr. Tipton?" I said. Hoisting my backpack onto my shoulder, I approached the front desk.

"Ms. Hayes," he said, surprised. "Our newest addition. How may I help you?"

"I didn't mean to overhear, but I have an idea that I think might benefit all of us."

"Is that right?"

I nodded.

"Well, let's hear it."

"It's just . . ." I paused. My heartbeat swished in my ears. "At my old school, whenever there was a new student, teachers would offer extra credit to volunteers who helped the new person get caught up. And so I was thinking that if Lynn—Lynn, right?" I asked, trying to play cool. She crossed her arms, but I could tell she was curious. "If Lynn already has a strong grasp of all the material, maybe she can earn some participation points by helping me get caught up?"

They both stared at me.

"I guess I'm feeling kind of overwhelmed with all my new classes," I added, punctuating the idea with a sympathetic smile. "I need all the help I can get."

Mr. Tipton pursed his lips as he considered, and though I'd been staring at him for the past fifty minutes, I felt like I was seeing him for the first time. Initially, he'd seemed much younger than the other teachers, perhaps because of his unconventional enthusiasm, but up close he just looked tired. As he glanced between us, I noticed his eyelids were heavy, in direct contrast with the liveliness of his tone as he said, "I think it's a great idea. Lynn?"

I grinned at her. For an instant I thought she smiled back, one side of her mouth curling slightly up—but I couldn't be certain. Her eyes bore into me. She nodded in agreement.

"It's settled, then. Lynn Chandler, Susannah Hayes—you are officially partners."

The sun was warm and white as I followed Lynn out of the classroom, across the quiet campus. Choir was my final class, but because I had not known my schedule that morning, I couldn't give my mother a time to pick me up. I told her I would call. We passed the two ancient pay phones still standing near the office building. I kept walking.

"That class is kind of a joke," Lynn said as we headed down the center of the parking lot. About half of the spaces were already empty. "You probably don't need my help."

"No," I said. "Probably not."

Lynn stopped. Her eyes glistened, suspicious, as she examined me. "So why'd you do it?"

We were standing by the trunk of an old dust-covered silver car. A single sticker embellishing the back window read *The Endless West*.

I shrugged. "It's my first day here. I haven't really met anyone yet."

Lynn was still watching me. Somewhere in the distance, I could hear the faint squeak of tennis shoes.

"You remind me of a friend from my old school," I lied.

"He probably would've let me off with another warning, you know. Tipton's a total pushover."

"He seems pretty nice," I said.

"That's his problem. He wants to see the good in everyone. It's kind of annoying, actually."

Lynn unlocked the trunk of the silver car, tossed in her coat, and began pawing through the clutter. Her tank top had a sheer back, and I could see the ridge of her spine through the fabric. Something about her frame—the graceful curve of each limb, the sharp protrusion of bones—reminded me of a ballerina: a body that appeared fragile, but was not.

"Thanks, though," she said suddenly, glancing over her shoulder. "For getting me off the hook."

My cheeks flushed. "It's no big deal."

Lynn located a pack of cigarettes, apparently what she had been searching for, and placed one between her lips before offering them to me. I shook my head. She began rifling through her backpack. "So where're you from?"

"LA," I answered, glancing around. "Eagle Rock. Are you allowed to do that here?"

"No," she said. Then, "I can never find my damn lighter."

Frustrated, she sat back against the trunk, and I remembered my father's matchbook, still in the pocket of my shorts, all twenty heads unused. I slipped my fingers into my pocket and felt the soft paper. This, I thought, is all I have of him now. Without our studio, without the guitars, this is what remains. I can't waste it. Not even for her.

And then I thought, maybe the whole reason I have these matches is for her. Maybe I was supposed to be here, right now, in this conversation, with my father's matchbook in my pocket. Maybe it means something.

Or maybe it was just a stupid pack of matches, and it held no significance at all.

"Here," I said, offering the matchbook.

"Fantastic," Lynn said. "Thanks." She turned the book over in her hand, and for a second I thought I saw a spark of recognition on her face, thought maybe she'd heard of the Sea Witch. "Cool matches," she said, and the spark faded to shadow. She tore out a stick, flicking it against the striker in one swift, practiced motion.

Handing the book back to me she said, "Now I owe you twice."

I must have been feeling lucky then, because I blurted out, "I saw you during lunch. Out by the baseball field."

Lynn narrowed her eyes at me.

"I was sitting nearby," I explained. "I heard the guitars. It was so . . ." I struggled for the words.

"Oh," she said. "I get it now."

"Get what?"

"Why you helped me." She inhaled. "Because of them."

My stomach sank. "No, that's not—I mean—I'm a musician too, and the way that they were playing, the uneven rhythm, it caught my attention. But that's not why I helped you. I would've helped you anyway."

Lynn laughed then. "Relax. It's cool. The boys have that effect on people."

"Do they go here?" I asked tentatively.

"Used to. They've all graduated now."

"So why were they here today?"

"Because I bribed them to visit me. They'll do almost anything for free booze, and it really fucking sucks here when all your friends are gone."

Closing her eyes, she took a final drag, trying to reach whatever tobacco was left above the stub of filter.

"You need a ride?" she asked, dropping the cigarette to the asphalt and squishing it with the ball of her foot. "It's the least I can do."

"Actually, yeah," I said. "Thanks."

"We just have to make one stop first. Well, two, if you want to get technical."

I nodded. Two stops couldn't take too long.

Lynn unlocked her door and then reached over to pop the lock on the passenger side. The interior was incensed with a thick, earthy scent that I couldn't place. She took another cigarette from her pack and said, "Did you know that Mr. Tipton went to high school here? Can you even imagine, being stuck here every day for the rest of your life, never escaping?" She laughed. "I honestly think that's my worst version of hell."

"Maybe he doesn't want to escape," I said.

Smoke coiled up and spread through the car. I wondered if my mother would be able to smell it on me. I didn't know what I would say if she did, and a small part of me already didn't care. I kind of liked the smoldering scent, the tiny piles of ash that had collected on Lynn's dashboard, in the cup holders, smeared in gray streaks on her steering wheel like the remnants of her own personal brushfire.

"As soon as I can get out of here, I'm gone," she said. "I'll have left this godforsaken state before anyone even realizes it."

"Where are you going to go?"

Lynn shrugged. "Somewhere out in open land, with no one around for miles."

"Arizona?" I offered.

"No deserts," she said. "Maybe Colorado, or Idaho or something. Some place that is nothing like here, without all the bullshit. Or traffic."

Lynn cranked down her window, turned up the radio. We pulled out of the parking lot.

I don't know what made me say it, in the end. Perhaps it was her laugh, the one I had heard in the trees, and the way it felt like I'd glimpsed an intimate part of this stranger. Or maybe it was the loneliness, black and bulbous, covering me in a tar-like daze that nothing had been able to rupture until that moment. Whatever the reason, I said it, just loud enough to be heard over the crackling sound of the stereo: "My dad's dead."

I had never actually uttered those words to anyone. Staring at the intricate layers of dust smeared around by her windshield wipers, I waited for whatever happened next. In my periphery, Lynn lifted her cigarette. She didn't look at me strangely, as I had anticipated, didn't stumble through apologies, or aphorisms, or the meaningless condolences that everyone but Nick had offered. She leaned her head back against the seat and exhaled. Then she said, "Mine too."

TEN

WE STOPPED FIRST at a liquor store, where Lynn bought a block of Tecate and a large bottle of Jim Beam. I watched the transaction from the car, amazed when the clerk swept through the process without even checking her ID.

"One down, one to go," Lynn said when we were back on the road. She wedged her knee up against the steering wheel so that her hands were free to light another cigarette. "Where do you live, anyway?"

"Orange Park Acres," I said. "I think that's what it's called."

She released a plume of smoke. "My very own Uptown Girl."

"It's my grandmother's house," I explained. "I'd never been

there before yesterday. Actually, before yesterday, I didn't even know she existed."

"Damn," she said.

"Yeah," I said.

There was a pause.

"Well, if nothing else, at least there's one benefit to having your life turned totally upside down."

I laughed. "What's that?"

Lynn tapped her cigarette out the window and smiled. "It's a lot harder to get bored."

I couldn't argue with that.

The streets in Orange were wide and calm. Lynn swerved habitually through the cluster of neighborhoods and I gazed out the window, trying—and failing—to memorize our path. The houses were all brown and nondescript, built in the same simple style, landscaped with similar drought-tolerant shrubs. So I was glad when Lynn finally parked in the driveway of a small, one-story home distinguishable by its disarray. Soaked in the stark light of afternoon sun, the house flaunted a lawn dry as burlap and a ramshackle porch that sagged in the middle. It looked out at a chain-link fence separating the street from two lines of train tracks—one, I would soon learn, that traveled south toward San Diego, the other running north to LA, and then anywhere.

"Is this your house?" I asked.

Lynn nodded, stepping out of the car. "Help me carry this stuff in." She unlocked the trunk and held out the jug of whiskey.

"I like it," I said.

She scoffed. "Sure you do."

"I'm serious. It kind of reminds me of my old house."

"It's a total shit hole. But at least it's my shit hole, so I guess that counts for something."

We were halfway to the front door when Lynn abruptly stopped. Dogs began barking from various backyards, a cat skittered beneath Lynn's car, and then the stillness of the afternoon broke—just for an instant. A breeze swept through, kicking up her skirt, my hair, a sheet of dust. I shielded my face but Lynn let the wind brush over her, opening her body as though in welcome. When the calm returned, she had a contented look on her face.

"Did you feel that?" she asked.

"Yeah," I said. "That gust came out of nowhere."

"No, not the wind. The shift."

Somewhere nearby, music started to play. "What do you mean?"

"Earthquake weather," she said.

My father had said something to this effect before, once or twice, when we experienced some particularly odd atmospheric change, but I couldn't remember the circumstances.

"Oh don't look so scared. It won't be the Big One. Not this time."

She spoke with such certainty then, and I wanted to know what else she could sense. Could she tell whether a fire would jump a freeway? Did she feel the Santa Anas coming like an itch across her skin?

But there wasn't time. She opened the front door and music flooded out.

"We're here," she called.

Even in the moment, I was struck by her simple choice of

phrasing. We. This might have been a casual, unconscious choice on her part, but to me the implications were overwhelming. I followed her into the hazy living room, suffused with a new sense of confidence, and there—slowly materializing through the curtain of smoke and dust—were the musicians.

Lynn had brought me right to them.

"Everyone, this is Susannah," Lynn said. "Susannah, these are the boys. Alex, Cameron, Gabriel, and Luke." She pointed around the circle of them, too quickly for me to register which name accompanied which face—except, that is, for Cameron. He was sitting on the mottled carpet, looking through a stack of scattered records. In his hand was *Electric Warrior*, I think—no, it was *Transformer*. At my introduction, he peered up from behind the image of Lou Reed, his soft eyes veiled by a thick curl of dark hair.

Yes. His name I'd heard clearly.

"Hi, everyone," I said.

The record skipped, jumping forward. The boys had already muttered their hellos, but when they noticed the bottles in our hands, they suddenly became much more interested.

This was the first thing I learned from Lynn Chandler: alcohol entices people toward you. And though I didn't yet understand the power that one could attain from this malleable hierarchy, I felt it. They were looking at us, faces expectant, as if we held a holy elixir and also the sole authority over whether they were worthy of it. All that power in my small, soft hands.

Lynn put the beer down on the coffee table. As the boy with bare feet tore through the cardboard, she motioned for me to join her in the kitchen. "Beer has too many calories," she said, taking two glasses from the cabinet and filling them with ice. She mixed our drinks—Jim Beam and Diet Coke—with a metal spoon, spilling over the sides. "Cheers."

"Can I get one of those?" Cameron asked from the doorway.

Lynn continued drinking, then licked the aftertaste from her lips. Cameron just smiled and crossed his arms. There was quite obviously something between them. I watched, waiting for an indicator (Was this harmless flirtation? A playful exchange between friends?), but if one came, it was too subtle to notice.

"I *guess* I can make you one," Lynn said, pulling another glass from the cabinet behind her. Her back now turned, Cameron's attention swung to me.

"What's your name again?" he asked, his voice deep and lingering. I wondered if he was the singer. "I'm really bad with names the first time."

Lynn clanked the spoon inside the glass.

"Susannah," I told him. "Hayes. Susannah Hayes." Then, after a beat, I added, "And yours?"

"Cameron Cabrera," he said.

"Right. Cameron. Hi."

"Hi." His smile hadn't flinched; if anything, it grew wider, and I noticed that one of his bottom teeth was slightly crooked, imperfect yet charming.

"Here," Lynn said, thrusting the glass at him. Cameron thanked her as she left the kitchen. Back in the living room, the other boys started talking over each other, over the music, and I heard Lynn say, "You know I always pay my debts."

"Have I seen you before?" Cameron asked.

"Doubtful," I said, gazing into my drink.

"Why's that?"

"Well, I've only known Lynn . . ." I calculated the time in my head. "About two hours."

He laughed. "That's a pretty good reason."

I smiled and glanced down, noticed his scuffed boots, and knew then that he was one of the guitarists. The song from the trees rushed back to me. God, it was good. Great, even. The kind of song I'd wanted "Don't Look Back" to be—though I'd have never thought to use that strumming pattern, or let the lead run rampant against the chords. And while I was (admittedly) attracted to him, what I really wanted in that moment was his skill and confidence. To get back to the one thing that had always mattered most.

So I gulped my drink. I looked directly at him. "I heard you playing guitar at the school earlier."

"Oh?" Cameron said, eyebrows arching. "Why didn't you come over?"

I shrugged. "I didn't know you yet."

"You sure it wasn't because you thought we sucked?"

"The opposite. I thought you were really good, actually."

"Now I know you're lying," he said.

"I'm serious! I don't know what you usually sound like, but what I heard had that—that *thing*." I took another big sip of my drink, and my mind flickered with a memory of my last night in the studio. "My father used to tell me that you shouldn't get in the way of a great song, that great songs get in the way of you. They create their own plane of emotion, you know? And your song captured that rawness perfectly. It wasn't conforming. It just *was*."

I stopped. Took a breath. My glass was half empty.

Cameron said, "Maybe you should find out."

"What?"

"Maybe you should find out what we usually sound like."

"Oh," I said, shaking my head. "I didn't—I'm sure all of your songs are great. I just thought that what I heard was really . . ." All the words that had gushed, unbridled, from my mouth were now collecting like lumps in my throat. I tried to swallow, to think, to climb out of whatever hole I had dug for myself, but my mind faltered.

"Weird," Cameron said.

"I was going more for 'unexpected.'"

"No, I mean . . ." He smiled, flashing the crooked tooth, and I felt something in my stomach clench. "You only heard this small part of one song, one time," he began. I started apologizing again but he spoke over me. "And somehow you've managed to pinpoint this feeling I've had about it. Like you understand the essence, without anything more than a verse."

"Chorus," I mumbled.

Cameron paused, searching me.

"What do you play?" he asked.

"Guitar."

"You good?"

I rubbed my left thumb against the smooth tips of my fingers. "I'm okay."

He nodded, and I thought that was that. I had blown my chance—hijacking the conversation and steering it right off a cliff.

Until he looked back to me.

"You're right," he said. "It's the chorus. It has to be the chorus."

Then he laughed. My heart fluttered with relief. And that's when it truly hit me: in this brand-new city, without the gauze of preconceptions or the shadow of my past, I could be anything. Anyone. I could make my history as mysterious as my father's. I could make my future whatever I wanted.

I could belong here.

"Listen," he said. "We're playing a show in Costa Mesa next Saturday to kick off this mini tour we're doing. Can you come?"

"I don't have a car," I said.

"Lynn will drive you."

"Would that be weird?" I asked, scrunching my nose. "We just met, and already I'm asking for favors?"

"Hey, Lynn," Cameron yelled.

"Hey, what?" Lynn yelled back.

"What are you doing?" I whispered.

"Can you bring Susannah to the show next Saturday? She doesn't have a ride." His body was angled toward the living room as he spoke, but his eyes stayed fixed on me, his smile the only invitation I needed.

"Sure," Lynn said. "I owe her."

I don't remember much of what else we talked about that first day as we sat in Lynn's living room and daylight began to wither. There were a lot of names I didn't know, bands I hadn't heard of, glasses and bottles becoming empty in our hands. At first the conversation was difficult to follow, but that hardly mattered; it was their energy that captivated me most, the way the current of their lives suddenly engulfed me and swept me along, as though I'd always been part of the flow. The boys, I learned, had played all over Southern California: at the Roxy, the Echo, the Whisky a Go Go—so many of the same venues my father spoke of. They had been there, were part of that world, and I didn't even want to get up and use the bathroom for fear of missing something that might bring me closer.

Ultimately, though, I had no choice.

Through the bathroom's narrow walls, I could still hear them laughing, recalling one funny show or another while someone picked at a guitar. I flushed, washed up, tried to rough my hair in the mirror, but it remained flat. I looked wan—like someone who spent too much time indoors watching reruns of *The Price Is Right*. And I had a strange urge then to press my left hand, full palm, against the grimy, water-spotted mirror. I counted to five before pulling back. For the first few seconds my imprint stuck, and then the markings faded, ghostlike. The mirror looked as though it hadn't been cleaned in years, but still I grinned at my own distorted reflection, knowing that even if this entire afternoon had been a mistake—some glitch in the cosmos—and I never saw any of these people again, the smudge of my hand would remain.

Back in the living room, the sun had fallen behind the horizon, outlining the train yard in a fuzzy orange glow. I sat down on the sofa, next to Lynn. She rested her head on my shoulder and her hair poured over my shirt, the red strands mixing with my black.

"You probably need to go home," she said.

"Probably." I knew that my mother would be furious by now.

I pictured her in Vivian's kitchen, tapping her fingers against a crystal wineglass, planning the precise words of her scolding. I imagined all the ways she would punish me. I didn't care.

"I could get used to you," Lynn said after a minute, after neither of us moved. "Having another girl around. Usually I only have Josie, and even Alex admits she can be a little much."

"Who's Josie?"

"Alex's girlfriend. Or ex-girlfriend, depending on the day of the week."

"Sounds complicated."

Lynn sighed. "Never a dull moment with those two."

"And you?" I lowered my voice, only half aware of the boundaries I was crossing. "You're with Cameron?"

Lynn let out a sharp laugh. "Oh God, no. I mean, yeah, we've found ourselves in a few incriminating situations, but that was ages ago, and it hardly counts anyway." She laughed again, quietly, and her whole body quivered, as if to shake the memory away. "It creeps me out just remembering. He's like a brother."

"I wasn't sure."

"You think he's cute, don't you?" she asked, turning to face me.

"No," I said.

"Liar," she said.

"I think he's talented—"

"I can talk to him."

"No! Please don't do that." My heart plunged, afraid that she was going to tell him, maybe in front of everyone. My eyes darted to Cameron, and I was fiercely relieved to find that he was busy rifling through Lynn's mess of a record collection, oblivious in his hunt. "Don't say anything. Please."

"Well, I didn't mean now," she said. "Don't freak out."

She stood up, throwing her head back, and stretched her arms toward the ceiling. "I've got to take Susannah home," she announced.

I said good-bye, trying not to let my eyes linger too obviously on Cameron.

We had just reached her car when we heard the screen door slam shut, a voice calling out for us to wait. I turned back, a nervous excitement pounding in my ears. But it was not Cameron who ran out after us that day.

"Wait up," Luke called again.

He had been on the floor across from Lynn and me all afternoon, but he hadn't said much, just sat with his legs crossed smoking hand-rolled cigarettes. Now, in the milky glow of dusk, I noticed that his dark eyes were swirled like marbles. He was taller than I expected too, thin and angular. Scattered tattoos adorned his right arm: a feather, a compass, the bear from California's state flag. He said, "I need more papers. Can we swing by Rod's after?"

Lynn popped the lock in back. "Get in."

Inside the car, Lynn turned up the radio. Luke centered himself in the backseat and began drumming on my headrest. I liked the way the vibrations felt on my shoulders, the gentle thudding sound his fingers made against the fabric. Lynn, I thought, must have liked it too; even though her teeth weren't showing, I saw that she was smiling as she glanced at him in the rearview mirror. I wondered if he was looking back. From my vantage point, I couldn't tell.

It must have only been seven or eight by the time we reached Vivian's house, but it was late fall in California and night had settled comfortably into the hillside. Before I got out of the car, Lynn scrawled her phone number on the back of an old receipt. "For all those urgent choir questions that I just know will keep you up at night."

"Thanks," I said, and got out of the car. "See you tomorrow."

Then Luke climbed into the front seat and they disappeared down the block, the orange flecks of burning cigarette paper trailing Lynn's car like a comet's tail.

ELEVEN

I DIDN'T HAVE a key yet, so I rang the bell.

"Hi," I said when my mother flung the door open.

Her expression was conflicted. I could tell that she didn't know whether to scream at me or hug me, and for a moment, she just stood there, helpless.

I said, "I'm sorry I'm home so late."

"Where the hell have you been?"

The rich coral flush in her cheeks could have corresponded to any number of things: daylight hours lounging in the sun, a glass or two of red wine. But the anger in her tone—how well I remembered it thundering through the walls of our house on Catalina Street. It stunned me to hear that tone, those words, directed at me, when before she reserved them only for my father.

"Do you have any idea how worried I've been?" she asked. "You could have been kidnapped, or dead. Worse."

My mother shook her head, obviously flummoxed by her own phrasing, but I knew what she meant. Dante's *Inferno* had taught me: so much could be worse than death.

"What do you have to say for yourself?"

My mind reeled. If only I could explain to her the electric surge of the music, the unexpected glimpse into my father's hidden world. The way it felt like something inside of me had been unlocked. But I knew she wouldn't understand.

"Let the girl come inside, Diane," Vivian beckoned from somewhere in the house. "There's no need to get the neighbors involved in this."

My mother hesitated, as if actually considering the satisfaction she'd feel when slamming the door on me. Then her body slackened. She stepped aside and let me pass.

And I thought that might be it. She would leave me with the shame of my disobedience, the tremendous guilt I felt for forcing her to imagine a world in which she had lost her daughter, too. Being left with my thoughts would be a harsh and fitting punishment. I turned toward my room.

"Susannah," my mother said. She folded her arms. "We need to have a talk."

Her anger was already waning, allowing a sliver of relief to shine through, and my father's wife fell from her like flakes of dry skin. We had all made mistakes. In that moment, I knew I was not the only who didn't want to repeat them.

"I'm sorry," I said.

"That's not good enough." She headed into the kitchen. "Do you have any idea . . ." She shook her head and started over. "If anything had happened to you . . ."

"Nothing would have happened. I made a friend. A girl from school. I just forgot to call."

"But how would I know that? You can't forget to call. Not ever. Do you understand me?"

I nodded. In the kitchen, Vivian sat at the table drinking tea. She was still made up for the day, with bronze dabs of eye shadow on her lids, smears of pink on her cheeks.

"We're just glad you're home," Vivian said. "Right, Diane?"

"Of course," my mother said, leaning against the counter. "Of course we're glad you're home." She paused, thinking. "What's that smell?"

"Patchouli," I said. Lynn had me slather my arms with the stuff before we reached my house. She claimed to have used it for years to cloak the scent of cigarette smoke. But from the way that my mother looked at me then and the odd expression striking Vivian's face, I knew I had answered too quickly. The question was not intended for me.

"I put one of those frozen pizzas you bought in the oven," Vivian said, one eyebrow just noticeably arched. "I figured Susannah might be hungry."

"I'm starving," I said, smiling, and sat down at the table next to her. "Thanks."

"So we've all agreed, then," Vivian said. "You made a mistake. You should have called. It won't happen again."

I said yes.

"Good. We got you something." Vivian slid a small white box across the table.

I looked from Vivian, who still had that same knowing smirk on her face, to my mother. "What is it?"

"Just open it," my mother said, a hint of excitement in her voice.

Bracing myself, I opened the box. Inside was a cell phone. "Why do I need a cell phone?" I asked.

"You could say thank you," my mother said.

"But I don't want this."

"Most kids your age already have them," she said. "And Vivian was gracious enough to get one for you."

"Well, thanks. But you can take it back." I put the lid on the box and shoved it across the table.

"Call this your punishment," Vivian said, pushing it back.

"It's so you can always call," my mother insisted.

"It's so you can keep tabs on me."

"Bingo," said Vivian.

"So I screw up one time, and you give me a twenty-four-hour monitoring device?"

"If that's how you choose to see it," my mother said, "then yes. You will have it on you at all times. You will not leave the house without it. If we want to talk to you, we will call you, and you will answer."

"You can't be serious."

"The world has changed, Susie," my mother said. "It's about time that we—all of us—accept that."

I thought back to Cara's party. My mother had no objections

then to my going out alone at night. And this was just an afternoon, a few daylight hours after school.

Of course, I understood that the difference was Cara, a girl who had been a part of my life since childhood, whose mother sat next to my own at all school functions, and the neighborhood I knew as intimately as the lines on my palms. Now, I was living in foreign territory. I wedged the phone from the box. It was a bulky thing, black, heavy as a paperweight. But as I glowered at the screen, ensuring that my disapproval was known, I allowed my mind to slip. Certainly, my punishment could have been worse.

"And you're grounded," my mother said. "Two weeks."

I laughed. I couldn't help it. "So why do I even need this, then?"

My mother took a bottle of wine from the refrigerator and poured herself a glass. She said, "There's an alarm on the phone. I'll expect you to be ready by seven fifteen for school." Then she left the room.

Vivian and I sat silent in the kitchen until the oven's timer beeped. She slid the pizza out onto a large cutting board and sliced it four ways, pulling two pieces onto a plate for me.

"Did you and Mom eat dinner already?"

"Your mother said she wasn't hungry," Vivian said.

"I didn't mean to scare her."

Vivian turned to the sink. "We rarely intend on doing the things that hurt the most."

Wetting a sponge, she began to wipe off the countertops, though from where I sat the granite already looked polished and clean. I watched her lips pull taut as she scrubbed, the trail of water gleaming beneath the lights, and I felt a nagging urge to say something else—defend myself. After all, hadn't I done exactly what my mother and Vivian wanted? Wasn't I making friends and moving on?

A beat passed. Between us, the countertops sparkled.

In bed, I spent an hour scrolling through my new phone's settings, perusing the manual and learning how to make the thing work, because once I'd stopped seething over the slices of frozen pizza, I realized that my mother was right: Everyone had cell phones. Lynn had one, and Nick, and Cara. All the boys probably, too. And the cell phone, despite what my father believed—what I'd always believed—was quite the opposite of a prison. It was freedom.

Perhaps out of habit, the first number I entered was Cara's. I pulled it up on a fresh text message and began writing, *Hey, it's Susannah . . .* but I couldn't think of anything to say next, and deleted the message. Instead, I wrote Nick.

Guess who finally joined the 21st century!

Give me a hint, he wrote back, punctuating the sentence with a smiley face.

I must have still been reeling from that afternoon—emboldened by the conversation I'd had with Cameron, my newfound mystery and the ability to be whoever I wanted—because I decided then to voice the ideas that had been bouncing around in my head all day, offering Nick a clue that I thought only he would be able to decipher. I wrote, *I'm surrounded by foreign faces / Close my eyes, pretend I'm not alone / This city might be bearable / if I wasn't bearing it on my own.*

Minutes passed without any reply and I began to fear that he didn't understand. Hoping to quell the twisting in my stomach, I busied myself getting ready for bed. I was brushing my teeth when my phone finally buzzed, but that didn't stop me from picking it up and grinning at the screen, toothbrush idling in my mouth as I read, *Roses are red / Violets are blue / Your absence is everywhere, Hayes / Los Angeles misses you.*

That night, I dreamed about a plane crashing. About turbulence so powerful it knocked me from my seat. The nose pointed south-ward and I began falling, legs flailing. My mother's hand was in mine. And then—the room rocking like the waves of the ocean, swaying like my childhood body in the arms of my father. The sound of him singing "Love Honey."

I woke on the floor, legs knotted in satin sheets and a cold sweat coating my skin. It was the middle of the night, but so different from the midnights I had known before. This was all-encompassing—no seeping streetlights infiltrating the edges of blinds, no murmur of freeway traffic. Only darkness so disorient-ing that at first, I didn't even realize the world was still shaking.

As children, we'd been taught to duck under our desks or stand beneath door frames, tuck our heads into our chests and cover them with our arms. I did none of these things. Lynn had known the earthquake was coming, and I felt a surprising complacency now. *It won't be the Big One,* she had said. *Not this time.*

I turned onto my back and stretched my arms over my head. The tiny trembles shivered against my spine, the larger movements like the undulations of water. Outside a coyote began howling, while in another part of the house something shattered. I wondered if my mother was awake, even thought about checking on her and Vivian. But once the earthquake stopped, I only wanted to talk to Lynn.

Feeling my way through the unfamiliar room, I crawled over to my backpack and fished around inside for the crumpled receipt. Then I grabbed my phone. The screen's harsh glare flooded the room. I shielded my eyes from the light, squinting through the cracks in my fingers as I saved her number and opened a new text.

I felt it, I wrote. Then, as an afterthought, *This is Susannah, by the way.*

I waited, staring at the bright white glow. After a while, the phone automatically turned off, casting the room once again in full, sweeping darkness. I pressed a button and the world lit up. When my phone finally vibrated against the sleepy silence of the room, my heart hiccupped.

I looked at the screen: *Told you.*

How did you know? I wrote.

Another moment passed. She said, *Here comes the aftershock.* And sure enough, the earth omitted one final, faint rumble before everything settled again.

Cameron really wants you to come next Saturday.

I grinned. My fingers hovered over the keypad. *I'm grounded,* I typed.

Shit. Was it the smoke?

I forgot to tell my mom where I was going. She completely overreacted.

The boys aren't scheduled to go on until at least eleven. Sneak out?

I'm not sure it's a good idea, I said, hoping that she would try to persuade me.

Then make it one, she replied.

I closed my eyes, my smile expanding, and rested the phone on my chest. *I'll think about it,* I said.

Good. We can talk logistics tomorrow. Meet me outside the library before first period.

Sure, I said. *But you have to tell me how you knew about the earthquake.*

She wrote, *If I told you, I'd have to kill you.*

"It says so right here. A four point seven, out in Riverside," my mother was saying when I entered the kitchen the next morning, the *Orange County Register* spread in front of her.

"Well that's comforting," Vivian said. "For a minute there, I thought it was just me."

My mother frowned across the table. "This isn't something to joke about, Mom. Tell me the truth. Do we need to call Dr. Hartford?"

I shuffled around the perimeter of the room, groggy and hoping to avoid detection for as long as possible, but when I opened the pantry in search of breakfast, the hinges creaked. Both heads snapped in my direction. "Morning," I said.

"Good morning, dear," Vivian said, making her voice sound chipper. It was only seven, and already she was dressed, her hair styled. She sipped her coffee through pink-painted lips.

"How'd you sleep?" asked my mother.

"Okay," I lied, hoping she hadn't heard my phone thrumming

in the middle of the night. I peered into the pantry, craving sugary cereal, or a cinnamon roll from the Last Bean. All I saw was wheat bran, granola, flaxseed meal, and—a flash of orange? I reached back, my fingers touching the smooth plastic of a tiny pill bottle. Covertly, I pulled the vial forward, examined the label. I saw Vivian's name, some other words I couldn't pronounce, and the directions: *Take two tablets once daily, with food.*

This seemed like a weird place to store medication, I thought, but in a strange way, I guessed it also made sense. Take with food, keep near food. My eyes drifted down the label: *May cause dizziness,* it read. *Avoid alcohol.*

"Susannah?"

I slid the pills back behind the boxes, as though guilty of something. "Yeah?"

"I asked if you felt the earthquake last night."

"Oh." I pulled out the granola. "No. I must have slept through it."

"You're lucky," my mother said. "A lamp in my room fell over and scared me half to death. I haven't felt one like that since you were a little girl. Do you remember?"

I did. Vividly. When I was maybe seven years old, I was awakened not by the rocking and swaying of the earth but by my mother scooping me from my bed, huddling over me in the door frame. Her body canopied mine. Because I had been half asleep during the incident, my tired young mind unable to divide the dream world from the real one, the memory is steeped in the surreal, the view from behind the waterfall of my mother's hair fractured and bizarre.

"Sort of," I said, and shoveled a heaping handful of granola into my mouth before excusing myself from the kitchen.

On the way to school, I couldn't stop thinking about my father and his own orange bottle of pills with the wording scratched off. I remembered my mother saying, *You're not supposed to drink with that.* I remembered my father saying, *Don't tell your mother.* From there, my mind whirled to Detective Melendez: there were no skid marks, he'd said, no sign of my father braking. And when he left our house that night, the overpowering scents of fermented oak and rye.

"Susannah," my mother said, startling me. "I want to talk to you about something."

"I already told you I was sorry about yesterday," I said.

"I know. It's not that." She paused as we slowed for a red light. "Your grandmother's having some health issues."

I turned to face her. "Is it serious?"

"It's nothing you need to worry about. In fact, she was adamantly opposed to me telling you, but I thought you should know, just in case you witness something . . . off. If she repeats herself, or forgets where she is in a conversation."

A warm swell of relief washed over me. "So she doesn't, like, have cancer?"

"No," my mother said. "Not cancer." We began moving forward. "She's started seeing a specialist and they're working to figure it all out, find her the right medications."

"I saw some of her medicine in the pantry this morning," I confessed. "By the cereal. I thought it was kind of a weird place to store it."

My mother nodded, her lips tightening into a thin line. "Yes, that is a weird place for it."

When we reached the drop-off zone, I hoisted my backpack onto my shoulder and had just opened the door when a black, half-formed thought nudged me. I looked back.

"But Vivian's going to be okay, right?"

"You don't need to worry," my mother said again. "And actually, I'd appreciate it if you didn't tell her you know. The last thing she wants is to be treated like a sick person, or for you to think of her that way. Okay?"

"Okay," I said, stepping from the car. If my mother said not to worry, then I'd try not to worry.

Still, my thoughts remained tangled as I set off across campus.

Due to several wrong turns, it took me longer than anticipated to find the library. But when I finally arrived Lynn was there, on a splintered bench in front of the entrance, wearing a lace minidress with torn black tights and Doc Martens. Her hair was electric against the delicate white fabric and the old, yellowing pages of the book in her lap. The sight of her filled me with buoyancy; until that moment, I hadn't fully believed she'd show.

She glanced up then. "Oh good, you're here," she said, and I felt a shock of familiarity. Behind my eyelids, I saw my father curled over a guitar, the spark of joy on his face when he finally noticed me standing in the doorway of our studio.

And then I saw him smashing through his windshield like a brick.

She said, "I wasn't sure you were going to make it before the bell."

I shook my head, ordering the images away. "If you're trying to finish a chapter or something before class, I can leave you to it."

Lynn plopped the book closed. It was the library's copy of *Anna Karenina*, equipped with stained filing stickers and a dust jacket covered in thick, murky plastic. "Oh, no," she said, gently patting the cover. "This is just for fun."

I sat down next to her. "I've never read it."

"You should. It's terribly depressing, which is exactly how I like it." She laughed then. "A story is only as good as its drama, you know?"

I said, "It seems long."

"I'm a fast reader. Plus, a few days a week I work at this costume rental shop that's completely dead most of the year, so I've got plenty of time to kill."

I tried to picture Lynn at work, in a small store brimming with carnival masks and poodle skirts. I smiled. A place like that suited her. All those relics of the past.

"You read much?" she asked.

I shook my head. "I love reading, but I've had trouble concentrating lately."

"ADD?" she asked. "I think I have something for that." She rifled through her purse and pulled out a small, scuffed Altoids tin. Inside were tiny pills of varying sizes and colors. She offered them to me. *May cause dizziness,* I thought.

"No thanks."

Finding an uncoated peach tablet, Lynn tossed it into her mouth. She swallowed it dry.

"You have ADD?" I asked.

She shrugged and said, "Sometimes it helps." She dropped the tin back in her bag. "Reading's always been my outlet, how I escape from all the fucked-up shit in my life. You must have something like that, right?"

I nodded. "Music."

"Oh," Lynn said, drawing out the vowel. "That's right."

"What?"

"You said you were a musician."

"I am," I insisted, but for the first time, this sounded more like a lie than the truth.

"It all makes sense now."

"What?" I asked again.

"Why Cameron was so taken with you. Don't get me wrong, you're very pretty—"

"Thanks," I mumbled, heat rushing across my face.

"—but the boys are frequently surrounded by pretty girls. It takes something else to actually hold their attention. Cameron wouldn't tell. But now I know."

I hesitated. "You lost me."

"I'm just thinking out loud," Lynn said, shaking her head. "Point is: Nothing in the world matters more to those guys than their music. And yesterday, you must have met him on his level. That's what made such an impression."

I felt caught between elation and annoyance. I wasn't trying to impress anyone. At least not then, not with Cameron. For that brief period, I actually felt like myself again (or, rather, the few remaining parts of my old self that I still liked combined with the few identifiable fragments of the new self that I wanted). So while I was naturally thrilled by my lingering impression, something about Lynn's comment, and the odd undertone clinging to her words, unnerved me. She had told me Cameron was like her brother, but maybe the situation was more complicated. Maybe she still had feelings for him. Liked to keep potential enemies close.

The first bell rang. All around us, people began to gather their things, give their hugs, shuffle away.

I turned back to Lynn.

"I wasn't trying to impress him," I began, the words leaving my mouth before I could process them. "Music matters a lot to me, too, but I haven't been able to talk about it lately. It was my thing with my dad. He taught me how to play guitar and sing, and write songs, and since he died, I haven't done any of that. My conversation yesterday with Cameron was the closest I'd come to getting back that piece of myself, but if I did something wrong then you've got to tell me now, because you're the only friend I have here and I'd really fucking hate to lose you already."

I was breathless, hot-cheeked, and full of adrenaline. I never cursed (never out loud, anyway). The word itself was like a shot of caffeine straight into my bloodstream. Fuck, I thought. *Fuck*.

And yet, as the seconds collected between us, my euphoria dwindled. What I'd said sounded so childish. I should have just stayed quiet.

"It's hard when you lose them," Lynn finally said, staring at some point out in the deluge of students. "And the pain doesn't get easier. It may lose its priority in your life, but it will always be a big fucking crater right in the center of you. The best you can do is try to keep it from swallowing you whole."

Though I wanted to know more about her father, how he died, how old she had been, and if the same devastating déjà vu consumed her every morning when she woke and remembered once again that he was gone, I didn't ask. No one could make you talk about that darkness unless you truly wanted to. I knew that better than anyone.

"But," she continued, "you need to get over whatever is holding you back. Try to think of the music as something your dad left you, rather than something that was removed with him. God knows a lot of my problems would be solved if I could just play a damn guitar."

She stood up, looking around, and roughed her hair with her fingers. "Jesus, I want a cigarette," she said.

"Yeah," I said automatically, also standing. Our time was almost up. "I'm sorry we've been talking about me this whole time. Is everything okay with you?"

Lynn's focus flickered back to me, her eyes a nebulous pattern of silver and white. "Never been better," she said.

"I'll see you at lunch, then?" I asked.

"Lunch," she agreed. As she merged into the crowd, she yelled, "You're one of us now, so cheer up."

I smiled and waved, watching the flame of her hair disappear down the hallway.

✢ ✢ ✢

When lunch finally came, I couldn't find her. At first I thought I just didn't know where to look. We had never actually designated a meeting spot, so I went first to the trees, then back through the quad and past my locker, ultimately ending my search at the library. I ate my lunch on the bench where we'd met that morning, in the cool shade of the concrete buildings, and wondered what other places I may have missed. Surely Santiago Hills had an infinite number of secret nooks where people retreated during lunch. I almost went back to the trees, thinking maybe I hadn't waited long enough, but the bell rang before I could get there.

She wasn't in sixth period choir, either. During attendance, Mr. Tipton asked me if I knew where she was, and I felt a soothing gratitude toward him then for the simple assumption that I would already know such things, but also unequivocally disheartened, because I did not.

After school, I sent her a text to make sure she was okay. She wrote back swiftly: *Wasn't feeling well. Got permission to go home, thank God.* I spent the rest of the night thinking about the fear that still—despite everything—lurked through me, and about the warm, woozy bliss that replaced it in Lynn's kitchen when I was talking with Cameron about music. I thought about what Lynn had said that morning: *You need to get over whatever is holding you back.*

The next day, when I saw her at lunch (the trees became our meeting spot after all), I knew exactly what I needed to do.

"Is the offer still standing for next Saturday?" I asked.

Lynn was lying on her back, her book bag beneath her head. "Of course," she said. "You going to sneak out?"

I nodded. "How should I do it?"

"Start by telling them you're really tired. Say the whole experience of moving and starting at a new school has been exhausting, and you're going to go to bed early. Don't offer anything more unless they ask, and then be entirely unspecific—mention an ailment that can connect to any number of simple or severe things. Like a headache."

"But what if they decide to check on me in the middle of the night?"

I glanced down at her. The dancing leaves above us were reflected in her big round sunglasses. "Why would they do that?" she asked.

It was the kind of thing I had seen in movies: a mother cracking open the door as a slice of light spread across the sleeping child, who was really no more than a strategically lumped cluster of pillows. I shrugged. I had no idea why they would do that.

"You've never snuck out before, have you?" she said.

"My mom never used to care what I did," I said, defensive.

"I'm only asking because if you've never done it, there's no reason for anyone to think you might. Trust me, it'll be a breeze. It only gets tricky when you're trying to climb down from a second story, but you don't even have to worry about that."

"I hope you're right," I said, lying next to her. Above us, the sun formed kaleidoscopic patterns as it blazed through the swaying leaves, and I struggled to watch the colors, how they changed from yellow to green with the angle, but I couldn't stop myself from squinting, and soon, closing my eyes. My own sunglasses were still at our house in LA, and my mother hadn't said yet when we would return for the rest of our things. Just as well, I thought; I wasn't sure if I was ready to go back there yet, pack up all my father's possessions, seal our old life in boxes. I'd rather buy a new pair. I'd ask Vivian to lend me the money when I got home.

A moment passed. The breeze blew my long hair across my face. Lynn said, "A successful liar knows exactly how much to give, and precisely when to stop."

This was the second thing I learned from Lynn Chandler.

TWELVE

THE NEXT WEEK passed slowly, considering that my grounding kept me from doing anything even remotely interesting. I went to school. I came home. I completed all of my homework assignments and read *The Awakening* for advanced English. I carried on text message conversations with Nick from the confines of my bland new bedroom. I thought about Cameron's show.

That Friday, in choir, Lynn passed me a note folded tightly in a triangle:

Cameron just texted me AGAIN. Can I tell him you're coming yet? PS: Mr. T looks kind of hot today in those khakis, don't you think?

I glanced at the front of the room and giggled. For an instant, Mr. Tipton's gaze rested on me. We continued practicing scales.

After the bell, as the class darted from the choir room, Mr. Tipton called out, "Susannah, can I have a word?"

"Shit," I whispered to Lynn.

"The note?" she asked.

My stomach tightened. I shoved her note in my back pocket and decided to plead the fifth as we approached his desk.

"Ms. Chandler?" Mr. Tipton said. "Is there something I can do for you?"

"I figured I would need to stay," she said. "Susannah and I are partners in this course, after all. You deemed it so yourself."

"Nice try," Mr. Tipton said.

Lynn feigned horror, one hand brushing the rigid bump of her collarbone. "I can hardly believe it, Mr. T. The one day I'm actually offering to spend extra time in your class and you kick me out."

Mr. Tipton leaned back in his chair. "Well, I've actually had some new ideas about extra credit, if you're looking for more—"

"As much as I would *love* that," Lynn interrupted, "I just don't feel right about causing you the extra trouble when I know you teachers already work so hard." She started backing up, slowly retreating toward the exit.

Right before she opened the door, she mouthed, *Text me!* Then she was gone.

Left alone, Mr. Tipton turned to me. My breath stuttered, and I coughed.

"How are you doing?" he asked.

The question seemed oddly general and I wondered if I had maybe dazed out for a moment, missing some crucial part of the exchange. "Fine?" I asked, hoping that my tone would elicit clarification.

"Ms. Grobler, as you must have guessed, alerted all of your teachers to your recent"—he searched for the right word—"hardships. You've been here over a week now, and I just want to make sure you're getting on all right."

"I'm fine," I repeated, looking down at the cluttered surface of his desk. Near the front edge lay a stack of worn hardcover books with a half-full *Santiago Hills Stallions* mug balancing dangerously on top of the heap. I stared at that mug, not blinking, certain that it would fall to the floor and shatter at any moment. I wanted to warn him.

"I'm fine," I said again.

"And Lynn? Is she helping you? You can be honest, Susannah. If she's not fulfilling her end of the agreement, I can speak with her."

"She's helped a lot," I said. "Really."

Mr. Tipton regarded me, as though waiting for something else. "All right, then. But I trust you'll let me know if I can help you in any way. Even if it has nothing to do with choir." He started gathering his things.

"That's it?" I asked.

"Yes. That's it." Mr. Tipton headed toward the door.

While his back was turned, I reached across the desk and moved his mug to a more central, safe location. "I thought I was in trouble," I said before following him.

He looked back. "Have you done something that might get you in trouble?"

I paused. "No."

"Then why are you worried?" Smiling, Mr. Tipton pushed the door ajar.

I exited first, emerging into the gleaming afternoon. The air was dry. Hot, too, but that I was used to; the crisp, dark mornings of fall always gave way to a bright wave of midday warmth. A drop of sweat dribbled down my temple and I wiped it away with my knuckles.

"Susannah, look," Mr. Tipton began. "I know how the passing of a loved one can consume you from the inside until you think you have nothing left. And I understand how hard it is to confide in someone unfamiliar, but it's important to me that you know my door is always open."

I nodded. His voice was gentle, but there was also a sense of candor in his words, a pain that hovered behind his kindness. His eyes searched mine, and I recognized something in him then—the peripheral shape of a sadness I was just beginning to understand. "Thank you," I said.

Then someone called my name.

"Susannah," my mother said again as she approached us. "Why didn't you answer your phone? I've been waiting out front."

I winced with embarrassment, even as Mr. Tipton began to explain that it was his fault for keeping me after class.

"She's not in trouble, is she?" my mother asked.

Mr. Tipton cast me a knowing glance, and smiled. "We were just chatting," he said, but his voice trailed off as he glanced— finally, fully—at my mother.

I had seen men look this intently at her before, but Mr. Tipton's gaze was different. It was filled with wonder, and my mother took off her sunglasses in response. Her lips parted slightly, her eyes so vibrantly golden and green next to all those pale cinder block and stucco buildings. An unfamiliar grin broke across her face. She tucked a loose strand of hair behind her right ear.

"This is my choir teacher," I started to say.

But she finished the sentence for me, his name distinct and alive on her tongue: "Roger Tipton."

"Diane Crane," Roger said, shaking his head in disbelief. "You look incredible."

They leaned in for a hug, arms crashing into arms, faces tilting the same direction. Laughing, they bobbed back and forth—a dance that culminated with a flustered touch and shoulder pats. And I knew right then, from the unmistakable awkwardness of their embrace and the smooth cadence of their names in the other's mouth, that at some point long ago, before my father appeared on that stage at the Troubadour and saw her face framed beneath the wayward glare of a broken spotlight, my mother and Roger Tipton had loved each other.

"All this time and you're still right here," she said, her head shaking lightly. "You always did love this place beyond reason."

A flush of pink crept up his neck. "And you never could wait to leave it. Last I heard, you were living in LA somewhere. Just like you planned."

"And that was what, twenty years ago?"

"Something like that."

They continued smiling, staring, unsure, no doubt, of whether one speaks of the past or the present when it has been this long, deciding instead to say nothing. Hours seemed to pass while I stood there with my arms still crossed, trapped on the outside of whatever was passing between them. Then Roger's gaze drifted, and his eyes darted briefly to me.

"You're Susannah's mother," he said, one hand smoothing down the front of his shirt. "Hayes?"

"That was my husband's last name." My mother's smile faded to a parenthesis.

"Your—" Roger paused, blinking, as though to recalibrate himself in the present. "Oh my God, of course. I'm so sorry."

"Thank you," my mother said.

"The musician," Roger said.

"That's right."

He forced a smile. "Well I can see now why Susannah wanted to take choir."

"Actually . . ." I began.

"Choir?" my mother interjected, her eyebrows rising, and I was sure that she'd admonish my choice of classes. Instead, she turned back to Roger. "You teach choir?" she said in disbelief. "But you never had a musical bone in your body."

Roger laughed. "You may be surprised by how much has changed."

"Around here?" My mother looked around brazenly.

"All right, fine. I'm an English teacher. But the choir teacher retired last year, and they needed a quick replacement, so I volunteered. Honestly, I'm really enjoying it."

My mother's smile widened again. "Same old Roger Tipton. Always trying to save something."

"If I remember correctly, we weren't so different back then."

"We should go," I said, my voice harsher than intended. I shoved my hands in my pockets and felt the matchbook hiding there. Nineteen sticks left. "I've got a lot of homework."

"Sure, hon," my mother said. She put a hand on my shoulder but her eyes were still stuck on Roger. "Homework comes first."

As we walked toward the visitors' parking lot, I kept my pace brisk and head firmly forward, but that did not stop me from noticing the way my mother glanced back over her shoulder. I kept walking. I didn't want her to know that I'd seen. Even more, I didn't want to know if Roger was still there, waiting.

On Saturday, I set about my preparations early. I moped around the house in my pajamas, occasionally moaning or resting a hand on my stomach as I watched TV. It was easy to act tired and ill. It was not easy to wait.

My mother paid little mind to my moods. She hummed as she went about her daily tasks, and kept mumbling cheerfully about her progress hacking away the overgrowth out in Vivian's feral yard—though I knew better than to believe her sudden glee was brought about by chores. After almost eighteen years on this planet, I was trained in the sharp joy of a crush. My mind was awash with them: Cameron's disarming smile and easy discourse, the unknowable mysteries of Cody Winters (whose quarter still lined a special pocket in my purse). And then there was Nick—his summery scent and the taste of his ChapStick, the way I imagined my body curling into his on my tiny dorm room bed. I wondered what he was doing, and sent him a message: *Will you remember me*

/ scattered between palm trees and train tracks / the years spent walk-
ing backward / hoping to outsmart the sun? (To which he replied:
Shall I compare thee to a starry night? / Thou art more splendid than
my meager words express / so I'll quit while I'm ahead. / Can you tell
that AP English has taught me nothing?)

No. My mother could not fool me.

That night, as the sky darkened like a bruise and Vivian called
me into the dining room for dinner, I had no trouble staring idly
down at my pork chop and roasted potatoes, pushing the various food groups around on my plate, and saying, "I'm not feeling
great. Can I be excused?"

"Hm?" my mother said. We had been sharing a silent meal—
each of us equally preoccupied.

"I'm really tired, and my stomach feels upset. I think I'll go to
bed early." My head had also begun to throb, but before I added
that to my list of symptoms (and these were real symptoms, more
or less, which made the whole situation seem a little less devious),
I remembered what Lynn had told me: to be believed, one must
know exactly how much information to give, and precisely when
to stop.

"Sure, honey," my mother said. "Let me know if you need anything."

"Just sleep," I said, and smiled weakly.

Amazed by the simplicity of my escape, I slid my chair back
and tried not to let the surprise register on my face. Lynn had been
right again; they did not question me. Why would they?

I was halfway across the room when Vivian spoke. "There's
some Pepto-Bismol under your sink," she said. "Brand-new."

Though the statement was clear enough, something in her tone gave me pause and I felt compelled to turn back. On the opposite side of the table, Vivian examined me through narrowed eyes. For a moment, our gaze remained locked. Then Vivian turned back to her plate, spearing her fork into a sprig of roasted broccoli. I flashed another feeble smile and said thanks before fleeing the room.

In the hallway, though, I decided that taking some medicine couldn't hurt, and it might even help sell my story if I left the bottle on the counter, looking less than full. But when I searched beneath my bathroom sink, I found no Pepto-Bismol. No medicine at all, in fact—only some rolls of toilet paper and cleaning supplies. Maybe Vivian meant *her* bathroom, I thought. Or maybe she forgot it at the store; after all, my mother had said that kind of thing might happen.

Once ready, I sat on my bed with the lights off and waited until Lynn sent word, my cell phone chiming with our code. *The phoenix flies,* she wrote. I unlatched the bedroom window and clambered out into the night.

A shock of cold wind grazed my skin as I hurried through the backyard, down the driveway, but it was too late to get a jacket. The new Susannah would not turn back. Sticking to the shadows, I crept forward, coerced by the night and the gentle whir of Lynn's engine idling in the street, just out of view.

"Well, well," she said as I slid into the passenger seat. "Your first official breakout. How does it feel?"

My pulse was racing. "So far, so good."

"So good," she repeated. "Welcome to your freedom."

She jerked the car into drive.

"The boys are supposed to play second," Lynn explained as we traced a path down from the hills, toward the freeway, "so we should be there just in time. The first band usually sucks anyway, and the later it is, the more crowded it is, the easier for us to get in."

In my mind, the opposite made more sense: the more crowded the venue, the less likely that any tickets would be left. I wondered if the boys had set some aside for us, and bit my lip to hold back my grin.

Our drive on the 55 South was fast and straight. After only ten minutes of whizzing past budget hotels and patches of stubby office buildings, brake lights began punctuating the night. It was a strange sensation, seeing a freeway end; we slowed to a stop and filtered out into surface streets, ultimately turning into the crowded parking lot of a strip mall. And there, tucked in the back corner, was the venue: Detroit Bar.

"Lynn," I said. "This is a bar."

Lynn gasped. "Impossible!"

"You know what I mean." I tried to sound casual. "It's just that I don't have a fake ID." If probed, I decided I'd tell her my mother had confiscated it.

"I don't have one either," Lynn said. "Lost mine last summer at a Fire Society party. But that's not the only way." She stepped out of the car and I followed.

Even from the edge of the parking lot, I could hear the bass buzzing. The drums, though muffled, were booming and full. Lynn headed down the row of cars, toward a black van parked near the bar's entrance, where Luke and Gabriel stood smoking.

"Who's the opener tonight?" Lynn asked as we approached. "They actually sound decent."

"They're called Pirate Idaho," said Gabriel, who had perpetually sleepy eyes, the wayward smile of a stoner. "From Long Beach."

"Why aren't you in there?"

Gabriel grinned in response, covertly pulling open his jacket. A flask filled the inner pocket.

"Share, please," Lynn said, reaching for the bottle.

"Just don't drink it all," Gabriel said. "And don't let the Rock over there see. I swear, he's had it in for me all night."

Peeking around the van, I spotted a security guard. Even while seated on a stool, he towered over most of the kids that came to the door, scowling at them as he examined their IDs with a black light, grunting acknowledgment when he allowed them to pass. I could not imagine what he did to those he caught deceiving him.

"Lynn," I said, unable to hide the uncertainty in my voice.

"Drink," she said, and handed me the flask. I took a long pull before giving it back to Gabriel.

"Glad you could come, Susannah," Gabriel said as he buttoned up his jacket. "Don't tell Josie about the flask." Next to him, Luke nodded in accordance, though I wasn't certain to which statement he was responding.

"Me too," I said.

I couldn't remember if Gabriel and I had even spoken that afternoon at Lynn's, but he obviously knew me, had known I was coming. Either he truly remembered me, or I had somehow become a topic of conversation among them. A thrill rushed over my skin.

"The others are inside?" Lynn asked.

"You know Cameron," Gabriel said. "He thinks these guys might really have something. And Josie is commandeering Alex's drink tickets, as usual."

"Three sheets?" Lynn asked.

"Maybe two," Gabriel said. "But the night is young."

"Well, I guess we should get in there." Lynn held out her hands. "Stamp me, kind sirs."

The boys looked at their right hands, which had been stamped in purple ink with some sort of emblem. Once it was decided that Luke's stamp was the most pristine, he proceeded to lick it, and then pressed it hard against Lynn's pale skin. They held the backs of their hands together for nearly a minute. When they finally pulled apart, Lynn was marked. The ink appeared slightly faded, but the design was clear enough. I would not have been able to tell the original from the fake.

After, with Luke's stamp too dim to transfer a second time, Gabriel licked his hand and held it against mine. My stamp came out slightly smeared, not quite as precise as Lynn's—Gabriel hadn't taken as much care as Luke, had not cradled my hand between his or waited patiently as the ink grafted—but the result was close enough. It was that simple. Too simple, I feared, but I smiled and thanked Gabriel, hoping that no one could sense the violent pounding of my heart while they leisurely finished their cigarettes, chatting about the other bands playing and the upcoming tour.

On our way to the front entrance, Lynn twisted her arm through mine, drawing us closer. "The trick is to act anonymous," she told me. "Once they know you, it can go only two ways. They like you and never ask for ID again. Or, they don't like you, and the next three years become a wasteland—no band, no bar, no fun."

"There are other venues," I said. "Other shows."

Lynn stopped, unlatching herself. "That's not the point. This is your chance to take control. You've come this far." She ran her fingers through my hair, arranging it aside my cheeks. "And once you know that you can get through those doors, you'll never be content in another parking lot again."

I gazed down at my hand, rubbing the pad of my thumb against the ink. "But what if he can tell?"

"You worry too much," she said, and proceeded in front of me. Pausing at the door, she lifted her hand to show the security guard. The whole endeavor took no more than a second: she lifted and he grunted. She was through.

Up close, I noticed the security guard seemed distracted. Though it had been easy to misinterpret the expression as perennial distaste for the entire concert scene, I saw now that his face held no scowl. Disinterest, maybe. Callousness. His mind was obviously elsewhere.

"I said go ahead," he growled.

"Oh—uh," I stammered, "thank you," and rushed through the door.

Detroit Bar was twice the size that it appeared from the outside, split in two, with the bar acting as the mediator between the sides. A wide lounge area lit only by tealight candles occupied the right, and on the left was the stage, where Pirate Idaho played in front of a small group, maybe twenty people drenched in darkness. I tried to find Cameron among them but the lights that ricocheted from the stage only turned the individuals further into silhouettes. In my ear the singer's smooth voice trilled, a somewhat tickling feeling that produced, strangely, laughter. It had been a long time since I'd heard anything so loud, so wonderful.

"They're not *that* bad," Lynn yelled.

"No, they're good," I yelled back, eyes roving across the stage, the bar, the dark, shadowed booths where groups sat huddled close, straining to hear one another. "They're really good."

"Wait until you hear the Endless West." She paused, fixing her gaze on me. "Looking for Cameron?"

I shook my head, not wanting Lynn to think I was more interested in the boys than the band. And besides, between the loud music and whatever had been in Gabriel's flask, I was having trouble focusing. Even I wasn't sure what I was looking for. But how incredible it was, just to look. To be there.

That's when Josie appeared, screaming. Like a flash, she emerged from some corner of the darkness, her bleached hair blazing as she clobbered Lynn in an off-balance hug.

"Finally," she said. "I've been stuck here since sound check. What took you so long?"

"Susannah, meet Josie."

"Hi," I said, extending my hand. I couldn't see much of Josie in that faintly lit room except black-framed glasses, the glint of a nose ring, and her hair, which was styled in a messy bob with full, swooping bangs. Though blond was clearly not her natural hair color, I thought it suited her; she was spry and unreserved, the opposite of Lynn in many ways. If Lynn was like a complex pattern in the sediment of tea leaves, then Josie was a billboard off the 5.

Her drink sloshed onto my arm as she enveloped me. She said, "It's so nice to meet you. We need another decent girl around here."

"Susannah just moved here from LA," Lynn explained. "Josie would have been at school with us, but she dropped out."

"You know that's not at all true. I got my GED and now I'm going to cosmetology school."

Awed, I asked, "And your parents are okay with that?"

She looked at me curiously. "What do they have to do with it?" Then she turned to Lynn and smacked her playfully on the arm. "By the *way*, you haven't even commented on my new hairdo yet." Josie posed, pouting her lips and angling her chin downward. Behind the glasses, her black eyes glittered.

"Totally classic," Lynn said, gently touching Josie's hair. "You'll be the stylist of the stars."

"It looks beautiful," I said.

"I like her," Josie said. Then, "I have to tell you about Andrew. Let's go get a drink."

At the bar, Josie proceeded to tell Lynn about the latest betrayals of someone named Andrew's most recent girlfriend, who, apparently, had been trying to sleep with Alex before she turned her sights on a more attainable target: the singer of a band called Great White Whales. But the myriad of unfamiliar names quickly became too cumbersome, and I didn't want to remind them that I had no idea who anyone was. Instead, I laughed and scowled and nodded when appropriate, offering just enough reaction to make my presence relevant while my mind focused instead on the arrangement of the music, the tinny timbre of the singer's voice. I wanted to know what he was saying but his mouth was right on the mic, more concerned with the pitch and flow of his voice than whatever he actually said. So I decided to make my own words.

Josie leaned toward Lynn, saying something about Saint Summer's bass player. I pulled a pen from my purse. On a cocktail napkin, I wrote.

> *Is this the beating of my heart,*
> *or the bass against my bones?*
> *This is the explanation*
> *for my broken words.*

I paused, thinking, listening to the music and the high pitch of Josie's voice, the crescendo of elements that made my heart surge. Ever since my father's death, I'd felt this deficiency within me—not the lack of him, which was an entire other realm of emptiness, but a lack inside myself. Like I'd lost a part of me that previously seemed as essential as water. But there at Detroit Bar, sipping on the round of whiskey-Diet Cokes that Lynn bought to commemorate the start of a new era in my life, I saw an end to the silence, the blank pages in my notebook. I could hear the words and their simple vibrato, the inflection produced with each vowel.

I'm speaking in fragments,
and I'm moving on.
I'll stay put if you do
(not).

As I read the lines back to myself, they made strange sense, as if I'd been writing from some future version of myself. I even felt them in my chest, bubbling in my throat.

"See?" Josie said to Lynn. "Susannah gets it." She placed a hand on my knee and leaned forward. "Isn't that the funniest thing?"

"Yes," I said, gripping her hand with my own. "It's hilarious."

When it was finally time for the Endless West's set, Lynn, Josie, and I ordered fresh drinks and stood near the front of the stage as the boys tuned and tested pedals. Around me, the sparse crowd had swelled into a sea. Heads trickled back as far as the entrance, most of the faces cloaked in shadows. Together, we waited. Anticipation turned into a subtle murmur.

"There are so many people here," I said.

"This is nothing," Lynn said. "You should have seen the show last month at House of Blues."

"That night was unbelievable," Josie said, laughing. "At least what I remember of it."

Lynn sipped her drink and rolled her eyes at me.

The Endless West started abruptly, without warning or welcome—just Luke with four counts on the bass drum quickly followed by the whooping cheer of an instantly captive crowd. Then, an influx of guitar: Alex strummed a clean rhythm wrought with reverb while on bass, Gabriel picked a slow, poppy groove. And only after the other instruments had built did Cameron's guitar begin whirling. He played lead, his fingers moving with effortless skill. Even as he harmonized with Alex's rickety vocals, his hands flowed across the neck of his guitar. A Fender Telecaster. It wasn't the same as my father's, but Cameron's sound was just as full—a perfect blend of progression and sustain. Each note reverberated, bouncing around in my rib cage until I felt the song's movement coursing with my blood.

There's no other way to explain. The music inhabited me, and my body responded first: a tap of my toe, a subtle twitch in my shoulder. A blaze, electric, burst across my skin. Before my brain could process the reaction, I was moving. I *needed* to move. The urge was primal and necessary—the only possible response to a sound so familiar that it could have come crackling out of my father's record player, and yet so wholly characteristic of now, of the four who produced it, and of the collective moment we all shared. All around me there were voices; everyone sang along. And after a while, when I glanced up at the stage, I was surprised to find Cameron looking back, the shadow of a smile on his face.

Right then, Lynn grabbed my hand. We came together, dancing, and raised our fists in the air. I closed my eyes, let the music rush over me. Our bodies smudged into the sway and my ears rang with the melodic howl of a hundred voices, and for the first time since my father died, I felt like I was home.

THIRTEEN

WE STAYED UNTIL the last band finished. It was after midnight. Cameron and I lingered in the small front patio, finishing our drinks as the parking lot began to empty. Though a half hour earlier the alcohol had made me feel energetic and unstoppable, I now felt anxious. Insecure. Lynn had gone missing sometime during the final set and Josie was still inside, searching for a way to elongate the party. For the moment, we were alone.

Because I didn't know what else to do, I checked my phone. Nothing from my mother (a good sign), but a new message from Nick: *Two freeways diverge at an off-ramp / one that takes me home, and one that leads south to Orange County / but I, being only one driver, cannot take them both. . . .*

I brought my hand to my mouth, smiling.

"Someone beckoning you?" Cameron asked. He pulled a pack of cigarettes from the chest pocket of his shirt and offered one to me.

I shook my head, but my cheeks had already flushed. I wondered if he could tell. "The opposite, actually, thank God. I'm not really supposed to be here right now."

"None of us are," he said with a shrug.

"Yeah." I laughed. "I guess that's true."

"It's a good thing that the big guy over there is completely oblivious. Without him, we'd all be banished to the parking lot. And I've been banished many times, so I speak from experience."

"Quick to cause a ruckus, are we?"

"Nothing of the sort. I'm a stand-up guy." Cameron cupped one hand around the tip of his cigarette, and with the other flicked a lighter. His face lit up in a warm yellow glow. "It's just a little bit hard to pass for twenty-one when you're only fifteen, sixteen, and still waiting for those final smacks of puberty. Trust me. It's not nearly as enjoyable out here."

I watched him inhale, his cheeks flattening. Smoke swirled into the murky black sky. "And the sound quality is really subpar," I added.

"All bass," he said.

"All bass," I agreed.

We smiled at each other. I remembered the feeling from Lynn's kitchen—a surprising lightness that emerged from the fluidity of our conversation, the soft lingering of his eyes. I held his stare. I don't know why, but it seemed important to me then, to not look away.

A few seconds later Josie appeared. Cameron diverted his attention to a group of girls talking loudly across the parking lot.

"Well," she said through an overzealous exhale, picking up my drink to refresh herself. "No parties tonight. That first band took off right after Saint Summer's set, and Saint Summer said they want to record a new song tomorrow before you all head to Vegas, so they've decided to ruin the night for everyone."

"About time they get that track down," Cameron said. "Are they going back to Diego?"

"I don't *know*," she cried, and slouched against the wall.

"How long are you guys on tour for?" I asked Cameron.

"A month," he said. "It's nothing official. We just called in some connections with other bands, set up a bunch of scattered shows. We're trying to expand our fan base."

"That's awesome." I pushed my voice up an octave, hoping the tone would cloak my disappointment. A month may as well have been forever.

Out in the parking lot, the girls hugged and got into their cars. Only a dozen vehicles remained. As a Honda pulled out of its space and circled toward the exit, I noticed Lynn and Luke standing near the boys' van. He disappeared back around the side as she crossed the parking lot toward us.

"What's wrong with Josie?" she asked.

"There's nothing to do," Josie moaned.

"So we'll go to Lynn's," Cameron said. "Your mom won't

mind if we go to your place, right?"

"She never does," Lynn said, and unconsciously brought a hand to her face. As she wiped a thumb beneath her bottom lip where her lipstick had smeared, her eyes caught mine. For an instant her face darkened, dangerous. Embarrassment gushed through me and I turned away.

A medley of voices seeped into the night as Alex and Gabriel emerged from the bar. "We got seventy-five bucks tonight," Alex said. "You guys want to go pick up some beer?"

"We always go to Lynn's house," Josie said, "or we go to my house, and we just sit there drinking and listening to records until we pass out like a bunch of fourteen-year-olds. Why don't we do something else for a change?"

"Like what?" Gabriel asked.

"Like . . . let's go to the beach."

There was a pause while everyone considered it.

"I'm in," said Lynn.

"Me too," said Cameron.

"As long as we get beer first," Alex said.

Josie grinned and draped her arm around Alex's shoulders, plastering his cheek with sloppy kisses. I glanced back at Lynn. The darkness was gone. Playfully, she tilted her head toward Cameron. I shrugged.

"So it's settled," Josie said. "A midnight swim."

"I don't have a bathing suit," Gabriel said.

Cameron laughed, patting Gabriel on the back. "At least you're a damn good bass player."

Lynn raised her voice, trying to reroute attention. "Not so fast.

I said *I'm* game, but it's not actually up to me. Tonight I'm in charge of this lovely lady, one Susannah Hayes, and, to no one's surprise, she's got a bit of a warrant on her head. If she feels this excursion might further her sentence, well, then, we're going to have to decline. So." Lynn turned to face me. I could feel all their eyes shifting but only saw hers, that perfect, pure cornflower blue, the way I imagined snow would look when washed in the filtered light of a smoke-shrouded moon. She said, "What do you think, Susie Q? Should we go?"

I said yes. Of course I did. After that night, that nickname, there was never another answer.

We took two cars—Lynn, Gabriel, Josie, and me in one, the rest in the other, tasked with finding a nearby gas station for beer. I sat in the front seat laughing as the radio blared Pat Benatar's "Heartbreaker" and Lynn cranked the volume up. "I love this song," she yelled out the open window, while Gabriel and Josie began performing interpretive seat-dances, singing in high, breathy voices. And through bleary eyes, as we curved back by the bar's entrance, I thought I saw Cody Winters standing on the patio, smoking a cigarette with one of the members of Saint Summer. It had to have been him; I knew the slick black swirl of his hair, the unconcerned shrug of his posture. But by the time I spun around to confirm, Lynn had already pulled onto the street and the bar had receded, the figures out front as indistinguishable as ghosts.

Newport Beach was maybe ten minutes away, but by the time we got there, Josie had already vomited out the back right window of Lynn's car and passed out in a slump against the seat. No one seemed surprised or concerned; they kept the windows cracked and locked her inside.

"She'll be fine," Lynn assured me. "She always is." So we pilfered her trunk for whatever we could find to stave off the cold, wrapped ourselves in Mexican blankets and fuzzy coats she'd gotten from the costume shop, and, leaving Josie to dream, headed down toward the water.

I thought that would have been the pinnacle of the evening—laughing about how silly Luke looked in Lynn's leopard-print jacket, how the emerald sequined sweater really brought out Cameron's eyes. We would drink to the soundtrack of the ocean until all our cans were empty, and then we would go home. But halfway through her second beer Lynn stood up, shook off her coat, and unzipped the back of her black dress.

"You're seriously going in?" I asked, rubbing my bumpy arms. The chill had punctured my skin, even beneath a thick white sweater.

Lynn's eyebrows rose as a challenge. "What?" she said as she shook the dress from her hips, dropping it to the sand. "You scared?"

"Of course not," I said, and began unlacing my shoes. I wanted to say that this was nothing—that I had learned to swim in the sea. I wanted to tell her how my father used to cannonball me into the Pacific and leave me tumbling beneath the plow of waves until finally the crest cleared and I broke through the surface, gasping and victorious. But that wasn't exactly the truth.

I'd learned to swim the same way as all the other kids: through weekly lessons at a high school with college-age instructors who gave me stickers and Tootsie Pops after each session. But, in a way, the story of the Pacific wasn't all lies, either. It was a game we had played, my father and I. He'd stand me on his shoulders and launch me toward the surf. I'd tuck myself into a ball, whirling around beneath the white water until I finally floated up. Even in winter, when the temperature dropped, we'd still race down from the shore to see who could dive under first. So who was to say that this wasn't my truth?

A seagull squawked somewhere above us, and when I tilted my chin up, I noticed the distinct outline of Orion winking down from the moon-bright sky. I pulled my shirt over my head and said, "I learned to swim in the ocean."

"I learned at the high school," Gabriel said, already undressing. "Pool was probably full of piss."

And then he took off running.

"Last one in has to clean up Josie's puke," he yelled over his shoulder. The rest of the boys flung off their clothes and chased after him.

For a moment, I didn't move. My head spun as their bodies blended into the black rumbling ocean, their voices stifled aside the swell of the waves. They crashed, and then there was static, like an amp before that first chord has been struck. In that instant, all I can remember seeing is her—the exposed skin of her back radiant beneath the twinkling sliver of moon, the vibrant red of her hair swirling around her head. And I thought that I had finally found her. The sea witch was here, right in front of me.

Sometimes, all you can do is make connections, charge half-naked into the freezing ocean and let the water pinch you a thousand times, enough to know you're crazy but not enough to make you stop because even though the hurt is so immense that it shocks every single muscle into near-paralysis, you know that the pain means something else entirely. You know that you're alive. And sometimes, when a boy who seems so kind and perfect reaches for you, his fingers curling around the curve of your waist, and glides you toward him through the salty foam, even if you aren't quite sure that it's the right thing, if you don't know him that well and don't know what any of it means, whether it's a promise or an instinct, you just open your mouth and say hello. Your hands rise up to grip the soft hairs that twist behind his ears. Hello, you say as you taste him. Hello, you say, and let the ocean determine everything else.

FOURTEEN

THE FOLLOWING WEEK the boys left for tour and the days of my new life rolled forward. The holiday break quickly approached, and without warning, another Southern California winter showed its strength. It was sharp and surprising as always, punctuated by ruthless winds and a cold that rolled down from the snow-spangled cusp of Mount Baldy. Under the veil of darkness the chill spread—yet that was always the strangest part. Our winters seemed to only exist during nightfall; somehow, the days remained bathed in warmth. And there was no snow, of course, not in our part of the state. The closest thing we had was the thin layer of ice that frosted our roofs before sunrise.

At Vivian's insistence, we bought a Christmas tree from the

pricey local Boy Scout lot. It was ten feet tall, full and fat, with branches that expanded farther than the length of my outstretched arms.

"Your grandfather was an Eagle Scout," Vivian told me that afternoon as she placed glitter-crusted glass balls among the boughs. "It just wouldn't do to buy a tree from one of those hardware stores, even after all these years. Do you remember, Diane? We would drive down there together, and you always insisted on saving the biggest tree you could find."

"Saving?" I asked. I was sitting cross-legged on the floor, unveiling fragile snowflakes from mounds of tissue. "All the trees are destined to die at that point anyway."

"Well, yes, but your mother didn't know that. As a child she thought that buying the tree meant that we were giving it a loving home for the season. And after Christmas, when we put it on the street with the garbage, she thought someone retrieved it, and replanted it in the forest. That secret was guarded more closely than Santa Claus. I still don't know where you got that wild notion."

"I guess I had a very active imagination," my mother said flatly, picking up one of the snowflakes. She examined it for a moment before walking over to the tree. "Children believe what they want the truth to be."

Vivian said to me, "Your mother wanted to save the world. The plants and the animals, anyway. People were not as much of a concern, but God forbid she saw a stray cat wander through the brush behind our house."

I couldn't help but laugh. "That's sweet."

"If your mother had her way, this place would have been turned into a zoo long ago. But the smaller creatures didn't fare well with coyotes, and the horses kept her busy enough, so we left it at that. Fitting," Vivian said, and showed me a ceramic horse ornament with my mother's name written on the side in elegant script. In my hands, it felt feathery, delicate. Much too breakable for a child.

"We never had any pets," I said, giving the ornament to my mother, who placed it on one of the higher branches.

Vivian stepped back now, examining the tree, her progress. She removed the horse. "It doesn't quite blend with the aesthetic," she explained, re-hanging it around the side where it was nearly out of view. Behind her, my mother's lips pulled taut.

"You didn't even have a cat, then?" Vivian asked me.

"Not even a cat," I said. My mother slipped around the back of the tree. "Or a hamster."

"Well I find that very surprising."

My mother covertly removed the horse ornament, hid it behind her back. "Your father was allergic," she said.

"To cats?" I asked.

"You knew that," she said, but I couldn't remember. I suppose there was a time when I had wanted a pet, and there was also a time when I stopped asking for what I knew I wouldn't get. In my memory, there wasn't much more than that.

But the idea that a cat allergy had afflicted my father bothered me. It was such a small, simple ailment, the banality of it offensive somehow. He was never sick. All those illnesses my mother made up—the flu, the stomach bug, strep throat. He never had any of them. At least, I didn't think so.

Then I remembered the pills.

"Mom?" I said, because in that instant, I had to know the truth. Headaches, he'd told me. Such awful headaches.

"Hm?" she said, glancing down at me.

I wanted his explanation to be the truth. But more than that, I needed him to be well. I needed what happened to be freak and unexplainable, because I could not have handled a clear buildup of symptoms and side effects. The possibility that his death could've been prevented would have destroyed me.

So I swallowed my doubt. "Never mind."

As Vivian kneeled down to unwrap more ornaments, my mother placed the ceramic horse back in the front of the tree. For a moment she smiled at her subterfuge, but the expression quickly dimmed, a shadow of sadness crossing over her face before she turned away and reached for more snowflakes. I wondered if Vivian would notice the horse, but she didn't. She just kept unwrapping ornaments.

"Your grandfather was an Eagle Scout," Vivian said.

"I know," I said. "You told me."

"Did I?"

"How about hot chocolate?" my mother asked. "I'll make some fresh whipped cream."

She retreated to the kitchen and plugged in the food processor. The machine began whirring. Vivian unpacked more ornaments. I flattened and refolded the pile of tissue paper while somewhere in the background, Bing Crosby continued singing about a white Christmas that would never come.

• • •

Later, I lay in bed beneath an assortment of blankets and quilts. A chill dashed through my body, and my mind plunged into the Pacific. I'd thought about the ocean almost nightly since the Endless West's show. Though, I suppose that when I say I thought about the ocean, what I really mean is, I thought about Cameron.

The memory of our kiss had swollen in my mind until I felt like I was bursting with it, because despite all the time I'd spent with Lynn since then, the subject of our midnight adventure was never broached. We talked a lot about the band, and what Josie had told her of the tour: the run-down motels, the wild parties, how the boys had decided to record a full-length album and were trying to write new material on the road. At first, I thought there must've been a reason why Lynn didn't mention our swim, and I wasn't sure how to bring up the topic on my own. But eventually I began to wonder if she had even seen the kiss—if anyone had seen. Then, the more I scrounged for validation, the more I began to consider that maybe it hadn't happened at all. The amount of alcohol I'd consumed did seem ludicrous, once I tried to quantify it. And yet the memory was too real; when I closed my eyes and let the Santa Anas surround me, I could almost hear the waves again, could feel the pressure of his fingers on my lower back, the way his thumb hooked around my ear, dripping polar water down my neck.

But that was all I had: an impression that glimmered when the cold punctured my skin.

Until my phone pinged with a text message from an unknown number.

I have a confession to make.

It was late and I must have been tracing the fringes of a dream, because I couldn't think of any reply better than, *Who's this?*

The response took a moment to come. *Cameron Cabrera.*

I sat up in bed, my heart thumping. Cameron had asked Lynn for my number. He hadn't forgotten about me.

Wanting to appear casual, as if boys kissed me and disappeared and then sent me midnight text message confessions every day, I wrote: *Oh hey. What's up?*

That night at the beach, he began, and my body turned hot. *Do you remember?*

I thought my heart might plow right through my rib cage. *Yeah.*

Something fell out of your pocket. I was going to give it back but then I read it and I couldn't. I'm sorry for stealing your poetry. And for smuggling it across state lines.

It's not poetry, I wrote back quickly, grateful that text messages revealed no tone or emotion. I would not have been able to hide my disappointment, the desire that filled me up like air. *But you're forgiven anyway.*

What is it then?

I said, *Lyrics.*

Yeah? I read it a dozen times. Each time I realize something else about the words. It's really good. Much better than what I write.

Thanks, I said.

More seconds passed. Worried that this might be the extent of the conversation, I searched for something further to add, typing and deleting various self-deprecating comments until a new message popped up.

I was wondering if you would do me a favor.

What's that?

I waited, giddy and nervous and hardly able to breathe.

Could you maybe help Alex and me with some lyrics for a new song? Most of the time we just sing a lot of gibberish. It'll sound good, but won't actually make much sense. And I want this one to have real meaning. Then, after another moment, he added: *I feel weird even asking, but I've never been great with words.*

Surprised, I stared at the screen. The brightness was almost painful. When I looked away, the afterimage of a white box punctured the darkness. *Sure,* I said. *I'd be happy to.*

We made a plan. After Christmas, I would go to their studio space and help them with the song—a simple collaboration between musicians. I could not imagine anything more exciting. Or terrifying.

I fell asleep to the sway of the wind, and woke the next morning to one final message: *Thanks, Susannah. I'm really excited about this. And seeing you. Merry Christmas, by the way.*

"Merry Christmas," I whispered to the empty room.

On the day I went to the studio, I told my mother of a study group for midterms, which would start as soon as school resumed. Then I borrowed her new (used) car and drove out to the back corner of an industrial park in Fullerton, where the Endless West practiced. It was Sunday and deserted; a few abandoned cars speckled the parking lot, but otherwise I saw no one—just building after building of concrete. Here and there a cement-sprouted tree teetered with the breeze, but it was not enough to dampen the glare. I left my sunglasses on—red "Wayfarers," courtesy of an Arco gas station—and removed my sweater as I stepped out of the car.

I think I'm here, I wrote to Cameron, *but I'm not sure where to go.* I leaned against the car and waited, arranging my hair in front of my shoulders. My skin appeared tanner in the tint from my sunglasses and I pulled them down, then up, admiring how quickly, how easily, I could change.

"Over here," a voice called from behind me. I spun around. "The numbers are actually on the ground." Cameron pointed to his feet, where I finally saw the address he had given me painted in bold, black stenciling.

I laughed. "I swear that wasn't there a second ago."

"You caught me," he said, flashing a smile. "Our studio is magic. But don't tell anyone."

He led me inside, down a short hallway that ultimately emerged in a long, narrow, windowless room—a veritable storage space. The front was equipped with a huge metal roll-up door where big trucks would have otherwise backed in for loading, but the platform had been converted into a stage. In every direction, the walls were embellished with splashes of color and a slew of thrift-store oddities ranging from weird paintings to macramé. And yet, beneath the erratic decorating, the room still felt raw: unfinished wood, exposed pipes, cement floor marbled with scuffs and ash stains, split down the center with a complex configuration of duct-taped cords. The way it existed as both rehearsal and commercial space reminded me of my father's studio—how our garage was always fighting to retain its artistic integrity despite the bulky plastic bins my mother insisted on storing there.

"So this is our space," Cameron said. "Fun fact: Fender was

started just a couple blocks that way." He nudged his head to the left, though I wasn't sure what direction that actually was. "Did you know that? Fullerton born and bred."

"I didn't," I admitted, but wondered if my father had known.

"The street's named after him now, but the original factory is long gone. I'll show you sometime, if you want."

"I'd like that," I said.

And then, for a few awkward moments, we were silent.

Cameron said, "You want the tour?"

I nodded, and he began pointing around the room. "That's the stage there, the bathroom, and the bar back there, but right now it just has a couple of PBRs and a really old bottle of Josie's Diet Coke. And up there's where we're going." I followed the direction of his hand to a second-story platform that jutted out over the makeshift bar. Orange extension cords draped from the edges, the way white twinkle lights still drooped from the roof of Vivian's house.

It looked sturdy, held up with numerous thick beams and enclosed by a railing, but still, I asked, "Is it safe?"

"Definitely," he said. "PBR for the climb?"

Beers in hand, we ascended the ladder to the balcony while Cameron explained that Luke's father owned the property, and thus gave them a good deal on rent. The location had also proved to be rather ideal; because the band practiced at night and on the weekends, they rarely encountered any other tenants and the possibility of a noise complaint was almost nonexistent.

Reaching the top, Cameron headed for a plaid couch that slumped against the back wall.

"So the tour was pretty great, huh?" I asked, sitting next to him. My body sank into the worn cushion.

He shrugged. "Not always the turnout we expected, but fun anyway. You been to Seattle before?"

I shook my head.

"Cool scene up there," he said. "Definitely some of our best gigs." Then he laughed at something. "Although the highlight was probably how after one of our sets, some girl cornered Gabe in the bathroom and gave him a hickey the size of a sand dollar."

I smiled at the story, not wanting to think about what kind of girls cornered Cameron.

"By the way, where is everyone?" I asked, suddenly aware of the empty warehouse and our proximity on the old plaid couch.

"They'll be here in a bit. I wanted to meet with you first." He picked up an acoustic guitar. "Do you remember the song we talked about before, the one you heard that day at the school?"

"Of course," I said.

"I want it to be ready for our New Year's Eve show, and the guys are easily distracted. I knew if we tried to do this while everyone was here, it wouldn't get done at all."

Before coming, I had not thought about the others, or how strange it would have been to embark on such a personal act in such a large group. I had only thought about Cameron. And I was grateful now that it would be just the two of us, because I had never collaborated with anyone but my father, and the pressure felt almost suffocating.

I took a deep breath. You are a songwriter, I reminded myself. Now is your chance to prove it.

"So I guess I should show you what I have," Cameron said,

striking a few swift chords. "I like the melody, but honestly, I'm not attached to the words at all. It's really just . . . well, you'll see." And he began to play.

He started with the song's major chords but broke up the progression with bits of embellishment—hints, I assumed, at the lead riff he was writing in his head. He sang in fragmented phrases, in melodic hums, sometimes with his eyes closed and sometimes staring directly at me but never looking at his hands, which bent and slid across the strings with unbelievable precision. The progression was beautiful but not without edge, and the first time he played it, I just listened, wanting to hear the feeling, the emotion. Halfway through, something strange began to happen.

Perhaps the empty warehouse provided an instant echoing effect, making the sound fuller and more intense, or maybe it was me, the hope pounding inside my rib cage as I watched him, this boy who saw gleaming the part of myself I'd always valued most. Whatever the reason, I felt everything at once: a coalescence of joy and sorrow, all the pain I'd internalized rising, a little more visible but at the same time a little less dense. And yet, this wasn't a reaction to what the song was right then, right in the moment Cameron played it. At least not entirely. It was a reaction to what I sensed it could be.

What the song was nudging awake inside of me.

Cameron broke into another chorus and suddenly I was back in the summer, back in the crux of those early Santa Ana winds, walking home from a shift at the Last Bean. I had just spent the night in the studio with my father. It was the last midnight we would share together, only I didn't know that then, didn't know anything except the simple fact that I had started to write what might one day become a great song. My father had said so: *You're getting better. Every piece you write is better than the last.* And as my mind waded through the dry August heat and Cameron struck a startling minor chord, hammering on the higher notes, I understood—the artistry in his discord, the harmony of the winds. My lips started moving, forming the words that had sat silent since that fateful afternoon. I could hear it clearly now— again—the drumbeat and drawl of bass, the hidden rhythm that had almost been forgotten.

I pulled my notebook from my purse. I needed to see the lyrics written on the page, immutable and unrelenting. My eyes swung from line to line. There was no mistaking it. Cameron's song was permeating the air around me, filling up my lungs. But in my head I heard "Don't Look Back."

I ripped out the page.

"This might sound totally weird," I said, holding the paper out to him, "but I started writing this song during the summer. I never managed to finish it. The music . . ." I paused, unsure of how to explain the winds, the rhythm. Coming home to find that my father had locked himself in the studio. I shook my head. "The circumstances aren't important. What matters is that when I heard you playing just now, it unlocked something that I hadn't been able to access in this song, and these lyrics—they just *fit*. We'd probably need to tweak a few things structurally, but, well. What do you think?"

Cameron glanced at the page. I could sense his uncertainty in the way he bit down on his bottom lip, how the fingers of his free hand twitched. He must have read my lyrics twice, three times.

My stomach twirled as the room swelled with silence.

"'Don't Look Back,'" he said when he was done. "That's the title?"

I nodded.

"I like it," he said.

After that, everything fell into place.

"And what if we end the chorus on the E," I said, "so it just slides right back into the verse?"

"And this line here," Cameron said. "'I won't forget who you are until you do.' Can we use that for the bridge?"

"And then at the end, after the last chorus, the tone could shift. It would stay in four-four, but what if the beat breaks down?" I slapped my hands on my thighs to show him what I meant. "*Da da da, da da, da da da.* But the vocals plunge forward, so the momentum quickly rises again, surprising you when the last chords finally ring out."

"Yeah," Cameron said. "Yeah. Fuck yeah. Let's try it from the final verse."

He started playing, and I sang:

> *Expiration dates tease me, and*
> *other possibilities tempt only pain.*
> *But I can't let go. I can't let go.*
> *I can't let go—oh . . .*

As the final line repeated, Cameron joined me with a reprise of the chorus (*Let's bury our woes and go back to the beginning*), our voices entwining until we had no breath left.

We grinned at each other.

"Again?" he asked.

"Again," I said.

We worked for an hour, maybe two. Maybe only twenty minutes. Time seemed to stop in that studio, without clocks or windows to the world outside. It was an endless midnight, so close to the one I had lost, and with it came bravado—the sense that everything felt a little more possible, a little more real. All I know for certain is that after a while, when we were giddy with progress, our fingers bumped atop the page. Our bodies inched closer. Our lips nearly touched. My eyes were closed but I knew that only a sliver of space separated us.

Then a herd of voices broke the moment and we split apart.

"Cameron," someone yelled. "You decent?"

"Fuck off," Cameron yelled back.

Downstairs, the boys had arrived. Cameron climbed down the ladder and I followed.

"Susannah was just helping me finish the new song," he announced.

"I bet she was," Alex said.

Gabriel nudged him in the arm. "Let's hear it."

Luke mounted the stage and sat behind his drum kit. He lit a cigarette.

"It's called 'Don't Look Back,'" Cameron said, smiling at me, and set his pick against the strings. He started singing.

The longer I stand here waiting,
the less I understand why . . .

I took the harmony, chiming in for emphasis. My throat stretched for the higher notes but I caught them, propelled my voice outward, louder, stronger, and as we sailed past the final chorus, I felt a chill inching down my arms. "Don't Look Back" was rough and wide-open and heartbreaking. I wished my father could've heard it.

When the song ended, the boys echoed unanimous approval. Cameron and I broke down the chord changes, the lyrics, and once everyone had it memorized, Alex decided to teach me the words to "Coastal Blues," followed by "Coming with Me." By the time night actually fell and I had to leave, I knew five of the Endless West's other songs. But no, that's not quite right; *knew* insinuates that I had learned them by proxy, by listening repeatedly, the way any other fan would have. What I did was different. I got inside the songs by layering my voice in the dips and grooves of Alex's melody, emboldened by the furtive glances Cameron cast from his side of the stage. My voice added a fresh texture, something that didn't exist yet in the band's songs. I thought nothing could possibly be better.

Then it got better.

As I was leaving, Cameron stopped me. "You should sing with us at the next gig," he said. "New Year's."

A hot current pulsed through me. "Are you serious? I mean, is that cool with everyone?"

"Hey, guys. What do you think of Susannah singing with us on New Year's?"

"Hell yeah," Gabriel said. "Your harmonies are sick. Some real Beach Boys shit."

"Okay," I said, attempting to tame the wild grin on my face. "That sounds fun."

It wasn't until after I'd merged back onto the 57 and began replaying the afternoon's events in my mind that my euphoria withered, and I was filled with something akin to dread. *Susannah was just helping,* Cameron had said. But I'd done more than that. I'd given him my lyrics, my chords. My ideas. An intimate piece of myself.

Or maybe I was overanalyzing everything. If they hadn't appreciated my contribution or acknowledged my skill, they wouldn't have taught me more of their songs. They wouldn't have wanted me to sing at their next show. There had been a consensual trade; I gave them "Don't Look Back," and they gave me a spot on their stage.

I felt a fresh rush of excitement just thinking about New Year's. No, the root of my worry had to be something else. I tapped my fingers on the steering wheel, and then it hit me: guilt. I'd spent the whole afternoon with Cameron and the rest of the boys, infiltrating the one place that I knew Lynn did not have unfiltered access. And I hadn't even told her.

It took five minutes of staring at my bedroom ceiling, typing and then retyping, before I finally sent Lynn a text. I settled on *Cameron asked me to help him with a song today.* It was simple and straight to the point; nothing hidden, nothing subverted.

How'd it go? she replied quickly.

Good. I met him at their studio and we worked on it for a while, then showed it to the rest of the band. They all seemed really happy with the result.

That's great.

I waited for more, unable to tell if her words were sincere. I'm not sure whether I had expected an assortment of exclamatory punctuation and smiley faces, or if I merely wanted something heftier, of greater consequence.

I just didn't want you to be mad that I went. Or that I didn't tell you first.

I don't care, she wrote back. *Figured something of the sort would happen anyhow.*

I thought back to how the whole thing started: Cameron had asked for my number. Of course Lynn would know, would've questioned him first. They were close. He was like a brother.

They asked me to sing backup at their next show, I added. *I guess those choir classes are paying off.*

New Year's?

Yeah. Although getting my mother's permission might be an issue.

We'll figure it out, Lynn said.

I hope so, I said, already imagining the stage and the crowd, the heat of a hundred eyes watching me.

A minute passed before Lynn replied. *I'm glad things are working out. I had no idea it would go this well when I told Cameron to text you. He can be a bit unpredictable.*

I read the message twice, not comprehending. Cameron had asked for my number. He found my napkin and saw my words and he wanted my help.

Didn't he?

My heart plummeted as I clicked back to that conversation and scrolled through all the messages he had sent, searching for some sort of validation of his interest. There was nothing. The exchange was gray and amorphous, based entirely on interpretation.

And yet—the longer I thought about it, the more I realized that the circumstances of Cameron's initial text hardly mattered. The results remained the same. All Lynn wanted to do was help. She was the reason I had met Cameron and the boys, the reason I might be onstage with the Endless West on New Year's Eve. None of this would've been possible without her. So what if she gave things a little push?

Thanks, I wrote back. *Looks like I owe you one now.*

FIFTEEN

ON A BRIGHT, hazy morning a few days before New Year's, I decided it was finally time to broach the subject of the party with my mother. I headed out to the garden bordering the stables, where I found her knee-deep in a rebellion of very tall, very resilient weeds. Her face was partially veiled, sandy hair spilling across her cheek, and for one sharp moment, I thought I glimpsed the girl from the old Spades photograph: mysterious and wispy with motion, features just barely captured beneath the spotlight of the sun. Then she turned to look up at me.

Though the gleam of her beauty remained, she was just my mother again. My mother dressed, beyond all logic, in old khakis and a safari hat. A laugh coughed from the back of my throat.

"What?" she asked.

"You look like Indiana Jones," I said.

"It's all I could find." She examined her attire with dismay before she also began laughing. "Wait. Doesn't Indiana Jones always carry a whip?" She patted her pockets, her hips. "See? No whip."

"Still. You look pretty ridiculous."

She pointed her trowel at me. "Keep that up and I'll start driving you to school like this."

I pretended to zip my lips. A smile remained on my mother's face as she stooped back down to assess the insurgence.

"How's your study group going?" she asked.

"Good," I said. "They really helped me understand *Portrait of the Artist*. I think I'll nail the midterm."

"I remember reading that book. I was probably your age. Maybe even in the same class. I thought it incredibly empowering, but at the same time, incredibly tragic."

This was such a simple statement, and yet it surprised me. I knew my mother was smart, always able to solve a problem, put food on our table, keep the electricity humming. But her literary history consisted mostly of *People* magazine and the occasional pick from Oprah's book club. I had only finished reading *Portrait* a few days prior, and I'd needed to consult CliffsNotes before I figured out how the story made me feel—let alone make sense of what actually happened.

"Such a lonely life," my mother continued.

"Yeah," I said, picking a feathery dandelion head from a weed near my feet.

She nodded, apparently pleased that we had the same reaction. "Mom?"

"Yes?"

"I was wondering if it would be okay for me to go to a party on New Year's Eve with my friend Lynn. I met her at school." Hesitating, I slid my fingers up the stem of the flower, releasing the fluffy seeds to the wind. "She's in my class with Mr. Tipton."

My mother stopped at the mention of his name, a fleeting pause that would have gone unnoticed by anyone other than me. "That seems fine. Will there be a chaperone?"

"I'm not sure," I said, and I suppose that was true enough.

"Well, if there's a chaperone, then you can go."

"Can I sleep over at her house after?"

At this request, my mother stood up again. "You haven't slept over at anyone's house since you were a little girl. And even then, it was only Cara's."

As a child, I always preferred my own bed. I didn't feel comfortable at slumber parties, all the cackling and pillow fights and boy talk, exchanging secrets and crushes like currency. I was a creature of comfort, unable to sleep with the strange creaks of an unfamiliar house, the unknown shadowy passages to the bathroom. I knew Cara's house so well that it almost felt like my own, but the others were uncharted territory, and I had no interest back then in what I did not already know.

"I'm not a kid anymore," I said. "Everything goes so late on New Year's, and it's completely out of the way for Lynn to take me back up here. I just thought it would be more convenient to stay at her house. Safer, too."

"I suppose you're right," my mother said, her tone still dubious. "But I want to talk to her mother first."

"Her mother," I repeated.

"Yes. If you're going to be spending a lot of time with this girl, I think her mother and I should at least have a conversation."

"Okay," I said. "I can do that. Let me see if she's available."

My mother nodded and squatted back in the dirt. At least she's in a good mood, I told myself. There were days when she looked wilted, when her movements were heavy and her crisp brown eyes turned muddy and red. I pulled out my phone.

My mom agreed to New Year's, but she asked to talk to your mom first. Probably wants to make sure we're being properly supervised. What should I do?

Give me two minutes, Lynn said.

I waited, watching the careful way my mother surveyed her foe.

My phone rang. "Hello?"

"Hey, Susie Q. Put your mom on."

I offered the phone to my mother. "Lynn's mom," I said.

My mother sat back on her heels and took off her gloves. "Hello?" she said. "Oh, hello, Lynn. Yes, it's very nice to meet you too. Okay, great. I'm glad we had a chance to say hi." There was a brief pause. I bit my lip, unsure of what exactly was happening. "Hello? Yes, hi. My name's Diane. I'm Susannah's mother. Yes. Well, she asked me if she could stay at your house on New Year's Eve, and I thought it best to touch base before agreeing. We only recently moved back to town and I haven't had the chance to meet any of her friends yet."

My mother listened. I could hear a voice chiming, high-pitched and jovial on the other end of the phone, but I couldn't make out the words.

"Oh good. I'm very glad to hear that. Well, that all sounds fine, then."

Across the pool, back at the house, Vivian tugged the kitchen's sliding door open. "Oh, Diane, there you are," she called.

My mother held up a finger. "Me too. I look forward to it. All right, then. Bye." She handed the phone back to me.

Immediately, I texted Lynn: *What happened?*

"Diane, you'll never guess who I ran into at the supermarket just now," Vivian said.

"You should have let me do the grocery shopping," my mother yelled back.

"I'm perfectly capable, Diane."

"At least let me go with you next time, okay?"

Just making all your dreams come true, Lynn wrote.

"Did you hear what I said?" Vivian hollered.

"Yes, I heard you. Who'd you see?"

"Roger Tipton."

A small sound broke from my mother's mouth.

"I invited him for dinner Thursday night," Vivian continued.

"Thursday's New Year's Eve, Mom," my mother replied.

"Yes, I know dear. And the poor man told me he planned on grading papers all night. It would have been cruel to not invite him. He was like family, after all."

The words ambled across the pool, floundering against the cusp of a breeze, but I was still unprepared when they struck. *Like family.* I looked to Vivian, trying to decipher her expression, but I could only make out her figure, reedy and slight, leaning on the door frame.

"Will you be joining us, Susannah?" Vivian asked.

I turned to my mother. "Can I go to the party?"

"Sure," she said. Her hand brushed my shoulder. "I'm glad you've made friends so easily here."

I threw my arms around her. "Thank you," I whispered.

Tromping out of the garden and back across the patio, I approached Vivian, who was still standing in the doorway. "I've got plans on New Year's," I told her.

Vivian examined me as though she had no idea what I was talking about. "Good for you," she said, and swerved around.

On New Year's Eve, my mother insisted on chauffeuring me to Lynn's house. The drive took twenty-five minutes—longer than I remembered, but I didn't mind. The length solidified the fears that I'd instilled in her: that was twenty-five unnecessary minutes on the road after midnight, after the parties had dispersed and the bleary-eyed drivers tried to make their way home.

"You don't have to walk me in," I said as we slowed to a halt in front of Lynn's house, but my mother turned the car off anyway.

"I know, but when will I next have the chance to meet your friend? I wanted to say a quick hello to Lorie, too."

As it turned out, Lynn's mother must have had the same idea. Before we'd even unbuckled our seat belts, a tall woman with skintight blue jeans and a nest of teased brown hair came trotting barefoot down the crumbling front path. My mother rolled down the front passenger window and leaned over me.

"Hi there," Lorie said. "You must be Diane. It's so nice to meet you."

I had not thought much about Lynn's mother, but I did not expect the figure in front of me: an effervescent woman in her mid-forties, as bold in manner as the thick swipes of blush on her cheeks.

"I'm glad to meet you too," my mother said, reaching across me to shake Lorie's hand.

"I'd invite you in, but . . ." She leaned into the window and a pungent whiff of vanilla pelted me. "I just haven't had the time to clean our little abode lately."

"I understand. I often wonder where the time goes."

In the background, Lynn headed down the path. Her hair was brighter, redder, blazing beneath the pink-smeared sky. My mother peered around Lorie. "You must be Lynn."

"Hi, Mrs. Hayes," Lynn said. "Thanks for dropping Susannah off."

"My pleasure. And please, call me Diane." My mother placed her cold hand on my arm. "You have your phone?"

I nodded and opened the door.

"Be safe tonight," she called.

"You bet," Lorie said. She continued waving until my mother's car disappeared around the corner.

We spent the next hour in Lynn's tiny bedroom, wading through the colorful heaps of clothing that collected like dust in the corners. The walls were painted a deep shade of mustard yellow, but otherwise, it felt like an enlarged version of her trunk—eclectic and chaotic, brimming with vintage clothing and accessories. And, like her trunk, she somehow knew where everything was.

"Which one?" she asked, holding two dresses in front of me—one sapphire and one olive green. I chose the green and she agreed, explaining that the color would "turn my eyes feline." I wasn't sure what that meant but her tone suggested it was a good thing.

Lynn laughed then.

"You have had sex before, haven't you?" she asked playfully as she placed other articles of clothing in front of me (lavishly torn tights, distressed jean jackets), trying to decide which layers worked best.

"Yes," I said. "Once."

And it could have been true, really, with just a slight shift in the truth. We were there, Nick and I, our hands grasping, our bodies prepared. That night felt so long ago, and I could imagine what didn't happen as easily as remembering what actually did. It was comforting to pretend that my first time was with him—to know that if it were, he would be sweet.

Lynn nodded, as though considering something. "Try this," she finally said, and handed me a camel-colored coat with a faux fur collar—the same one, I realized, she was wearing the day we met.

I donned the jacket and spun in a circle.

She smiled. "Perfect. Now all you need is some makeup."

In the other room, Lorie turned on her stereo. "Runnin' with the Devil" vibrated through the walls. She sang in a wobbly falsetto, stomping her feet out of rhythm as she clicked through the hangers in her closet. I liked her exuberance, the way she seemed young and careless, even if her clumped, sticky lashes and puttied coat of foundation suggested otherwise—but Lynn just shook her head and sat me on the edge of her bed.

"Your mom's really coming tonight?" I asked as Lynn kneeled in front of me. She slid cool, liquid liner across my eyelids. It tickled and I wiggled slightly.

"Don't move," Lynn said. The base of her palm rested on my cheek and I tried to hold still, centering myself on the scent of patchouli oil, the audible draw of her breath as she concentrated. "And not if I can help it. She had other plans, anyway, but talking to your mom inspired her. She decided she needed to be a good parent and go with us—not that she has any idea what good parenting means. She was already halfway to Saturn by the time you got here."

"You should have gone without me," I said.

"Don't be ridiculous." Lynn swiped the mascara, began lining my lips. "It's just an excuse for her to party with us. A few weeks ago, when I had people over here, she tried to go home with Davis from the Vile Bodies. She actually got in his car and I had to drag her out. Smack your lips."

I smacked my lips.

Lynn sat back, head cocked to the side as she studied me—or, not me, exactly, but the image of me, my aesthetic components. She brushed another dash of powder across my forehead and then nodded. "Done," she said. "What do you think?"

Examining myself in her full-length mirror, I was arrested by the strange sensation of seeing someone beautiful and unfamiliar gazing back. As Lynn predicted, the olive dress had emphasized my eyes, turning them a crisp, emerald green that radiated from within the smoky contours of black eyeliner, and my mouth was full and shiny—smirking, I noticed after a moment. Later, when a hundred sets of eyes rested on me, this is what they would see. I felt buoyant with anticipation of that moment.

Lynn gazed over my shoulder with a pleased look on her face. "You're going to knock them dead," she said. I grinned. A glimmer of my old self shone through, so I shut my mouth, letting only the slight upward curl of my lips remain.

Her phone dinged then. While she scanned the message Lorie whizzed by the door, heading for the bathroom. "Just give me a few more minutes, girls," she cooed.

Lynn sighed and typed something on her phone. "For one night," she said, looking up at me, "I just want to be a normal kid, breaking the rules, not worrying about the inappropriate advances of my mother."

"So what do we do?" I asked.

Lynn thought for a second. Then she tossed the suede coat at me and said, "Run."

"What?"

Lynn grabbed her purse and raced from the room. "Come on!" she yelled.

I grabbed my bag and chased after her, all the way out the front door and down to her car. We jumped inside. The ignition thundered to life and her foot pounded the gas, a cloud of dust exploding behind us as we screeched down the street. In the side-view mirror I saw Lorie teeter out of the house in tall black boots, hands signaling in the air. My eyes stayed glued to those streaks of motion until we zoomed out of view.

"She's not going to tell my mom, is she?" I asked, breath short with the thrill of escape.

Lynn cranked down the window and laughed. Even now I can still hear that sound, its mischievous peaks and falls. "No," she said. "She won't remember any of this tomorrow."

We must have all gathered in the wide backyard while the first two bands played, talking or laughing, but I don't actually remember much of what happened before our set. I know I'd had a few sips of whiskey, needing warmth in my stomach and a calm in my nerves. Otherwise, I recall only the waiting, a general feeling of anxiety that had spread to all ends of my body. My fingers, in particular, trembled.

"It's going to be weird singing without any instrument in my hands," I said to Luke once we'd mounted the stage, while the other boys tweaked treble and bass. "I'm not sure what to do with them."

I held out my hands, palms up, as if to display their awkwardness, and noticed the cuts were completely healed. They must have been healed for weeks, at least. But I hadn't noticed.

Luke leaned over and rummaged through the old suitcase where he kept the tools of his kit and other small percussion pieces. "Here," he said, and handed me a tambourine.

I laughed. The tambourine was an ornament, a prop. Something people did when they couldn't play anything else. I took it anyway.

Behind me, Alex said something to the crowd. Luke picked

up his sticks. I turned around, awed by how infinite the audience appeared, almost magical, just a thousand tiny movements in the dark.

Then Cameron started strumming the opening progression of "Coming with Me."

I lifted the tambourine.

The Endless West and I had only practiced together once, that first Sunday after Christmas, but no one would have been able to tell. I made sure of that. Cameron had given me the Endless West's most recent EP before I left the studio that day, and every night, outside in the driver's seat of my mother's car where I thought no one could hear, I practiced along with the gruff recording, bellowing against the cool evening wind until I knew every lilt and creak of Alex's tone, every dip of Cameron's harmonies. Now, Alex's voice came barreling through the speakers. Cameron's guitar wailed. I struck the tambourine against my palm, and as the first chorus approached, I stepped toward my own mic stand. I opened my mouth and began to sing.

How to explain the fluster in my chest, the unconscious motion of my hands, the way a slight upward tilt of my chin expanded my entire range? With my father I always held back, but that night, I offered the crowd everything I had. Without my guitar I could still create urgency as I shook, banged, pivoted my wrist in rapid whirls, the tiny brass cymbals that circled the tambourine's crescent clanging. And at the conclusion of each song, a barrage of cheers erupted. The whooping howls sent a rapturous chill down my back once the knowledge finally settled: those cheers were, in part, for me.

We ended the set that night with "Don't Look Back." With the full band behind it, the song became faster, heavier. I embellished Luke's drumbeat with swift rolls on the tambourine, grinning as Alex vigorously delivered my lyrics and Gabriel's bass broke out of its background riff. The shadowy crowd danced as we drove into the chorus:

This can't be as far as it goes
(this can't be, this can't be).
Let's bury our woes, and
go back to the beginning.

Our three voices trilled together, sometimes overlapping, sometimes in tandem, galloping forward as the song approached its penultimate shift. And when the final strum of guitars faded into feedback, the crowd exploded; their cheers echoed into the night, drowning out the sound of illegal fireworks crackling down the street, and I was filled with euphoria like nothing I'd ever experienced.

I had finally done it. The crowd's reaction was proof. "Don't Look Back" was my first great song.

Afterward, everyone wanted to know me.

While I was walking across the yard, a girl with black discs in her ears and tattoos spiraling down her arms leaned forward, across the conversation she was having, to say to me, "Hey, that was awesome."

"Sick beats, Stevie," quipped a boy nearby.

Near the patio, another guy stopped me to ask, "Who'd you play with before?"

I didn't even hesitate. "The Midnights," I said, "out of LA." I paused before adding, "I played guitar with them, too."

"Cool," he said, nodding vigorously as though he'd heard of us. I waited for him to inquire further about the Midnights, perhaps even hoped for it. Instead, he said, "The harmonies on that new song were killer."

I found Lynn draped in a rusty patio chair, her slender legs stretching lavishly from the hem of her dress. Next to her sat Josie, with newly dyed turquoise hair.

"There she is," Lynn announced when she saw me, raising a red cup in salute. "We can say we knew her when."

"How'd it sound?" I asked them.

"Fucking incredible," Josie said.

"Fucking incredible," Lynn repeated.

"It looked like you were possessed or something," Josie said. "In a really good way, though."

"Maybe she was," Lynn said, raising an eyebrow.

A girl I didn't recognize came up behind Josie then and the two hugged. Josie twisted around in her chair, and as they talked, I saw the girl's focus bouncing curiously off me. A thrill zipped across my skin. I wondered if this was what fame felt like.

"That last song," Lynn said to me. "That's the one you were working on with Cameron?"

I nodded.

"It's going to be a big hit."

"You think?"

"I know," she said. "Your pops would have been real proud."

"I just wish . . ." I began, but I was no longer sure what I wished, was not certain that I would want to go back and risk changing anything that had happened to me since he died. I wouldn't want to risk changing tonight. "I just wish he could have heard it," I finished.

"Maybe he did. If you believe in that kind of stuff."

I sat on the arm of her chair. "And I wish I knew what happened."

"To what?" Lynn asked.

"To my father. To his band. I have all these pieces, but they don't completely fit together. I just want to know the truth."

"The truth isn't all it's cracked up to be," Lynn said, her tone hard.

"It has to be better than not knowing."

She opened her mouth as if to argue further. Perhaps if she had let the words formulate, had tried to express the fear that sat, rotting, inside her, everything would have turned out differently. But she just took another drag of her cigarette, and after a while said, "So what're you going to do?"

"I actually found one of them," I told her. "One of my father's bandmates. He lives in Pasadena. I was planning to go see him, but then we moved here, and I got sent back to school, and for a while my mother was watching my every move. And now . . ."

"Now what?"

I shook my head. "Pasadena is so far away."

Lynn laughed. "It's really not. I mean, yeah, traffic's a bitch.

But if we go early, like on a weekend morning, it wouldn't be too bad."

"We?" I asked.

"Well who else would drive you?"

I grinned, and threw my arms around her. "I don't know how to thank you."

She said, "I'm sure you'd do the same for me."

Up onstage, the next band was setting up and I watched as the boys filtered out across the yard—Cameron, I noticed with a jolt of pride, heading straight toward me. My mind buzzed with excitement. I wasn't sure what would happen next with him or the band, but I knew this for certain: with Lynn by my side on the drive up to Pasadena, fear did not stand a chance. Maybe that's all I ever needed, a friend, some support. I was finally going to meet Kurt Vaughan.

Driven by blissful audacity, I picked up Lynn's cup (she was drinking straight that night, no chasers), and took a long sip.

For a few minutes after Cameron joined us, the conversation floated around the table, loose and untethered. Only after the next band had started playing did he come stand next to me, saying something indiscernible.

"What?" I yelled.

He placed one hand on my back and leaned in closer. "You were amazing tonight," he said into my ear. His breath was hot, sultry. My heart jumped sideways. I set my focus on the stage.

This time, when I saw Cody Winters, there was no uncertainty. His voice cut into me, that sandpaper snarl I knew so well reverberating through the yard the way it used to ring out in the hallways of my old high school. His hair had been cropped around the ears but it was still long in front, curtaining his forehead with a thick, familiar swoop. Every now and then, between the jaunty melodies jangling from his Les Paul, he'd shake his head to clear his eyes, but the hair fell right back into his lashes. I wondered what it would be like, brushing those stray hairs away.

Two songs passed before I noticed that Cameron's hand was still pressed against my back. My breath tugged at my throat, but whether it was because of Cameron or Cody, I couldn't tell.

The yard was packed as the final minutes of the year ticked down. All the quick, chattering voices created a drone that made me sleepy, but I forced myself to stay alert. I looked around, trying to find Cameron, but sometime after Cody's band (which Lynn told me was called Fire Society) finished, Cameron and Alex went inside to get more drinks. And though Alex had returned, Cameron still had not.

The temperature must have dropped because I saw a number of girls throughout the backyard shivering, but I no longer felt cold.

"My resolution," Josie was saying, "is to go on a road trip this year. A real one." Her arm hooked like a boomerang around Alex's neck. "Just get in the car and drive."

"You always just end up wanting to go to Salvation Mountain," Alex said, his eyes glassy. "And then you want to come home. You can't handle being in a car for more than two hours."

"That's why they call it a *resolution*, Alex, and not a fucking *unassailable fact.*"

"Resolutions are bullshit," Lynn said to me, her voice barely audible over Josie and Alex's argument. "You always think that your life's going to be different this time, but then you make the same mistakes." She fished a pack of Camels from her purse. "It's the human condition, to be stuck in cycles."

"Yeah," I said, though I didn't fully agree. I could hardly even remember the girl I was last New Year's Eve.

I scanned the yard again for Cameron but did not see him. Cody, too, was gone. Next to me, Lynn started typing something into her phone and all of a sudden I was consumed by a fierce, brimming sadness that I didn't understand. Already, this had been one of the best nights of my life. I'd performed on a real stage, and "Don't Look Back" was a wild success—far beyond what I'd imagined it could become last summer in my father's studio. So why did I feel this ache of loneliness in my gut? I swigged from a cup of whiskey. My thoughts zipped to Nick.

Just that morning he'd messaged me about my plans for New Year's, to see whether I'd be coming into town. So I told him briefly about Lynn and the boys, my songwriting and impending stage debut with the Endless West. Being one of the few people who had witnessed the evolution of my music, he was thrilled for me. *But don't forget about the little people back home*, he added at the end of our conversation.

Now, glancing at my phone, I saw that I had received another message from him, over an hour earlier. *Good luck tonight! I know you'll be great.* Then, a few minutes later: *Happy New Year, Hayes. Wish you were here.*

I smiled, felt the sadness abating, and wrote, *Another year has disappeared between us / but I won't accept regret / so let's close our eyes and count backward / relive the memories that haven't happened yet.*

Happy New Year, Nick.

I put my phone away then, glancing up just in time to see a sliding glass door open near a gloomy back corner of the house. From the darkness, Cody Winters emerged. He was alone, removing a cigarette from the top buttoned pocket of his jean jacket. A bolt of energy tore through me. I stood up, not knowing what to do, but knowing I had to do something.

"Can I bum one of these?" I asked Lynn, picking up her cigarettes.

"Go for it," she said, swooping her thumbs over her phone's keyboard, and I was already heading across the yard before I'd even figured out what to say.

When I reached him, his face was cupped in his hands, a tiny firelight flickering across his jaw.

"Hey," I said. Lynn's cigarettes dangled from my shaking fingers.

"Hey," he mumbled, glancing briefly up. "Nice set. That last song was pretty epic."

The stampede beneath my rib cage quickened, and I thought for an instant that I might spontaneously combust. "Thanks," I said. I reached my hand into my purse, feeling around for the book of matches, but just as I reached them, I let them go.

"Can I borrow your light?" I asked.

He struck the flint twice before it sparked again. I had only ever been that close to him once, at the Last Bean, and then I was nothing more than a barista pouring his coffee, pocketing his change. Now, the small glow of his lighter warmed my face.

When the smoke hit my throat, I coughed. I was sure he would laugh at me, or worse, that he would leave. But he didn't even seem to notice.

"You look familiar," he said. "We met before?"

I thought about all the lunch hours I'd spent trailing his voice and the airy pluck of his acoustic guitar, the way my name slid from his tongue that day at the Last Bean. What satisfaction I would have had if he'd recognized me. But too much had changed since then; I was no longer the girl hiding in hallways.

"No," I said. "I don't think so."

He nodded, unaffected. "I'm Cody."

"Susannah."

For a few minutes we just stood there, leaning against the sliding glass door and looking out into the yard. Though the stars had seemed electric an hour ago, they were hazy now, as if a thin layer of gauze had been pulled over the sky. Not even Orion was visible. From the corner of my eye, I tried to watch Cody, but I couldn't see anything more than the wispy tendrils of his smoke. Still, I had that feeling—that prickling of the skin when you know someone is watching you. I tapped my cigarette the way I'd seen Lynn do it, an index finger lightly on top. People started counting: "Ten! Nine! Eight!"

That's when I noticed Cameron, perched on the edge of the stage, chanting the diminishing numbers with a group of people (mostly girls) I didn't know. And that was the problem—I didn't know anyone yet, did not know their histories or intentions. I didn't know if those girls had boyfriends or had interest in

Cameron, didn't know if Cameron, perhaps, had interest in one of them. In that moment, all I knew was what I saw in front of me: Cameron, with his breezy, crooked smile and eyes that glistened beneath the backyard twinkle lights, was not looking for me, and Cody Winters was the only person at that party whose history converged with mine.

"Seven! Six! Five!"

"I'm not big on this shit," Cody said.

"Me either."

Our eyes met there in the shadowy corner. When he retreated back inside the dark room, I followed.

It was midnight and the sounds of the party penetrated the wafer-thin walls. People were shouting "Happy New Year!" and banging keys against beer bottles, or clinking together cans. Down the street confetti poppers exploded. Inside, Cody and I were silent.

The assured way that he leaned into me then was terrifying. It was not fierce and sudden, the way Cameron and I had grasped each other in the ocean, and it wasn't comforting but clumsy like the night I spent in Cara's guest room with Nick. Cody knew exactly what to do. He knew where my mouth was, where my hands would be waiting, how all the buttons and clasps flicked apart. His movements were quick and precise. And though I could not see much more than a shape in front of me, darker and fuller than the surrounding shadows of the room, every other aspect of him had heightened. I smelled the sweat that still dampened his shirt from the show, the tobacco coating his fingers. His hands, as they gripped my face, were rough from the friction of sinking guitar strings and beating on drums. I wondered if he could feel the weight of my breath before covering my mouth with his own.

As he laid me on the bed, I realized I had no idea whose room we were in. Someone could have walked in at any moment. But Cody tasted like barley, like the smoldering cinders of a forest fire. His skin burned against my fingers. I opened my hands wide, splaying them across his back, and pulled him toward me.

When it was over, we peeled apart and dressed and he left the room first. It was a small, unconscious act, but I was glad. The party still raged outside, louder and more reckless now that midnight had passed, and I sat on the edge of the bed, my dress half zipped, willing the room to stand still. I wasn't sure what happened next, what I was supposed to do. My mouth was dry. His scent lingered on my skin. I kept waiting to feel different somehow, but I didn't. The only change was the taste in my mouth—the remains of his tiny fires igniting on my tongue.

This is the truth: After we were done I wanted nothing more from him. I had no desire to date him, nor did I harbor any misconceptions of love. I didn't even know him. But for so long I had wanted him, had wanted him to want me, and for that brief moment, he was mine. It was that simple. All I had to do was take control.

In the dark, I couldn't find my tights, so I felt around until I located a light. Illuminated, the room seemed sad. It was mostly empty, the walls white. Locating my tights, I pulled the fabric up my legs and only then did I notice the bruises, yellows and blues blossoming on the outside of my right thigh. I couldn't even feel them yet—there was too much alcohol in my system for that—but

237

the composition was mesmerizing. My left palm had the same bud of color, too, and as I examined the patterns climbing toward my hip, expanding from thumb to pinkie, I knew that I would need to harden myself, build up new callouses; I was far too soft and pervious if a tambourine was enough to break the blood vessels beneath my skin.

SIXTEEN

SCHOOL RESUMED. AMID the flurry of the new quarter, Lynn and I made a plan to go to Kurt's on the first Sunday morning we were both free. Until then, though, I was stuck waiting, wondering what it would be like to drive again on those streets. If it would feel sort of like going back in time.

Even though we'd been living with Vivian for months now, my mother still hadn't taken us to retrieve our stuff from the old house. I thought about it frequently, wavering between a ravenous urge to submerse myself in all my father's possessions and an urgent need to not touch a thing. The knowledge that he was preserved back in our studio, in our home, gave me comfort. His scent would still be thick between the walls of shipping foam.

His fingerprints would still perforate the dust that rimmed the record player. His T-shirts, each one adorned with its own unique constellation of holes, would still be hanging in the closet. And in these small ways, my father continued existing.

At least I thought so, until the day I came home from school to find the front entryway cluttered with boxes.

"What's all this?" I asked my mother, navigating a path through the mess. "Are we going somewhere?"

"The opposite, actually. We're finally moving in."

"You mean this is our stuff?" I crouched down to decipher one of the labels. It might have said "Master" something, but the penmanship was almost illegible. It was not my mother's hand. "When did you have time to go?"

Vivian's voice emerged then from behind a pile of boxes. "You didn't think we were going to move it ourselves, did you?" She was so slight that I hadn't even noticed her in the sea of brown cardboard. "That's what men are for, dear—to lift things."

"I put your stuff in your room," my mother said, releasing me with a nod of her head.

I hurried down the hall. Turning into my bedroom, I saw only five meager boxes slumped below the window. Even before I tore them open, furiously searching for what I already knew was absent, the dread that had sprouted in my stomach began to expand. I flung the contents behind me.

Out of all five boxes, I found only two things that mattered. The first was a dollar bill that had been folded into the shape of a heart. Nick had given it to me when we were in middle school, and I'd kept it pinned to the center of my bulletin board ever since.

I breathed in the worn, softened chemical smell. Then I snapped a picture and sent it to Nick with a caption that read, *We're all struggling for a piece of immortality / but sometimes just a memory is enough.*

The second item had been wedged halfway beneath one of the box's bottom flaps, and I almost missed it: a guitar pick. It was not a pick of any special meaning—just a medium weight tortoiseshell Dunlop—but as I held it up between my fingers, the sunlight caught the mottled brown plastic and the swirls of color inside sparkled. Minutes passed while I stared, sitting on the floor among the ruins of a past life. Finally, when my eyes began stinging, I got up.

"Where's the rest of it?" I called down the hallway.

"The rest of—?" my mother started to ask. "Oh, well we donated all the furniture. Nothing was worth much, old as it was. And because most of our dishes were chipped—"

"Dad's stuff," I interrupted. "His guitars and his records. All the recording equipment. Where is it?"

"Susannah," she said gently, "you couldn't have thought that we'd bring everything. There was too much."

"Where is it?" I said again, louder, aware of the tears that swelled in the corners of my eyes, not bothering to wipe them away.

"In storage," my mother said.

The air around me seemed to sigh with relief. "I want to go get it."

"Later," my mother said. "After we sort through all of this and see—"

"I'll go by myself. Just tell me where it is."

The tears started falling then, hot and incessant, and even as I acknowledged that it would only be a matter of time before I was reunited with what remained, a part of me must have understood then that something monumental and intangible had been lost.

Muffled by the discord between sorrow and rage, my voice was a whisper when I said, "I can't believe you didn't even let me say good-bye. You left me nothing."

"Now just wait a minute, young lady," Vivian began, but my mother held up one hand, stopping her. How sad she looked right then—how tired. Her eyelids drooped with a weight I couldn't fathom.

"Go into the living room," my mother said evenly.

"Why?" I said, voice burning. "Because you don't want me to see how you finally got exactly what you wanted?" The words erupted from some dark place inside of me and I couldn't cage them. I just wanted her to look at me, to scream—anything that would make me stop—but her focus remained on the floor. "This is a new low, even for you. Banishing me to another room just so you don't have to be held accountable. That's what you're doing, isn't it?"

My mother winced. It was a tiny, almost imperceptible twitch in her eye, at the farthest crease of her lips, but I felt it more forcibly than a hundred slaps.

"Isn't it?" I repeated. This time, my voice broke.

"Just go," she said, and turned back to the boxes.

So I went to the living room, my vision blurred behind tears, terrified by how well I already knew those hallways and rooms—scared, most of all, by the way Vivian's house already felt like home.

When I turned the corner, I stopped. My father's Martin had been laid carefully on the sofa.

I picked it up, turning it over in my hands. Not long before, that guitar had swallowed me, but it didn't seem so big now. It was glistening, unscratched. A distorted reflection gloomed up from the varnish and I stared at the smeared image, my tears slick across the glossy body.

"She's not as cruel as you think," I heard Vivian say behind me. But after a moment, when I didn't reply, she walked away.

My mother and I had argued before, many times, but our fight that afternoon was different. In the past, our disagreements were always secondary to the dominating blur of my father's problems, easily forgotten when more pressing matters were at hand. Now, I feared even running into her in the kitchen, and the fifteen-minute drives to school were excruciating. I knew that I had made horrible accusations; my behavior sickened me, and I was guilt-ridden and sorry, but I didn't know how to say this to my mother. So instead, I hid from her, tried not to engage in any conversation, and moved forward in the only way I knew how: through distraction.

Once again, I set my sights on finding Kurt Vaughan.

It was a bright morning during the peak of an eighty-eight-degree winter heat wave when Lynn and I made the trek to his Pasadena home. The drive had felt eternal, but it was easy, like she'd said. Light traffic, no accidents. When we arrived, we parked on the opposite side of the street. Though his muddy truck sat in the driveway, the shutters were angled down and the place looked dark. The only motion was the gentle swaying of the American flag over the lawn.

"You do plan on going in, right?" Lynn asked after a while. "At least ringing the doorbell? If he's not home, then . . ." She shrugged, insinuating that we would turn around and go back to Orange.

But I couldn't give up. Not this time. I unbuckled my seat belt. "Let's do this."

At the front door, I pushed the button. A chime echoed inside the shut-up house. We waited. Nothing.

"Come on," I mumbled, and pushed the little white button again. And again. The bell rang in harsh, frantic snippets.

"Susie Q," Lynn said, but her voice was distant. "Susannah, stop."

She put her hand on mine. The touch of her skin stunned me.

"Maybe some things just aren't meant to be known. We tried. We really did." She squinted out at the street, then focused her gray eyes back on me. "Maybe the only thing left to do is to stop at that diner we saw by the freeway and get some coffee, huh?"

A laugh climbed in my chest but it emerged as a cough.

Lynn twisted her arm through mine and smiled. We were halfway down the driveway when the door opened behind us.

"Can I help you girls?" a man said, peeking out from the darkness.

He had a kind voice, but underneath that gentle tone I detected a trace of fear—not for himself, but for us. Or, more specifically, for me: the girl who had rang his doorbell in a panic two dozen times.

"We're fine," Lynn said when I didn't immediately respond. She gripped my arm tighter in assurance.

"Are—are you Kurt Vaughan?" I asked.

"Yes," the man said, hesitant.

All morning I had thought about this moment, what to say. I'd worried that he would be brusque, displaying immediate disinterest as if we were selling magazine subscriptions, and close the door before I'd even mentioned my father's name. But Kurt Vaughan was waiting for me to speak. I could see past his feet into the front entryway, where a basketball and dirty sneakers rested.

"I think," I began, "you knew my father. James Hayes."

Doubt clouded Kurt's face for a moment before the name struck, and then his expression alighted. Surprise registered first, tinged perhaps with a shade of joy. Solemnity quickly followed.

"Yes," he said, shaking his head, looking at the ground. "Yes. Please, come in."

The white, glaring winter sun cut harsh diagonals through the patio overhang as Lynn and I waited on the back porch while Kurt poured us all glasses of iced tea. Most of his yard was paved in patio stones, but around the perimeter trees and ivies thrived, outshining the teal of the small swimming pool. A bag of fertilizer waited, still open, near the back fence, muddy gloves tossed aside.

"I was very sad to learn what happened," Kurt said as he distributed our teas.

"Thank you," I said. "How did you hear?"

"It didn't happen too far from here. The papers ran the story."

I nodded, again questioning if my father had known Kurt's whereabouts—if he'd ever thought about visiting or trying to reconcile what had been broken between them. And I wondered, with sudden hope, if that's where he was headed on the night that he died. It didn't make much sense in the grander scheme of that evening, of the summer, but I preferred this new possibility to my only other options: one, that he was leaving us, and two, that he was leaving the world.

"Had you talked to him recently?" I asked.

Kurt shook his head. "Not in many, many years, I'm sorry to say."

A dull ache gripped my stomach, and I sipped my iced tea. It was bitter, unsweetened.

"How'd you and my father first meet?" I asked next. I knew my father's story, of course, but it seemed important to start this way, with a safe memory, to see the shades that separated his version of events from Kurt's.

"Well, let's see," Kurt began, leaning back in his chair. "I'd been working in this used record shop in West Hollywood."

"Half-Life," I said.

Kurt smiled. "That's right. Half-Life Records. It was this tiny hole in the wall, a blink-and-you'll-miss-it kind of place that survived entirely on our regulars. Collectors, mostly—guys who'd come in every day looking for first pressings of some obscure jazz ensemble, or rare alternate B-sides. That must sound funny to you, but we didn't have the internet back then. Most of those albums only had so many pressings, and then they were gone."

"I don't think it's funny," I said. "I grew up with my father's records. They're some of my most valued possessions. And Lynn has a pretty great collection too."

She nodded. "Mostly secondhand stuff, but a lot of it."

"I guess I should have expected that," Kurt said through a laugh. "But the whole experience was so different back then. We lived for that hunt. Most weekends, at the crack of dawn, my boss and I would drive around garage sales, estate sales, buying up entire collections for next to nothing. Sometimes, we'd even find albums that were still wrapped in plastic. Can you imagine? Having an entire record collection sitting in your garage, completely untouched?"

Kurt grew more and more animated as he spoke, and even though his memories of Half-Life Records unfurled a different set of details than those already etched in my brain, the dreamy way he spoke of the shop—of that time—made him sound just like my father.

"I'm sorry," Kurt said, scratching his neck. "I'm way off track. It's been a long time since I've talked about any of this."

"I was actually just remembering all the stories my father told me about Half-Life," I said. "You wrote your first song there."

Kurt smiled, the same sweeping smile that carried from one photograph to the next, making his eyes small and pulling creases around his cheeks. Visually, he looked older than my father had, and yet he didn't seem to carry any of the invisible weight that sagged beneath my father's eyes.

"We sure did," he said. "We had some great times there, your father and I."

He looked past us, watching something out in the yard, and I yearned to know what his life was like now, what his son's name was, and how many years he'd been married to his wife. Did she know him back then, have any idea what the Vital Spades could have become? The questions rubbed and shifted inside me, but I knew I had to be careful. Kurt wanted to talk; I merely had to wait until he was ready.

"I was twenty-one when your father first came into the shop," Kurt said a minute later, his smile fading to a rueful glow. "God, that seems like so long ago. But I guess that's normal. You get older, you move on, and the past fades into white noise."

"My father wasn't normal," I said, fingering a bead of sweat on my glass.

"Don't I know it. From the second we first spoke, I could tell that together, Jimmy and I had the potential to do something huge."

"Jimmy?" I repeated.

"That's what everyone called him back then. Except your mom. She always preferred James."

"Did you know her well?" I asked.

"Sure," he said. "We all did."

I considered this, anchoring my gaze out in the garden. Though I'd been prepared to ask dozens of questions about my father and the Spades, I suddenly found my interest shifting to what Kurt knew about my mother.

But I hadn't planned for that. I didn't know what to ask, or where to start.

"Was she Yoko?"

Lynn's voice scrambled the careful trail of my thoughts. I shot her an irate glance.

"Well, you weren't going to ask," she said flatly.

Opposite us, Kurt frowned. "If you're wondering whether she broke up the band, then the answer is no. Diane was probably the only reason the Vital Spades stayed together as long as they did."

I shook my head. "But that doesn't make sense. I always thought . . ." I stopped, swallowing the second half of the sentence.

"Thought what?" he said. "That she was the bad guy? Far from it. Her leaving was the only reason Jimmy got clean. Without her, he may not have even lasted long enough to see the band break up." Abruptly, he paused, one hand rising slightly above the table. I thought maybe he wanted to cover his mouth, to will the words back in, but it just perched there above his chest.

"I'm sorry. I've said too much."

"Please," I urged, my voice strained. "Tell me what happened."

His eyes darted between Lynn and me, uncomfortable under the weight of what he could not take back.

I said, "I need to know."

Kurt sighed. "When your mother got pregnant," he said, "she left him. Jimmy was volatile. The Spades were breaking apart. Everyone knew it, but Jimmy pushed on, doing whatever it took to keep going. Your mother didn't want either of you to be a part of it. We weren't sure if he'd still be standing, when everything was said and done. Of course we tried to help but he wouldn't listen. Not even to her, in the beginning."

When he turned back to me his expression shifted, darkening like the world when a cloud floats over the sun. "I'm sorry. No kid should ever have to know those things about a parent. But you have to believe me when I tell you that it was his choice. Jimmy chose, of his own free will, to leave the band and go after you. And thank God he did. Thank God for all of us."

I suppose it should have made me feel better, Kurt's insistence that my father chose my mother and me over the Spades—that maybe he really did love us more than the thing I always thought he loved most. The truth was, it made me feel worse. If the band's dissolution was inevitable, then my father merely made the survivalist's decision. No one would choose to stay in a burning building.

And that's when I remembered the matchbook. "Have you ever seen this before?" I asked Kurt, fishing the matches out of my purse.

"Well I'll be damned," he said. He flipped the book over in his hands, his face lightening again. "Yeah, I've seen this. Jimmy always kept it in his pocket, would fiddle with it if he was nervous before a show." Kurt thumbed the worn cover. "I can't believe this thing hasn't disintegrated."

"Do you know what it means? Did he ever talk about the Sea Witch, or about Iowa?"

Kurt shook his head. "All I know is he kept it on him. We all had our superstitions."

"Yours was argyle socks," I said.

"That's right," Kurt said, surprised.

"And not washing your hands."

He couldn't help laughing at that. "He really did tell you everything, didn't he?"

I forced a smile, but something was pressing at the edges of my chest, rolling in like a fog.

"Are you still in contact with the other Spades?" I asked. "Or do you know how I might find them?"

"Dan and I stayed in touch for a long time after the Vital Spades broke up," Kurt said, "but he moved to Ohio about seven, eight years back. His father-in-law was ill. We finally lost contact after that."

"And Jason?" I pressed. "Do you know where he is?"

"Jason," he started, and then paused.

"Please," I said. "I need all the pieces. I don't want to let my father disappear."

Kurt took a deep breath. "Hang on a moment," he said. Then he stood, retreated into the core of the house. Lynn and I waited on the patio. For a while we were silent.

"Are you sure you'd want to do this again?" she asked.

"I don't know," I admitted. "I just need to have the choice."

Lynn frowned, but didn't argue. "Where do you think the rest of Kurt's family is?"

"Church?" I suggested, and suddenly my mind flung to Cara, what she'd said the last time I saw her: *He's in a better place now.*

Maybe I should just let him rest, I thought. Stop digging up the past. But the truth was that I hadn't been doing any of this for him. I'd been doing it for me.

The back door opened.

"Last I knew, Jason was living here," Kurt said. "Not sure if he still is, but it's all I've got."

He handed a scrap of paper to me. I rubbed my thumb over the address. "Thank you."

Kurt nodded, a barb of sadness in his voice as he said, "I hope you find what you're looking for."

As we waited for to-go coffees at the diner, I worried the edges of the paper into tatters, folding and unfolding until the creases began to tear. The physicality of the thing no longer mattered, anyway; I'd already memorized the address, and had looked it up on my phone. It led to the outskirts of Venice Beach, far west of Pasadena. The opposite direction from Orange.

"What now?" Lynn asked. "Do we try to find Jason?"

It was after noon, the heat barreling down. Traffic to the beach would be terrible by now—and on top of that, my mind was spinning. The conversation with Kurt had left me feeling unmoored, obscured by a thick veil of conflicting thoughts. I needed time to process everything.

"Not today," I said.

Armed with our coffees, we merged back onto the freeway. We'd only been on the road for ten minutes when I saw a sign for York Boulevard, a street that cut down across the bottom of Eagle Rock, below Occidental College. "Exit here," I said to Lynn.

"What?"

"Now, get over now!"

Without signaling, Lynn swerved across two lanes of traffic toward the exit. Cars honked and braked behind us but we made the off-ramp.

"Jesus," Lynn said, clutching her coffee. She slowed as we curved down toward the stoplight. "What's the deal?"

"We need to make a detour," I told her.

"Can you please be more cryptic?"

"My house," I said, though the thought had already started to feel foreign. "We need to stop at my house."

I directed Lynn in a circle, down York to Eagle Rock and then up around Colorado, passing the strip mall that lodged the Last Bean. I wondered if Lou was working. I wondered if my handwriting was still displayed on the chalkboard menus hanging behind the register. From the street, I couldn't tell.

I continued giving arbitrary directions, and I wasn't even sure where I was leading her until we approached the street that led to Nick's and Cara's houses.

A heaviness rooted in my stomach as the intersection grew near, and I realized that I hadn't talked to Cara since that day she showed up at my house with a carefully assembled binder of missed homework assignments, months ago. At the time, I'd told myself we were already drifting apart. And yet it occurred to me now that maybe I was the only one drifting. The heaviness bloomed into guilt. So much had changed; I wouldn't have even known what to say if I saw her. But Nick . . .

There were a thousand things I wanted to say to Nick.

Had I been alone, I would have called him, or maybe just shown up at his door. I was certain the sight of him would ease everything contending inside me—but I wasn't alone. And more than anything else, I wanted to keep Nick as he was: constant, reliable, separate from Lynn and my new life. Something good that was only mine.

So we kept driving.

A few minutes later we coasted up Catalina, my old street. Even from half a block away it was obvious that no one currently lived in the house. Still, the driveway felt too personal, too familiar. I told Lynn to park at the curb.

Somehow the place looked exactly the same, and yet completely different. The blinds were drawn, making it the only house on the block that was not infiltrated by sunlight, and the grass, while never particularly verdant, had turned haystack brown. I looked at the garage. The windows were still covered with cardboard.

Turning toward the house, I found our spare key right where we'd left it: under a loose brick lining the flower bed where my mother and I had planted poppies and sweet alyssum in the days following my father's death. Now, all those flowers were dead too.

"I'm going to stay out here and have a cigarette," Lynn said.

I nodded, and went in alone.

Inside, I floated from my bedroom to the bathroom, through my parents' room and back to the kitchen. I'm not sure what I'd expected to find, really, but in the end, I didn't wander those rooms for long; a few minutes were enough to preserve the empty spaces in my mind. It was no longer home. It was just a structure, some walls and a roof. Everything that mattered was already gone.

Outside, Lynn leaned against the avocado tree, typing into her phone. The hint of a smile played on her lips.

"I'll be done in a minute," I said, locking the front door and returning the key to its space beneath the loose brick.

"Take your time." She tapped a flutter of ash to the ground. The flakes camouflaged with the lawn.

"Can I bum one?" I asked.

Lynn handed me her pack. "You're not getting addicted, are

you? I'd hate to think that it was my fault."

I slid out a cigarette. Lynn handed me her lighter, but I shook my head. "I'm not addicted. I just need to feel something else." From my pocket, I withdrew my father's book of matches and struck one. When I inhaled, it tasted like Cameron, like Cody, like the smoke of a hundred tiny fires dancing on my tongue.

"Sounds like what you really need is a drink. And this time I don't mean coffee."

"Isn't it still early?" I asked.

"For some people," Lynn said, "it's just really, really late."

I smiled, allowing the cigarette to settle me. "Who were you talking to?"

"Just a friend," she said.

Can you be more cryptic? I thought, but did not have the energy to push. We smoked, thoughts drawn in opposing directions, our papers burning down toward the filter. There was only one thing left for me to do.

I headed for the studio.

Thank God the door was unlocked. There was no spare key, not since my father's truck was salvaged for scraps with his key chain somewhere inside. I flipped the light switch and watched as the overhead bulb flickered with disuse before the room brightened. It was empty, of course, but unlike the house, which my mother had cleaned and treated before leaving, the garage made apparent all that was gone. Patches of tape residue pockmarked the walls, and trails of staples swirled across the ceiling—all the places that had once held up shipping foam, blankets, our makeshift soundproofing. The spots on the floor that had been hidden beneath amps and storage bins were lighter, free from all the dirt that had painted the rest of the cement over the years. Even his scent still clung, faintly, to the shadows. It wouldn't last much longer, I knew, not with the door open and the smoke from my cigarette. But at least the dissipation was on my terms now.

I closed my eyes and I could see him there: the gentle curve of his back as he leaned over his Telecaster, his eyes full of possibility. I could still hear the buzz of the amps like an unspoken promise between us.

"I'll never know what was going through your head," I said out loud. My stomach knotted, though I was talking only to air. "I'll never know all your secrets, or if you regretted the choices you made, but maybe that's for the best. Because I have to believe you didn't do it on purpose. You understand that, don't you?"

I opened my eyes once again to the desolate room, and for the first time in a long time I thought about Lance and Travis. I wondered if my father had revealed different stories to them. I thought again about his final tape, now lost forever, and whether they had heard it. Even just the possibility made anger simmer inside me, so I beat it down. What did that matter now, anyway? I was never going to see them again. I was never going to see any of this again, and I did not come here for a bitter good-bye.

"I wish you could've heard me," I said to the emptiness. I wished he could have seen me onstage, listened to the final version of "Don't Look Back," wished he'd have stuck around long enough for me to show him my cover of "Love Honey." I wished I hadn't spent so long being afraid.

A flurry of white ash fell from the end of my cigarette and, smearing the powder beneath my shoe, I created a sooty arc on the cement floor. The mark was impermanent, easily erased by a wave of the hose, but it would still serve as a reminder to whoever ultimately bought the house that someone else had been here first. I continued inhaling, flicking the cigarette's tip until I had enough ash to draw a full circle around me. For a while, I stood in the center of it, wondering if the new residents would think about us, who we were, what we were like. Probably not. We had really shared something special here, my father and I. But no one else would ever know about it.

SEVENTEEN

IN THE WAKE of New Year's and my encounter with Kurt Vaughan, I began playing regularly with the Endless West. Practice happened a few afternoons a week, and gigs were scheduled on most weekends, all around Orange County and Long Beach. With school back in full effect, I found it easy enough to account for my busy schedule by developing a plausible rotation of academic alibis: small reading groups for advanced English, larger review parties for pre-calc and history. I even made flashcards for physics, dutifully filling the sides with key vocabulary and equations so that I could review with my imaginary lab partner. Incidentally, I began doing much better in physics.

Neither my mother nor Vivian doubted me; as long as I did

well in school and obeyed their rules, I was treated (more or less) like a responsible adult—allowed to borrow the car, given a tolerable curfew—and the more I asked to sleep over at Lynn's house, the less resistant my mother seemed to the idea. I thought perhaps she wanted to give me my space. Every time she agreed, I made sure to thank her. The ice between us slowly began to thaw.

And as the sharp hint of winter seeped back into spring, Cameron and I continued skirting the razor-edged line that encompassed our relationship, suspended somewhere between friendship and more. After a few awkward practices, I thought I'd finally figured out what was happening: the band was a sacred space, and our professionalism could not be tainted. Occasionally, I caught the boys regarding Cameron and me, their expressions slightly concerned as though we might all of a sudden throw down our instruments and start making out. But nothing happened between us in public—only the brush of a hand, the graze of a shoulder. What transpired with Cody hadn't changed the way my stomach bottomed when I saw Cameron, and I told no one about what happened on New Year's Eve—not even Lynn. Cara was the only person who would have understood.

When Cameron and I were alone, though, the entire infrastructure of our pretending crumbled. Every time I wondered, with a torrent of anticipation, if he would kiss me. And every time, when he did, his smile rising from the left side of his mouth like a crescent moon, I knew that all those other days when we kept ourselves apart were meaningless. It didn't even bother me that we never went any further than that.

Of course, I wanted to define what was between us, had

decided dozens of times that I would ask. And once, I almost did. But as the words formulated, I sensed that needing to present the question meant I would not like the answer. So instead I asked about his family.

"There's not much to say," Cameron said. We were lying on the plaid sofa, the one on which we'd finished "Don't Look Back." That had become our place. "My dad's an engineer. My mom works at an elementary school. And I've got two older siblings, a sister and a brother. She's finishing up at UCI and my brother lives down in San Diego."

"So who gave you the music?" I asked.

"What do you mean?"

"Who inspired you to start playing?"

Cameron rotated onto his back. Facing the ceiling, he thought for a minute. I watched his eyelashes twitch with the memories. "I don't know. I grew up listening to my brother's CDs. At the Drive-In, the Pixies, the Strokes—that kind of thing. And my dad used to blast, like, Cream and Santana when he'd work in the garage on the weekends. But no one in my family plays anything."

"So you just decided one day to start playing guitar?"

"I asked for a drum set first, but my mom wasn't too keen on that idea. Too much noise. Guitar seemed like the next best option."

For some reason this nonchalance—the simplicity of his skill—impressed me more than anything else.

"Your dad plays, right?" he asked.

I sat up on my elbow. "How'd you know that?"

"You told me."

"No I didn't."

"Well you may as well have." He pulled me on top of him, twisted my hair behind my ear. "That day in Lynn's kitchen, when you told me not to get in the way of a great song. You said your dad told you that."

"How do you even remember that? I was spouting nonsense."

"Here's the most profound thing my dad ever told me about music," Cameron said. "When I was just starting out, unable to even hold down a barre chord, he said, 'You should really get a stand for that thing. Don't want it to fall over and break.'"

I laughed. "Sometimes the most sage advice is simple."

"And some of us are luckier than others." When he bent up to kiss me I could feel his stomach muscles tightening. He said, "I'd like to meet him sometime. Your dad."

I traced my fingertips across Cameron's cheek, down his soft lips, and considered lying, saying that my father would love to meet him, making up excuses every time the date drew near.

"He died a few months ago," I said.

"Shit," Cameron said, "I'm sorry," and he held me against his chest. I closed my eyes as his hands waded through my hair, down the curve of my neck.

"If you could play a show anywhere in the world," I said, "where would it be?"

Cameron took a while to answer. "The Filmore East. Or West. I'd take either, as long as it was in 1970."

"Time travel, huh? That's a tall order."

He laughed. I felt it rumble through his rib cage. "What about you?"

"The Troubadour," I replied instantly.

He said, "I'll see what I can do."

"Really?" I looked up at him.

"Sure. I actually know someone whose band is playing there in a few months. I'll talk to him, see if we can tag along as an opener."

I grinned. He kissed me again.

Outside, the world kept turning, progressing further away from the place where my father once lived. But with Cameron, inside the Endless West's studio, the world felt still, like my life was finally angled in the right direction again. Like nothing could ever go wrong.

Then one Friday I came home to find Roger Tipton reclining on our living room sofa.

"Susannah," Vivian said when she saw me. "Where have you been?"

I'd just returned from the studio where the boys and I planned on practicing our set for an upcoming gig at the Prospector, but Lynn and Josie were there too, and pretty soon we were all just drinking or smoking, the halfhearted refrains of "we should probably start playing now" getting quieter and less insistent until they ceased altogether. Though I planned on rushing off to shower before encountering anyone, afraid of the scents that might cling to me, the sight of Roger in our house left me frozen.

"Study group," I said, but in my head I thought, *Shit. Busted.* "What's going on?"

"We have a guest over," Vivian said. "Don't be rude. Say hello."

My heart beat jagged melodies against my chest. "Hi, Mr. Tipton."

"Hello, Susannah," Roger said through an uncertain smile. "Long time, no see, huh?"

I stared at him. Silence congealed between us until my mother entered the room through the side hall, holding a tray of wineglasses. "I have red for Roger, and white for Mom," she said, handing out drinks. She took the third glass for herself and rested the tray on the table before she even noticed me standing there.

That's when it struck me: New Year's. This all had to be connected to their New Year's Eve dinner, which I had never asked about, because frankly, I didn't want to know if it had gone well.

"Susannah!" my mother cooed. "When did you get home?"

"Just now," I said.

She smiled at me. "Why don't you get cleaned up and come join us? Dinner will be in ten."

I headed to the shower without another word.

For dinner, we sat around the small square table where we always ate, but the room had transformed. Tall white candlesticks towered out of polished silver holders, and the usual place mats of woven fern had been swapped for embroidered textiles that matched the ivory napkins. Even my mother was dressed up in an elegant blue dress that swished at her kneecaps. A pearl bracelet—Vivian's, I guessed—shimmered when her wrist turned. I sat across from her, hunched in my father's faded Flying Burrito Brothers T-shirt, my wet hair corralled into a messy bun. The ends wept cold streams down my back.

"Why don't you tell us about your day, Susannah?" my mother

asked after a while, when I still hadn't said a word.

"There's not much to tell," I said, and squeezed the chicken breast with my fork until the feta stuffing oozed out. Any other day, I would have devoured my meal in a matter of seconds, but as I watched the casual way Roger cut into his meat, listening to his effortless banter and the laughter that lingered in that high-ceilinged room, my appetite waned. "I went to school, then to Lynn's to work on an Economics project. Now I'm home."

I stared at Roger, daring him to challenge me. He just kept eating.

My mother said, "I'm glad you've found a nice pattern here. And friends. It's so important to have friends."

"Yup." I attempted to stab a pomegranate seed from my salad with the loud clang of metal against china. "Patterns and friends."

For a moment, I felt the weight of all their eyes on me. Then Roger cleared his throat.

"This chicken is incredible, Vivian. You'll have to give me the recipe."

"Are you much of a chef these days?" she asked, once again refilling the wine.

My mother picked up her glass and swirled it around before drinking. "Actually, Roger's always had a flair for cooking. He used to make a mean mac 'n' cheese. He'd even throw in little hot dog slices, if he was feeling fancy." She flashed a grin across the table.

Roger laughed. "Well, I guess not much has changed, then. I still tend to eat simply. I make a lot of pork chops, a lot of spaghetti. Burritos." He threw me a knowing smile. I glared back.

"But this might be the best meal I've ever had."

"It's a lot easier than it looks," Vivian said. "I don't have the patience to bother much with recipes these days. All you really need are fresh ingredients and common sense. Even a man of mac and cheese could make this."

"I think you're letting yourself off easy. This is truly delicious."

"Well, eat more, then. Please. We still have tons of food."

"Maybe just another bite of salad. Do you mind passing the salad, Diane?"

As the bowl changed hands, their fingers touched. It was only a second, but I saw something jolt between them.

"Can I be excused?" I asked.

"May I," Vivian chimed.

I gritted my teeth. "*May I* be excused?"

"You've hardly touched your dinner," my mother said.

"I ate a big lunch."

She sighed. "Well, I suppose I can bring out the dessert now."

"I'll clear the plates," Vivian offered, but my mother insisted that she sit down.

"Susannah will help, and then she can be excused."

I grabbed my plate and the basket of bread and followed her into the kitchen.

"What are you doing?" I whispered when we were alone.

My mother took the dishes from me and placed them next to the sink. "I'm not sure what you mean."

"He's my teacher, Mom."

"Roger and I have been friends a long time." She began loading the bread into a Ziploc bag.

"He's my teacher," I said again, louder, though I must have recognized that the teacher part wasn't actually the problem. I liked Mr. Tipton at school—I really did. But the man here at our dinner table was not the familiar teacher or the kind, curious choir dilettante who rushed around the room trying to get us to sing louder as he slapped emphatic time signatures against his knee. This was somebody else. Somebody from my mother's world, her past, the place before my father existed. A place I never wanted to be.

"Susie, please," she begged. "Lower your voice."

"It's barely been six months since Dad died, or did you already forget?"

My mother stopped, one hand hovering above the bread basket, and turned to me. "That's not fair."

"Isn't it?"

"I'm not trying to replace your father," she said. "No one could ever do that. And yes, perhaps things are a bit more complicated than—"

I scoffed. "Complicated. Right. Twenty years have passed since you were kids. You don't even know him anymore and yet you're throwing yourself at him, like you can just pick back up right where you left off. Like nothing ever separated you—"

"You're being completely irrational about this—"

"—but something did separate you. I'm right, aren't I? There's a reason why you didn't pick him. And maybe there's a reason why he never got married."

My mother looked past me, frowning.

I swerved around. Roger stood behind me, a tall stack of dishes perched in his hands, the remnants of a smile fading from his face.

"The cooks shouldn't have to clean," he said, and walked toward the sink. He turned on the water and began wiping the scraps from our plates into the garbage. Every few seconds he stuck his finger beneath the faucet, testing the temperature.

"Roger, please don't," my mother said. "I'll take care of that later. You're our guest."

"I was married once," Roger said. He picked up one of the plates and rotated its surface through the water. "Nine years."

My mother and I just stood there watching as he arranged the plates in the dishwasher, gently scrubbed the empty wineglasses with a sponge. Little phosphorescent bubbles floated up from his hands, dawdling through the air before popping.

"What happened?" I asked.

My mother shot me a look of warning. "Roger, you don't need to talk about this. We have dessert. You still like white chocolate macadamia cookies, don't you?"

His hands kept moving beneath the stream of water. "She passed away," he said, as if he hadn't even heard my mother, and I knew then that he was talking solely to me. "Lung cancer. Never smoked a day in her life." He trailed off, shaking his head.

For a while, no one spoke. I wanted to leave, to make the conversation and the evening end, but my limbs felt too heavy. So I watched Roger wash our dishes. Next to me, my mother stared at the floor and bit at the inside of her lip, her expression pained but not surprised. Clearly, she already knew about Roger's wife. I wondered what else she knew about him, how often she had seen him, what had transpired since the day she ran into us outside the choir room. I wondered what had happened on New Year's Eve.

"Well," Roger said, turning off the water and drying his hands on one of Vivian's dish towels, "this isn't how I hoped the evening would unfold, but there it is."

"Roger." My mother's voice emerged as a whisper.

"I'm just going to give my regards to the chef, and then I'll be out of your hair."

My mother and I did not move from our spots on opposite sides of the kitchen sink as Roger walked out of view, offering a muffled thanks to Vivian in the dining room. The two spoke for a minute in hushed voices, and then moved toward the front door.

"He's a good friend," my mother said quietly, twisting Vivian's pearls around her wrist. "A good man."

I wanted to tell her I knew. Despite everything I had said, I knew Roger was genuine and caring, the kind of man who made the best of bad situations, who would volunteer to save a dying choir program and greet the challenge with zeal and warmth— only, I didn't know how to express that out loud, or how to explain the inconsistencies that had split Roger the choir teacher and Roger the potential boyfriend into two separate people in my mind, because in that moment, I was hit by a more immediate truth: I just wasn't ready to see my mother move on.

I wasn't sure if I'd ever be.

Out in the foyer the front door clicked shut. My mother waited a few more seconds, her jaw set. Then she turned away. Left alone, I looked around the empty, half-cleaned kitchen. In the big bay windows that overlooked the pool, I saw only darkness and my own reflection painted with shadows.

"Well, that went horribly," Vivian said when she entered the kitchen. She rummaged around for a minute, putting away spices, shaking the dirty linens over the sink. Then she opened the pink baker's box that sat in the center of the island. "Cookie?" she asked.

I shook my head. Vivian took her time before choosing one. "I always try to pick the one with the most chocolate. Why indulge at all if you're not going to indulge completely?" she said, and began nibbling on the sweet, placing one hand beneath her chin to catch the crumbs. She tossed her head back and made an *"Mmm"* sound. My stomach roared.

"You didn't just randomly see Roger that day at the grocery store, did you," I said.

"Your mother told me that they ran into each other at the school. She seemed hopeful. Happy, for the first time since you came here. And your mother needs a distraction." She took another bite of the cookie, dabbing a napkin at the corners of her mouth. "Don't get me wrong—I adore that she's single-handedly raising my property value, and the new view is marvelous. But what your mother really needs is a friend. She's known Roger a long time."

I crossed my arms. "Everyone keeps saying that."

"I think Roger needs a friend, too."

"Why didn't you like him?" I demanded.

"Who, dear?" Vivian asked.

"My father."

Vivian watched me sternly, no doubt deciding whether she should tell me the truth—not that she would lie. Whenever there were elephants in the room, she was the first to pull out a gun. This was one of the qualities I liked most about her, despite how harsh she could sometimes be, and I felt a strange prick of pride when she looked directly at me and said, "He wasn't good enough for her."

"In what way?" I asked.

"In every way."

"You didn't even know him."

She sat on a stool at the island, as if the conversation had already exhausted her. "He was wild and uneducated and he didn't have a stable job. He had no way of providing for a family, and no intention of doing so. He would disappear for days at a time and your mother would call me, crying. I'd tell her to leave him and come home."

Though I wanted to argue, to defend my father and all the pieces of him that Vivian couldn't even pretend to know, a separate thought struck me. "So when exactly did you two stop talking?"

"I needed to free her," she said. "I thought he would ruin her life."

"What did you do?"

Vivian sighed. "I did what I thought any sane parent would do. I gave her an ultimatum, an offer with only one logical choice. I told her to leave him and come home, or I'd cut her off. She'd already taken a leave from school by then, but we were still paying for her apartment, her gas, her groceries."

A fragment whirled back to me then: a warm door, a dark hallway. My parents' angry voices rubbing up against each other before pulling apart. I stared at the black expanse beyond the kitchen window and focused, harder, willing the memory into precision. *This was bigger than the amount of zeros on a check,* my father had said. *Your exact words.*

Then I remembered what Kurt told me the day we sipped iced tea on his patio in Pasadena.

"But she did leave him," I said. "Before I was born. She didn't come to you?"

"Did I ever tell you about your mother's bike-riding routine?" Vivian asked. Her voice had softened, rounded to a supple lilt.

I shook my head.

"Your mother used to love riding her bike in the driveway when she was a little girl, but before she could, she had to walk back and forth across every inch of the pavement looking for bugs. Anything bigger—snails, worms—she would pick up and place in the grass, but if something like a trail of ants marched across the pavement, something she couldn't easily relocate, she would mark the spot with a chalk line, so she knew not to cross it. Only then could she get on her bike and start riding. She couldn't bear the thought of accidentally squishing any creature. Not even a—what do you call those little things? The gray ones that curl up?"

"Roly Poly?"

"Yes. Exactly."

As Vivian shifted on her stool, the light caught the sheen of her blush. It looked too orange, almost tawdry, and her lipstick had rubbed off. I'd never thought Vivian looked particularly old, but right then, lost in her reverie, I could see in the lines of her face as she smiled just how many years she had already lived.

"What was I saying?" she asked suddenly.

"That my mother refused to ride her bike over bugs."

Vivian furrowed her eyebrows, as though straining to orient herself in her own story.

"She'd pick them up and move them out of her path?" I said uncertainly. "Roly Polies?"

She nibbled the cookie, thinking. "Hm," she said. Then, "Well, your mother would have made an extraordinary marine biologist."

"She wanted to be a marine biologist?"

Vivian nodded. "She always loved animals, but as she got older, she became fascinated with the ocean. There were so many possibilities out there, so many more unknowns. And she was so inquisitive. She had her father's brain."

The only link I had between my mother and the ocean was the ratty old SeaWorld hat she used to wear when she gardened. When I listened to the waves, I thought of my father, not her. Not what might be living underneath.

"My grandfather was an Eagle Scout," I said hollowly, reciting the one thing I felt I knew with any certainty in that moment.

"That's right." Vivian nodded, pleased that I remembered.

"What happened to him?"

"The same thing that happens to all of us, eventually."

"But how?" I asked before adding, "I should know these things. For, like, when I have to fill out all those forms at the doctor's office, about family health history and stuff. I already have a big blank on one side."

"Heart attack," she said. "Such cruel irony, isn't it? The healthiest among us are often first to go." She sighed, her narrow shoulders visibly rising, falling. "Your mother was only a teenager when he died. Younger than you, I believe."

"She never told me that."

"Yes, well. We were dead anyway, weren't we?" When Vivian

laughed, her voice echoed off the granite. Then she picked up the baker's box. "Cookie?"

"Still no."

"I always try to pick the one with the most chocolate."

I shook my head, not wanting to be led off track. "Doesn't it make you angry that she let me believe you were dead?"

"Love can make you do otherwise unthinkable things. None of us are immune."

"Well *I* think it was unfair," I said. "To both of us."

"Your mother did what she thought was best. I can't say I blame her. I didn't make it very easy." She paused. "You must understand. Things were different when I was a girl. Women had different roles. I heard the most awful stories about these young girls who fell in love with musicians. They would hop on to one of those tour buses and come home in a box, their arms pricked more times than a pincushion."

"But you could have called," I said. "You could have visited, tried to make it right. She would have forgiven you."

"Perhaps." Vivian looked toward the black window. "Perhaps not. Your mother's a strong woman, Susannah. I'd like to think she got that much from me. But we're stubborn too. Proud. It took me a long time to admit that the world was changing. To understand that your mother's choice was not a direct stab at me."

The refrigerator started humming, its buzz filling the quiet room. Vivian said something else but I couldn't hear her. "What?" I asked.

She shook her head and placed two fingers on each temple, began rubbing the skin there.

"Be a dear and fetch me a glass of water, will you?"

I did as she asked. When I handed her the glass, she wrapped her fingers around mine, preventing me from letting go.

"Don't be angry with your mother," she said, her eyes boring into me. "This family has been broken for far too long." I started to protest, to explain why I was mad, but Vivian swept on. "Your mother is not the villain. If this story has one, I imagine that the most likely candidate is me."

She let my fingers fall. My whole hand fell, heavy, to my side. "I always thought I was the villain," I said.

"What a preposterous thing to say."

"If it weren't for me, none of this would have happened. You wouldn't have had to give her an ultimatum. No one would have had to choose."

"I'm sorry to be the bearer of bad news," Vivian said, cutting me off, "but the same decisions would have been made without you. She saw in him a man worth saving. I saw a man who was wasting his life. You might have sped things up a bit, but the same bridges would have been crossed. Or burned." She stood. "Both seem applicable, in this case."

"But—"

"She loved him," Vivian snapped. "No one will ever take that away. But he isn't coming back. Do you understand that?"

My entire life, I had always fractioned everything into sides. My father and me against my mother. My father, Lance, and Travis against me. My father versus Roger. Versus Vivian. Versus me. And maybe it didn't have to be that way. I had spent so much time floundering beneath the weight of regret, thinking that if I had done something differently, he might still be alive. But I suppose all of us are doomed to think this way. We are, after all, the stars of our own stories.

"Do you understand?" Vivian said again. I nodded. She placed one hand back on her head, trying to steady herself, and smiled. "Occasionally I forget that I'm not young anymore, but the world never tires of reminding me." She shuffled toward the hallway, glancing back before leaving the room. "So you'll give him another chance? I'm not saying tomorrow or even the day after that, but sometime?"

Maybe I hadn't inadvertently destroyed my parents' lives all those years ago, I thought, but the asperity I had shown toward Roger? For that, the blame fell solely on me.

"Yeah okay," I said. "Sometime."

EIGHTEEN

LATER, AFTER I called Lynn and crawled out my window and edged down the dark driveway, I got into her car and we sped away from Orange Park Acres. Someone Lynn knew was having a party. The boys were already there.

Lemon Heights had no streetlamps, and as we curved through the neighborhood, only the slim fan of headlights guided us. I would have been terrified driving like that, hardly able to see as the car climbed higher, the houses getting both larger and farther apart. But Lynn knew those streets well. Now and then we swung around a stretch of road right on the edge of the hill, and through a break in the foliage I could see the entire city blazing like a circuit board. From that vantage point, I could block all of Orange with my hand. My father's voice echoed in my ears: *Doesn't every-thing look so calm from up here? It's much smaller than it seems.*

"So are you going to tell me what's wrong, or do I have to guess?" Lynn asked once we'd parked on a block cluttered with cars and headed in the general direction of distant music. Above us, dense clouds loomed, veined with moonlight. A breeze shivered over my arms.

"It's just stuff with my family," I said, rubbing the goose bumps.

"Nuh-uh. You don't get to use that with me. I am the queen of 'just stuff with my family.' You've met my mother. There's nothing you could possible say that I haven't said myself."

Lynn offered me her cigarettes and I took one, unearthed the matchbook from my purse.

"So you've said before that your mother is secretly dating your choir teacher—who, it appears, just happened to be her rather serious high school boyfriend? Likely the first man she ever loved, and maybe someone she *still* loves, has always loved? And here I thought I was special."

Lynn's mouth dropped open, and smoke streamed out like dried ice. "Shut. The fuck. Up."

"I win," I said drily, continuing toward the music. "I expect you to abdicate the throne by midnight."

"That's completely unfair!"

We rounded a corner and the party's noises amplified.

"Unfair how?" I asked.

"Mr. Tipton was supposed to be *my* secret lover."

Abruptly, I stopped, scrunching my face in an attempt to push the ensuing mental images from my head. "That's disgusting. I can't believe you just said that."

"It's true. I've always thought he was kind of sexy, in this totally geeky way."

"*Sexy?*" I cringed. "*Lover?* Who are you right now? I want the old Lynn back, because this new version is making me really uncomfortable."

"I'm sorry, Susannah," Lynn droned. "I'm afraid I can't do that."

I couldn't help but laugh, recognizing the voice from *2001: A Space Odyssey*—a movie Nick had forced me to watch during winter break our junior year.

"I'm afraid the old Lynn has been replaced with a sex-crazed robot, charged with taking over the world one lowly high school teacher at a time."

"Please stop," I said, a cramp forming in my stomach, "before I vomit the nothing I've had to eat today all over you. And don't tell anyone about this, all right? I mean it."

"But you feel a little bit better now, don't you?"

I shrugged. Lynn hooked her arm in mine and steered us left, up an inclined driveway.

"Let's forget all about your mother and Mr. Tipton and my deviant, secret fantasies, and go get ourselves a drink."

"Make that a hundred drinks," I said. "Maybe one hundred and two, after the conversation we just had."

Inside, the house was dim and gloomy. The party poured from every crevice—not crowded, necessarily, but always apparent in a cluster of empty bottles and cups on a tabletop, a swell of voices seeping from a dusky room. Some people greeted us as Lynn and

I snuck toward the kitchen, but many were already too drunk or distracted to notice. After we each drank a shot, we made our way to the yard.

Though the air was brisk and the wind biting, the patio was far more crowded than the house. Bodies spilled across the lawn and around the sides of the luminescent lap pool. We spotted Josie's lavender hair near Gabriel in the back. Behind them, Alex stared past the wrought-iron fence, into blackness—an expansive mass of undeveloped land.

"He's brooding," Josie explained when we approached. She leaned in close to me and put one hand on my arm—maybe for camaraderie, or for balance. "He thinks it makes him more mysterious, though I can't figure out who he's trying to impress." She changed her voice to a mock-whisper. "Granted, half this party wants to fuck him. But I'm pretty sure the other half already has."

She pulled back then, suddenly. Behind the wide lenses of her glasses, her eyes were dark and slick as coffee beans. "*You're* not trying to fuck him, are you?"

"What?" At first, I wasn't sure I'd heard right; all the smoke in the yard made me feel light-headed, and the shot—or two, or three—that I'd slung was starting to tingle in my fingers. "Josie, I'd never—"

Josie erupted in laughter. "Oh my God, you should see your face."

"Oh," I said, and glanced around, waiting for someone else to laugh or tell me that this conversation was normal, but Lynn, I realized then, had vanished. Gabriel and Alex had also shifted into another circle.

"I was just kidding," she said. "We've been together five years, you know. Don't believe what everyone tells you." She paused then, strained her gaze across the pool. "Plus, I know you wouldn't do that."

And though she was right, I would never try to sleep with her boyfriend, in that moment I found myself fostering a surprising thought: Josie didn't actually know me at all.

"It's common knowledge"—she threw back whatever was left in her cup—"who you're fawning over." Then she yelled his name: "Cameron!"

I reached out, trying to stop her from saying something embarrassing. But it was too late. He emerged from the throng and headed toward us, his cheeks pinched with red, a bottle in his hand. When he saw me, his eyes glinted.

"I didn't think you were going to come," he said to me, voice thick and fizzy. He had no jacket either, but seemed unaware of the frigid night air.

"What made you think that?"

"Hand that over," Josie demanded, snatching the bottle from Cameron's grip. She splashed an inch of liquid into her cup before floating off.

"You're welcome," he called after her.

But I was grateful to be left alone with him. "Aren't you freezing?"

He moved closer. "We can keep each other warm."

When he laced his fingers through mine, my heart surged. Our hands were fully visible. *We* were fully visible, but of course no one else was paying attention. Still, my nerves twitched, our proximity unbearable. Like that night in the ocean—we were so close, and yet I'd never felt more aware of the distance between us.

My brain spun. I didn't know how to traverse that final inch, how to make my body say all the things my mouth couldn't. So I slipped the bottle from his hands, and drank.

"You know," I said finally, my throat on fire, "I've been thinking . . ."

"Oh yeah?"

I laughed, and hit him playfully on the shoulder.

"What were you thinking?" he urged.

"I was thinking that we should write again. A new song."

"You got some ideas?"

"Tons." I smiled. "And maybe . . ." I willed my body forward, just a fraction, a centimeter. "Maybe I can sing more, too."

"I'll have to talk to the guys," he said. "Alex is really the singer."

"I know. I don't want to change that. I just want to be more involved. I thought that because 'Don't Look Back' was so successful—"

"We'll figure it out," he said. "By the way, I think I might have found us a gig at the Troubadour."

"Are you serious?"

"Why would I lie?"

"I don't know." I grinned. "Maybe you're trying to put me in a good mood."

"I'm not trying to do anything," he said. "Not even this."

And then he kissed me, right there on the deck, in full view of whoever wanted to see. It must have only lasted a few seconds, but those seconds felt suspended, floating above the grasp of the party.

Everyone else drifted away, muffled in some other reality that was less real than the heat of Cameron's hands as they crawled beneath the hem of my shirt, my skin prickling like a current of static air—until a burst of white brightened my eyelids, and suddenly, too suddenly, we pulled apart.

My eyes flapped open to a camera. Behind the lens a guy with shaggy hair turned to capture some other moment with some-body else. There were always a handful of guys like him around, bringing their expensive camera equipment to shows, perusing the parties after to snap "candids"—though it was obvious that people hovered in the photographer's periphery, always turned to their best angle, praying to be preserved with that perfect, practiced expression. Before, the desperate way people paraded themselves in front of the lens always made me uncomfortable. But now that the camera had been turned to me, I felt suddenly proud.

"Let's go inside," Cameron said, and he led me through the mob, past the kitchen, down one hallway and another. He opened one of the doors and my mind reeled with questions. I did not ask any of them.

We found each other easily in the dark, in secret—the place where we felt most comfortable. Cameron kissed me hard. His hands navigated the hills of my body. I stumbled backward, grip-ping his hair. Maybe, I thought, this was also the place where everything started.

Briefly, my mind flashed to New Year's. I was glad this wasn't my first time, that I knew now what to expect, what I wanted. And I wanted this. It didn't matter that he was drunk, or that I wasn't drunk enough. All that mattered was what happened next.

"Wait," Cameron said, pulling back.

"What?" My breath was heavy, my heart rasping.

"Not like this."

It was the most steady his voice had sounded all night.

"Like what?" I asked, though of course, I already knew. "It's kind of exciting, though, isn't it?" I offered, remembering Cody, the sliver of light that splashed in from the yard and the barrage of high-pitched voices just outside the room. The way it felt to be that connected to another person.

"Not like this," Cameron said again, peeling away from me. "I'm really drunk."

I nodded pointlessly.

"My head is spinning."

"Want me to get you some water?" I asked.

"I just need to lie here for a minute."

I nodded again.

"I'll meet you back out there, okay?" He plopped back onto the mattress.

As I groped my way to the door, a wave of disappointment dizzied me. I didn't understand. Hadn't he wanted this? Hadn't he kissed me in the backyard, led me to this room, stretched his hands across my bare skin? A lump unfurled in my throat. I inched open the door, glancing back, but there wasn't enough light to reveal anything more than a silhouette. When I finally slipped into the hallway, I was so consumed by confusion that I nearly slammed into someone.

Luke.

"Jesus," I gasped. "You scared me. How long have you been there?"

He examined me with sullen detachment. I felt myself blushing beneath his stare. Luke and I had only had a couple of one-on-one conversations, all of which had been brief and band related, and it felt strange now to have his eyes on me. Gratifying, but also unnerving. The rest of party seemed impossibly far away.

"It's never going to be enough," he said.

A dangerous feeling lodged in my chest. "I don't know what that means," I said through a smile.

"You're wasting your time."

"What are you talking about?" I asked, but he was already stepping past me, walking further into the depths of the house. "Luke?"

He disappeared around a corner—a habit of his, I realized with a start. I rushed forward, trying to catch him before he was gone again, but found only another dreary hallway and a series of closed doors.

I retraced my way back to the yard.

"Susannah," Josie yelled, parting the crowd to approach me. "You haven't seen Lynn, have you?"

I shook my head.

"I swear, that girl is Houdini incarnate. At least I've got you. Smoke?"

Staring at the gleaming turquoise pool, I drew from my cigarette while Josie talked. When necessary I nodded or shook my head, smiled blankly while trying to trick my thoughts away from

Cameron and Luke. I didn't even want to think about Alex then, and all the girls he may or may not have slept with. Gabriel, however, was still safe; he'd never attempted to be anything other than exactly what he seemed: sweet, aloof, defined by his persistent sideways grin. When he came over to borrow a light from Josie, I rested my head on his arm, allowed myself to imagine standing onstage at the Troubadour. He combed his fingers through my hair.

And I thought maybe there was just something in the air, putting me on edge—something about the peculiar angles of the wind-rustled trees, or the sky that had filled up, threatening to spill over. Almost a year had passed since the last rainfall, and even then it was more of a mist, the kind that floats in over the Pacific and speckles the lawn like crystal dust. Most people would probably praise the storm as a miracle, considering the severity of our drought. But I sensed something different stirring.

Though outsiders always assumed Southern California is perpetually soft and subtropical with the perfect beach breeze, that sweet lick of sunshine, I knew the truth. The real Southern California exists in extremes. It's a place of spontaneous wildfires, and Santa Ana winds, and droughts that turn lakes into craters, splintering the earth like pottery that has crazed. It's a place of storms that transform streets into oceans, and I had no doubts now: the rain was coming.

But the foreboding feeling that had bloomed behind my rib cage remained—even when Lynn finally appeared, saying she'd been in the kitchen the whole time, that we must have walked right past her, and once we traced back through the sleeping hills to Vivian's house. When the sky finally broke with a crackling sigh and the first drips of water splattered ceremoniously on Lynn's windshield, I thought I'd feel better, but I didn't. She dropped me off down the street as usual and I ran the half block home, crept up the driveway, the quickening raindrops catching on my eyelashes and arms until I climbed in my window. Peeling off my clothes, I crawled into bed.

For a long time I lay awake, wondering what was wrong with me. I wanted to believe Cameron was waiting for the right time, that *not like this* meant later, a promise for the future. And yet, even then, a nagging, irrepressible piece of me had already accepted that belief changed nothing. Hope changed nothing. All that mattered were the choices people made: what they did, and what they didn't.

NINETEEN

AND IT RAINED.

Hurricane winds hurled in from the tropics and the clouds burst open, sparking vines of lightning through the low-hung sky. All weekend I stayed indoors, watching the torrents pummel the pool, listening to the drumroll on the roof. I used Vivian's computer to scour the web for the photograph that had been snapped of Cameron and me mid-kiss at the party, scrolling through every photographer's site I could locate and every social profile that flaunted images from Friday night. I clicked and clicked and somewhere along the line, I started to understand why people needed the proof. But I never found the photo.

During those long, anxious hours, I wanted to text him. We

hadn't spoken since I left him alone in that bedroom, and I was afraid of how much I wanted him, how badly I needed everything to remain the same between us, even if we never existed in public. And yet, I was more afraid of revealing this. So I texted Nick instead.

Sitting in the kitchen while Vivian chopped vegetables for a beef stew, I asked, "Should we be preparing or something?"

A small TV perched on a shelf near the cabinet of wineglasses, and I'd been watching the footage on the news: roofs collapsing in San Clemente, power lines torn down by ferocious winds in Garden Grove.

"I am preparing," Vivian told me. "I'm preparing dinner."

"You know what I mean."

She said, "We're on high ground."

I wondered if she had seen the backyard lately. Outside, the world had been repainted in grayscale, filtered through fog. Water from the overflowing pool lapped across the patio, closer and closer to the house. Even my mother, who hardly batted an eye at that autumn's fire, seemed affected by the storm; she'd been in bed for two days, her nose red and skin pale. She said she thought she might have the flu.

"We need this," Vivian affirmed, nodding to herself as she sliced a carrot into smooth, even slivers. She dropped the pieces in the pot and began rifling through the cabinet. "Susannah, have you seen the cabernet? I just bought a brand-new bottle for this recipe, and now it's not here."

I shook my head. "Nope."

"Are you sure?" She turned around, eyeing me sternly. A sudden sharpness tinted her voice. "I won't be mad if you took it. Just tell me the truth."

"Why would I take it?"

"Why have teenagers been smuggling family liquor since the dawn of time?"

"You probably just forgot it, like the Pepto-Bismol."

"Pepto-Bismol?" Her brows knitted together. "What are you talking about? I haven't bought that in years."

I rolled my eyes. "Nothing. Never mind."

"Don't use that tone with me, young lady," Vivian warned.

"I'm sorry," I said through my teeth. "But I promise you, I didn't take the wine, okay?"

After that I left the kitchen.

In my bedroom, I picked up the Martin. A fine fur of dust coated the varnish, and I wiped the body clean with the hem of my shirt. I wanted to write a new song, to have something ready when Cameron broke the silence between us—but my fingertips hurt from disuse, and for some reason the only chords I managed to form were the ones that made up "Love Honey," the only sounds I could glean the howling wind and ravenous rain. Baritones of thunder echoed through my head. I sighed, put the guitar down, and grabbed the Endless West's CD.

Glancing at my bedroom window, I tried to gauge how drenched I would get in the short distance across the driveway to my mother's car where I always practiced vocals, but all I could see was the rain battering the glass. And what if she decided, beyond all logic, to go somewhere—the store, perhaps, for medicine? Vivian wouldn't leave, though. Not in this weather.

I headed to the garage.

I'd only been shut inside Vivian's car for a moment, had not even managed to slip the CD into the player, when I noticed the smell. Something rotten. I crawled into the back, peered over the last row of seats, and there, slumped in the trunk, was a forgotten bag of groceries. Nestled between Greek yogurt and a pint of strawberries lay a dark bottle of red wine.

I hesitated, unsure of what to do. My mother had explicitly stated that Vivian did not want me to know she might be ill, or to treat her as such. Besides, if I brought in the groceries, then I'd have to explain why I'd been in the car. So I left the bag where it was, the yogurt curdling, the fresh fruit growing fuzz. I snuck back into the house, and knocked softly on my mother's door.

"Mom?" I said through the crack when she didn't answer. "Are you asleep?"

I could hear the bed creak as she rolled over. "What is it, hon?"

"I just . . ." A knot yanked in my throat. I inched into the dark room and lowered my voice. "I just wanted to ask you about Vivian. Is everything still okay with her?"

"Did something happen?"

I sat on the edge of the bed and looked toward the window, where a tunnel of rain was no doubt drowning all the plants and crops we had hoped it would save.

"No. Well, sort of. She just accused me of stealing some wine. I didn't, though," I added quickly.

My mother sat up. The dim light of the TV splashed across her face, soaking her skin in a strange shade of blue. It was disconcerting to see her like that—eyes puffy, nose rubbed raw. We were safe inside our house, on high ground, and yet I felt like the world around me was slowly sliding apart.

"You don't need to worry," my mother said. Her frozen hand grazed my cheek. "It's just a side effect. Everything is under control."

The rain continued for a week. The following Monday, during morning announcements, we were told that there had been a mudslide out in Silverado Canyon, and a junior named Annie Young had died. The principal omitted the details over the loudspeaker, but soon enough, the facts dispersed: a boulder had crashed through the roof of her bedroom, crushing her instantly beneath its weight.

Though I had never met Annie, her death struck me hard. I was used to the ground trembling beneath me and had prepared for fire, spent hours considering what possessions I would grab if the winds ever changed and the flames swept toward me. But this—how could anyone prepare themselves for this?

The school held vigils and grief counseling sessions on campus. Ms. Grobler even offered to excuse absences for any advisees that came in to talk. I didn't go. I didn't think I had the right to mourn someone I'd never met, to walk around with my head slung or huddle in the groups that hugged and cried, spilling tears into each other's hair. I couldn't even picture her when the principal said Annie's name, or in the minute of silence that my homeroom teacher requested in her honor.

But by lunch, I saw nothing else.

"It's kind of creepy, isn't it?" Lynn asked when we met at her locker.

Sometime after the announcement, the school had been plastered with photocopies of Annie's yearbook picture. The rain had finally eased and everywhere I looked, through the vaporous air, she smiled.

"Yeah," I said, turning in a slow circle. There she was, staring out from the doors of all the classrooms she wasn't in, from the concrete walls and the bulletin boards. She had a round face and thin lips, a single freckle on her left cheekbone. She wasn't looking at the camera, exactly, but just beyond, over my shoulder. As though she saw something I didn't. I shivered.

"It's really surreal," I added. "I wish the copies hadn't been made so big." The breeze clipped the corner of the paper and in that instant, it looked like she was moving. "Did you know her?"

Lynn shook her head. "Never seen her in my life."

For some reason, this made me more sad than anything else.

"Let's get out of here," Lynn said then, turning away from Annie Young. "I can't handle this place right now."

Traffic was sparse as we zipped down the 55 South, and I was glad to leave the grieving campus—even more so to miss choir. Just thinking about the harrowing evening I spent across the table from Roger Tipton filled me with dread, and seeing him every day made it impossible to forget. In class, he tried to remain impartial toward me, but that only made me feel worse. I resented the casual sound of my name in his mouth, as if I were any other student passing through his classroom.

At the beach, we parked on a residential street a few blocks inland and wandered down to the ocean. The wind was rougher than it had been in Orange; every few seconds a massive gust kicked up and the seawater sprayed our faces, lacing our skin with a delicate coating of salt. I wondered if we were at the same beach we'd visited the night Cameron and I first kissed.

"Looks like we're the only ones twisted enough to be out here in this weather, huh?" I said. The shore, as far as I could tell, was empty.

Lynn nodded at the sea. "There are others."

Even from where we stood, the waves towered over us. They were huge and vicious, each break thundering down with so much force that it was almost impossible to see them at first: surfers. There were a dozen at least, maybe more scattered down the coast. Their shiny black wet suits glistened beneath the veiled rays of sun.

Lynn spread a blanket on the sand and we sat down. "I think there's something really peaceful about the ocean on days like this."

"You mean days when the waves are deadly and it's freezing cold?" Teeth chattering, I pulled my knees to my chest.

"When there's no one here except the surfers."

We both turned our attention back to the ocean. Not a single body had moved since we arrived; they simply floated up and down, bobbing over the waves.

"I'm terrified just watching them," I said. "Terrified and mesmerized."

"Do you ever think about how you'll die?"

"What?"

I looked at Lynn, but she was still focused on the surfers.

"Sure," I said when it was clear that she would not elaborate. "I spend so much time trying not to think about death that I end up thinking about it constantly."

She said, "I've always had this feeling that I'm going to die young."

"Why would you think that?"

Lynn shrugged. "I've just never seen it for myself, that life that you're supposed to have. A husband and a house. Kids." She shook her head. "I can't imagine any of it."

"But that doesn't mean anything. You can't see your future because it hasn't been decided yet. That's all."

"I guess," she said, but I still felt flooded by some grim feeling.

"Is something else bothering you?" I asked.

She offered a thin smile and said, "No."

Despite Lynn's reassurances, I knew Annie Young's death must have rattled her, too—reminded her that we were all breakable. That at any moment a boulder could crash through the ceiling of our small, safe world and end everything.

Shoving my hands in my pockets, I felt the soft edges of my father's matchbook.

"I want to find Jason," I said. "The other Spade." A moment passed, but she didn't respond. "You don't think I should?"

"I just don't want you to get your hopes up. Digging up the past rarely leads to anything good—and that's *if* he even still lives at the same place."

"But he might. And he might know something important. I have to at least try, before . . ." *Before it's too late*, I thought.

Seagulls floated along the shore, cawing as they searched for stray crabs or scraps of food. Beyond them, a surfer paddled into a forming wave, climbing with the crest. I could feel my muscles tightening as I watched his arms struggle to gain momentum, but the wave built too fast. He couldn't catch it. My body unclenched as he disappeared behind the swell.

"You're afraid of it, aren't you?" Lynn said. "Death."

"Yes." My answer was hardly more than the whisper of wind.

She turned to me. "What if he'd survived? Have you ever really thought about it? He could have ended up in a coma, or on life support. He could have drooled from a wheelchair for the next twenty years. Would that have been better?"

I'd never considered the other possibilities. Of course I hadn't—there was only the man my father had been, and the lack of him.

"Trust me," she said. "Sometimes death is a preferable alternative."

The breeze picked up again, spritzing us with saltwater. Lynn lay down on her back and closed her eyes. I kept watching the surfers. I thought about the rainwater that had pooled across campus, drowning the flowers my mother had planted in our backyard. I thought about the picture of Annie Young and the way she smiled from every surface of the school, her eyes seeing something that the rest of us could not. Words nudged me; I pulled a notebook from my backpack and began to write.

> *I won't believe it. No, I won't believe*
> *that all eternity can be spent looking*
> *for the soul you lost after a single mistake.*
>
> *A single regret is all I can take.*

· · ·

It was four o'clock in the afternoon and the 55 was jammed as we headed back to Orange. Because it rained so infrequently, most Californians never learned how to drive in it. The asphalt was still slick with oils, the cars skating on tires that were old and worn. There must have been an accident somewhere up ahead. We merged into the carpool lane, but even then our progress was sluggish.

I sank into my seat as we crawled forward, my mind hazy with thoughts of Cameron and the Troubadour. I'd been desperate for details, or at least a date, but since the party Cameron had only texted me twice—once to inform me about band practice, and once to cancel it because of the weather. When I tried to turn those dregs of contact into conversation, the messaging quickly fizzled and died. Truthfully, I couldn't remember if our earlier texts had been all that interesting, or if the fact that he had messaged me with any frequency at all made me think there was something special between us.

"Can I ask you something?" I said after another futile cell phone check.

"Shoot," Lynn said.

"What would you do," I began, and then stopped. Above the cramped lanes of the freeway, a plane coasted toward the Santa Ana Airport. It grew bigger and bigger until I thought it might land right on top of us. "What would you do if you were involved with someone who didn't want the relationship to be public?"

"Correct me if I'm wrong here, but didn't Cameron practically swallow your face the other night at that party?"

"I wouldn't have put it that way, exactly, but yeah. You saw that?"

Lynn lit a cigarette and rolled down the windows. "I know he can be a bit sloppy when he's drinking, but the instinct was there."

"I guess you're right," I said through a sigh. The confirmation of our kiss seemed satisfying enough, and I would have left it at that—gladly. But Lynn continued.

"Look. I've known these guys for years," she said, "and I'm not suggesting that I agree with it by any means, but I've learned to accept it."

"Accept what?"

"Their need to . . . exude a certain image." She waved her fingers. "They're incredibly talented, but that's not enough. Even if you're the best band out there, it doesn't mean a goddamn thing anymore. You need buzz. You need people talking about you, coming to shows, spending their money on your tickets, your albums, your fucking T-shirts. And the boys know that, so they project themselves in a way that makes them seem attainable, even if they aren't. It's part of their intrigue."

"What about Alex?" I said.

"What about him?"

"He's been with Josie for five years."

She exhaled a hard, straight line of smoke. "I'm assuming she's the one who told you that?"

"Well, yeah."

"Let's just say that neither one of them has the greatest track record when it comes to fidelity."

I felt something creak through my gut. But hadn't Josie also warned me not to believe what everyone else says? Only the two people in any relationship ever knew the truth about it—and sometimes, I supposed, only one.

Sighing, I dangled my arm out the window. "What was it like when you were with Cameron?" I asked.

"I wasn't *with* him," Lynn said, tossing me a thorny glance. "We didn't date or anything. Just fooled around a bit."

"But you slept with him," I said, hoping to sound indifferent.

"A few times," Lynn admitted, and my heart dropped. "It wasn't a big thing. We just drank too much."

The carpool lane began to move, and Lynn pressed lightly on the gas. We must have only been going thirty, thirty-five at most, but the way we raced past the other cars made our acceleration seem much faster.

"Cameron's flighty," Lynn said. "Easily interested, and easily spooked. The best way to keep him is to be comfortable letting him go."

"And if I don't want that?"

"I guess you have to ask yourself what you're willing to sacrifice. But if you can't sacrifice him, then he's probably already gone."

"So I lose either way."

"What did you expect? To marry the guy? If that's what you want—and God, please tell me it isn't—then this thing you have going with Cameron will never be what you want anyway, and you shouldn't waste your time waiting around for something that will never change."

Leaning my head back, I gazed up through Lynn's windshield.

The sky was an ashy gray smudge of blank, undefined clouds, and for some reason then, I thought of my parents. I wondered if my mother had spent all these years waiting for my father to change, to deliver on the promise he made when he left the Vital Spades and came back to her, or if she'd been forced to slacken and shift, accept that she was the only one who could save them. There in the passenger seat of Lynn's car, one hand coiled around my quiet phone, I finally began to understand what my mother must have felt living with my father, always outnumbered by the phantoms of what had been and what could be. I understood what it must have felt like to love someone who was only ever half present. And I couldn't decide which would be worse: having only a piece of something, or having none of it at all.

"I guess it must be true, then," I said. "You're the second person to say so."

"Who was the first?" Lynn asked.

My phone vibrated and I yanked my hand from my purse, stomach tumbling through tangled nerves. But the text message wasn't from Cameron.

Oh Susannah, Susannah—wherefore art thou, Susannah? Deny thy caffeine indulgence and refuse to ever go to the Last Bean again if that new girl doesn't figure out how to serve a freaking iced coffee . . .

A smile fought its way to my lips. I typed, *Oh, Nick—you're kind of like a rainstorm, and just as unexpected.*

Lynn spoke again. "What?" I asked.

"Who was the first person to say that?"

"Luke," I told her.

"Luke?" Lynn turned to me, confusion furrowing her brows.

"Yeah, it was the weirdest thing," I said, slipping my phone back into my purse, but before I could explain, a car slammed on its breaks in front of us. "Lynn watch out!"

Our car screeched to a stop, bodies whipping forward against the seat belts before knocking back again. My heart skidded through my chest but we were static—no crash, no clang. We must have only been centimeters from the bumper in front of us, and I just kept breathing, gulping in air, staring at the bright red sticker in the car's back windshield: *Do you follow Jesus this close?*

Only once we'd exited the freeway did one of us dare to speak.

"I'm sure you've got nothing to worry about with Cameron," Lynn said lightly, as if our conversation had never been interrupted. Her voice was unconvincing, quivering. "But you probably shouldn't be taking relationship advice from me. It's not like I've figured any of this shit out." She glanced at me just long enough to confirm that I noticed the sad way she tried to smile.

My hands were still trembling when she added, "Sorry for the scare. This day has completely fucked with my nerves." She shook her head. "Goddamn Boulder Girl."

A few days later all the rain clouds had cleared but the school was still shrouded in the death of Annie Young. Students continued to wear black, and at lunch, a hushed, collective calm swept across the otherwise boisterous quad. Even the teachers remained somber—a fact that, Lynn and I realized, rendered many of their ironclad attendance policies temporarily flexible. Knowing there would likely be no consequences, we decided once again to skip out at lunch. This time, though, we drove in the opposite direction.

"Are you sure you want to do this?" I asked Lynn as we pulled away from campus. "I can find another way out there. You already drive me around enough as it is."

"You know how much I love driving," she said. "There's nothing better than the freedom to go wherever the hell I want, whenever I want. And maybe today, I want to go to Venice." She flashed me a smile. "Besides, it's your gas money."

"And your time," I said. "So thank you."

We took the 405 North, toward Jason Miller.

The address Kurt Vaughan had given me led to an old, grungy apartment building hidden at the back side of a gas station—the kind of place time had neglected, with rusted bars covering the windows and exterior walls patchworked with paint in a vain attempt to remove old tattoos of graffiti. Lynn and I climbed to the second floor, curving around the balcony until we reached number 6B. I knocked on the door.

Inside, something clanged. "Yeah, coming," a raspy voice grumbled through the wall. I looked to Lynn.

"At least he's home," she said, "whoever he is."

A strange amalgamation of hope and unease pounded through me. The door flung open.

"Oh, hey," the man said, leaning against the door frame as though he'd been expecting me. At the same time, though, he looked like he'd just woken up. He was half-dressed in a tank top and boxer shorts, with unkempt hair and murky brown eyes that appeared somehow sunken as he squinted against the sharp gleam of sun. He snapped his fingers, searching for a word that dangled just out of reach. "Vanessa."

"Susannah," I said, stunned.

"Susannah," he repeated. "Right, yeah. I meant to call."

My mouth fell open. "You did?"

"I think you have her confused for somebody else," Lynn interrupted, severing the connection, and only then did I understand what was happening.

I decided to start over. "Are—are you Jason Miller?"

"Maybe." A sudden suspicion tinted his tone. "What's it to you?"

"My name is Susannah Hayes. My father was James Hayes. From the Vital Spades."

He straightened up at the names, a short laugh springing from his mouth as he said, "No shit."

Jason's apartment was tiny: a one-room studio with a detached kitchen at one end, a pullout sofa bed that he'd hastily pushed in at the other. Takeout containers decorated the tabletops, along with ashtrays and empty bottles and a grimy glass rimmed with red lipstick. In the far corner, I noticed crates of records stacked next to scattered music equipment: a mixing board, a Gibson SG, an amp. The air smelled faintly of sweet-and-sour chicken—emphasis on the sour.

"Can I get you anything?" he asked, opening the fridge. "I've got . . . beer. You guys want a beer?"

"No thanks," I started to say, but Lynn accepted. As Jason popped off the caps I caught Lynn's eye. Shrugging, she mouthed, *What? Free beer.*

"We don't want to take up too much of your time," I said, sitting on the sofa's edge.

Jason plopped down next to me. "I got nothing but time. How is ol' Jimmy, anyway?"

"He died," I said. "A few months ago."

"Man, I'm sorry to hear that. What happened?"

"A car crash."

"Shit." He ran his hand through his hair. "Bad way to go."

I thought about telling him the rest of the story: the circumstances of the crash, the detective's theory. Instead, I picked at the label on my beer and let the silence swell until it felt almost unbearable.

"So you still play music?" Lynn asked, breaking the quiet.

"Never stopped," Jason said proudly. "Got a band right now called Folly Goes, maybe you've heard of us?" When we didn't respond, he said, "And I also DJ at this bar off the boardwalk called the Black Crab."

"Oh cool," Lynn said. "The Black Crab."

I could tell by the upward tilt of her voice that she was faking.

"Yeah it's pretty great. I get free drinks, too." He fished a pack of cigarettes from amid the mess of a side table, then offered them to us. Lynn took one.

"By any chance had you talked to my father recently?" I managed to ask.

"Not in at least . . ." Jason thought. "Ten years? I can't remember."

"But you spoke since the breakup?"

"Sure, yeah. Talked about jamming sometime, but it never happened. Too bad, really. He was one hell of a musician, but he just couldn't compromise. It was always all or nothing with

Jimmy. For a while it was all. Then, it was nothing."

"Because of—" The word jammed in my mouth. "Because of drugs?"

Jason shook his head. "He had his vices, but man, we all did. I'll be the first to admit that. Vices are what keep life interesting, know what I mean? They're how you *live*. Am I right? She knows what I'm talking about." He nodded to Lynn.

"No argument here," she said, dragging casually on her cigarette.

"See, I just want to have a good time. That's why I do it. And when it stops being good, I move on to something new."

The beer label had become a soggy ball wadded in my hand. "So you don't fight? You don't try to hold the good together even when everything else starts falling apart?"

Jason exhaled, crinkling his eyes against the smoke. "That's just not my style."

Something caught in the back of my throat, like a pill swallowed dry. Before Lynn and I arrived here, I'd assumed Jason would be similar to Kurt—married, well adjusted, with a proper career. Yet while Kurt seemed to welcome the arrival of "middle-aged," Jason clearly did everything he could to rebel against it. And I didn't buy the act. I refused to believe that he hadn't cared about the Vital Spades with the same depth and passion as my father and Kurt, that he didn't sometimes mourn what could have been—or at the very least miss it. He had to be hiding something, covering up his own wounds.

But I had not come here to find out the truth about Jason.

I said, "What do you remember most about my father, when

you think of him now?"

Jason took a deep breath and lounged back, gazing into the hazy air. "When he was on, he was on, you know? You could see it in his eyes, this wild clarity taking over. He heard rhythm in everything, like the whole world was a secret symphony. And then he'd have these fits of inspiration that kept him up for days, tweaking a strumming pattern or a slide or something that no one else really noticed. He'd insist that the almost imperceptible elements mattered most, like some sort of melodic subliminal messaging." Jason laughed then. "Sometimes, I really thought Jimmy was a genius."

And though I knew I should have stopped there, allowing myself to float through a superficial glimmer of goodness and hope, I pressed on. "And the other times?"

Jason was still smiling, but something about his expression had emptied. "The other times," he said, "I knew he was just as lost as the rest of us."

Throughout most of the drive back to Orange, I remained silent. The time we'd spent inside Jason's apartment elongated in my mind, stretching and warping until I felt even further away from any one singular truth about my father. Every time I thought I was getting closer to him, a dozen more unknowns emerged, and I was even less sure now of the things I previously felt with absolute certainty. I was even less sure his crash was an accident.

"I'm sorry," I said to Lynn once we'd reached her house.

"For what?"

"For making you drive all the way out there. I thought—"
We were walking up the driveway and for a moment, I paused,

convinced I felt something, that supernatural flash of wind. But it was only my imagination. "I thought he would be different."

"Not like I had anything better to do," she joked as she slid her key into the front door. "But seriously. If this is what you needed to move forward, then I'm glad we—"

Abruptly, she stopped.

"What?" I asked. I stood on my toes, craning to see what had halted her. In the living room, reclining back on the sofa, was a man watching television.

"What are you doing here?" Lynn said, stepping into the house.

The man stood and turned off the TV. "What do you think? I wanted to see you."

"Wrong answer," Lynn said, crossing her arms.

"I don't know what else you want me to say, kid. That's the truth."

The man had a deep voice, weighted with weariness, as though he were accustomed to fighting off suspicion. I could understand why; though at first glance he seemed well put-together—tall and thin except for a small gut that protruded above his belt buckle—I sensed a roughness escaping in unexpected places: the tug of his tucked-in T-shirt, the faded ink of his tattooed arms.

"Who's your friend?" he said after a moment. He must have seen me gawking and my body bristled with tension, though I wasn't sure why. He reached out to shake my hand. The start of a smile softened his face.

"Don't talk to her," Lynn snapped.

"Whatever you want," he said, hand falling. I watched his fist open and close.

"I want you to leave. I didn't see your shitty car out there, so I guess you'll have to walk."

"I got a new one," the man said, brightening. "Used, technically. But new for me."

Lynn's eyes crackled with distrust. "Technically?"

"If you don't believe me, check the papers. It's the Ford right out there." He dug the keys from his back pocket and offered them to us.

"Not interested."

The man laughed sadly. "Come on, kid. I'm trying here."

"Oh, I'm sorry," Lynn said, "but you don't just get to show up here and expect me to welcome you with a hug."

"I didn't come here for that. I just wanted to talk. So much has changed in the last year. Let me buy you a cup of coffee—both of you." He looked at me again. I felt my lips parting, the urge to speak.

"How'd you even get in here?" Lynn asked.

"This was my house too, Lynn."

"Give me the key."

"I'm not trying to move in, but I do have rights—"

"None of this belongs to you," she said. "We don't owe you anything."

The man scratched his neck. "You can't keep punishing me forever."

"That's not for you to decide." Lynn stepped back, exposing the doorway, and put out her hand. "You can either give me the key or we'll change the locks. Your choice."

I took a step backward then, too, not for any particular reason other than to get out of the way, but the man must have taken my action as an emphasis of Lynn's because he glanced down at his keychain and began twisting one of the small bronze keys from its ring.

"I'm not going to leave it like this, kid," the man said, shaking his head. "You think you're always right about me, but not this time."

Lynn's lips were taut, her body tightened in a way that reminded me of a toy set on springs. I'd never seen her like that before— wholly affected, and trying so hard not to be. Or maybe that's not right; maybe it wasn't really the first time I had encountered her vulnerability, just the first time I'd had no choice but to see.

The man placed his key in Lynn's open palm before passing through the door. On the porch he glanced back, just for a moment, and I was surprised to find that the look wasn't for her. Instead, his eyes found me.

For the next few moments, until his car rolled out of view, I stood frozen.

"Let's go to the thrift store or something," Lynn said, swiping at her cheek with the back of her hand. "I just—I need to get out of here."

"Okay."

Without another word, Lynn led us to her car.

We drove with the radio down low. Lynn stared straight ahead. In profile, without the full coverage of her sunglasses, I could see that her eyes were spiderwebbed with red.

I still sometimes wonder how it all might have turned out, had I just been able to keep pretending. But I couldn't. My mind flooded with the image of the man's final glance, gray and nebulous, saturated with lament for a past he could not change but begging anyway, begging *me*—knowing in some abstract way that I would want to give him another chance.

"That was your dad," I said, voice clouded with disbelief. But something about hearing the words aloud caused my body to react with a throb of recognition, and I had to knot my hands in my lap, fix my eyes on the road ahead of us, just to keep steady. "Your dad is alive."

The truth hovered between us, dense and impenetrable—though part of me expected, even wanted, her to deny it.

She said, "Not to me."

"Lynn," I said, with more force now. "You told me he was dead."

"He's been gone for most of my life. Saying he's dead is easier than trying to explain. It had nothing to do with you."

"This whole time, you've been acting like you knew what I was going through. But you don't. Your dad is here. He wants to be in your life."

"So? He's never going to change, and I'm not still the little kid who waits around for him to come home, to pick me up and take me wherever the fuck he said he would. It's done." Lynn secured the steering wheel with her knee and rolled up the sleeve on her right arm before offering it to me, elbow down, fist clenched. Her skin was unblemished except for a tiny series of ripples near the top of the forearm, about an inch below the elbow's bend. "You see that? Doesn't look like much now, but it hurt a hell of a lot at the time."

"What happened?" I asked.

"Daddy dearest dozed off with a cigarette in his hand, decided to use me as an ashtray."

"But it was an accident, right? He didn't do it on purpose."

Lynn scoffed. "Sure. An accident."

As she tugged her sleeve back down, I thought about all the nights I had lain awake in bed waiting for my father, listening to the Santa Anas as they whirled down from the canyons. I thought about the nights he did come home, drenched in the scent of whiskey, someone else's voice still ringing in his ear. The way his hand slammed against my shoulder that final night. His eyes glistening with tears in the red-hot darkness.

And I swear I tried to understand why Lynn would refuse any possibility of reconciliation with her dad. I really did. But I would have switched places with her in a heartbeat. I'd have taken a thousand more disappointments if only my own father were still alive.

She pulled into a parking lot and turned off her ignition. For the first time since we left her house, she looked at me. "Do you want an apology or something? Okay, fine, I'm sorry. I didn't plan on ever seeing the scumbag again, and definitely didn't think he'd have the audacity to show up at my house. If I could take it back, I would. All right?"

It would have been hypocritical of me to not forgive Lynn when chastising her for not forgiving, so I did.

At least I meant to.

TWENTY

JUST WHEN I thought my search was over and I had finally exhausted all the roads that might lead back to my father, I received an unexpected text from Cameron. It was simple, totally lacking in congeniality, and yet I felt my heart slip out of rhythm when I read it, because it was the exact message that I had stopped hoping for.

He wrote: *We're playing the Troubadour on Saturday.*

It was April, and this was the most he had willingly texted me in a month. His brevity, of course, was still upsetting, but I refused to let his waning interest affect me now. The Troubadour was too important.

The mere possibility of being there, on the same stage that

hosted the debut of Buffalo Springfield and enabled the formation of the Byrds—the stage where my parents first glimpsed each other—glittered in my mind with a brilliance so stultifying that I couldn't focus on anything else, and I nearly convinced myself something had to go wrong. Even as we drove up the 5, the boys, Lynn, Josie, and me all smushed in the van between amps and various pieces of Luke's drum kit, I was certain the frequent chirping of Cameron's phone meant bad news. But we kept creeping forward, winnowing through pockets of afternoon traffic. And then, after what felt like hours, we arrived, unloaded our equipment, set up for sound check, and repeated "Check-one-two" into our mics, gazing out into the strange luster of the empty room as we breezed through the opening verse of "Coastal Blues": *Tell me your secrets so that I can tell you the things you already know. . . .*

"All right guys," the invisible sound engineer said through the monitors, halting us. "You're good to go."

The boys pushed their equipment aside and ambled toward the bar, the same way they would at any other venue. I stayed on the stage. The Troubadour was known for its intimacy, yet the room was so much smaller than I'd imagined, grungy almost, with dark wood-paneled walls and the stench of beer hanging in the air. Near the front entrance, a mess of torn posters advertised upcoming gigs. Bands had been making history here for decades, but instead of feeling exhilarated by all that had been sweated and beaten and bled into this stage, an ache gathered in the center of my chest. I was finally here, at the pinnacle. The literal origin point of my existence. But it felt just like everywhere else.

Disappointment ricocheted through me, so sharp and

unexpected that my eyes welled. I didn't understand; I'd felt the electric energy of this place just listening to my father's stories, so why did I feel so disconnected now? I closed my eyes, lifted my face to the warm glow of the overhead lights. I tried to imagine what he'd felt when he stood here, tried to imagine the flutter in his chest when he first glimpsed my mother's blond hair haloed by that broken spotlight in an otherwise imperceptible crowd. Maybe that was the problem—the doors weren't open yet, the lights weren't down. Maybe when the room dimmed and the crowd swelled, when the music was so loud that it drowned out the pounding of my heartbeat . . .

"Watch out," someone growled, lugging a guitar case and an Orange amp head up to the stage. Behind me another band was setting up for their sound check.

"Sorry," I mumbled.

At the bar, I ordered a Coke and pulled out my cell phone, opened a message to Nick. I couldn't think of anything clever or poetic to say, so I wrote, *You'll never believe what is happening.* Then, too anxious to wait for his reply, I added, *My band is playing the Troubadour tonight!*

A minute passed without response. Sighing, I put my phone away and looked around for Josie and Lynn, only to have my eyes hook on the rough, unmistakable profile of Cody Winters.

So that was how we got here.

Cody was talking to Cameron, something about set times. I'd only been watching them a moment when Cody's eyes flicked to me and I felt the air pull tight between us. I remembered the heat of his mouth, the way our bodies fit together and the salty taste of his skin. Then I remembered the party in Lemon Heights, and how Cameron had pulled away from me. How I hadn't been enough.

Cody smiled at me, an almost indiscernible movement, and I wondered what it would be like to sleep with him again—what it would be like if this time, everyone found out. From our split-second glance, I knew he'd want to, but right then he was talking to Cameron and I felt sick just standing there, watching the two of them, waiting for the sun to recede and the sky to grow black while I drank my complimentary Coke, maybe chased it with swigs from a flask in the bathroom, as Lynn and Josie must have been doing, tumbling now out of the hallway with vociferous laughter.

"First band doesn't start for an hour," I said, approaching them. "Smoke?"

Together with Luke and Gabriel, we emerged back into sunlight, walked down to the corner where we'd seen a small, triangular slice of a park. Heading toward the fountain in the center, I dug around in my purse for loose change. My father and I used to always do that, offer our spare pennies and nickels to fountains in exchange for a wish. He'd nestle me into his hip and say, "I think we're getting the better end of the bargain, don't you?" even though we were broke and neither of our wishes ever came true.

"Do you know who's played here?" Gabriel asked, lighting one of Luke's hand-rolled cigarettes.

There, at the bottom of my purse, a quarter: the meager tip Cody had given me all those months ago. At one time, I had cherished the bumps and ridges of the coin's surface. Now, I knew it was just a dirty piece of metal.

"Bruce Springsteen," Gabriel continued. "Fleetwood Mac."

"Metallica," Josie said.

"Metallica?" Luke questioned as he sat in the grass opposite us.

"So I had a metal phase. Don't judge me." She pulled a water bottle filled with brown liquid from her bag and sat on the rim of the fountain.

"Guns N' Roses," Lynn said, snatching the bottle from Josie with a grin.

"Poco," Luke countered.

"Van Morrison," Gabriel added.

"My father," I said, and flicked the quarter. They turned to look at me but I aimed my gaze at the fountain, pretending to notice only the tiny plunk of the coin smacking water.

"Dude," Gabriel said. He stared at me with unusual focus. "Van Morrison's your father?"

Lynn and Josie burst into laughter. On the opposite end of the park, a man who'd been napping beneath the shade of a jacaranda turned over, smashing a dirty sweatshirt against his ears.

"What?" Gabriel asked.

"No," Josie said in the deep, drawling baritone of Darth Vader, "I am your father."

She held her arms out in front of her like a zombie and Lynn's laughter escalated. I tried to laugh too. Though it may not have been obvious to the others, my friendship with Lynn had remained strained since I met her father. We still hung out almost every day, but our interactions were tense and hesitant, often punctuated by awkward stretches of silence. I didn't think I could handle any more of it. I'd lost so much already—my father, my old friends, my old life—and everything I had now, everything I'd become, was tied to her.

So when she smiled at me, her expression soft with familiar ease, I smiled too. I just wanted to go back to the way things were.

She handed me the water bottle and I took a bold, burning sip, allowing the whiskey's warmth to cocoon me. I sat down next to her.

"I just meant that my father has played here," I told Gabriel.

"Oh. That's cool. Not as cool as Van Morrison being your dad, but still pretty awesome."

"When?" Luke asked.

He was facing away from us, examining the unending traffic on Santa Monica Boulevard, and for a moment, I wasn't even certain he was talking to me.

"I'm not sure of the exact dates. A number of times in the nineties."

"They were really good," Lynn said. "Imagine if Joe Cocker had a love child with Paul McCartney, and that child was raised by, like, Cheap Trick."

Josie shook her head. "You lost me at love child."

"Why didn't you ever tell us about him?" Gabriel asked.

"I thought I had," I said, but of course, the only person I'd told was Cameron. He was the only person I had told a lot of things. The rest of the boys must have known very little about me.

Luke turned to me. A tiny thrill crept across my skin. "What were they called?"

"The Vital Spades."

He tapped his ash into the grass, nodding.

"You've heard of them?" I asked.

He shrugged as if to say, *Maybe.*

"They broke up right on the verge of a major record deal," I said, compelled to explain, "so they only ever released small-press EPs. Limited runs." With my fingers, I plucked at the tears in my tights as if they were guitar strings. "Isn't it weird? Back then the internet barely existed, and if your band broke up, everything was gone. Now, the music can still live online forever. I guess we're all lucky in that way. Pretty much everything the Spades had is gone by now."

"Except you," Lynn said, resting her head on my shoulder.

"I don't think I count," I said.

"It all counts."

I sighed, hoping she was right.

"Speaking of recording," Josie said, "what's the deal with Cody's guy? Has he set dates yet?"

"Should be soon," Gabriel said. "He wants to finish up with Deerskin Ocean before we lay anything down. Says he doesn't like to be in two sounds at once."

My pulse quickened. Recording? With Cody's guy? No one had mentioned this to me.

Josie and Gabriel continued talking about the band Deerskin Ocean. Across from us, Luke reclined in the grass. His demeanor did not suggest that I had purposely been left out of the recording conversations, but Luke's demeanor rarely revealed anything. He always seemed so quiet, uninterested, and I had started to question whether he merely feigned detachment. He must have been

317

scrutinizing Cameron and me for months before I ran into him at that party, noticing what I didn't—what I couldn't. I wondered if Luke sensed it now, the interminable ache I felt for Cameron despite (or perhaps because) I was losing him. I wondered what else he'd been able to glean.

Above us, the sky had mellowed into a dusky mauve. Because there were no clouds to catch the rays of light, I knew the night would be dark and clear. Perhaps I would even be able to see Orion. Next to me, Lynn lit a cigarette and squinted out in the direction of the setting sun. She appeared to be looking at Luke, too, and I wanted to know what she'd heard about Cameron and me. Probably everything. She had predicted this, after all.

"He doesn't like me anymore," I said softly, so that only Lynn could hear.

A moment of silence passed between us, and then she offered me her cigarette. I inhaled, so grateful for the staggering lightness slipping through me that when she finally spoke, voice almost inaudible against the whoosh of evening traffic, it took a few seconds before I understood. "You and me both," she had said. And maybe it's selfish, but in the moment, I didn't really care who she was talking about. I found comfort in the fact that she felt the same way I did, because the only thing worse than suffering is having to suffer alone.

The Endless West played second that night. Everything began as planned. Onstage, Luke unearthed the tambourine from the depths of his suitcase and handed it to me—a preshow ritual that we'd engaged in ever since my debut on New Year's Eve. Then he led us in with four counts on the kick. Our set list was solid, the same five songs as always, with the same transitions and a variation of the same interlude banter. And yet, from the very first verse of "Coastal Blues," I knew. Something had changed.

At first I assumed the shift was just a result of that day, my already-edgy emotions altering what would have otherwise been a decent performance. And I really do believe that if we'd been anywhere other than the Troubadour—if this had been any other show, any other venue, any other night—I might have never noticed anything wrong.

But this wasn't any other show. I knew exactly where we were.

The room had filled in during the first band, and from the stage it looked like a black, swirling ocean. Before, that view had always fascinated me; no matter how many people were in the crowd, whether three or three hundred, you couldn't really see them, transformed into phantoms by the angle of the lights. Most of the time, I lost track of the crowd completely. That night, though, I gazed out from the stage more than usual.

This is the truth: I was still searching for my father, for answers, for the past. For the stripe of a broken spotlight that had long ago been fixed.

Instead, I saw face after face alighting behind cell phones. I saw bodies crashing into each other like storm-churned waves. I kept singing, forcing the words to barrel out of me as they always had, but for the first time I felt truly apart from them. And nobody—not even the boys—twitched when Alex accidentally repeated the first verse of "Runaway" for a whole two bars before correcting himself, or when Cameron dropped his pick during the solo of

"Coming with Me" and tried to overcompensate, hitting a handful of muted notes. It was as though no one else was actually paying attention. As though they hadn't been listening at all.

And maybe they weren't. People came to see the Endless West because they wanted a good show, to have a good time, to get wasted. The boys, too, coveted these things, and even I'd had a lot to drink that night, most nights, becoming used to the way whiskey calmed my nerves and gave me courage. I beat the tambourine against my palm. I could barely feel the impact.

But when was the last time any of the boys had written a new song?

When had I?

The week of the rainstorm, I hadn't even been able to play the Martin for more than fifteen minutes because my hands had grown too soft and awkward. When I pressed my fingers against the strings, I felt like I was a child again, sitting in my father's studio beneath an instrument I couldn't decipher—only my father was gone, and the studio was gone, and his final tape was gone. Everything he'd had, gone. Except me.

We ended that night with "Don't Look Back." The song hadn't been recorded yet, but somehow, over the months, a surprising number of people in the crowd had learned the beat. They knew when to clap their hands, when to speed up, when to stomp the ground and thrust their fists in the air. They'd even learned my lyrics, chanted the chorus like an anthem. I waited for elation to fill me up, to buoy me like helium in a balloon, but as the crowd kept singing, projecting my lyrics back across the narrow room, the words turned hollow and tasteless in my mouth. I knew then that my song, with its once weepy guitar and raw, windblown melodies, no longer existed. "Don't Look Back" had transformed into something else.

When our set was finally done, I threw the tambourine in Luke's suitcase and helped him carry his drum kit out to the van, deflecting the usual post-set pleasantries. I used to thrive on these tiny approvals, however routine they might have been. But this time the words ignited in me a quiet, smoldering rage. It wasn't a great set. The boys fucked up. I fucked up. Luke was the only one who didn't, and thank God for that, because if the drumbeat had crumbled, we'd have had nothing left to hold us together.

As we finished wrestling our equipment into a Tetris-like configuration in the back of the van, I wanted to tell Luke how grateful I was. He shut the trunk. Alex and Cameron had already gone back inside. Gabriel was smushing the butt of a cigarette beneath his shoe, angling toward the Troubadour's back door, obviously waiting for us. I turned to Luke, blinking, my lips pulled taut.

Somehow, I knew he understood.

He tilted his head toward the venue. "Coming in?"

I nodded, and followed them inside.

We had just merged back into the sway of people when I heard someone say my name. I swerved around, unsure of where the sound had come from. Even between sets the room remained dark, and so many people were packed together, some raspy punk band straining from the house stereo. My eyes swung past a scraggly blond curtain of hair. I kept walking.

Then, my name again, more certain this time, and the shock of fingertips grazing my forearm.

"Have you forgotten me already, Hayes?"

"Nick," I said, stunned to find him in front of me—stunned that I'd looked right past him. "What are you doing here?"

"I got your text," he said. "Surprise."

I shook my head, momentarily confused. Then I remembered: I'd texted him after sound check. At the time, I'd just expected him to be excited for me, for his own enthusiasm to reinvigorate my own. I never imagined he would actually come—yet here he was, solid and real and exactly how I'd remembered him all these months, his chlorine-curled hair, a glaze of freckles bridging his nose. The sight of him in that moment produced such profound comfort that I smiled, even though my insides felt tangled and torn apart. I leaned in for a hug. "It's so good to see you."

The warmth of his voice sinuated my ear. "I want to kiss you," I thought he said.

"What?"

"I've really missed you. And when you said you were here?" He grinned, eyes sparkling like the surface of water. "There's no way I'd have skipped this. You were amazing up there."

I bit the inside of my lip, fighting the urge to tell Nick everything I felt onstage that night, because "everything" also included Cameron—someone I'd conveniently never mentioned to him. I said, "It wasn't our greatest set."

"Well, from out here, it sounded pretty damn good. And that last one"—Nick whistled— "I remember those lyrics."

"You do?"

He nodded. "I read them in the Last Bean. Had to tear them

out of your hand first, though."

I laughed. "That was so long ago."

"Yeah, but how could I forget gold-record material like that?"

"You should have heard it originally," I said. "It was really beautiful, and really different from what the band played tonight. Just acoustic guitar and vocals, with this great dueling harmony between us."

"Who's 'us'?" Nick asked.

A flush flared in my cheeks. "The lead guitarist," I said, as evenly as possible.

"Ah." His mouth pushed into a tight line.

I said, "No one knows I wrote it."

"Why not?"

I shrugged, felt something tug in my gut. It was such a simple, impossible question. "I guess the origins just never come up. It's the band's song now, so people probably assume the band wrote it together."

Even as I said this, I knew it wasn't true. People probably thought Cameron wrote the whole song, as he'd written all the others. And people probably saw me as nothing more than a tambourine player, an unnecessary flourish. Not a real musician. Not a songwriter.

"Well, I know you wrote it," Nick said. "I'm really proud of you, Hayes. And really impressed. Like father, like daughter, right?"

Up onstage, the next drummer started beating his tom while the other band members checked their tunes. My eyes bounced from one to the next, some distant awareness yanking at me.

Something about the front man, in particular. He was tall, gangly. As he tucked his long hair behind his ears, I couldn't shake the certainty that I knew him.

"School doesn't feel the same without you," Nick said.

"That's probably just your senioritis."

"Maybe. I honestly can't wait for this year to end. Did I tell you? I just received acceptances from USC and Chapman. I'm still waiting to hear back from a few places, but at least I'm going to college, you know? It's all starting to finally feel real."

"You were always going to college," I said. "But I'm really happy for you, Nick. Congratulations."

"What about you? Heard back from any schools yet?"

"A few," I lied, realizing for the first time that I hadn't received a single letter from any of the schools I'd hastily applied to. Rejections wouldn't have surprised me, but the lack of any response seemed, suddenly, alarming. "I'm not sure what I want to do yet, though," I added.

"Hey, everyone," the singer called from the stage. "Thanks for coming out. We're Los Funerals."

And then his voice pealed across the room, gruff and atmospheric, backed at first only by the sultry reverb of simple chords on his guitar. With eyes scrunched tight, he let the words overpower him: *It's old news now that everyone has done you wrong.* On the far right, the pianist began striking spiky, off-kilter keys. Each vibration pulsed through the floor, piercing me with a jab of movement: the twitch.

"Have you heard this band before?" I asked Nick.

"No, have you?"

I shook my head. I didn't think so.

In between songs, Nick and I attempted to talk by shouting in each other's ear. He told me about his final water polo season, his continued patronage at the Last Bean, and the short film he'd worked on to advertise the school's annual spring carnival, which raised a record amount of funds that year.

"The treasurer must've been thrilled," I said then.

"She was," he agreed.

"How's Cara doing?"

"Good. Really good. She got into Berkeley."

"That's incredible! Berkeley's been in her top five since we were in, like, seventh grade. I can't believe—"

But I didn't finish the thought, because that's when Lynn appeared at my side. She tossed her arm across my shoulders, her voice booming into my ear. "I've been looking for you," she said. "Hey, who's your friend?"

For a moment I hesitated, but there was no escaping the introduction now. "This is Nick, from my old school. Nick, Lynn."

"Nice to meet you," he said, reaching across me to shake her hand.

"Likewise." She flashed a smile as their fingers intertwined.

I interjected myself between their grip. "What's up?"

"I just thought you should know," Lynn said, leaning into my ear. Her breath was sharp, biting.

"Know what?"

She placed her hands on my shoulders and spun me around, guiding my sight in the direction of the bar. In the far corner, I spotted Cameron pressed up against some girl. I couldn't see her face. He dipped forward, spoke into her ear, and she threw her head back, laughing.

"I don't know what's going on," Lynn said, "but I didn't want you to go over there and get sideswiped. Maybe he's just doing the same thing you are."

The last chord of a song rang out, filling the room with its echo. I could not peel my eyes away. "I'm not doing anything."

"You and Surfer Boy sure looked—"

"He's just a friend," I said, and though I hated the thought, it emerged anyway: Would Cameron be jealous if he saw me with Nick?

I doubted it. Nick was a stranger, an outsider. But Cody . . .

My eyes flicked around the room in search of him, only to remember that Fire Society was playing last. Cody must have been upstairs somewhere, preparing.

I shook my head, ashamed at the course of my thoughts.

"Fine," Lynn said. "Whatever. I'm on your side. I'm just saying that if it was me, I'd want to know."

"Would you?" I said, but the singer started talking again, and Lynn did not seem to hear me.

"We've got one more for you tonight," he announced, and I veered my attention back to the stage. I'd been expecting this, I reminded myself, imagining Cameron with another girl for weeks—and yet the foresight made no difference. In the end, the reality was still crushing.

"You okay?" Nick asked.

"Fine," I said.

"This is a very special song, written by a brilliant artist who passed away a couple months ago. Before he died, he said we should play it *every goddam show*"—laughter pierced the air, and my vision snapped into focus—"so that's what we're doing."

The singer put one fist to his chest and angled his face toward the ceiling, where his features caught the light. I looked to the bassist—but no, he wasn't familiar. Nor the drummer in the back. Then, there, on lead guitar. Though his round face was mostly hidden now behind facial hair, I could still make out the faint traces of acne scars, and suddenly, I saw the two of them as clearly as if they'd been standing on the curb in front of my old house.

Lance and Travis.

Lance said, "This one's for you, man," and around him, the band launched into the song. The crowd cheered and whistled. On my left, Nick might have said something, or maybe he just cleared his throat. All I could hear were my father's lyrics coming out of Lance's mouth:

> *I'll give you all my love, honey,*
> *pull the moon down from above,*
> *but I know that it will never be enough*
> *to make you see you are everything—*
> *you are everything to me.*

My lips moved involuntarily, unable to deny my father's words, but I was shocked to find I wasn't the only one singing. Smashed up against the front of the stage, with hands thrusting wildly in the air, a whole group of people shouted the lyrics. The clamor of their voices sawed through me; I thought about my mother, the unidentified muse, my pulse darting as her lyrics flung around the room. Behind my eyelids, I saw the girl in the photograph: a twenty-year-old ghost who had no idea that loving my father meant she would be forever frozen in the shadows of his stage.

Although my mouth continued moving through the entire song, the rest of me had stiffened with an anger so pronounced it felt physical. Only after Lance said, "Stick around, Fire Society is up next!" and the crowd started loosening did I regain my motion.

After that, everything happened quickly.

I shoved my way through the horde, toward the stage where Travis was lacing a cord through the hook of his thumb and down around his elbow.

"Hey!" I yelled. Despite the punk music raging once again from the speakers and the contending buzz of conversations in the crowd, he heard me, turned around. A glint of recognition crossed his face.

"Oh, hey," he said. "Cool set earlier. You guys have a good style."

"You can't play that," I snapped.

"Play what?"

"'Love Honey.' It's not yours."

"We're not trying to steal credit," he said through an unsettled smile before tugging another cord from his pedal board. "Bands cover songs all the time, and most of them don't even have permission."

"Neither do you!"

"Whoa," Lance said, crossing the stage. He glanced, confused, between Travis and me. "What's going on?"

"We were there," Travis said to me. "Just days before he died. He told us to keep the song alive, like he knew something was going to happen."

"You don't know anything about him!" I shouted. They didn't know anything at all—not the way my mother looked beneath that spotlight, or when my father pulled her into his arms, twirled her around the kitchen, and whispered in her ear. They didn't know how he used to pick me up and sing "Love Honey" to me when I couldn't fall asleep, the sway of his arms how I imagined waves would feel out in the middle of the ocean. And they didn't know I'd covered "Love Honey" myself, that I was actually proud of it, and that I abandoned it before ever even showing anyone. But most of all, they didn't know what I felt right then with devastating certainty: that my father would have been more proud of them than me.

In some very real, very visceral way, I understood I had no right to hate them. I couldn't blame Lance and Travis for anything that happened, for stealing a song they hadn't actually stolen, for doing exactly what my father had asked. But I did anyway. I blamed them for all of it, because in that moment, it was easier than blaming myself.

"You have no fucking clue what was going through his head," I continued, "or what he wanted. He probably only kept you around to feel better about himself."

Lance laughed—a harsh sound, crisp with hostility. "And what the hell do you know about it?"

That's when it hit me: they had absolutely no idea who I really was, only recognizing me from the Endless West's set an hour earlier. Last summer, Lance and Travis had been such a prominent presence in my life, lingering like a giant thorn in the flesh of my relationship with my father. But to them, I was nothing.

My anger boiled over, drumming in my ears. I said, "I'm his daughter, you asshole."

I felt a hot pull of gratification when both their faces blanched.

"Come on, kid," said the security guard who had appeared, suddenly, next to me. "I think you need some air."

He gripped my upper arm—a gentle grip, admittedly, there to guide more than force, but I wrenched myself free of him. "Get off me!"

"Watch it," he warned, seizing me again with greater strength. He steered me away from the stage.

"You didn't know him," I yelled over my shoulder. "He didn't leave you anything."

As the security guard escorted me from the room, I noticed that a few people nearby had halted their conversations in order to stare. I tried to twist loose, but my effort was futile; we reached the front and the security guard waited with stiff, knotted arms until I huffed through the door.

Emerging, bleary-eyed, out into the night, my shoulder knocked into someone. "Hey!" he yelled, but I didn't stop. Traffic zoomed down Santa Monica, smearing taillights through the dark as I veered west. Above me, smog smothered the stars. Not sure what else to do, I turned the corner and swung into the alley behind the venue where our van was parked.

"Susannah," a voice called, and I thought instantly: *Nick*. He must have followed me. Relief fluttered in my chest as my head swarmed with images of the next few seconds (collapsing in his arms), the next few months (entwined on a tiny dorm bed). I scanned the darkness for his blond flop of hair. My eyes caught on the sparkling orange tip of a cigarette.

"You all right?"

Shadows danced across the ridges of Luke's face and I stared at him, mute. A flicker of worry clouded his expression—something I'd never before glimpsed.

"It's okay," he said, reaching toward me. The rough pad of his thumb slipped across my cheek, clearing the tears. I closed my eyes.

So much was already clashing inside of me, and I didn't have the strength to question his touch or the rapid swell beneath my rib cage. When he asked what had happened, I shook my head. What could I say? The harder I fought for something—anything—to hold on to, the further away stability always seemed. I'd been searching for my father all over Los Angeles, in the creases of record sleeves and the patterns of songs on the radio. I'd been certain that some clue would rise up from the bottom of the emptying whiskey bottle each time I took a swig. But he was really gone. No matter what I did, or how hard I looked, or how many fragments of his past I found and wound together, there would always be a wilderness of what I didn't know.

I cupped my palm around Luke's hand and pressed it harder against my face. The heat of his skin felt electrifying.

"It'll be okay," he said, words floating almost inaudibly on the cusp of his breath. The scent of embers wafted from his tongue.

I leaned forward.

In a way, what happened next was as unimaginable as a room full of people singing a song my father had written about my mother as though they, too, could hear his voice jangling through every facet of their memory. And yet, I wasn't really all that surprised when Luke met me there.

TWENTY-ONE

THE CAR RIDE home was quiet. I sat in the back row of seats with Gabriel, exactly where, not quite two hours earlier, Luke and I had tumbled into each other. We hadn't even fully undressed then, our limbs too clumsy, too impatient as we'd clambered into the backseat. Already, the whole night felt a lifetime away—or maybe that was a mere effect of the pot, which Luke had dug out of the glove compartment once we'd finished, sprinkling the green pebbles atop crispy wisps of tobacco before rolling it all into a tight cigarette that tasted not like the aftermath of a fire but like the spark had just started. Other than the secondhand highs I'd experienced in Lynn's living room, I'd never actually been stoned before, and I let my body sink fully into the sweet weight of lethargy. My mind slipped through a state of half sleep, allowing only simple sensations to reach me: the strange tinge coating my teeth and the incomprehensible heaviness of my limbs. The remote tendrils of Cody Winters's voice wending out of the venue and down the alleyway toward me, like the edge of a dream.

But now Luke was driving, and I was so exhausted that I felt brutally awake. In front of me, Josie snored shamelessly. Because of construction, the 5 Freeway had tapered down to two lanes and I stared at the directional flares as we rolled forward, each slow bump of road pitching my stomach into my throat. Though I'd planned to stay at Lynn's house, as I often did when I knew we would be out far later than curfew, I did not think I could bear anything now other than my own room. My own bed.

"I don't feel great," I announced to no one in particular. "Do you mind dropping me off at home?"

I'd expected grumbles, or perhaps even disappointment. No one responded—not Cameron, who was bobbing his head to the Los Funerals CD that seeped from the stereo, or even Lynn, who rested her cheek against the cool glass of her window, feigning sleep.

"Luke," I said, a flush rising in my cheeks as though his name in my mouth would reveal everything. "Is that all right?"

For an instant, our eyes met in the rearview mirror. Then he shrugged. "Fine with me."

I tilted my head back, anxious for sleep. Though I tried to think of nothing, tried to aim my focus on a universe of blank, white, untouched space, guilt gnawed at my periphery. My mind sprang for the hundredth time to Nick. I opened my phone, reread the hail of text messages he'd sent, which I saw only after we were back on the road—the appropriate time for rectification having long since passed:

Come back soon, Hayes—I'm wandering lonely as a cloud out here.

Where are you?

Are you okay? I'm kind of worried. Lynn said she'd also look for you, so if she finds you first, I'm still by the stairs.

Look, I'm sorry if you didn't want me to come tonight. Maybe I just misinterpreted everything, but I really thought you wanted to see me, so if that's not the case, then please, just tell me.

I'm going to leave. See you around, I guess.

Even after the construction zone finally ended, after Luke dropped me at the corner of my street, after I stumbled up the driveway and began hoisting open my unlocked bedroom window, Nick's texts still tormented me. I tried to conjure excuses and explanations, the magic combination of words that could fix what I'd done, but part of me also thought that I deserved this. I'd hurt the one person I could always count on. My mind lurched with the single, agonizing, pointless wish that Nick had been in that alley instead.

The thought was only severed when my foot caught the bedroom's windowsill, and I toppled, clamorous, into my room.

I had just stood up again when the door sailed open. The lights leapt on. Instinctively, my face dipped down, an arm rising to shield my eyes from the cruel exposure of the lamps.

"Mom," I gasped. "I can explain."

But the voice that thundered back was not my mother's: "I

should damn well hope so."

"Vivian?" I put my arm down, eyes fluttering to thwart the brightness.

"How many times must we discuss this?" Vivian asked. She appeared frail in her white silk nightgown, hair matted on the left side from her pillow. "I don't care what you say to your friends, but when you are in my presence, you will not refer to me by my first name. It's disrespectful."

"I'm sorry," I stuttered, too bewildered to remind her that she'd basically told me not to call her Grandma on the first day we met. I was about to try "Mrs. Crane," the most reverent choice I could think of, but Vivian spoke again: "What in God's name are you wearing?"

She was staring at the runs that climbed up my tights from my knees to the hem of my dress. My fingers instinctively touched my thigh.

"They're just tights," I said.

"You look like a two-bit hooker."

A smile caught the corner of my mouth. Admittedly, there was a certain sexuality to the tears in my tights, the visible slivers of skin—but little seemed more horrifying than discussing my sexuality with Vivian, so I simply said, "I guess we just have different concepts of fashion."

She sat down on the edge of my bed, shaking her head. "Where did I go wrong with you?"

"I don't really think you have anything to do with what's wrong with me," I told her.

"I know you were with that boy again."

My heart plunged. "Boy?"

"I'm not completely oblivious."

My eyes roved helplessly around the room in search of an explanation. It was still, all things considered, a guest bedroom, blank and impersonal. I had no secret boxes of notes under the bed, no private diary or incriminating mementos shoved to the bottom of my underwear drawer. Briefly, I thought of my lyric journals, which were accessible in a messy stack at the corner of the desk, but those wouldn't have given away any concrete evidence. I crossed my arms over my chest, trying to anchor myself. The weed was still lapping through my blood. "It's not what you think."

"All those boys are after one thing," she said, "and this Roger is no different."

"Rog—?" The name snagged in my throat. "Did you just say Roger?"

"Don't tell me there's already another."

My mouth dropped open. "You think," I said carefully, "that I was out with Roger."

"Colleen Johnson saw you kissing in the hallways."

"Colleen Johnson," I repeated.

"Mrs. Johnson, the administrative secretary." She brought her fingers to her temples and began rubbing in a circular motion. "Eleanor Johnson's mother."

The names still meant nothing to me, but as I scrambled to find some frayed strand of logic in the net of an otherwise stymieing conversation, Vivian spoke again, exasperated. "You know Eleanor. Her father gave you your first horseback riding lesson."

A flurry of conflicting emotions tore through me. "I'm not—" I began, but then some instinct that I couldn't quite identify, or maybe just the deep trill of disquiet that was expanding inside my stomach, stopped me from continuing. I shook my head, felt the irrepressible urge to start over. "Of course," I said, barely able to control the quaking in my voice. "Eleanor Johnson's mother. I'd forgotten for a moment."

"You're too young," she said.

"Too young for what?"

"How can you possibly know whether or not he'll be good for you?"

I paused, trying to radiate calm. Trying to act like my mother. "I know he's a good man," I said.

Vivian scoffed. "He's hardly a man."

"He *will be* a good man," I amended, this time with more certainty, "and he's going to make someone very happy one day. I'm sure of that."

"He's not good enough," Vivian said, and despite myself—despite the night and the conversation and the position I'd unwittingly found myself in—I smiled. She may have had valid reasons for being suspicious of my father, but it was obvious now that she had set the bar unreasonably high. If Roger Tipton could not have passed her test back then, no one could.

I sat down next to her on the bed. "You'd say that about anyone."

"What are his plans?" she demanded, turning her head just enough to look at me.

"He wants to be a teacher. He's really smart, and he's compassionate—"

"He should come to the door," she interrupted. "Not make you sneak out in the middle of the night."

"I'll invite him over, then. I know he would love to meet you."

"He hasn't made a very good first impression."

"Give him another chance," I said. "Please."

Vivian brought a bony hand back up to her forehead where a parabola of sweat glistened. "Only if you promise to start obeying the rules of this house," she said. "I'll be damned if I let you screw up your life while you're living under my roof, understand?"

I nodded, aware of a loosening in my limbs, the physical relief.

"No more lies," Vivian said.

"No more lies," I echoed, and wished, achingly, that I could mean it.

Vivian sighed. "Let's not concern your father over this," she said then, standing. A brief, tight smile crossed her face. "The poor man is working himself to the bone. He's always so tired these days."

As she spoke, a new swell of fear dazed me. The night had me so twisted around that I nearly forgot who we were, when we were, had to physically repress the urge to shout, *He's not tired, he's sick—please take him to the hospital!* For an instant, I actually thought that if I acknowledged the signs and took the precautions, maybe I could save him.

Then, without warning, all the worry and the sadness fell away, replaced by a soft, blanketing equilibrium. In the morning,

I knew, everything would change—but right now, wherever we were in Vivian's memory, David Crane, my grandfather, was still alive, and I wanted her to keep him for as long as possible.

"No," I agreed. "Let's not worry him tonight."

My eyelids pulled apart to a white morning, bright and fresh as stretched canvas. I wasn't sure how long I'd been sleeping but it felt early, the sun-dusted air hushed with the quiet of dawn. After flopping uselessly around my bed for a while, I got up and washed my face, brushed my teeth, attempting to scrub the tissue-paper taste from my tongue. The previous night swirled around me in fragments but I was locked inside the dominating fog of a hangover. I could hardly think. I needed food, and ten thousand glasses of water.

In the kitchen, the sun had already broken through the wide windows, fanning ivory light across the tile. My mother sat in her usual chair at the table, the Sunday *Register* propped in one hand. I shuffled toward the sink.

"Good morning," my mother said, surprised. "When did you get home?"

I bit my lip. "Last night. I wasn't feeling well and wanted to sleep in my own bed, so Lynn drove me home."

"I see," she said. "And now?"

"What?"

"How do you feel now?"

"Oh. Fine."

I chugged a glass of water straight from the faucet, staring out at the backyard. Sometime in the night, the wind had started blowing again, and the pool was strewn with a fresh layer of fallen leaves. An unsettling familiarity swirled in my stomach.

Then Vivian entered the kitchen, and the reality of last night slammed into me.

Did she remember what happened? I couldn't tell. The version of Vivian worrying my mind was incongruous with the woman I saw in front of me now: elegantly dressed, with hair already curled and makeup applied. She looked so normal. I felt a knot of hope.

Vivian poured herself some coffee. To no one in particular, she said, "I can't seem to find my pills."

"Which pills?" my mother asked.

I detected the briefest pause. "The ones for my headaches," Vivian answered.

"Have you checked that hidden zipper compartment in your purse?"

"I think I'd know if they were in my purse, Diane."

"What about the glove compartment in your car?"

"No, no, they're not there."

"Could they have fallen beside the sink?"

As Vivian checked off all the places on my mother's list, I tried to think about whether I had seen her pills since that time I found them in the pantry, but my head throbbed, like my brain had become too thick for my skull, and I could not summon a single new place to look. I just kept thinking about what my mother had told me all those months ago, in front of the school: *You don't have to worry.* And: *Don't tell her you know.*

"Well, please keep an eye out for them, both of you," Vivian said. "This pain—"

One flinching hand rose to her forehead. Without finishing the sentence, she strode back down the hallway, deserting her coffee on the kitchen counter. A minute later, I heard the clacking of heeled footsteps in the entryway, the rumble of the garage door opening. Vivian's car whirred.

"Where's she going this early?" I asked, unable to disguise the strain in my voice.

"Sometimes she goes to church." My mother licked her fingers before flipping the page.

"Since when does she go to church?"

"Always. I mean, she doesn't always go. But she's always sometimes gone. Why do you ask?"

I shrugged, sat down at the table.

"She's back long before you wake up. You usually sleep until noon on Sundays, if you're even home."

"I guess I'm just surprised. Vivian doesn't really seem like the religious type."

My mother paused then, lowering the paper. Even upside down, I could read the top headline: "Coyote Snatches Cat During Daytime Birthday Party in Huntington Beach." There was a photograph of a little girl crying. It must have been her party, I thought. Her cat.

"I think it can be a nice feeling for people," my mother said, "thinking that there's a greater force governing us and life isn't just a random, meaningless series of events."

I knew she was right. People crave order in chaos. Ever since my father's death, I'd been functioning under a skewed iteration of this exact idea. Right then, though, I preferred the opposite; I *wanted* last night to be a random, meaningless event. A momentary chemical imbalance caused by missed medication, provoking an old fuse in Vivian's brain to spark. It happened all the time, didn't it? My mother told me not to worry. Vivian was fine. She would be fine.

But what if she wasn't?

Suddenly, my secret felt unbearable. Whatever happened last night was so far beyond a lost train of thought or a forgotten bag of groceries, and if there was any chance I could prevent something worse from happening to Vivian next time, or prevent the next time entirely, I had to tell my mother everything. I didn't even care if I implicated myself and was grounded for the rest of my life, because somehow I'd traveled so far away from the person I thought I'd become when we moved here—when I sat in Ms. Grobler's office and vowed to be different.

"You look pale," my mother said. Standing, she walked around the table and hunched over me. Her knuckles were frigid as they brushed my forehead. "You're burning up."

"I don't have a fever," I said, batting her hand away. "You're just always cold."

"I think we should take your temperature anyway."

"I don't have a fever," I repeated.

"At least let me give you some Tylenol."

"Mom," I said. "Stop. Please. Just sit down."

Outside, the sun had climbed above the hillside. It beamed viciously through the windows, glinting against the gold specks in my mother's eyes as she lowered herself back into her chair.

I said, "I have to tell you something."

The basic facts were easy enough to explain: Vivian had come into my room in the middle of the night and was, for some reason, misplaced in time. She thought we were twenty years in the past. She thought I was my mother. Disoriented myself, I decided to play along.

After I relayed these details, though, the more delicate questions arose: Why did she come to my room in the first place? Why had I been making noise? Why had I still been awake at such an hour? I had not expected my mother to be more interested in my role in the story than Vivian's, and instinctively, I evaded, resisting once too often with a shifting gaze and a shrug. I'd grossly underestimated how difficult it would be to tell the truth.

My mother rubbed her hands over her face and spoke through her fingers. "Why must everything be a secret between us?"

"What did you expect? You've been lying to me since the day I was born." My voice emerged more harshly than intended. "And anyway," I added with a half-moon smile, "aren't all parent-child relationships like this?"

My mother lowered her hands. She said, "You didn't lie to your father."

Her words tore through me with a sharp sting of guilt. Of course I'd lied to him. I did so constantly, internalizing my true feelings until the pressure of everything I never said made me want to explode. But my mother wouldn't know that; she had always been on the outside of our music, our midnights. To her, we must have seemed so connected. So impenetrable.

"I'm in a band," I said.

At the edge of my vision, I noticed my mother's fingers tightening around the grip of her mug.

"And—" I swallowed. "I lied to you earlier. About last night. Where I was."

"So where were you?"

"The Troubadour," I said, looking back to her. "I played a show at the Troubadour. That's why I came home so late, when Vivian heard me."

For an instant, I thought I saw some spark of surprise—maybe even pride—cross her face. Then her expression darkened.

"You're mad," I said. "I knew you'd be mad."

"Of course I'm mad. You've been gallivanting around the city in the middle of the night."

"See? This is exactly why I didn't want to tell you. I knew you wouldn't approve—"

"You're right," she interrupted. "I probably wouldn't have approved. But I wouldn't have stopped you, either."

The wind kicked up outside, skittering a trail of leaves across the patio.

"What do you mean?"

"What could I have done? Put locks on your windows? Chased you down the street?" She paused for a moment, and I wondered if she expected me to answer. "I know what music means to you," she said. "And besides. You've got his spirit. You'll do what you want, regardless of what I say."

"That's not true. When you grounded me, I stayed grounded." The words shot from my mouth before I could stop them. "Mostly," I amended. Then, "I'm sorry."

My mother sighed. "I know what happens when parents try to dictate your life. And you were already so far away from me. I know we've never had the same relationship you had with your father, but after he died . . ." For a moment, her eyes pinched closed. "I was afraid. I didn't want you to make my same mistakes."

"I'm not you," I said.

"No. You're not."

I waited for her to continue, to punish me. I waited for her to tell me how to atone.

"So I guess I'm grounded?"

"You've already admitted that doesn't work," she said. And then her mouth crept into a tiny smile. "Maybe I should come up with a punishment that's particularly cruel and unusual instead—something public. Humiliating." She sipped her coffee. "Your grandmother used to threaten to show up at the high school in a bathrobe and curlers, face covered in an olive-green skin mask, the whole Sunday night routine on full display as she shouted my name through the hallways."

Her smile tilted, firmed.

"Vivian threatened this often?" I asked.

"Once or twice," she said.

"Well, I have it on good authority that you were quite the troublemaker. Running around with boys. Out all hours of the night."

"And where did you hear that?"

"Vivian."

My mother smiled again, shaking her head. "I can't believe she told you that."

"She didn't," I said. "Or not exactly."

Immediately, a shadow seemed to spread across us. Whatever memory had previously enveloped my mother flickered and was gone.

"I'm sorry you had to experience that," she said. "You did the right thing, letting the episode play out."

The way she said this made something tighten in my chest. "You already knew, didn't you? That this was happening?"

"I'm not sure 'happening' is the right way to put it. But I know it has happened, yes."

"Why didn't you tell me?"

My mother hesitated. "Because I wanted to protect you." I tried to protest, to remind her that I wasn't a child anymore, but she swept on. "It seemed like you were finally starting to be happy again, and until we knew something for certain, I wanted you to be able to live with one less worry. Not to mention Mom's insistence that no one know."

"But I'm not just anyone. I'm family."

"I know. But your grandmother is very stubborn, and very proud. She couldn't bear the thought of meeting you for the first time, and having that be the way you viewed her. Her heart was in the right place. You're really so special to her."

I crossed my arms. "She has a funny way of showing it."

"I know. She makes me furious sometimes, but that's just who she is. It took me a long time to understand that. When my own father died"—she reached for her mug, studied its center—"she went about her days as though nothing had happened, and I hated her for it. I know that's harsh, but it's true. And now . . ." My mother looked up. "When overwhelmed by all the things we can't control, we grip tighter to the few we can. We have to give her that."

"So what do we do?"

"We wait. We schedule regular appointments with her doctor, and we monitor, and we wait."

"Does the doctor even know what's wrong?" I asked.

"It's not quite that simple, Suz. The brain is such a complex thing, affected by so many other parts of the body. But the good news is that the medications seem to curtail almost all of the symptoms. Unless, of course, she doesn't take it."

"And she hasn't been taking it," I said, "for who knows how long."

"I know she had it Friday," my mother said. "And if it doesn't show up by the morning, I'll call her doctor to get a new prescription first thing."

"But should she be driving? Shouldn't we go after her, make sure everything is all right? What if she gets a migraine?" What if she swerves, or forgets, even for a second, what she's doing? What if she crashes into a telephone pole, takes out the power, shuts down a freeway?

"I know this is hard, but your grandmother is a tough woman, and she's always adhered to a very independent lifestyle. Like I said, we'll consult the doctor tomorrow, but at this point, we have to trust her to know when she's not okay."

"Sometimes the healthiest are first to go," I mumbled.

My mother frowned. "That's a rather pessimistic thing to say."

"It's Vivian's phrase," I told her. "She said it about my grandfather."

My mother sat up straighter, her mouth opening slightly.

"What? Did you not want me to know I had one? Kind of figured, biology and all."

"She's not the biggest sharer of sad stories. I'm just surprised you two talked about him."

"We didn't, much. She told me how he died. When. I still know hardly anything about him."

"Well," my mother said, "what do you want to know?"

I thought about all the concrete questions: where he was from, where he worked, how he met Vivian, what hobbies he liked. Did he also get dressed before coming into the kitchen for breakfast? Did he do crosswords on Sunday, or stay up late watching TV? Had he spent his teenage years driving down PCH with the windows open, the tinny sound of the Beatles rattling from the AM radio?

There was so much I would never know, but this time, it was nobody's fault. No one's choices kept me from him.

Perhaps for this reason, I decided there was only one question worth asking. "What was he like?"

My mother thought for a moment. "He was kind," she said slowly. "Thoughtful. Particular in his own ways, but understanding of those who differed. And he had these big, firm hands that would have been great for a carpenter or a farmer or something. I remember he drank coffee every morning, right here in this seat, and our mugs looked so small in his grip. Like a child's toy." My mother smiled. "Maybe he just preferred the smaller mugs or something, but in my memory, his hands were giant."

At first, I had trouble picturing it. My mother's hands, like Vivian's, were slender, small but long. "Piano fingers," my father had called them. I'd always marveled at their elegance, so different from my bitten nails and bumpy knuckles, and figured I'd inherited my father's hands. Now, I wondered if my hands were really a version of my grandfather's.

"He always told me I worried too much," my mother continued. "That I was too young for that. I think he'd probably say the same thing, if he was here now."

"You still miss him?" I asked.

"Every day," she said, and while I knew this was the right answer, the only possible answer, it struck me—not because of how incredibly she'd hidden the feeling, but rather the idea that you could miss someone forever. Even my mother, strong and unwavering as she always seemed, acknowledged it would never get easier. Over twenty years could pass and still the wounds would not have healed.

And right then, as I gazed out at the sun sloping down the hillside, something else began to frighten me even more: the possibility that the wounds inflicted by the living might not heal either.

"Did you miss Vivian, too?" I asked.

"Of course," my mother said sharply. "She never stopped being my mother."

"But if Dad was still alive, and you didn't need her help, you wouldn't have called her. I still wouldn't know she exists."

"I may have been the one to break our silence, but, as you

know, I was not the only one who needed help."

A memory sped across my mind from the day Vivian showed up at our door in Eagle Rock: the perfect frame of her face through the peephole, the myriad misconceptions I had before discovering who she really was—misconceptions that were only now being rectified.

"That's part of why we moved here," I said, working the pieces together out loud. "Isn't it? She needed us, too."

My mother nodded. "Now you know everything." She sipped from her mug, and her face scrunched in disgust. "My coffee is cold," she said, but kept drinking it anyway, and in that moment I felt something open between us.

I said, "If I ask you a question now, will you answer me honestly?"

"Yes," she said.

I took a deep breath, considering all the mysteries. All the unknowns.

"Do you think the crash was an accident?"

My mother stood, moved toward the coffee decanter. She refilled her mug. I watched her back heave up and down. "I think your father had demons," she said carefully. "And I think he made many wrong decisions because of it."

"That's not really an answer," I said.

She turned around, folded her arms. "Susie, I don't know what happened that night. We never will, and dwelling on all the things we'll never know only makes it harder to move forward."

"I'm not asking for an irrefutable truth. I'm just asking you to tell me what *you* think happened."

When my mother finally answered, her voice emerged slowly, soft, as though dispatched from somewhere far away. "No. I don't think he meant it."

"You don't sound very certain."

"Do you remember the day we scattered his ashes out on the ridge?" she asked. "I thought you had a death wish, the way you walked right out to the edge of the cliff. I felt like I was going to have a heart attack, I was so scared. But then it was over, and you were fine, just like you said you would be, and you told me that he didn't do it on purpose. You were so sure, despite everything the detective said. You knew that the facts only accounted for so much, and that day I decided to believe you. I still do. So don't tell me you've gone and changed your mind now."

In the dark, remote caverns of our psyches, we both must have recognized that the pieces didn't quite add up. But if my mother was lying, I knew it was for her sake as much as my own.

"I haven't," I told her. "I just keep thinking, if I'd done something differently—"

"What happened wasn't your fault," she said quickly. "We loved him with everything we had, and that's what matters. That is the *only* thing that matters."

"Love," I said. "It can still be present tense."

She sighed. "Yes. It's present tense. It will always be present tense. But we can't let that keep us from moving on."

All of a sudden, the conversation shifted, and I knew were talking about something else.

"How is he?" I asked. "Roger. He hasn't been around in a while."

My mother smiled sadly. "You'd know better than me."

I wanted to tell her that I was sorry, that I'd reverted to instinct, erecting defenses without knowing entirely why. If only she'd told me about him in the first place—their history, their existence— then maybe the possibilities wouldn't have seemed so frightening.

But my mother spoke first.

"So the Troubadour, huh?" Her eyes brightened. "How was it?"

"Not like I expected."

"Why not?"

"The way Dad always talked about it . . . I guess I just thought it would be different." But no, that wasn't right. That wasn't the truth. "I thought *I* would be different." I paused. "I thought, if I ever made it to that stage, he'd be there."

"I'm sure he'd have been so proud of you," she said.

I shrugged, because I didn't want to argue. I didn't want to think any more about last night, what would or would not have made him proud. He was gone.

We were still here.

"How do you remember it?" I asked then.

"Remember what?"

"The Troubadour. I've heard Dad's stories a hundred times, but not yours."

"Oh, geez. That was so long ago." My mother laughed slightly, looked up at the ceiling. "I guess—I guess I remember the *feeling* more than anything specific. The music being so loud that it filled you up until it felt like it was part of you. I remember the way it echoed in my chest. And I remember feeling like I never wanted it to stop. The music, the dancing. The song. The moment."

She smiled, her eyes misty, and my mind itched with the image of the young woman in the photograph—how desperately I'd always wanted to know her. Yet suddenly here she was, right now, right in front of me. All this time, and it never truly occurred to me that that woman and my mother were still the same person.

All this time, and I just needed to ask.

"That's not really about the Troubadour, though, is it?" my mother said, looking back to me.

"It's close enough," I said. And it was. It was everything I'd ever wanted to know.

"That was my very first time there, the night I met your father."

"He never told me that."

She nodded, seemingly pleased to have surprised me. "I didn't know who he was, who the band was. A friend from school asked me to go with her. Her name was Karen Matthews, I think. God, I haven't thought about her in years." My mother put one hand on the side of her face, shook her head. "One innocuous decision, a girl who lived down the hall in my dorm, and my entire life changed course."

"Do you . . ." I began. The words congealed in the back of my mouth. "Do you ever wonder about what would have happened if you hadn't gone?"

"I wonder about a lot of things," my mother said, "but I don't regret any of my decisions. Not for a second."

Down the hall, the garage door growled open. My mother turned around, wet a sponge, and began wiping the coffee spills from the counter as the thin echo of heels clicked toward us.

"I brought bagels," Vivian announced as she entered the

kitchen. She hoisted a plastic bag onto the counter, began unfurling the paper pouch nestled inside. Then she looked at us. "Everything all right in here?"

"Yes," my mother said, replacing the sponge on the rim of the sink. Her eyes flashed to me. "Everything's great."

"Well, are you hungry?" Vivian pulled butter, cream cheese, and a beefsteak tomato larger than my fist from the refrigerator.

"I'll take half a bagel, if you want to split one," my mother said.

"Susannah?" Vivian took out a cutting board.

"Sure," I said, looking into my mug of cold coffee. "Thanks."

"Need any help?" my mother asked.

"I'm perfectly capable of chopping produce," Vivian said tersely, slicing through the slick tomato skin with a thud of knife on wood. "But if you want to scramble some eggs."

As they continued talking, chopping, and whisking, I excused myself from the kitchen. I needed a moment alone. I'd been so sure that the conversation with my mother would go terribly, and I was stunned to find that in many ways, I felt better. Last night seemed so far away. I wasn't going to be that girl anymore. I wasn't her now.

And yet, I knew I still had to answer for her mistakes. So I went to my bedroom and pulled up Nick's number in my phone.

The thorny wilderness of a blank, fresh text message shone from my hands and I almost turned the phone off, too daunted by the task of finding the exact right thing to say. But I didn't. I began typing: *Is it too late for apologies / to tell you my eyes have blurred behind county lines / and I'm not always sure who I am?*

Minutes ticked by. Nick didn't respond. I tried again.

I'm so sorry about last night.

Another minute passed.

It's fine, he wrote back.

The words echoed in my head, clipped and curt, as I imagined he must have meant them—just two vague, tiny words, practically meaningless when removed from context. They shoved through the bulk of my newfound contentment with a weight so heavy and expansive that when my bagel was finally done toasting and the scrambled eggs were fluffy and firm, I wasn't even hungry anymore.

TWENTY-TWO

MAY BROUGHT LONG, hot, monotonous days. I threw myself into school. There was just over a month left before graduation, but it was still enough time to salvage my grades, and I was studying for a history test one Saturday when my phone pinged with a text from Gabriel: *Constellation Room canceled. Warehouse show instead. Be here by 8, cool?*

I wrote him back right away: *See you then!*

This would be our first show since the Troubadour—as far as I was aware, anyway. No one had bothered to tell me about the Constellation Room. I wondered what else they hadn't told me. I wondered if they'd been recording.

I texted Lynn. *Warehouse party tonight. Want to meet up before?*

Can't, she replied. *See you there.*

A weird, restless feeling stirred in my chest. We always went to parties together, and what kind of plans could she have that excluded me? Something with Josie, I guessed. It was true they'd known each other far longer, but even after our fight and the enduring awkwardness, I still considered Lynn my closest friend.

For the first time, I began to wonder whether she felt the same.

When the sun sank behind the hillside and the gloomy, moonless night descended, I got ready alone in my bedroom. I attempted to paint narrow streaks on my eyelids the way Lynn always did, but my hand was not as precise, the lines too wide and uneven. Wiping my face clean, I settled for simple swipes of mascara and red-tinted lip balm. Casual, I thought. I let my hair down and gazed at the mirror. I didn't look like my father anymore, or like Lynn. Just me.

At exactly seven fifteen, I marched into the living room and presented the night's plan to my mother and Vivian. In a spate of full, excruciating details, I explained that four bands would be playing a show, unregulated and unchaperoned, at the Endless West's practice space. I expected my mother to stop me each time I inhaled or shifted course, but she didn't. When I finally finished speaking, they both sat quiet. The television grumbled in the background.

My mother asked, "And when will you be home?"

"Two?" I tried, awaiting the harsh curl of the word *no*, or *youhavegottobekiddingme*. On the adjacent sofa, Vivian noisily flipped the pages of her TV guide, though she was obviously listening. "One?"

"Twelve thirty," my mother said, "and not a second later."

"Twelve thirty," I repeated, stunned. Despite the time I'd spent getting ready, I didn't fully believe my mother would let me go.

"Be safe," she added, veering her attention back to the TV, and I left the family room unable to tell whether the remaining tension in my stomach was relief or disappointment. My mother was, I realized, not going to punish me. Though part of me wonders now if perhaps she actually did.

By the time I arrived at the warehouse, the place was already packed, dense with the humid scents of spilled beer and sweat, chatter straining to be heard above the stereo. I surveyed the room, checking off in my mind all the people I knew by name or face.

Then I pulled out my phone.

Want to come to a party tonight? I asked Nick, jokingly adding, *I promise I won't disappear in the middle of it!*

I stared at the screen, waiting. Maybe he was at a swim meet, I thought uselessly, or working on a project for the video yearbook. I sent him the address anyway, emboldened by a glimmer of hope until I saw Lynn rushing toward me. She approached so suddenly—tripping, perhaps, on one of the duct-taped lumps of cord on the floor—that she fell into me, and my phone shot from my hand.

"Susie," she said, laughing. "Where have you been hiding, huh?"

"Home?" I said, scanning the area around me. "I just got here. Do you see my phone? I dropped it."

I crouched down, peering between legs. Lynn squatted next to me, but instead of helping me search, she stared directly at me.

Her eyeliner had clumped at the corners, smeared across the crease of her lids. Her skin was splotched and pink. When she leaned into me, I could smell the booze on her breath. "I know what you've been doing," she said.

"What?" I asked, not sure if I heard right.

"Oh, here!" Crawling on her knees, she moved a few inches forward, tapping calves out of the way. The crowd parted for her. When she returned she had my phone.

I smiled, standing, wondering if maybe I'd overanalyzed her earlier text. "Thanks," I said. The phone was scuffed and screen cracked, but otherwise it seemed fine. Then I tried to turn it on. Nothing. "Shit."

Lynn grabbed my hand and started swinging my arm back and forth like a child. "Oh, say that you'll be true," she sang, spinning beneath my fingers, "and never leave me blue, my Susie Q." As she danced, her hips sloshed in sync with whatever was in her cup. Frothy drops plunged over the side. I shoved my phone in my purse.

"Looks like you're a few drinks ahead of me, huh?" I joked, though something ominous bristled through me.

"Dance with me!" Lynn spun again, but this time she lost her balance and knocked into some girl standing next to us, who then shot me a hostile look.

"I think we should get you some water," I said.

"Good idea." Lynn gulped down whatever remained in her cup. "Let's go get a drink."

"Of water," I said, but Lynn wasn't listening; she had already begun dragging me through the crowd, bumping, unconcerned, into more bystanders as we hurried toward the plywood bar in the warehouse's back corner. "Excuse me, sorry, excuse me," she called to each person we rammed. I had never seen her act so clumsy, not even when we were drinking. That night, though, it was clear: something inside her had come apart.

"Let's do shots," she said as we sidled up to the bar.

"I'm driving tonight," I said.

"So? Drink now, sober later."

That's when I noticed Cameron behind the haphazard bar, cracking open cans of Natural Ice in exchange for a dollar.

"Hey," he said, looking between us. "Beer?"

"Come on, Cam," Lynn said, reaching out to tuck a loose strand of hair behind his ear. "There's no need to be *weird*."

From my vantage, that gesture seemed alarmingly intimate, but he didn't even twitch. She must have touched him that way a thousand times before, as friends, as more. Even when he and I were together, I'd been too hesitant to imagine such an action.

"Susie Q's already over it, anyway," she continued. "You've moved on, she's moved on, so let's just all forget it."

Laughter crackled somewhere behind me and my breath caught in my throat. I wanted to run, hide, shout that what she said wasn't true (or maybe it was—I really hadn't figured that out yet). But the capacity for language had deserted me.

"Now, I just happen to know," Lynn continued, lowering her voice, and I couldn't help noticing the way her tank top draped open when she leaned forward. "Josie has the good stuff back there. I'll come around and get it myself if I have to. You know how much I hate Natty Ice."

"Fine, but I won't cover for you," he said. "If she notices, I'm pointing fingers."

"I'll take my chances," Lynn said sweetly.

He grabbed a bottle from beneath the slab of plywood. "You too?" he asked me.

My reply came out as a squeak. Clearing my throat, I said, "No thanks. You got any water?"

As Cameron poured Lynn a shot, her attention shifted to the boy on her right. I recognized him from Surreal Killers, another band scheduled to perform that night, but I couldn't remember his name. Lynn playfully gripped his forearm, flirting. I turned back to Cameron in time to see his gaze brush away from mine, as though afraid of what might happen if it lingered.

"The weather," I blurted, regretting the words the instant they left my mouth. I'd meant to suggest that the sudden influx of thick, arid heat had a way of spiking nerves—but my mouth couldn't formulate the rest of the thought and those two futile words hung there like a pathetic jab at small talk, spotlighting the strangers we'd become. Or maybe, I thought, we'd always been strangers.

It struck me then that this was how most things end: seemingly slow and then all at once. As the last trace of him slipped like sand through my fingers, all I could do was smile bleakly, drink my water, and watch him go.

"To Boulder Girl," Lynn said, clinking her cup against my bottle. Then she knocked back the drink in one swift sip.

Shortly after that, the first set began. Surreal Killers followed almost immediately. The bands all used most of the Endless

West's equipment, slipping black braided cables in and out of guitar jacks, so the music rarely stopped. Tall plastic trash cans filled up around me with empty beer cans. Lynn did not leave my side.

I wondered at first if she and Josie had fought that afternoon, and a remote satisfaction wafted through me. But the sensation was fleeting; when Surreal Killers came to an end and I mounted the stage with the Endless West, Lynn shimmied to the front of the crowd where Josie was standing, rainbow colors streaking her bangs. Lynn said something to her that I couldn't decipher, and I waited for them to fight or yell but Josie just pushed up her glasses and squinted at me.

The boys plugged in their instruments. At the corner of the stage I sipped my water, sharply aware of the noises clashing through the crowded room and the way people's eyes kept flicking to the stage, to me. Cameron, unsurprisingly, kept his attention diverted, but a strong, prickling ache overcame me when I realized that Luke was ignoring me, too. I lingered, awaiting his glance, the tiny offering of his tambourine. But that night, Gabriel had been searching through the suitcase for a spare tuner. When he ultimately handed me the tambourine, smiling in a way that should have brought me comfort, I felt only a deeper pull of despondency.

We played. Nothing about that night's set stands out in my mind. The songs had lost their luster, that hypnotic edge I detected when I first heard the boys' music wafting out from the trees. Even when Alex strummed the first chords to "Don't Look Back," as the crowd cheered and chanted and stamped their feet against the stained cement floor, I felt only the routine of the song coursing through me. I still sang, *I can't let go, I can't let go, I can't let go*—but I was no longer sure of what I was even holding on to.

When our set ended, Alex announced that Abandoned Nova Brigade would play next and the boys unplugged their instruments. Plunking the tambourine in Luke's suitcase, I hurried from the stage, scanning the room for the sunny fluff of Nick's hair, his blue coral reef eyes. But he wasn't there. Of course he wasn't. It had been useless to think a meager apology would make everything okay between us, or that he'd drive all the way down here on a last-minute invitation. Emerging through the back of the crowd, I made my way to the bar and paid a dollar for the beer—not because I particularly wanted it, but because I wasn't sure what else to do with myself. I took a sip. A metallic taste lingered in my mouth.

I turned to the guy next to me. "Hey, you want this?" I asked him. "I only had one sip."

"Cool, thanks!" the guy said, and disappeared back into the mob.

I sighed. All around me were people I recognized, but I didn't actually know any of them. I couldn't spot a single person I wanted to talk to, until Gabriel slipped behind the bar. He cracked open a beer for himself, then offered one to me. I shook my head.

"Did you know," he said, "that John Lennon and Harry Nilsson got kicked out of the Troubadour?"

"John Lennon?" I asked. "Nuh-uh."

"True story—1974. The Smothers Brothers were playing, doing their comedy thing, and apparently Lennon and Nilsson just started yelling shit at them, as though they were part of the act. Which they obviously weren't."

I laughed. "It's hard to imagine John Lennon as the heckling type."

Gabriel, now playing bartender, did not quite look at me when he said, "Same goes for you."

Because no one ever said anything about my outburst that night at the Troubadour, I'd assumed it must have been relatively subdued, massive only amid the scrim of my drunken memory. After all, there were no mosh pits or punches, no broken glass. Apparently, though, I'd been wrong. I wondered if everyone knew—if they saw me now as that girl who screamed and made scenes. And suddenly, I was reminded of Detective Melendez, the nervous way he watched me as my mother and I sat in his office. As if he knew, just by looking at me, the mess I was capable of causing.

Gabriel grinned and bumped me with his elbow. "Pretty badass of you."

I could have kissed him right then. Instead, I let myself smile and said, "Thanks."

Gabriel continued handing out beers, one after another like cookies at a blood drive until Abandoned Nova Brigade's first song galloped from the crackly speakers and everyone's attention turned. I held my post next to him. Sometime after our set Lynn had vanished, and I hoped she was sleeping—in the loft, maybe, or out in someone's car—but I couldn't deny that without her, I felt like I didn't belong.

I leaned toward Gabriel and yelled into his ear. "I think I'm going to go."

"It's still early," he argued.

I shrugged, and gave him a hug. "I'll see you around, all right?"

"Yeah, okay," Gabriel said, sounding genuinely disappointed. "I'll see you."

I squeezed him one last time before letting go.

Outside, the sky was that dusky shade of purple it becomes when there are too many lights and a thick, low-hanging shroud of smog—the kind of sky that never feels dark enough. I headed down the parking lot toward my mother's car, pulling out my phone to text Nick. *I wish you were here*, I would say. Or, *I still mean every word I said.* Then I remembered my phone was broken.

I'd only just rounded the corner when I became aware of voices—or, more accurately, a single voice. I couldn't make out what she was saying but I quickly recognized the sharp strain of her tone, the note of panic. Only once before had I heard Lynn's voice rise with such reckless distress: the day her father came back from the dead.

Guided by the sound, I crept closer. I hid in the shadows and crouched behind cars until, finally, I spotted her. She was facing away from me. I couldn't see who she was talking to so I snuck forward, careful to remain in the dark, and there, visible over the hood of the car, stood Luke.

"Just tell me why," she said. Her voice was high-pitched. Unstable.

"We're not together," Luke said sternly. He dragged on his cigarette, smoke writhing up from his fingers. "We haven't been for months."

"That hasn't stopped you from sleeping with me."

My heart detonated. Luke's mouth moved in response but my ears had become clogged with hot air. I leaned farther over the hood, my face dipping into the brume of light as I struggled to hear.

"Do you have feelings for her?" Lynn demanded.

He flicked a speck of tobacco from his lips before saying, "No."

"Why, then?"

"Why does it matter?"

"Because I love you," she cried. "Don't you fucking get that?"

Some small aversion unsettled Luke's face, and I knew he didn't love her back. Maybe he had at some point, before they'd been consigned to whatever they were now, a secret played out in parking lots and the back rooms of parties. But it was obvious as he glanced up, to the side, anywhere other than Lynn, that all he wanted now was an escape. Though I knew I should leave, I didn't.

That's when his eyes caught mine.

I can't imagine he wanted to look at me then for as long as he did. Everything would have been so much easier had his eyes bounced off me like a ray of light, but they stuck, pinning me behind the hood of the car. Before I could react, Lynn whirled around.

In that instant, I hardly recognized her. Her cheeks were glistening, wet in the dreary gleam of the streetlights, the black of her mascara smearing down her face. On her lips, a small, uncertain parenthesis had formed, and a dangerous swirl ravaged the edges of her eyes. This was not the same person who floated into Roger's classroom on my first day at Santiago Hills, mysterious and indomitable and everything I wished I could be. She was just another infatuated, vulnerable girl. She was just the same as the rest of us.

Maybe I only understood all of this later, after that instant had crashed against the walls of my memory so many times that it finally became smooth and clear. All I know is that when I look back now, I still see this moment, this single second before I ran the rest of the way to my mother's car, in painfully sharp relief: the entirety of our friendship crumbling right in front of me.

But I guess that's not true, either. The collapse had begun long before this, and I didn't do a single thing to stop it.

Over a week passed before I saw Lynn again. She wasn't in front of the library in the mornings, or lounging in the heart of the pine cluster during lunch. She didn't show up to choir class, either, and after a few days Roger asked me if I knew why she'd been absent.

"She's sick," I told him, because it seemed better than admitting I had no idea where she'd been, if she'd be back, if I'd ever know these things again.

He eyed me curiously, waiting for elaboration. "Must be pretty bad to keep her out this long."

I shrugged. "The flu. It's been going around."

"Well, send her our best, will you? We hope she can join us again before the school year's over."

From the smooth levity of his voice, I knew he didn't believe me. Still, I told him I'd pass along his regards.

Then, the following Monday, she was back. I didn't know until choir, and even then I didn't notice right away. In her absence, I'd become one of the first people to enter the classroom every afternoon, not knowing how else to occupy my time. It was only as Roger began checking off his roll sheet and said, "Ah, Ms.

Chandler. Welcome back," that I realized she had slipped into the classroom, taking a seat in the back corner closest to the door.

She offered a brief smile in response to Roger's comment—proof, I guess, that she was present. She seemed paler somehow, sunken, and I wondered if maybe she'd really been sick. I waited for her to look at me. Eventually, I had to turn back to the whiteboard.

At the end of class, after the bell rang and everyone began scurrying from their seats, I shoved my notebook into my backpack and sped toward Lynn, determined to catch her. But Roger called out first.

"Ms. Chandler," he said across the bustle. "A word?"

I waited outside the choir room as the seventh period bell echoed and students disappeared into classrooms, the locker room, the emptying parking lot. The sky was blazing, bright and dimpled with tufts of clouds. To the north, intricate plumes of gray smoke billowed. It was fire season again, always, and though that small conflagration appeared to be controlled, my thoughts were not; they'd drifted so far that when Lynn finally blew through the door, charging straight past me, for the first few seconds I just stood there, dumbfounded.

Then I ran after her.

"Lynn," I yelled.

Somewhere, a car alarm started wailing. Lynn kept moving.

"Lynn," I called again. "Wait!"

She stopped, turning around so fast that I nearly rammed into her. "What? What could you possibly have to say?"

A lump climbed up the back of my throat. "I didn't know."

She laughed—a sharp, razor-edged sound. "How could you not know?"

"You never said anything."

"I know you're a smart girl, Susannah, but you act so goddamn dense sometimes."

The harsh stab of her words twisted in my stomach and I said nothing.

"I've seen the way you watch everything, studying us, making all these little notes in your head." She tapped on her forehead. "But of what? What is it you see? Because we both know I'm not that good of an actor. The only person you're fooling is yourself."

"But that's not—" I began, voice creaking. Lynn was wearing her favorite pair of sunglasses, the big round ones with the tortoiseshell frames, but I had none that day, no protection, and my own eyes felt hot and blurry in the sunshine. If I only had my sunglasses, I thought, I could block out the light, stop the tears, shield myself.

"I never would have—" I tried again, but the words still broke. I wasn't even sure I believed myself anymore.

Lynn sighed. "Look, I don't think you *meant* to hurt me, okay. I know no one is loyal anymore. No one is faithful. I should have known you'd be no different from the rest of this fucking city. That's on me, I guess."

I didn't want to cry—would have given anything to stop it—but I felt like I was falling, whooshing past reality into a place where I had no control. My voice was a whisper, lost somewhere else in the air. "Please don't hate me."

Lynn crossed her arms. "I'm not going to spread rumors behind your back and try to ruin your life, if that's what you're worried about. But you fucked up, and I'd rather not be anywhere near you right now."

As if to stop me from following her, she put out a hand. The gesture summoned a swell of anger from somewhere inside me. She was not the only one who had been wronged.

"So that's it? You get to be mad at me but I'm not allowed to be mad at you?"

Even through the tint of her sunglasses, I could feel the intensity of her stare. "For what?"

"For pretending your father was dead."

She cocked her head to the side and regarded me with a vague sadness that I soon realized was something far worse: pity.

"I don't owe you anything anymore, Susannah," she said. "So I'm sorry your dad went and crashed his car into a telephone pole, but you've got to realize that your life is not the epicenter of the universe."

Heat flooded my face. I said, "He doesn't love you."

I didn't mean for the words to shoot out the way they did, had not meant them to sound so cruel. But I think I knew, even in that split second before the words left my mouth, that they would only come out mangled. And right then, everything inside of me felt mangled. So I said them anyway.

Lynn's body tightened, face constricting in a callous half smile. "And I suppose you're going to tell me he loves you instead?"

"No," I said. "There's nothing between Luke and me. There never was."

But she wasn't listening anymore.

Sometimes, I still marvel at what came next. She didn't scream, pull my hair, or make me bleed. She didn't pretend everything was fine and wage war against me when my back was turned, reinventing me as a traitor, a slut, a thief. In the end, Lynn just coughed, or laughed—some final, caustic sound of offended disbelief—and then she walked away.

I don't know how long I stood there staring at the space where she had been before I heard my name, spoken with such gentleness that at first I thought I'd imagined it.

"Susannah?" Roger said again. "Are you all right?"

A moment passed before I found my voice. "No," I said. "I'm not."

A few minutes later, I found myself sitting in Roger's decades-old SUV—a boxy, silver thing with a dented back bumper and leather seats time had marbled with cracks.

"Do you want to talk?" he asked as we curved onto Chapman Avenue.

I shook my head, nailed my eyes to the window. The Santiago Hills perched brown and dry in front of us; to the right, an upscale Mexican restaurant with a wide patio draped in pink bougainvillea was setting up for dinner. I took note of every business we passed, a weak attempt to reroute my mind. My body had stopped convulsing but the tears continued to push up through my eyes.

After a minute Roger said, "Shall I put on some music?"

I didn't answer. He flipped on the radio. Ahead of us, a light changed to yellow.

If we'd sped through the intersection like everyone else, I

might not have felt the urge to speak, might have let the weight of the past few months slip by. But the car glided to a stop, and all of a sudden I was too conscious of Roger driving me home, the unbearable silence as we idled. Around us, the air had turned taut and fragile—like a guitar string tuned too tightly.

"I'm sorry," I said.

"It's no trouble at all. It may be a little unorthodox, but it's hardly out of the way."

"I mean, for what I said. For before."

From the corner of my eye, I could see that his mouth hung partially ajar. He must have known what I was referencing, but he didn't reply. The light turned green.

"I was really upset," I said.

"It's okay," he said.

"It's not."

Behind us, a car tapped its horn. Roger shifted his foot to the gas and we began moving again.

I said, "No one tells you how to keep living."

"You're doing the best you can."

My bottom lip trembled. I tilted my head against the warm window. "I've messed everything up."

"I'm sure that's not true," Roger said. "Anything worth fixing can be fixed."

His voice held such conviction that for the rest of the drive, I let myself believe him.

"Well, here we are," Roger said when we pulled up to my house. His foot was on the brake but the engine still rumbled. At the end of the driveway, my mother's car glimmered in the sun.

"Aren't you coming in?" I asked.

He tapped his fingers nervously on the steering wheel. "I should probably head home."

"She wants to see you."

"I'm just not sure if it's a good idea right now."

"When, then?" I said. "When else?"

For the first time that afternoon I turned to fully face him, and I was not surprised to find Roger looking away. I'd seen myself in the side-view mirror while we were driving and knew how I must have appeared to him then, a crazed, hormonal teenager with my red-webbed eyes and swollen lips. He must have been embarrassed to see me like that.

"Do you know why I was so upset that night?" I said. "It's not because I thought you were trying to replace him, or because my mom has feelings for you." I paused, wiping away the new stream of tears that trickled down to my jaw. "I was upset because she was happier than I can remember seeing her in a really long time."

Roger shook his head and tried to say something, but I pressed on.

"I'm done now," I said. "I'm done being the reason why my mother is unhappy. I'm done punishing her for living, even though my father isn't, and I'm done punishing myself. So, please, just—come inside."

Roger gazed up at the house, eyes flickering across the brickwork and wide windows. As the lines on his face softened, I sensed the familiarity he felt with this place.

He took a deep breath. "Okay."

Inside, sunlight slanted through the back windows, fanning

a haze of amber light across the tile floors. A faint aroma of citrus hung in the air. My mother must have been cleaning. For a moment, Roger and I stood in the front entryway, both unsure of what to do next. I called to my mother.

"In here," echoed her voice.

I led Roger toward the kitchen. "I brought someone with me," I said.

My mother was hunched over the sink, scrubbing ferociously at some object I couldn't see. Her hair had been bound in a messy ponytail, and streaks of sweat colored the back of her T-shirt. Without turning around, she said, "Is that Lynn?"

Her assumption caught me off guard, and I didn't know how to answer. She glanced back over her shoulder.

"Oh," she gasped when she saw him. She turned off the faucet and spun around. Water dripped from her hands to the floor as she smoothed her hair, her dirty T-shirt.

"Hi," Roger said.

"Hi," she said. Behind her, tiny soap bubbles waltzed through the golden air. "What are you . . ." She broke off and her eyes oscillated between us, uncomprehending. "What happened?"

"Roger drove me home," I said, as though it were that simple.

"You didn't call," she said. "I figured Lynn was driving you."

"We kind of got in a fight."

My mother's head fell to the side. "Oh, honey," she said, walking toward us. For those few seconds, her eyes didn't leave me. It didn't matter that Roger—a man she had loved, might still love— was standing at my side. She cupped my face in her cold, soft hands. "I'm so sorry."

When my mother wrapped her arms around me, my mind whirled back to that earthquake all those years ago, and the way she'd protected my body with her own as we crouched in the doorway of our old house and waited for the world to stop shaking. So much had changed since then; foundations had cracked and split, relationships had frayed. But some bonds, I saw now, were stronger than friction.

My mother's hands remained on my shoulders. "Do you want to talk about it?" she asked.

"Not really."

She touched my hair. "Remember that whatever seems like life and death now will become trivial in time. I promise you that."

I nodded, but "in time" was too abstract to comfort me. Even if after a year, ten years, what transpired between Lynn and me began to feel like some petty, childish rift, that wouldn't change the fact that I had lost her, that I had lost almost everyone I cared about. I tightened my lips to keep them from quivering.

My mother turned to Roger. "Thank you," she said. "For being there."

"It was no trouble."

His gaze had been fixed on the floor, perhaps in an effort to give us some semblance of privacy, but when my mother spoke to him, he looked up. It's true what they say: sometimes, a single glance can express far more than any number of carefully conceived words. They both smiled, shy and unsure, their eyes darting away and back, away and back. The energy was kinetic between them.

"Can I get you something?" my mother finally said. "Coffee? Tea?"

"Tea would be great," Roger said.

My mother filled the kettle and rummaged in the cabinet. "What would you like? We've got green, Earl Grey, chamomile, cinnamon apple—"

"Earl Grey." Roger took a step forward. "Please."

I began backing out of the kitchen. "I'm going to start on my homework."

"Oh, Suz, before you go—" My mother turned back, motioning to the island. "You have some mail."

Uncertainly, I approached the counter where a mound of envelopes waited. Some were short and thin, some were tall and fat. I shuffled through the few on top. All were addressed to me.

"Apparently our change of address overlapped, and these were all sent to the old house. I'm sure you've been waiting for some of them."

There was likely a smirk on her face, or some remnant note of pleasant surprise in her voice (because of course, by then, she had already sifted through the envelopes herself and knew exactly what I was receiving), but I wasn't paying attention anymore. I thanked her, and left the kitchen.

In my bedroom, I tore through the smallest envelopes first: rejection after rejection from half a dozen universities throughout the state of California. I was not scared of rejection; in fact, the two larger envelopes worried me far more, and with them I took my time. I slid my finger beneath the flaps and gently pried open the seals. My eyes swung across the page, savoring the words as the unimaginable began to gain shape and form: *On behalf of the faculty, administration, and staff, I am pleased to inform you . . .*

I leaned back against my headboard, stunned. Both Cal State Long Beach and San Francisco State had accepted me for the fall semester. Despite myself, I laughed out loud, eyes falling again to the letters. I read each one twice more. Even then, I still struggled to believe it.

I'd been accepted. To college.

I'd applied without declaring a major, unsure if this would be seen as a fresh breath of honesty (after all, what seventeen-year-old *really* knows, without any shred of doubt, what she wants to be doing for the rest of her life?), or some subconscious confession of ineptitude. Now, though, I was overwhelmingly thankful for this decision. In a few months, I'd be at college, and I'd have the chance to finally figure out my life. I'd have the chance to figure out myself.

In a few months, everything would change again.

But I had to act fast. Because of the delay in delivery of my acceptance letters, I only had a week before my deposit was due.

Overcome with possibility, I gathered up the two packets and had just jumped from my bed to go tell my mother the news, when I stepped on something bulky—a small manila envelope that must have slipped from the mail pile as I ravaged through the initial lump of rejections. I put down the college letters and bent to the floor. The surface of the envelope was scuffed and frayed, pock-marked with ink. A pale yellow *RETURN TO SENDER* sticker had been adhered at the bottom, and in the center, an address had been scribbled in the unmistakable scrawl of my father's hand:

Capitol Records A&R Dept.

1750 N. Vine St.

Hollywood, CA 90028

It was unclear why the tape was returned. Had they not been accepting unsolicited submissions? Had my father not addressed the package properly, neglecting some delivery specification—a floor or suite or name? Or had it been something even more simple, some unnecessary oversight, like the requirement that all demos now be submitted as CDs, or digitally through email? A deep, prickling sadness welled within me. I could have opened a hundred more college rejections letters—a thousand—and still I would not have felt quite the same despair as I did then, holding in my hands the rejected remains of my father's final opus.

As I turned the package over, I felt tears once again springing to my eyes. In many ways, this tape was just another piece of my father's story that I would never really have access to, exposing a whole slew of new questions. And yet, as I looked closer, one thing became certain. Discernible from the precise mound of crisscrossed tape and the resistance of the glue beneath the envelope's flap, that same adhesive layer I'd torn through so many times already that afternoon, I knew: the package had never been opened.

TWENTY-THREE

That night I couldn't sleep. I lay awake in my bed, winding the tape's reels back and forth with my pinkie finger while my father's songs reverberated in my mind. It was only an EP—four tracks that I'd already listened to repeatedly on an old Sony Walkman unearthed from Vivian's garage. Some of the melodies I recognized, pieces of which we had tinkered with during our various midnight sessions, but most of the progressions were unfamiliar. The final song, in particular, struck me: a wailing rock ballad built around delay, undoubtedly derived from the one we'd played that last night we spent together in the studio. "Before I Go," he'd titled it. My father strummed slowly but the chords howled, echoing behind elongated, bellowing vocals and an upbeat drum track. The juxtaposition was brilliant, the guitar tone heartbreaking, but the production felt rushed and unfinished, which lent the recording a strange, hollow quality. Something was missing, and I couldn't stop trying to figure out what. It wasn't like my father to release a song into the world before it was perfect—especially one that was so good, so close.

In the end, though, I was forced to admit that the state of his songs didn't really matter, because I was the only one who was ever going to hear them.

Unless I wasn't.

Gripped by sudden, urgent clarity, I got out of bed and grabbed the house phone. Turning it on, the dial tone droned in my ear. My mind hesitated at first but my fingers still knew the number by heart. The phone rang four times before Nick finally answered.

"Hello?" he said groggily.

"Hi," I said. "It's Susannah."

For a moment, there was only silence. I wondered if he had fallen back asleep.

"Tell me something," he said.

My heart thumped against my ribs. "What?"

There was a scratching sound, like fabric rustling against the receiver. I imagined Nick in bed, in the dark, nestling his phone between his cheek and the pillow. "Tell me a joke."

"Um," I mumbled, raking my mind. "What's the difference between a piano and a tuna?"

He thought for a moment. "I give up."

"You can tune a piano, but you can't tuna fish."

On the other end of the line, I heard a soft, reluctant chuckle.

"All right, Hayes," Nick said, and I could almost feel him smiling. He yawned emphatically. Pleasantly. "All right. You have my full attention."

Nick's bedroom looked exactly as I remembered, from the framed poster for *The Empire Strikes Back* that hung above his desk to the lumpy forest-green comforter tossed crookedly across his mattress. He had attempted to clean for me, I noticed, by shoving a heap of clothing beneath the bed, but the bookshelf remained in happy disarray. A small, thin TV perched atop his dresser, beside which waited the tangled controllers of an old Nintendo console we had played with as kids. But one alarming difference between the room in my memory and the one I found myself in that Saturday afternoon prevailed: though the summer sun raged outside, shriveling lawns and evaporating reservoirs, inside, we were drenched in darkness.

After my arrival, Nick had barricaded us in the room; he'd drawn the shades, closed the door, wedged a blanket in the narrow crack above the carpet. "It's to keep the vibrations from kicking around," he explained. "I've spent all morning trying to optimize the tone in here. It's no Sunset Sound, but for what we've got?" He glanced proudly around the dimly lit room. "I think it's pretty good."

"I'm sure it's perfect," I said. "Thank you so much for doing this, Nick."

"My pleasure," he said. "You know I live for this stuff. Now, let's see this tape."

I handed over the Walkman, my father's final cassette still

nestled inside. Nick sat down at his desk and plugged a cord into the headphone jack, pulled up a complicated-looking program on his computer. Then, he pressed play.

For the next hour, with his ears cupped in headphones big as earmuffs, Nick translated my father's final cassette tape directly from the Walkman to a digital file. Periodically, I glanced over his shoulder at the squiggly sound waves on his monitor, but mostly I just waded through the shadowed room, touching Nick's belongings, immersed in his smell. I felt jittery and elated. I'd never really recorded before. Against the corner of his bed, the Martin waited.

"The quality on this," Nick yelled suddenly, unaware of how quiet the room was. He spun around in his chair and slipped the headphones down to his neck. "It's incredible. There's no way you'd be able to tell it was recorded in your garage. The levels will need to be tweaked a tiny bit, so they'll match you, but your dad really knew what he was doing."

I smiled, though a strange heaviness filled my gut. "How'd you even figure out how to do all this?" I asked.

He shrugged. "The internet."

Standing, Nick pulled two mic stands into the center of the room, began checking their plugs, adjusting their height. "You ready?"

I picked up the Martin and tossed the strap behind my head. I could see the letters *TAL SPADES* branded in the worn leather near my left shoulder. "As ready as I'll ever be."

We began recording with "Night Lives," the catchy, pop-infused folk song that opened my father's EP, and worked our way to "Before I Go." Each track had its own personality, and I'd spent every spare moment of the past week practicing and planning, debating how to best emphasize my father's complicated guitar riffs before ultimately deciding to do what I'd always done best: strum a simple rhythm that swirled through the hollow spaces of his songs. Together, our two guitars created a melody that was sometimes rueful, sometimes bounding with upbeat urgency, and sometimes, somehow, both. At carefully chosen moments, I layered my voice behind my father's. I sang with my eyes closed, his final lyrics echoing in my ears: *We're all on our own, trying to do right, trying to get by.*

After I'd recorded each track three, four, five times, taken two breaks to temper all the emotions teeming inside of me, and paused to restring the Martin's high E, I was finally done with my father's songs. The decision resulted less from my being satisfied with my work, or thinking I had done my father's album justice, and more from the sudden wave of exhaustion that felled me. But I wasn't quite finished recording. Not yet. I needed one more take.

"There's one more thing I want to do," I told Nick. "Can you create a new track?"

"Something of yours?"

"Not exactly," I said. "A cover."

Nick nodded. "All right, give me just a minute." He clicked around on his screen. "And we're rolling."

I clasped a capo on the third fret, took a deep breath, and started to strum the opening bars of "Love Honey." I tapped my right foot in a metronomic pattern against Nick's carpet, trying to quell my tendency to rush as the lyrics streamed from deep in my chest. I gave the take everything I had, because I knew I wouldn't have the strength to do it again. I knew that after this, the song wouldn't be mine anymore, but that no longer seemed like such a bad thing. More than anything else in that moment, I wanted the song to live.

When the final chord died out, Nick began clapping. "That's a wrap," he said. "I've always wanted to say that, you know."

I took off the guitar. "And pretty soon you'll be saying it for your first feature film."

"I hope so." He smiled.

"I know so. Not everybody can do this."

"On the contrary, Hayes. Anybody can hit record. But lucky for me, that's not where my skill set ends."

As I leaned over to rest the Martin on the floor, a dizzying white light swarmed my head. "I think I need to lie down," I said.

"You okay?"

"Just tired." I kicked off my shoes, tipped backward into the plush comfort of Nick's bedspread. "I haven't slept much this week."

"Well, it's going to take me a little while to put together a rough mix of this, so feel free to rest in the meantime."

"Thanks," I mumbled, smushing my cheek against the clean spring scent of his pillow.

I woke sometime later, wreathed in the tendrils of a distant memory—or was it just a dream? Though a golden slit of light crept in from the covered window, the room was still dark and musty. I wondered why Nick hadn't opened the curtains. Maybe he'd thought it would help me rest.

Nick was right where I'd left him—hunched comically close to his computer, making tiny movements with his mouse. Sidling up behind him, I placed a hand on his shoulder.

He whirled around and yanked off the headphones. "Hey. How you feeling?"

"Much better," I said through an unexpected yawn. "How's it sound?"

Nick grinned. "You'll just have to listen." He offered the headphones to me, the spiral cord stretching as it extended from his desk to the bed. "I think you're going to be pretty pleased."

"We'll see about that," I joked, and put on the headphones. Nick said something I couldn't decipher but I smiled anyway. A few seconds later, static crackled in my ears.

The music began.

I was seized by disappointment.

Nick, I quickly discovered, hadn't always picked my best takes, or the ones I thought he would use, where I had nailed the tone on my harmonies and the timing of my strums. Instead, he favored the earlier versions, the ones brimming with uncertainty. Right at the start, I noticed a few muted notes in a barre chord. I heard my voice waver as I grasped for a higher note. It was wrong—not at all the way I had imagined I would sound, and I was about to take off the headphones, to make him start over, but then "Night Lives" surged into the chorus, and I was struck by something else: the mix, I realized, had been carefully split in stereo. All of a sudden spatial relationships existed between our voices, our instruments. As though I were on one side of the room and my father was on the other.

Closing my eyes, I pushed from my head whatever faults I thought I'd heard in myself, because if my father had taught me anything, it was that the whole of a song was always greater than the sum of its parts. And Nick, I was starting to understand, had chosen the takes that matched the passion in my father's recordings—the takes that felt the most true to his songs. It was because of this choice that I could see us there, sitting on opposite sides of our studio, my father cradling his maple Telecaster in his hands. Between lines, I could hear the sharp inhales of his breath, could practically smell the whiskey on it. We were living there, inside those songs, in an alternate midnight that went on and on, even when the sun began rising, and when it never would again.

I took off the headphones.

"He would have really liked you," I said.

"What do you mean?" The mattress squeaked as Nick sat next to me.

"It just sounds so . . . real."

Nick laughed. "It is real."

"I mean, like we were really sitting in a room together. My father and I. Recording this."

"So you approve?"

"Nick," I said. I shook my head, struggling to navigate my thoughts. Next to me, his face softened into a full, gleaming smile, and a jolt seemed to pass between us. The physicality of the feeling was overwhelming; my heart began thrashing and I tried to tether myself to the rhythm of Nick's breath, certain that I could hear his thoughts creaking into sync with mine as he waited for me to speak. I closed my eyes and let go of my nerves, and the timing, and all the reasons I'd been telling myself to wait, all the excuses I'd invented to keep him at arm's length.

I let everything go, and I kissed him.

For a few exhilarating, extended seconds, there was nothing else. No noise or background or history, just my zipping pulse and our lips pushed together, the taste of Nick's ChapStick, the salt of his tongue.

And then Nick pulled back. "Susannah—" he began. I couldn't remember the last time he'd said my first name and I tried not to think about the strangeness of the sound, or the way he started chewing on his bottom lip as his eyes slanted downward.

"I got into Cal State Long Beach," I blurted, fully aware of the frantic note that had wormed into my voice but unable to stop it. "Well, and San Francisco State, but what if I stay here? Long Beach really isn't that far from USC, and I can come up on days you don't have classes, or you could come to me, and we can make it work. Just like we imagined."

"We can't," he said.

"Of course we can."

Nick rubbed his hands over his face. "There was a time when all I wanted—" He paused. "When this—"

He stood and walked to the window. Parting the curtain slightly, he glanced out into the street. A shard of sunlight invaded the room, sliced right through the darkness, across my chest.

"I'm going to NYU," he said. "I leave at the end of July."

His words knocked the breath from me.

"I meant to tell you earlier."

My voice sounded thin and far away as I said, "Congratulations. I'm really happy for you."

"I care about you a lot," Nick said. "You know that, right? But this just isn't the right time to start something. It doesn't seem fair to either of us, when I'm about to move to the other side of the country. And you're going to Long Beach? That's awesome."

Tears began burning behind my eyes. "Yeah."

"This doesn't have to change anything," Nick said. But I think even he knew, as the words left his mouth, that everything had already been altered.

A rogue tear dripped onto my cheek and I brushed it off with my knuckle, pretending it was an itch, a fly, a speck of dust. "I should go," I said, and shoved my feet into my shoes. "Thanks for all your help. Really." I gathered my things, tugged the blanket from beneath the door—and yet, how swiftly I turned around when Nick said, "Wait."

"The songs," he added after a moment. "Let me burn them for you real quick."

I was stunned to realize I'd forgotten, and I hovered in the doorway while Nick swiveled around in his chair, fed a blank CD into the disc drive. The next five minutes felt eternal.

"You're still one of my best friends," Nick said as he handed me the CD.

"You're one of mine, too," I told him, though I wasn't really sure what that meant anymore. I didn't seem to know anyone as well as I thought I did. But I wonder now if maybe you can't ever truly know another person. Maybe all you can do is hope that one day, you'll know yourself.

I left Nick's quickly, forcing myself to not look back at his bedroom window as I loaded the Martin into the trunk and sped away from view—yet despite the urgent need I had to leave, I was not actually ready to go home. After turning a few corners, I pulled over and parked, and only then did I notice where I was: Cara's street. My eyes caught on the familiar sight of her house, and the muscles in my throat began to tighten. But her car was not in the driveway.

I wasn't sure why I thought it would be, or why I felt such immense, grating disappointment to discover that she wasn't miraculously here, waiting for me to show up. My thoughts blurred with the muggy air seeping in through my cracked window. I sat in front of Cara's house for what felt like a long time before finally turning the ignition back on.

It was then, driving away from Eagle Rock for the last time, away from Nick and Cara and the place where I'd grown up, that I understood what I needed to do next.

When I got home, I went straight to the computer in Vivian's office.

I opened up the website the Endless West used to stream their music, and, creating a new account, began filling in what few details I could—my band name, a brief description, the title of each track on our EP. The old machine grumbled as the CD uploaded. Eventually, the page refreshed, and it was official. *The Midnights EP* was live on the internet.

For a moment, I stared at the screen, stunned and overwhelmed by how long it took me to get here. And sure, it was entirely possible that no one would ever listen to what my father and I had made. Right then, though, that didn't matter. Our music existed—and not just in the middle of the night, in the privacy of our studio, in the past. This was real, permanent. Available to anybody. Just as my father would have wanted.

But what I did after surprises me still: I searched the site for Los Funerals. They had a well-trafficked page, replete with photos and videos and tour dates, and three times as many listens as the Endless West. I spent a few minutes scrolling through their content, but didn't find any recording of "Love Honey." No mention of it, either. I opened up a new direct message and began typing:

Lance and Travis,

I'm sorry about what happened at the Troubadour. I hope you're still playing "Love Honey." Play it every goddamn show. You were right—it's what he would have wanted.

It's what I want too.

Susannah Hayes

Before I could change my mind, I hit send.

Though so much of me still felt wounded and scraped raw—still felt the snarl of Lynn's voice slashing through me, the momentary flutter of Nick's eyelashes against my cheek—I couldn't help it. I sat back in my chair and smiled, because in that moment, I also felt free. My future was definitive and simultaneously unwritten, the next step as clear and unknown as the gleaming red suspensions of the Golden Gate Bridge, even through a sheet of fog.

Yes, I was certain now: I was going to San Francisco.

But I had one more mistake to fix first.

The phone rang four times before Cara answered.

"Hello?"

She sounded breathless. Happy. Like she'd been laughing.

"Hi. It's . . ." *It's me*, I wanted to say—what I've always said—but I wasn't *me* anymore. Not the version of me that Cara once knew.

I swallowed, traced my fingers over the computer's keyboard. "It's Susannah."

There was a pause.

"I thought I recognized your voice," she said.

"I finally got a cell phone," I told her, and laughed awkwardly. "But then I broke it. So I'm back on a house phone for now." Silence. "And I heard you got into Berkeley. I'm really, really excited for you."

"Thanks," she said. "Nick tell you?"

"Yeah. I . . ." I didn't know how to explain, how to tell her that I'd sat in my car in front of her house six months too late, uselessly hoping that everything would change. So I said the only thing that felt absolutely, unequivocally true. "Cara, I'm so sorry."

"For what?"

"For everything. For being a bad friend. For disappearing. For not . . . for not calling you a long time ago."

She sighed—a loud, heavy sound—and I knew that dwelling on the past was pointless. I couldn't *fix* the mistake at all, couldn't change how I'd acted. All I could do was try to be better. Start putting rights in the place of wrongs.

"I'm going to San Francisco State next year," I swept on, "and I was thinking, you know, you'll only be across the bay, so if you wanted to, maybe we could meet up sometime. Get coffee or something. I mean, if you're not too busy. If you even want to."

There was another pause, and in the background, I could make out the distinct murmur of voices. Behind that, I detected the splash of the ocean.

"I'd come to you," I added.

For a moment, I feared she'd stopped listening—that she'd left me there, speaking into nothing, as I likely deserved. The wind scraped against the receiver. I closed my eyes, could almost feel it rustling my hair.

"Yeah," she said. "I'd like that."

My eyes shot open. "Great! Okay. So, uh—I'll talk to you later?"

"Yeah," Cara said. Then: "Hey, Susannah?"

"Yeah?"

A deep breath. "I'm glad you called."

"Me too," I said. Two simple words that I'd never meant more in my life.

TWENTY-FOUR

THE DAY I graduated high school, a hot, skin-cracking wind blew down from the San Bernardino Mountains, knocking mortarboards from heads and flipping dresses up at knees. The sun reflected harshly off our football stadium's bleachers, where the spectators struggled to hang on to their programs. From time to time, a particularly forceful gust swung through the crowd, whipping a slew of unguarded papers into the air, and I watched as the pages twirled higher and higher, finally settling like premature confetti across the AstroTurf.

After the ceremony, I ushered my mother and Vivian from the stadium, anxious to leave Santiago Hills behind. The summer may have stood before me like an open wound, but soon enough

I'd be gone, and I held on to that knowledge as though it were holy. I'd sent in my acceptance to San Francisco State a few weeks earlier and had already started packing in my head—not that I really had much to bring with me. Just clothing, toiletries, my notebooks, and my father's guitar. His matchbook, with only one head left. I found it both soothing and sad that even though years seemed to have passed since we first left Los Angeles with Vivian, my life could still be reduced to the same small stack of possessions. I told myself I wouldn't miss anything about Orange. Most of the time, I believed it.

And then there were the other times, when a mere flicker of memory could dissolve my future oasis into something that seemed as distant and unreachable as a mirage. Walking through the parking lot after graduation, it was the fleeting hint of patchouli trailing a tendril of wind. Instinctively I halted, turned my head toward the scent. There, in the corner of my eye, a familiar glimpse of red flashed between the scintillating metal of parked cars.

Lynn.

She was still wearing her graduation gown but had left it gaping open, smoke swirling from the cigarette in her hand. I could tell she'd spent time in the sun lately, her skin that particular shade of gold and her hair ablaze, freshly dyed. Josie and Gabriel were standing next to her, and their laughter pealed into the hot air as they looked toward the field. I wondered if Cameron was here, and what any of them would say if they saw me. I wondered what Gabriel would say. Lynn had probably told them about me. Or, maybe she told them nothing. Maybe, when I never came back, she just let me disappear.

"A friend of yours?" Vivian asked.

Her voice startled me; I hadn't realized she also paused, and was now tracing my gaze to Lynn. "Not really," I told her, and a stinging, deep-rooted sadness lodged itself in my throat as the truth of that response resonated.

Later that night, my mother rapped her knuckles against my door, poked her head into my room. "You're going to be late for Grad Night," she said.

"Not interested." I rolled over on my bed, toward the window. Outside, a slim sickle moon glazed the backyard with a milky shimmer.

"What about your friends?"

"What friends?"

I tried to smile—not in a cruel way or to make my mother feel bad, but in an attempt to show I was fine on my own. Or that I would be.

My mother nodded, as though she'd been expecting my response. "Well, Vivian and I . . ." she began, and stepped into my room. "We wanted to give you a little something. A graduation present."

"You already gave me something," I said, and dangled my new phone from my fingers. I let it drop with a dull thud onto the mattress.

My mother lowered herself onto my bed and handed me a non-descript white envelope. On the front, she'd written my name in thin, precise cursive. I lifted the flap. Inside was a check.

Stunned, I sat up. "Vivian already gave me the deposit money," I said, sliding the check back inside. I held the envelope out to my mother. "I sent it in weeks ago."

She cupped her hands around mine, and pushed them back. "We're really proud of you," she said. "*I'm* really proud of you. And we want you to have this. You're going to be on your own pretty soon." My mother reached out, touched my hair. "I see so much of him in you. That used to scare me, you know, but now—" She smiled. "Your future will be full of great things, Susannah."

In the yard, wind whistled elegiacally through the trees. She said, "I know what it's like to feel suffocated and stuck and alone. When I was your age, I would have given anything to live in some far-off city."

She glanced around my room—*her* room, actually, with the bed that rested her growing bones and the desk where she wrote her own college applications—and I wondered if that's what she saw now, the place it had been back then, when she was still a child, still dreaming. I wondered when those dreams had stopped.

"Why didn't you?" I asked.

With a shrug, she said, "I guess I just thought there'd be more time."

"There is time," I urged. "You don't have to worry about me anymore. I'll be at college, and you can do whatever you want. You can go too."

My mother shook her head. "My place is here now. And that's okay. It's good."

Of course. She had to stay for Vivian.

Growing up, I'd been so concerned with my father's ambitions and sacrifices that I left little time to consider what my mother had given up. Now, I was all too aware of how much I'd overlooked.

Though I believed that she'd found solace in the trajectory of her life (or, at least, resigned herself to its present course), this did not make up for what she might have lost because of me.

"You know," my mother began, examining me, "that being your mom is the best thing that ever happened to me. Right?"

She'd said these words many times before but never quite like this, with her eyes burrowing into mine as though she could see straight into my thoughts. As though she knew the exact phrase I longed to hear.

I said, "I know."

For a few seconds we sat there, allowing the words to settle over us.

"And one more thing." My mother pulled something else from behind her back. "This is just from me."

"You've already given me too much," I said as she offered me some small object wrapped in delicate mulberry paper. Her eyes gleamed with excitement, but her smile was tight and uncertain when I unwrapped the gift: a brand-new leather-bound notebook. The cover was a supple brown, soft and worn. Just like my father's wallet, I thought. I opened the book, fanned through the blank, ivory pages. I could smell the thick spice of the tanning oil, the sweet must of the paper.

"Do you like it?" she asked. "I wasn't sure if you had any pref-erences, lines or no lines, hardcover, softcover. But I thought that you needed something a little more grown-up than those cheap composition books from the grocery store, so—"

I pummeled my mother with a hug.

"It's perfect," I said. Gratitude burned through me, and not just for the notebook, or even the money, but for pushing me, insisting that I take those college applications. For knowing I'd want this, even when I didn't.

My mother stood. Her eyes were glossy. Out on the hillside, coyotes cackled at the sliver of moon. Maybe, I thought, I would miss this place after all.

"Thank you," I said, still clutching the notebook.

"You're welcome."

My mother smiled and headed for the door, but she'd only made it halfway when I felt the urge to call her back.

"I have something for you, too," I said.

In the instant that followed, I considered giving her the CD Nick had made of my recording over my father's tape, or maybe even the near-empty matchbook—the few fragments of him that I'd selfishly hidden away for myself. Instead, I angled toward my desk. I rummaged through my stack of old composition books until I found the one with the photograph nestled inside. Then I took one final look at the half-obscured figure of my young mother. I said, "I've had this for a long time, but I think maybe now you should have it back."

My mother took the photo, confused. Her eyes swung across the image for a few seconds before recognition bloomed. She touched her fingers to her lips, and I wanted to say something more, something important and profound, but a wave of sorrow washed all the words down. I was no longer sure why I had kept the photograph secret for so long, or why my curiosity had always seemed so forbidden. Though I must have had a reason, I couldn't remember it.

"I thought I'd lost this," my mother said after a while, voice knotted with disbelief. "Where did you . . . ?"

Caught in the nebula of her thoughts, she never finished the sentence. In the end, I don't think the circumstances really mattered. I watched her face soften, observed the tiny twitching movements of her thumb at the edge of the picture, refusing to shift or speak until the spell broke and she looked up from behind the gauze of whatever memory had grazed her and remembered that I was still beside her, in her childhood bedroom, on a windy, slim-mooned night.

I couldn't give my mother much, but I let her have this moment.

A week later, I left.

It was a lot easier than I thought it would be; a simple procession of Google searches led me to a site associated with the university, in which students traveling or going home for the summer tried to sublet their rooms. After clicking through a handful of listings, I found the one that stuck: an African Studies major was doing a summer program in Ghana. Her roommate, an artist, was staying in the city to work on her senior show. They wanted someone to move in as soon as possible. I had no reason to spend the summer in Orange.

The morning was quiet, exploding with sunlight as my mother and Vivian drove me down Chapman Avenue to the small train station in Old Towne Orange, just a few minutes away from where Lynn lived. I'd become so familiar with that drive, the roundabout with the quaint park in the center and the liquor store where we'd stopped one sultry afternoon to buy a case of beer for the boys. *Earthquake weather,* Lynn had said that day. But it was June now, the air calm. The ground had not quaked since.

We waited silently in the depot's small parallelogram of shade until we heard the train's whistle shrieking in the distance.

"You'll call me when you get there," my mother said. This was not a question.

"Yes," I told her.

"And when you're settled in at the apartment."

"Yes."

"And—"

"She'll call you," Vivian said, wrapping her arm around my mother. She squeezed her shoulders and flashed a sympathetic smile—more, I think, for my own reassurance than my mother's. They would be fine. They would take care of each other.

After boarding, I collapsed into a window seat and waved one last time. The train lurched into motion. I kept my nose pressed to the glass, watching their bodies shrink until they finally receded from view.

Then I took out my new notebook.

Now, as my train chugs through the last stretch of open land before San Francisco, I can't help thinking about the strangeness of these in-between moments, these points of intersection amid one thing and the next. People often forget how big California is, how varied its two ends. They forget that San Francisco is actually as far away from Los Angeles as Phoenix, Northern and Southern like completely different states. It's funny how perception changes; not so long ago, LA and Orange County seemed like opposite ends of the world.

And sometimes, it still feels impossible that I moved to Orange less than a year ago, only met Lynn in October, and played with the Endless West for five months. I wonder (more often than I like to admit) if any of them will even remember me five months from now—a year from now. I wonder if Cameron will ever think about our first kiss in the freezing Pacific, or how time seemed to stop inside the walls of his studio. I wonder if Lynn will remember that day we bellowed "Go Your Own Way" out the wide-open windows of her car so emphatically that our throats felt scraped raw—and if these moments, so vibrant and dominant in my mind, matter less if their memories of me cease completely.

I wonder: Is this moment—this train ride—the in-between, or was my in-between the entire past year?

My name has never appeared on the Endless West's websites or in any of their articles or interviews. But I know I was there. However brief my appearance, however unnoticed my mark, I lived for a time in the center of it all. I stood on that stage and felt the glow of the spotlights beaming down like an angry sun. I wrote lyrics that gushed from the mouths of strangers in a wave of sound so massive that my own voice was submerged in the swell. I felt the bass line pump with my blood, stomped my foot against the tape-scuffed floor, slammed the tambourine against my palm until my hand turned blue, and as long as they continue playing "Don't Look Back," as long as they sing my words, that piece of me will still exist there. The rest of me, though, has let that piece go.

It's when I start thinking about all of this that I'm reminded of something my father once said, not long after my very first midnight in the studio. My amateur fingers were newly healed and my

C had transformed from a mangled clang into a clear, precise lull that I struck over and over, awed by my ability to create a sound so beautiful and strong.

"There are many ways to tweak a chord," my father told me in the pauses between my strums. "You can use pedals and treble and distortion. You can jiggle a whammy, or glide an EBow across the neck. Even the specific instrument you're playing will affect your sound, whether the body is solid or hollow, the action and gauge of the strings. It all matters. See?" He twisted the nobs on my amp as he spoke, making my strum fuller, deeper, adding a light twinge of distortion. When he was satisfied with the results, he sat back in his chair, picked up his Telecaster, and began tinkering over me.

"There's one thing you have to remember, though," he continued. "Sustain can only resonate for so long." He played an elaborate series of notes and then suddenly muted the strings with the base of his palm, plunging the room into silence. All the while his blue eyes tunneled into me.

He said, "It comes down to control. You decide how long each chord lasts. *You* decide when to let it linger, and when it has to end."

My father's voice may have grown quieter, as Lynn said it would, but I can see now that he actually left me something after all. He left me these little plucks of wisdom that spring forth when I need them most, and his perfectionist's insistence on finding the perfect tone for every song. He left me the twitch, that sudden jolt of my muscles when I see someone else on a stage, or when I realize my hands have been idle for too long. And he left me the yearning I get in the deepest fold of midnight when the rest of the world is sleeping, when the dark is too quiet or the air is too still, and something begins to strum in my gut.

So maybe he didn't fail. Maybe neither of us did.

My calluses are reemerging now, and the Martin is tuned, waiting in the rack above my head. Even though I can't hear it yet, don't know the next chord or progression or line, I know that a new song is forming. It might be hidden in the rhythm of the decelerating train, or in the pulse of this brand-new city, the chorus of dinging streetcars and the buildup of summer fog—just waiting there, ready to be discovered, as long as I'm willing to trust myself, my instinct, my heart. As long as I'm willing to listen.

And I'm listening. I'm ready. My mind, finally, is clear.

I can't wait to hear what the winds sound like in San Francisco.

ACKNOWLEDGMENTS

So many incredible people have given their time, dedication, and support to this novel. I owe the most effusive, eternal gratitude to:

Jess Regel, my rock-star agent. Thank you for believing in this book from the very first line you read—even as I sat across a table from you, mumbling nonsensically about my half-complete manuscript. Your faith in Susannah's story played a huge part in my ability to actually finish it. I feel so lucky to have you in my corner.

Emilia Rhodes, my brilliant editor, whose kindness knows no bounds. Your insight and guidance have made this book a hundred times stronger. I'm still amazed by how smooth and joyful this process was, and I know that it's entirely because of you.

Jen Klonsky, Sarah Kaufman, Alexandra Rakaczki, Tyler

Breitfeller, Laura Kaplan, and everyone else at HarperTeen whose hard work helped transform this book from long-time dream to tangible reality.

Mia Nolting, the incredible artist behind the stunning cover.

Amy Kurzweil, Elisha Wagman, Katie Peyton, and Rebecca Nison—some of the most amazing, talented, and hard-working women I've ever known. Your feedback has been indispensable. Thank you for always holding the flashlight steady while I waded around in the dark, searching for the roots and sinews of this story. Thank you for always inspiring me to push forward and be better.

Valerie Aper, Emily Amodeo, James Suffern, Brian Morgan, and Danny Goodman, who have all so graciously offered to read (often multiple) versions of this book. Your comments helped shape the story in the most surprising and lovely ways.

James Blaylock, Tim Powers, and Chapman University's creative writing program for your astounding generosity in helping a strange, aspiring poet find her voice in fiction all those years ago.

Helen Schulman, Ann Hood, and the New School's MFA program for teaching me so much, always asking the hard (but essential) questions, and for the wisdom you've shared.

Teddy Wayne, who chose an early excerpt of this book as the winner of the New School's alumni fiction chapbook contest, and made me feel like a Real Writer for the first time.

Dana Spiotta and the Tin House Summer Writer's Workshop for allowing me to see my story through a different lens, precisely when I needed it the most.

My parents, Cindy and Daryl Smetana, for always encouraging my creativity, and for always pursuing their own. To my father, the musician: Thank you for filling my childhood with music and inspiring me to play the guitar. That decision changed my life. To my mother, the visual artist: Thank you for supporting every single one of my endeavors, and for all the beautiful art you have made and continue to make. I am an artist because you showed me how, and I know how fortunate I am to have a family that values these things.

My sister, aunts, uncles, cousins, in-laws—basically the whole extended family. Your love and enthusiasm mean the world.

And, most of all, Justin. Thank you for moving across the country with me so I could get my MFA. Thank you for supporting me when I'm immersed in my work, and also for leading me back into the big, bright, beautiful world. My life is infinitely better because you are in it. I couldn't have done this without you.